EVIL NEVER SLEEPS

I almost regretted having Awareness. Without it, I wouldn't have noticed a thing; I would have been as oblivious to the danger as everyone else.

I took a deep breath and tried to isolate the power to pinpoint who was using it, and—perhaps even more importantly—who was the victim of it. And, for the first time in my life, I failed miserably. The power was too great. It permeated the whole room and I could not track it down. I'd never seen the red taint of dunmagic spread so widely before. I'd never seen it roil its evil way so strongly.

I wasn't used to my Awareness failing me—and I was frightened . . .

The Aware

BOOK ONE OF THE ISLES OF GLORY

GLENDA LARKE

ACE BOOKS, NEW YORK

THE BERKLEY PUBLISHING GROUP
Published by the Penguin Group
Penguin Group (USA) Inc.
375 Hudson Street, New York, New York 10014, USA
Penguin Group (Canada), 10 Alcorn Avenue, Toronto, Ontario M4V 3B2, Canada
(a division of Pearson Penguin Canada Inc.)
Penguin Books Ltd., 80 Strand, London WC2R 0RL, England
Penguin Group Ireland, 25 St. Stephen's Green, Dublin 2, Ireland (a division of Penguin Books Ltd.)
Penguin Group (Australia), 250 Camberwell Road, Camberwell, Victoria 3124, Australia
(a division of Pearson Australia Group Pty. Ltd.)
Penguin Books India Pvt. Ltd., 11 Community Center, Panchsheel Park, New Delhi—110 017, India
Penguin Group (NZ), Cnr. Airborne and Rosedale Roads, Albany, Auckland 1310, New Zealand
(a division of Pearson New Zealand Ltd.)
Penguin Books (South Africa) (Pty.) Ltd., 24 Sturdee Avenue, Rosebank, Johannesburg 2196, South
Africa

Penguin Books Ltd., Registered Offices: 80 Strand, London WC2R 0RL, England

THE AWARE

An Ace Book / published by arrangement with HarperCollins Australia

PRINTING HISTORY
Voyager Books edition / 2003
Ace mass market edition / April 2005

Copyright © 2003 by Glenyce Noramly.
Cover art by Scott Grimando.
Cover design by Annette Fiore.
Interior text design by Stacy Irwin.

ISBN: 0-441-01277-9

ACE
Ace Books are published by The Berkley Publishing Group,
a division of Penguin Group (USA) Inc.,
375 Hudson Street, New York, New York 10014.
ACE and the "A" design are trademarks belonging to Penguin Group (USA) Inc.

PRINTED IN THE UNITED STATES OF AMERICA

10 9 8 7 6 5 4 3 2 1

This book is dedicated to the
most patient man I know—even though he
never reads fantasy—
my husband, with love.

THE ISLES

Surveyed by the 2nd Explor.
Ex. Kells 1782-1784.

THE MIDDLING ISLES
Discovered by Sallavuard i. Rutho, 1780.

The Keeper Isles

BETHBASTION

Bethany Isles

BETHANY HOLD

Breth Island

THE HUB

Xolchas Stacks

XOLCHASBARBICAN

CIRKASECASTLE

Cirkase Islands

Mekaté Island

The Stragglers

The Spatts

MEKATÉHAVEN

STRAGGLERFORT

The Dustels

SPATTSHIELD

THE SOUTHER ISLES
Discovered by Sallavuard i. Rutho, 1781.

O F   G L O R Y

Calment
Major

CALMENTCITADEL

FEN TOWER

Fen
Island

Quiller
Island

Calment
Minor

QUILLER
HARBOUR

THE NORTHER ISLES
Discovered by Huwight, 1781.

N

SCALE OF NAUTICAL MILES
0   50   100   200

STATUTE MILES
0   50   100   200

ISLAND MILES
0   50   100   200

© P Phillips

THE NORTHER ISLES

Discovered by Huwight, 1781.
Surveyed by R.V. *Seaward Congress*.
2nd. Explor. Ex. Kells 1784.

*Calment
Major*

SITTIM COAST

ITAM I.

Anten

CERA I.

Janaty

CALMENT CITADEL

Quindy

QUINDIN I.

METAN R.

TANTA I.

QUINDIN REACH

INAM GAP

IS BAY

Tanta

METAN REACH

CARLAN HILLS

STRAIT

THE KARKIN

KARKIN BAY

ELMINI I.

QUILLER
HARBOUR

Gismady

*Calment
Minor*

SKYTHAN

QUILLER'S NOSE

JESTIL I.

AKINI HEAD

*Quiller
Island*

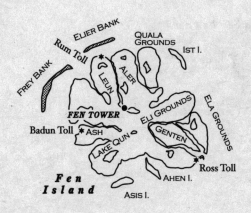

ELIER BANK

Rum Toll

FREY BANK

QUALA
GROUNDS

IST I.

LEUN

ALER

FEN TOWER

ELI GROUNDS

ELA GROUNDS

Badun Toll ✷ ASH

GENTEN

LAKE QUN

Ross Toll

AHEN I.

Fen
Island

ASIS I.

SCALE OF NAUTICAL MILES
0 20 40 60 80 100   200

STATUTE MILES
0 20 40 60 80 100   200

ISLAND MILES
0 20 40 60 80 100   200

N

© P Phillips

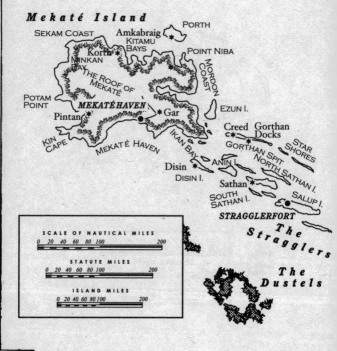

Mekaté Island

SEKAM COAST

Amkabraig
KITAMU
BAYS

PORTH

POINT NIBA

Korth

MINKAN
BAY

THE ROOF OF
MEKATÉ

MORDON
COAST

POTAM
POINT

MEKATÉHAVEN

Pintan

Gar

EZUN I.

Creed   Gorthan
Docks

STAR
SHORES

KIN
CAPE

MEKATÉ HAVEN

IKAN BAY

GORTHAN SPIT

NORTH SATHAN I.

ANIN I.

Disin

DISIN I.

Sathan

SALUP I.

SOUTH
SATHAN I.

STRAGGLERFORT

*The
Stragglers*

*The
Dustels*

SCALE OF NAUTICAL MILES

0 20 40 60 80 100   200

STATUTE MILES

0 20 40 60 80 100   200

ISLAND MILES

0 20 40 60 80 100   200

THE SOUTHER ISLES

Discovered by Sallavuard i. Rutho, 1781.
Surveyed by R.V. *Horn*. 2nd. Explor. Ex. Kells 1784.

N

The Spatts

ILGA I.

Est
AWAY I.

EHEN I.

IGA I.
Igashiel

IFSTA I.

INGEN I.

SPATTSHIELD

Ubensha

IAAB I.

UBEN I.

ANKEN I.

Atenshiel

ATEN I.

© P Phillips

THE MIDDLING ISLES

Discovered by Sallavuard i. Rutho, 1780.
Surveyed by R.V. *Seaward Congress*. 2nd. Explor. Ex. Kells 1782.

```
SCALE OF NAUTICAL MILES
0   20  40  60  80 100              200

        STATUTE MILES
    0  20  40  60  80 100           200

        ISLAND MILES
      0 20 40 60 80 100             200
```

© P Phillips

Yebaan YEBETH I.

THERAN
REACH

BRETHBASTION

*Breth
Island*

Kysis 'Ikkon' Keret

SEDIN
BAY

Sedin Kovo AYIN I.

Binaan TWO
PAPS THE KITAL

ATIS COAST

YAWOON STRETCH

N

XOLCHASBARBICAN

*Xolchas
Stacks*

The Keeper Isles

Bethany Isles

FIRST SPOKE
SECOND SPOKE
THIRD SPOKE

Sidami
Magreg
Kanenby Dunan
THE EDANA
Golbun
Korby
Breckby
THE HUB
Senthan
Anby
Milkby

BETHANY HOLD
FOURTH

Fis I.
Idistaig

ASAN I.

SPOKE
IDIS I.
ABAN I.

FIFTH SPOKE
Areth
CIRKASE SEA

HORN HAVEN
SIXTH SPOKE

SINA I.
Azadesen

CHIS I.

ELEVENTH SPOKE

TENTH SPOKE
TENKOR I.
NINTH SPOKE
ADIO HARBOUR
EIGHTH SPOKE
GANNON REACH
SEVENTH SPOKE

Lem
CIRKASECASTLE
Aralisen

AKASE I.

KELM WATER

ANDANI I.

Cirkase Islands

Letter from Researcher (Special Class) S. iso Fabold, National Department of Exploration, Federal Ministry of Trade, Kells, to Masterman M. iso Kipswon, President of the National Society for the Scientific, Anthropological and Ethnographical Study of non-Kellish Peoples.

Dated this day 7/2nd Darkmoon/1793

Dear Uncle,
Here is the first of the packets I promised you: my preliminary conversations with the woman Blaze Halfbreed. It is a transcript, translated of course, of interviews I conducted in the presence of a scribe—Nathan iso Vadim. You may remember him: I introduced you on the docks when RV Seadrift *was about to leave for the Isles of Glory. But that was three years ago now, so maybe you don't recall. Nathan and I became good friends on the tedious sea journey and he proved an invaluable asset to the research expedition because of his language skills. I was also ably assisted by Trekan i. Cothard, the expedition's assistant botanist, who proved to be a gifted artist. All of the sketches accompanying this packet are his work.*

The interviews have been partially edited, with all my questions removed. This was done to give the tale more continuity, but care has been taken not to change the substance or to tamper with the narrative style of the speaker.

I intend to use the material enclosed here as the basis for the first of the two papers you have asked me to present to the Society. I am calling it Social Conditions in the Isles of Glory Prior to the Change. *The second paper I think I will entitle* Power of Belief: Magic in the Isles of Glory, *but I haven't started that yet.*

I am still confined to my bed with the fever, but am improving daily. Please thank Aunt Rosris for the items she sent over: I am drinking the possets and reading the books!

I remain,
Your obedient nephew,
Shor iso Fabold

CHAPTER 1

SO YOU WANT TO KNOW WHAT THE ISLES of Glory were like back then, eh? In the days before the Change, in the years before you people found us—and we found out that we weren't the only islands in the ocean. *That* was a shock, I can tell you! But you know about that.

What you want to hear is quite different. You want to know about our lives. I'm not sure I'm the person to tell you, mind; I was always more one for thinking and acting rather than talking. Still, there wasn't much I didn't know about the Isles then, and most of it I remember better than what happened yesterday. I'd visited every islandom, except for the Dustels, before I was twenty-five, and the Dustels didn't exist then anyway.

Yet it's hard to know where I should start. The islandoms were more diverse then than they are now, you see: each had its own way of doing things, its own way of looking at life. The people differed from island group to island group. After the Change there was more uniformity; after you people happened along, the differences faded still more.

Perhaps the Keeper Isles would be the logical place to begin because they were at the center of things. But no, I think I'll start with a place that wasn't even a proper islandom: Gorthan Spit. It wasn't a proper island either, if it comes to that. True, it took a few days to sail the length of it, but you could have

walked the width in less than a single day. There was one raised
patch of rock on the north coast, but the sea cliffs there were
hardly higher than the mainmast of your sailing ship. The rest
of the place was just white sand: think of a silver sand-eel, long
and thin, with a bit of a scab on the middle of its back, and there
you have Gorthan Spit. Not the sort of place where things of
import would occur, or so you'd think; yet if I tell you what happened there it'll not only show you what the Isles of Glory were
like before the Change, but it'll help to *explain* the Change, because the seeds of that were sown on the Spit, although none of
us who did the planting realized it then!

And if nothing else, the story will tell you what it was like to
be a woman and a halfbreed back in those days. And that's really the sort of thing you want to know, isn't it? Don't look so
surprised! I may not be as schooled as you are, but I've lived
long enough to hear what is not spoken. I know what you are interested in. You may give it a fancy name, and call it science, or
what is it? Ethnography? But render it down, and it's just people
and places . . . people like me, and places like Gorthan Spit.

THE SPIT WAS ONE OF THE SOUTHER IS-
lands, a middenheap for unwanted human garbage and the
dregs of humanity. A cesspit where the Isles of Glory threw
their living sewerage: the diseased, the criminals, the mad, the
halfbreeds, the citizenless. Without people, Gorthan Spit would
have been just an inhospitable finger of sand under a harsh
southern sun; with them it was a stinking island hell.

The first time I went there I swore I'd never go back. The
time I'm going to tell you about was my third visit and I was
still swearing the same thing, even while I cursed the sheer perversity of the events that had made a trip there necessary.

You had to be mad, or bad, or just plain greedy to go to
Gorthan Spit voluntarily. In those days there were many who
said I was the first, a few who swore, with reason, that I was the
second, but I'd only admit to the third. Mind you, I had reason
to be greedy. My purse might have been filled with fish scales
for all the weight there ever was in it and that was reason
enough. Money and I just didn't seem to get along—no, that
isn't quite true. I could *make* money all right, I just didn't seem
able to *keep* it. I'd made two fortunes before this particular trip
to Gorthan Spit and lost them both. The first went down with a

ship in a whirlstorm and very nearly took me with it. The second, over two thousand setus, was stolen when I was thrashing around in bed with the six-day fever. I almost died that time too.

Anyway, there I was, prompted by my search for wealth into returning to Gorthan Spit, and wondering if it was a good move. So far that third fortune seemed very elusive.

I rented a room in the main port of Gorthan Docks, in the best inn on the island, The Drunken Plaice, which meant that I actually had a room to myself, with a window, and it had a bed instead of just a pallet. I doubted that there was any difference in the vermin between Gorthan Spit's best hostelry and its worst, but one could always hope. I'd even managed to get some hot water out of the drudge for a wash. The clam shell that acted as a basin was small and none too clean and the water was half salt, but I knew better than to complain. I washed and went downstairs to try the food in the taproom.

I took a seat in the corner where I could see the rest of the room—a wise precaution in a place like Gorthan Docks—slipped off my sword harness, and looked around. The room hadn't changed much in the intervening years: a little more dirt ingrained into the driftwood floorboards and a few more knife gouges in the table tops, but otherwise it was as I remembered: bare necessities, no fripperies. With a first cursory glance, I saw pretty much the people I expected to see as well. A number of slavers, a few seamen-traders who were probably pirates on the side, and an assortment of unsavory characters who had only one thing in common: they all looked as villainous as sharks on the prowl. In Gorthan Spit people came and went like the tide and it had been five years since my last trip, but there were one or two familiar faces.

I attracted a fair amount of attention myself. Any woman on her own in such a place would have, but one as tall as I was really swung the heads around. I heard the sniggers and the tired jokes I'd heard a hundred times before; I tended to have that effect on people. To be fair, even without my height I would perhaps have excited comment: I wore a Calmenter sword on my back and there weren't too many women who did that, especially not ones with coloring that made it clear they weren't from Calment. Calmenters were invariably honey-eyed blondes and I was brown—brown-haired in those days, as well as brown-skinned—while my eyes were the kind of green you sometimes see in clear water along the Atis coast of Breth

Island. And that was a combination which made it obvious I was a halfbreed. In those days, everyone knew that green eyes were the exclusive property of the Fen Islanders, and the Fen Islanders weren't brown-skinned Souther people . . .

Of course, halfbreeds were a setu a score on a place like Gorthan Spit, but I was distinctive enough to be noticeable.

While waiting to be served, I took a second more careful look around that room, and saw that it contained no less than three tall men. It was second nature to me to notice a tall man; not that I had anything against shorter men, you understand, but I'd found over the years that a normal-sized male who could bring himself to bed a woman more than a head taller than he was, was rare indeed. The trouble was, there weren't all that many men who were as tall as I was. To find three of them in one room was unexpected—and promising.

I should have known I was looking at trouble. That kind of luck can never be all good. Especially when all three of them were handsome.

The first, the tallest of the three, was seated with the slavers. He looked faintly familiar, but I couldn't remember where I'd seen him before. He was close enough for me to see his earlobe tattoo: a "Q" inlaid with gold. Which made him a Northman, a Quiller Islander. He was well dressed, too smart for a slaver, I would have thought, and he was long and lithe rather than big. Fair-skinned and dark-haired with a pleasing smile, he was about the finest-looking male I'd seen in a sea full of islands. Moreover, he noticed me—and liked what he saw. The smile really was charming.

The second man, while not as tall, was a great deal larger. Broad hands, broad shoulders, broad chest, and not an ounce of excess flesh on him. He sat alone in the corner diagonally opposite from me; a handsome man with a humorless expression, tan-colored skin, shrewd blue eyes and a complete lack of flamboyance in the way he was dressed (all in black); a man who took life seriously and yet didn't wear a sword—a surprising omission. Perhaps he thought his large size was protection enough. He looked at me without any change in expression. And that piqued; men usually showed *some* reaction.

The third was the youngest. Too young for me. He looked about twenty, but he might have been a little older; fair-skinned, fair-haired and a face that was so innocent of guile you wanted to ask him what the hell he was doing in a midden like Gorthan

Spit. He had dimples, for god's sake, and lashes that hit his cheeks like the curling foam of a wave hitting the beach. When he saw me his eyes registered his distaste. He obviously didn't like low-life halfbreeds.

My stomach knotted with anger. Nobody should have had the right to look at me with such contempt, especially not a man as young and as untried as this one. It was at moments like this that I would have done anything—almost anything at all—to have had a citizenship tattoo on my earlobe.

For all my inner anger, I returned his gaze calmly enough. I'd had plenty of practice at ignoring contempt.

I was about to switch my attention back to one of the other two when the waiter lurched over from a neighboring table and asked what I wanted. I knew the answer to that one: fish. In that hostelry there was never anything else but fish. And I doubted that I had much choice about the way in which it was cooked, not unless the culinary standards had done an about-face since I'd last stayed at The Drunken Plaice.

"Grilled fish," I said, "and a mug of swillie." And then I had a whiff of dunmagic that prickled my spine in warning and made me take a very good look at that waiter.

He wasn't an attractive sight. He was in his middle years, I supposed, but it was hard to tell because he was only half normal. The right half. The left half of him was a travesty of a human being, and I didn't really need the stink of dunmagic to tell me he had been its victim. It was as if a giant had pinched his left-hand side between two fingers, squashing it out of shape to make that side of his face a twisted mess and that side of his torso a humped deformity. His left eye drooped down, the left side of his mouth jerked up. The cheek between, as rough as dead coral, was pitted with scars. The jaw below petered away without definition into his neck. His left foot was clubbed, his left hand a set of gnarled claws at the end of a foreshortened limb. The lobe of his left ear was missing, deliberately cut away, taking with it any proof of his citizenship—or lack of it. What made it all worse was that there was enough of him that was normal to indicate that he had once been at least as handsome as the Quillerman sitting with the slavers. For one fleeting moment I glimpsed something disturbing deep in his eyes: tragedy. A tragedy of such epic proportions as to be beyond the understanding of most people: more than even I could begin to comprehend.

I was stirred to compassion, and that didn't happen very often. "What's your name?" I asked and held out a coin to show that the inquiry was made with the best of intentions. On Gorthan Spit you had to be damned careful about asking personal questions.

He leered at me, and a dribble of spit ran out of his twisted mouth down onto his chin. "You can call me Janko. Any time you want, jewel-eyes." He managed to drawl out that last sentence into an obscene suggestion, then he grabbed the coin, laughed in a high-pitched giggle that seemed curiously at variance with his appearance, and stumped away.

I sighed. So much for compassion in a public house like The Drunken Plaice. I wondered if I was growing soft; there had been a time when I would not have wasted a moment's pity on such an unprepossessing specimen. Perhaps I was mellowing with age, as pearls do. The thought brought me no joy. For a person with my disadvantages, the anger the fair youngster's contempt had aroused in me was of more value than any feelings of compassion could be. I needed to be as hard and as rough as the shell of the oyster, not smooth like its pearl. To be soft was to jeopardize my dream of attaining wealth, of having enough money to buy the comfort and security I wanted. Bleeding hearts were rarely rich. Worse, in my line of business, they too often ended up dead.

The swillie came quickly enough, delivered by the tapboy who was probably more in need of my compassion than Janko, if the bruises on his cheek were anything to go by. I smiled at him but he ducked his head, dumped the mug down, spilling some of its contents, and scuttled away as fast as he could. I didn't usually scare people *that* much. I settled back to sip the brew and watch the room.

And found I hadn't reached the end of the surprises the place had to offer, for just then the most beautiful woman I'd ever seen in my life came down the stairs into the room. She was a blue-eyed, yellow-haired, golden-skinned dream; a Cirkasian, of course. No other islands produced that kind of coloring. She wasn't much older than twenty; she had legs long enough to set every man in the room drooling, and curves that were just obvious enough to hint at sexual pleasures without being too flagrant. Like me, she was wearing the drab standard travelers' garb of trousers and a belted tunic, but it wouldn't have made any difference what she wore. Every head in the room swiveled her way—and stayed looking.

Including my own. I'd never wanted to bed another woman—still don't, if it comes to that. It wasn't her sexual attributes that interested me. Yet I edged the empty chair opposite me into a more inviting position with my foot, and hoped, without much reason, that she'd settle for my table. A bird, a small nondescript blackish thing, flew in and perched on the back of the chair instead. Apparently fearless, it cocked its head at me, and eyed the crumbs on the floor. I tried to shoo it off, but it ignored me.

The woman paused on the bottom step and looked around the room for a place to sit. There wasn't all that much choice: the seat at my table, several empty chairs at the tall, broad man's table, another next to the young man with the curling lashes. The bird hopped, agitated, along the chair back. When a sunbeam caught its plumage, it turned iridescent with a shimmer of deep blue on the wings and purple across the breast, like a bolt of shot silk catching the light.

That was when the stench of dunmagic evil hit me, so potent I almost gagged. The whiff I had caught earlier from Janko was nothing compared to this; that had been the traces of a past spell, this was immediate. Someone was operating right then and there, and he—or she—had to be a dunmaster. This was no novice, no small-time operator with a modicum of talent. I'd never sensed such power, and I'd never been so aware of the sheer *badness* of dunmagic before. The place fairly reeked with evil. I put my mug down before I spilled the contents, and made sure my sword hilt was within easy reach.

A red glow skittered across the floor, intangible and rotten, touching us all with its foulness as it ran between the chairs to leave patches of ruddiness behind like bloodied turds. It was an effort not to jerk my feet away as it streamed under my table and over my boots, tainting them with color. I wanted to shake my feet—as if I could rid myself of the residue it left—but I withstood the temptation. It was safer not to let the dunmaster, whoever he or she was, have an inkling that I could see it. I did risk another downward glance a moment later, to see that the red glow on the leather of my boots was fast fading, but I hid my relief just as I had hidden my revulsion. I almost regretted having Awareness. Without it, I wouldn't have noticed a thing; I would have been as oblivious to the danger as everyone else.

I took a deep breath, and tried to isolate the power to pinpoint who was using it, and—perhaps even more importantly—who was the victim of it. And, for the first time in my life, I failed miserably. The power was too great. It permeated the whole room and I could not track it down. I'd never seen the red taint of dunmagic spread so widely before. I'd never seen it roil on its evil way so strongly. The only thing of which I could be reasonably certain was that it wasn't directed at me. Still, my mouth dried out and my clenched hands were clammy. I wasn't used to my Awareness failing me and I was frightened.

God, the things I did for money! I should never have returned to the Spit; too much that was bad could happen there, especially when magic was involved. I felt a momentary doubt about whether it was all worth it: a chilling notion that crept up on me like an unexpected rain-squall, and was quickly thrust away.

Janko lurched across the room to deliver my fish, the bird on the back of the chair near mine flew off and the girl on the stairs made up her mind. She ignored a seaman-trader who had tipped a drunken companion out of his chair and was patting the empty place invitingly. She walked across to the youngster with the eyelashes. I could have sworn he actually blushed when he saw where she was headed. He stood up, came close to knocking over his chair, swallowed in embarrassment, sat down again and gave a good imitation of a man hit over the head with a cudgel. The girl smiled a smile that would have charmed even Janko on a bad day, and sat down.

I turned my attention to my fish. I wanted to get out of the taproom quickly. If there was anything I didn't need, it was to be mixed up in dunmagic.

I had almost picked the fish bones clean when the empty chair next to me squeaked across the floor and I looked up to find the Quillerman, that lithe length of male beauty from the slavers' table, slipping into the seat. The charming smile I'd already noted tilted not only his lips but also the corners of his eyes as he said, "Niamor. Also known as the Negotiator." The name had the same faint familiarity as his face.

I reciprocated with a smile and gave the only name I'd ever considered to be mine, although I'd used a number of others at various times. "Blaze Halfbreed."

He looked a little startled. The last name I used was obviously contrived, and it must have puzzled him that I had chosen to accentuate my status in such a way; he wasn't to know that perversity always had been a fault of mine. Still, he didn't remark on it. He said, "I've seen you before somewhere."

"Perhaps. I've been in the Docks before."

He clicked his fingers. "I remember! You were here, oh, five years or so ago, looking for work as I recall. You finally shipped out as a deckhand on a slaver." He gave a chuckle. "I never expected to see you alive again. That ship had a reputation, it did. Some said its captain was a dunmagicker."

I grimaced at the memory. "They were right." It had been a hellish voyage and I'd almost ended up as food for a sea-dragon, but I'd been offered a lot of money to wrangle myself on board that ship as a crew member and there wasn't much I wouldn't do for money in those days. I doubted I would do it now, being a shade more cautious. And possibly a shade less greedy.

"You arrived this morning," he remarked.

I nodded. We were getting down to business.

"I believe you're still interested in the slave trade. I hear you've been asking around for a slave. Before you even got a room here."

I poked into the fish head, extracting the last bit of succulent meat from the triangle above the eye. "That's right." Typical of Gorthan Docks: gossip traveled as fast as the smell of rotten prawns, and everybody minded everyone else's business, or tried to, if they could do it discreetly.

He persevered: "And you want a very particular piece of merchandise."

The sweet morsel of fish melted in my mouth. Not even The Drunken Plaice could entirely ruin fresh solfish. I said, offhand, "My employer is very particular in his tastes."

" 'A Cirkasian woman. Must be young.' They come expensive, they do." His eyes slid across to the Cirkasian beauty at the next table, assessing her potential as a slave with callous dispassion.

I pushed my plate aside. "Uh-uh. Don't even *think* it, Niamor. In case you haven't noticed, that woman has class. I don't want any trouble. I'll take one that's already a slave, not a lady who doubtless has backup somewhere or other."

He shrugged regretfully. "That might be more difficult."

"I understand that there was a boat in from Cirkase with a cargo just yesterday."

"True. But the merchandise was direct from Cirkasian jails, courtesy of the Castlelord himself. The Castlelord takes a very dim view of the export of Cirkasian lovelies to the slave trade, but he doesn't mind foisting his male crims on to the unsuspecting public."

I snorted. From what I'd heard, the Castlelord of the Cirkase Islands would have sold his own mother if the sale had brought him enough money and no trouble. He and the Bastionlord of Breth who ruled another of the Middling Isles were both tyrants of the worst kind, and the world would have been a better place without either of them, but I kept that view to myself. I'd discovered it didn't pay to make political statements; they had a habit of being repeated just when you wanted to appear neutral.

"Look about for me, will you?" I asked. "I've a feeling you can find me a suitable candidate if you put your mind to it. What's your fee?"

"Five percent. Plus expenses."

I nodded. "Just don't pad the expenses." I had no intention of ever paying him, any more than I intended to pay for the slave, if I ever found her.

The business disposed of, he moved on to the personal. (He had his priorities right, Niamor. Doubtless he wasn't called the Negotiator for nothing.) He nodded at my sword. "Your employer a Calmenter?"

"Perhaps. What does it matter?"

"It doesn't. I'm just interested, that's all. I heard the Calmenters don't make their swords for just anybody. Very proud of their workmanship, the Calmenters. I did hear they'd only make a sword for an off-islander if there was a blood-debt involved."

"You may be right," I said, noncommittal. He *was* right, of course; the sword was payment for a debt. I'd once saved the life of the son of the Governor of Calment Minor. I might even have told the story to him if it hadn't been for that dunmagic in the air. For all I knew, Niamor could have been the source of it, and not even his extraordinary good looks and charm were going to entice me into a non-business relationship until I was sure he wasn't. Pity really, because just looking at him was enough to have me feeling randy. It had been quite some time since I'd had a man in my bed.

I finished my swillie and stood up. "I have a room here, if you have any business to offer." I nodded affably and started toward the stairs. On my way I glanced across at the Cirkasian, thinking that a beauty like her didn't belong in a place like this, any more than the youth she was sitting with did. She wouldn't last twenty-four hours unless she found herself a protector. Always assuming, of course, that *she* hadn't been the source of the dunmagic. But if she wasn't, she'd made a bad choice of table. She would have done better to sit at mine. I didn't give a damn about her safety, naturally, but I would have been prepared to offer her protection in exchange for information, whereas that pretty lad would be as much use to her as a mast without a sail—the fundamentals were fine, but without the right accoutrements, what's the point?

I gave a mental shrug and started up the stairs.

Just as I reached the first landing I looked back, and my eyes met those of the tall, broad man, the sober Southerman dressed in black. His face had not changed, but something made me stop. A strong emotion: *recognition*. His . . . or mine? Strangely, I couldn't tell. I couldn't remember ever having seen him before, and his face still seemed without expression—yet the emotion hung there in the air between us.

I felt about as happy as a crab about to be dropped into boiling water. Intuitive feelings always meant trouble.

Fearful of what I couldn't understand, I turned and went on up the stairs.

Once in my room I barred the door and flung open the window shutters to take a deep breath. It was a relief to leave the stench of dunmagic behind, even if the alternative was the strong scent of fish. My room overlooked the drying racks of the fishermen's wharf, but it wouldn't have made much difference if I'd had a room on the other side of the building. Fresh fish, salted fish, pickled fish, dried fish, smoked fish, rotting fish—everywhere you turned on Gorthan Spit there were fish. Fish flopping in boat holds, fish roasting inside ovens, fish drying on racks, fish pickling in barrels, fish preserving in smoke-houses, fish being scaled, gutted, filleted, dried, fried, skewered, barbecued, sold, eaten. When you walked the streets anywhere in the Docks, dried fish scales a handspan deep scrunched underfoot. You think I exaggerate? Well then, you've never been to Gorthan Spit.

Beyond the drying racks, seven or eight fisher folk were seated on fish boxes grouped around wicker baskets of fresh solfish, some of which gave proof of their freshness by flopping out onto the rough boards of the wharf. The fisher folk, both men and women, were gutting their catch with deft skill. Innards and scales flew along with laughter and coarse chatter. I wondered what they found to laugh about; it was hot out there, even in the shade of the inn, and I wouldn't have liked their job.

I raised my eyes. Farther away, on the other side of the wharf, I had a view of a row of ramshackle buildings. The predominant method of construction in the Docks was to hammer together whatever materials were to hand and to stop when you ran out of anything you could use. In this land without trees, most building supplies came—in one way or another—from the sea, although on my first visit to the Spit I'd seen a hostelry built entirely out of beer barrels and a shop with walls made of empty bottles. In the row I was looking at, most were obviously fashioned from general flotsam that included tree trunks, hull staves and deck planks. The nearest house had made extensive use of whalebones, another had a roof of shark skin and walls of barnacle-encrusted wood from a shipwreck. The overall effect was bizarre, yet not without a sort of misshapen charm.

(I must have been out of my mind. Did I ever think that? Gorthan Docks? *Charming?*)

I couldn't see much of the rest of the port from my window, but as the coast curved outward after the town ended, I could just make out, in the far distance, the beach beyond and the steep-sided dunes that rose behind the shore. The white sands there danced in the heat haze and shimmers of dune mirage dissolved into the air.

I closed the shutters, blocking out the light along with a little of the heat. I slipped out of my boots, unfastened my sword and lay down on the bed. I was going to be up most of the night and I needed to sleep first.

CHAPTER 2

I WAS AWOKEN ABOUT AN HOUR LATER BY
the sound of someone groaning. The noise was so close I
thought they must actually be in my room. They weren't, of
course; it was just that the walls of The Drunken Plaice were
built of driftwood planks so warped and poorly fitted together
that whatever went on next door could be clearly heard through
numerous cracks and chinks. I tried to ignore the sounds, but
there was no way I was ever going to be able to get back to sleep
while someone did a good imitation of a death rattle in my ear. I
sighed, strapped on my sword and padded out in my bare feet.

As it was still afternoon I didn't take a light—a mistake because the narrow passageway was as dark as it was airless.
Away from the outside smells I scented dunmagic again, and
my insides tightened. Distracted by the stink, I foolishly took a
step into the darkness, right into the path of someone passing
my door. I had an impression that the room next door was also
his destination.

For some long moments we both stood still, so close that our
bodies were actually touching. I couldn't see him well but I
knew exactly who it was: the tall Southerman dressed in black.
The serious one. What I couldn't understand was the effect he
had on me. Ordinarily, in a situation like that, I would have
stepped back and apologized—hand on sword hilt just in

case—but we stood there, nearly nose to nose, and a whole gamut of emotions tumbled about in my mind and my body. The trouble was, I couldn't decide what they were trying to tell me.

The predominant feeling was again one of recognition, possibly his, and equally possibly mine. Was my Awareness acknowledging the presence of a dunmaster or a sylvtalent, or recognizing a kindred Awareness? Or was my memory telling me I should know this man? It might even have been my physical needs recognizing a man who could have satisfied them . . .

When I did step back I was breathless. With fear, certainly, but also with a tension I couldn't identify. Part of me wanted to turn and run.

Before either of us spoke, the groaning from the other side of the door resumed with sharper pathos.

"There's no need for you to involve yourself," the man said urbanely. There was a moment of charged silence, while neither of us moved.

Arrogant sod, I thought, without rancor. His coloring had told me he was a Southerman. His accent, as smooth and as rich as thick honey, pinpointed the island group: the Stragglers. I glanced at his left earlobe and, now that my eyes had adjusted to the dim light, I could make out the tattooed sea-snake inlaid with turquoise bands that confirmed he was a citizen of those islands.

"Someone has been taken ill. I shall attend to it," he said, with a firmness that suggested he was used to being obeyed.

Unfortunately, there was quite enough authority there to prod my cursed contrariness to the fore. A moment earlier I had been a reluctant investigator looking for an excuse not to get involved. Now I was being offered a chance to return to my room with a clear conscience and I refused to take it. As I've said, perversity always was a fault of mine. "Perhaps I can help," I replied politely. "I have some medicines in my kit." Before he could protest, I had opened the door to the neighboring room.

The man on the bed was the young innocent with the lovely lashes, and he wasn't alone. The Cirkasian woman was with him. The man beside me hadn't expected that; I could feel his surprise. I was surprised myself, but it was the smell in the room that was more arresting: the perfume of sylvmagic, as pure and as sweet as spring flowers, overlaying an unpleasant putrefaction.

The Cirkasian was sitting on the bed, the young man's leg on her lap. She had pushed back his trouser leg and we could see

from where we stood the cause of his pain: a sore, green and suppurating, on his ankle. Seen through my Awareness, it was indistinct, its edges blurred with dunmagic red. I knew now who had
been the victim of the dunmagic spell downstairs.

Untended, it would grow, spreading tentacles of rottenness
through his flesh like gangrene and he'd be dead in a week, his
healthy flesh literally eaten away into one open oozing sore . . .
It was a vile way to go. I'd seen it happen once and I never
wanted to see it again.

The man next to me gripped my arm, his eyes narrowing. "I
don't think either of us are needed here after all," he purred in
my ear. He nodded to the woman. "Sorry to have bothered you."

He pulled me out of the room and shut the door.

Then, without another word, or even a glance in my direction, he went off up the passage the way he had come.

The Stragglerman was right about one thing: we weren't
needed. And I'd been wrong about the Cirkasian woman—she
didn't need a protector. She already had all the protection she
needed: sylvmagic. No wonder she could stroll so calmly into
the taproom of The Drunken Plaice looking the way she did,
without even bothering to wear a sword.

I felt all the old stirrings of jealousy. Dark, murky feelings
that always shamed me, but which I could never quite control.
Sylvmagic. Damn it. Damn her.

As I returned to my room and reopened the shutters, I
stopped feeling and concentrated on thinking again. Firstly, I
could have sworn she hadn't known that young man before
she'd entered the taproom. Secondly, if she had sylvmagic, she
must have known immediately that he was the unfortunate re-
cipient of a dunmagic spell, even before he knew. Practitioners
of sylvmagic had no ability to see dunmagic as I had, but they
were more skilled at sensing the physical damage done by it.
And so my next thought was if it had been neither a previous
acquaintance nor coincidence that had sent her to the seat next
to that young man, then it must have been an acknowledgment
of his need of her healing magic, his need of her protection. I
decided the Cirkasian was as foolhardy as she was beautiful. A
dunmaster could not sense from afar the annulment of one of
his spells, but if he saw his victim again he could hardly fail to
notice that he was alive and well. And a thwarted dunmaster
tended to be a vengeful one.

And the Stragglerman? His swift assessment of what he'd

seen in the young man's room and his subsequent remark seemed to indicate that he, like me, had Awareness.

I stood at the window, looking down on the now deserted wharves, only half noticing the sea-mewlers as they squabbled over the fish remains, their normally pristine feathers bloodied with offal, their serrated beaks jabbing and slashing bad-temperedly at one another. I was thinking that the last thing I wanted to do was involve myself in affairs of magic; being Aware gave me protection against the magic itself, but those who practiced dunmagic loathed both the Aware and sylvs. A wise possessor of Awareness, and a wise sylvtalent, kept their ability hidden around a dunmaster. There were many nonmagical ways to die, after all.

I felt a sick fear. I had a nasty feeling that magic, in the person of the Cirkasian, was mixed up in my affairs already. It seemed too much of a coincidence that, just when I was looking for a Cirkasian slave, this woman should turn up. Cirkasian women were rare enough outside the shores of the Cirkase Islands at the best of times. To find two such women on Gorthan Spit at any one time, without a connection between them, would have been quite a coincidence. I was after a particular slave girl and I was fairly sure she was on the Spit; I was even more certain that this could not be her, yet I felt there must be *some* connection. But what? It was puzzling. And worrying.

My thoughts were swimming around in fruitless circles like pet fish in a jar, when a furtive movement from below caught my interest. The tapboy had sneaked out of the back door of the kitchen and was scuttling between the drying racks on the wharf. When a fishermen walked by carrying a lobster pot, the lad hid under some nets until he was gone. I watched, fascinated. It was like attending the theater back in The Hub, the Keeper capital, and looking down on the stage from the balcony at one of those awful melodramas. I always used to laugh in all the wrong places . . . But this drama was real, especially intriguing since everything that I'd noted about the boy while he was serving in the inn had indicated that he was a halfwit. He didn't move like a halfwit now. He disappeared behind a stack of rotting fish boxes that had seen better days and emerged a moment later with something in his arms. He sat down on the wharf, surrounded by boxes. At a guess, the only place he would be visible from was my bedroom window.

It was a dog he held, a mangy bundle with an oversized tail

and huge feet. He fed it, played with it for a while, then shoved it behind the boxes once more. A few minutes later he was back in the kitchen.

Even tapboys had their secrets on Gorthan Spit.

WHEN I WOKE UP FROM A SECOND SHORT nap, the worst of the heat had gone from the day and a breeze was beginning to rattle the shutters.

Everything was quiet in the room next to mine.

I found the drudge and, by means of a coin, persuaded her to get me some ordinary skin unguent. When she returned with some, I added dried herbs that were supposed to be good for skin ailments, then went downstairs to the kitchen and persuaded the cook—also for a price—to give me some seaweed bread and fish paste. Finally I strolled out onto the fishermen's wharf. It was still deserted, although the strong smell of fish offal remained and there were people working on the boats tied up there, rebaiting fishing lines. One of them raised his eyes, grinned and seemed about to say something—until he spotted the hilt of my sword poking out of the sheath on my back and thought better of it.

It didn't take me a moment to find the dog; it was much more of a problem persuading it to trust me. Gorthan Spit curs learned a thing or two about trust and survival, none of it good, very early in life. Eventually some of the bread spread with fish paste made him decide I couldn't be all bad and he allowed me to rub him with the salve I had concocted. His initial growls turned to ingratiating whines and then to slobbering licks.

I hadn't expected to have the good luck to be caught at what I was doing, but that was what happened.

The tapboy found me.

He stood there gaping for a while, not believing what he saw. I guessed him to be about twelve, or perhaps an undersized fourteen. He'd been fair-headed once, if the freckles were anything to go by, but he was so dirty it was hard to tell. He had no ear tattoo that I could see. In the taproom he had looked at me with dulled, unintelligent eyes. There was nothing stupid about the way he looked at me now.

"No lad," I said as he turned to run off. "There's no need to be frightened. I won't harm you, or your dog." I held out the jar of salve. "Here, take this. Rub the animal with it once a day and he'll soon be rid of that mange. You won't know him once he has a proper coat of hair."

He stepped forward as gingerly as a cat in snow and took the jar, while the dog thumped its tail in happy acknowledgment of his presence. "What do you call it?" I asked.

I had to ask him to repeat the barely decipherable mumble, and finally grasped that he'd said "Seeker." An interesting choice of name. Perhaps there was much more to the boy than I'd hoped. I fumbled in my purse for some coppers. "See these? They are yours if you will try to answer some questions. It doesn't matter if you don't know the answers to some of them; you just say so. Understand?"

He backed off a little. He guessed now that the help I'd given his pet wasn't prompted by just the kindness of my heart, and he was wary.

"What's your name?" I asked.

"Tunn," he said and then added doubtfully, "haply." I wasn't too sure whether he meant his name was Tunn Haply, or that he was, perhaps, called Tunn but he wasn't sure. However, I didn't pursue that question any further. Instead I asked him if he knew a man called Niamor the Negotiator.

He nodded.

"Tell me about him."

That was when I discovered we had a problem. Tunn evidently spoke so rarely that he had just about forgotten how—if he had ever known. He could understand all right, but his speech was about as articulate as the chatter of a retarded parrot. He wanted to be obliging, but the tangle of sounds that came out of his mouth could hardly be called words. His first effort, as far as I could determine, was something like: "N'mor gudly tulk. Him sy summat—rightful allus. Bilif itn." I managed to translate this as: "Niamor talks good. If he says something, it's always true. You can believe him."

He wasn't unintelligent: he knew much more than he could say. I felt a momentary anger at a world in which no one had bothered to spend the time to teach a child to speak, but I wasted no time with that fruitless emotion. Instead, with a lot of persistence and many carefully worded questions, I managed to find out that Niamor had been on Gorthan Spit for as long as Tunn could remember. A rumor—which I now vaguely recalled having heard on my last visit—said that the Quillerman had been involved in a daring but disastrously unsuccessful embezzlement back on his home islandom, the uncovering of which had necessitated his exile. Now, from what Tunn said, it seemed he was not an embezzler any more than he was a slaver. He was more a go-between. An entrepreneur, although the lad did not know the word. Because Niamor had a reputation for being absolutely trustworthy in all his dealings, he was trusted. That did not, of course, make him entirely honest. He was as capable of making a self-serving deal in stolen goods as the next Spitter, but if he told you something, you could believe it. And in the dark world of slavers, thieves and pirates, a go-between who would faithfully deliver a message or undertake a negotiation was very much in demand. Niamor never doublecrossed, and therefore kept his head on his shoulders, even though the game he played was a dangerous one.

It seemed he was now a useful man to know. He had obviously honed his skills since my last visit to the Spit. I certainly didn't remember him then being such a prominent figure in the murky business world of the Docks.

Once I had all I wanted on Niamor, I turned to some of the others who interested me. "Do you know the name of the tall Stragglerman wearing black?" I asked. "The man who sat by himself in the taproom at lunch?" And who, unless I was very much mistaken, was one of the Awarefolk.

Tunn nodded. "Tor Ryder."

The name meant nothing to me. Further questioning told me Tunn didn't know anything about him either, except that he had arrived a week back on a two-masted trader coming in from one of the Middling Islands and that he had a room at The Drunken Plaice.

The young man, the one who had been given the dunmagic sore, had arrived two days earlier than Ryder on a fishing vessel, although he was no fisherman. Tunn couldn't make him out at all. He'd given his name as Noviss, but Tunn was sure that wasn't his real name. He didn't do anything except sit around looking as tense as a sand plover nesting on an exposed stretch of beach.

"And the Cirkasian?" I asked.

He rolled his eyes eloquently. "Cum yesty."

"She came yesterday? There was only one ship in yesterday—the slaver from Cirkase." I'd checked that out already.

He shrugged.

In other matters, Tunn was even less helpful. He didn't know anything about a Cirkasian slave woman—or why a slaver ship's crew and its captain, as devious a load of ocean-going rats as ever I'd laid eyes on, had told me earlier that morning that they had never seen any female Cirkasian, never had one on board, wouldn't know anything about one. They'd said their whole cargo was male and they'd had no passengers at all, and not even the offer of a bribe had changed the story one whit. But then, they'd also denied being slavers: their story was that they carried indentured servants on their way to Souther employers.

When I was sure I had extracted all the information I could from Tunn, I gave him the coppers and sent him back to the inn.

I took another look at that pet of his before I put it back behind the boxes. He had rounded ears that seemed far too small for such a sizable beast, and oddly slitted nostrils. His red coat, at least in the areas where there was no mange, was short and thick. There was a look in his eyes that belied his appearance: a shrewd calculation that had nothing to do with being a mongrel born on the docks. I'd seen that look before in lurgers, the hunting water-cannies of Fen Island, but they were never red-haired and had much shorter legs. Following a hunch, I picked up one of Seeker's oversized front paws and spread out the toes. They were webbed. I almost laughed at the irony—he was part dog, part lurger. A Fen Island halfbreed, just as I was.

Aware that he had my attention, he thumped his heavy tail with more enthusiasm than good sense, whacking it against the fish boxes like a cudgel. He whined, groveled and then slurped at my face. Fortunately I was quick enough to dodge this time, but saliva went flying in all directions. I ordered him back behind the boxes and he went meekly enough. In spite of his size, he was hardly more than a puppy.

I went on my way into the heart of Gorthan Docks with a certain reluctance.

The more I found out, the more convinced I was that I had stepped into something that was way beyond what I could cope with. There were countless plots inside every intrigue in Gorthan Spit, numerous eddies within every wave, and in my search for a Cirkasian slave, I felt I was somehow placing myself right in the middle of waters that I knew nothing about—and there was a good chance I'd be drowned.

* * *

EARLY AFTERNOONS ON GORTHAN SPIT
were usually hot and still. The glare from the white sands daz-
zled unbearably and even the harsh glitter of the sea was hard
on the eyes. It was at this time of the day that the smells of the
Docks were at their worst too, saturating the air, making every
breath an unpleasant effort. All those who could afford to do so
went indoors, closed their shutters, and slept as I had done.
Even the stray dogs dozed, sprawling in the shade with their
heads and tails wilting.

By the time I left Tunn's pet, late in the afternoon, things
were beginning to come alive again. It was then that the phe-
nomenon that resident Docksiders called "the Doctor" came to
revive the port with its ministrations. The Doctor was a breeze
that swept in from the ocean, bringing cooling moisture with it
to banish the heat and alleviate the stench. It was then that the
night fishing boats put out to sea, tacking their way out of the
harbor against the wind, and it was then that the town itself
shook off its lethargy. Shopkeepers threw open their wooden
shutters, hawkers cajoled passersby, beggars dragged their diseased bodies on to the busiest corners, and dogs loped along on
the lookout for whatever they could steal. The contrast to the
torpidity of the earlier part of the afternoon was startling, but it
never lasted, I knew. As soon as night fell, the atmosphere
would change as the shops closed and the bars and brothels
opened. The bustle and legitimacy of the afternoon trading soon
degenerated into the quieter and more menacing stealth of the
business of the night; a stealth punctuated by the rowdiness of
drunken violence, or worse, by the kind of noises that were best
not investigated. It was a rare night without a murder or two.

With my sword within easy reach in its back sheath, and
keeping one hand clamped to the purse on my money belt (the
Docks' pickpockets were notoriously skilled and I could ill afford to lose what little money I had), I went to find an acquaintance who had been helpful on my last visit to the town.

I didn't find him. The shop he had owned didn't exist anymore. It, and the rest of the street, had been burned to the
ground, not an infrequent occurrence in a place where most
buildings were built of wood and thatched with seaweed, and an
unusually large number of the inhabitants were either crazed or
habitually drunk, or both. No one could tell me what had happened to the shopkeeper. Gorthan Spit was like that: people
came and went, they died or disappeared, and no one cared.

I stopped in a nearby fish-and-swillie bar, all seafood again, of course. This time I settled for a cheap dish of seaweed and rayfish. Staying at The Drunken Plaice was an extravagance. I had to economize somewhere.

I was just finishing the food when I heard my name bellowed from across the room. My hand automatically dropped to my sword (now resting across my knees) before I realized there was no need. The bellow was one of pleasure, not anger, and the voice belonged to Addie Leks, a woman I had inadvertently helped on my very first trip to the Spit. I'd been twenty-three then, and Addie about the same age. I was hunting a man, a renegade sylv, who had a price on his head—a substantial bounty that I coveted—and she'd been that man's lover. In those days she was an attractive and much abused woman wanting to escape a relationship that contained nothing but pain and violence, and I'd been only too glad to relieve her of the cause. (That part had been easy; it was getting the bastard back to the Keeper Isles to collect the reward that had given me problems. He knew he was going to die if he reached The Hub, and he'd done his level best not to arrive, preferably by killing me along the way. I'd finally handed him over, minus several fingers I'd severed during one of his many escape attempts, but it was the hardest delivery I'd ever made.)

Addie wasn't quite as attractive now. She worked in the kitchen of the fish-and-swillie place and she'd grown fat. Her skin had reddened and coarsened. She flopped down in the seat opposite me and launched into a new tale of marital woe; it seemed that although she'd grown older, she hadn't grown any wiser in her choice of men. With surprise, I realized that she was hinting that I help her out of her present relationship as well. I'm not too sure what she had in mind, because I didn't give her a chance to tell me. I changed the subject and asked her about Niamor instead.

She said very much the same things that Tunn had, adding, "Nice fellow, Niamor. Always good for a laugh and a bit of fun. No more morals than a bitch cur on heat, of course, but he doesn't like to hurt people's feelings. Kindhearted is Niamor, as long as it doesn't cause him any trouble." It was a view of the Quillerman that agreed with my first impression of him.

"You should remember him," she added. "He was around that last time you was here. Shacked up with that sylvtalent woman. You must remember her. She was exiled from the

Keeper Isles for misuse of power—some said she'd used her talent illegally to help her non-sylv lover become rich. What was her name again?"

"Oh. Samiat. Yes, I remember now. What happened to her?"

"The Keepers forgave her. Took her back into the fold when they thought she'd learned her lesson."

That figured. The Keepers were always loath to lose one of their own.

Addie sighed. "I thought she and Niamor made a lovely pair. So refined, the both of them. Yet when the time came, she left him without a backward glance . . ." She sighed again, caught up in fantasy, even though Niamor was the most unlikely candidate for a hero. He was about as romantic as Blaze Halfbreed. "He was broken-hearted, I could tell. Hasn't looked at anyone, not serious like, since. Reckon that's why he can't settle on just one—"

I just stopped myself from snorting.

She leaned toward me conspiratorially, resting her elbows on the table. The fat of her forearms wobbled as she clasped her hands. "People say he came from a princely Quiller family. That he actually has a title. D'you think that's true? Could he be noble? Thrown out for some youthful indiscretion perhaps . . . Or even a son of the Quillerlord, d'you think? He has *such* nice manners."

I'd never thought that nobles had particularly good manners myself, but said vaguely, "Anything's possible."

I went on to ask her where I might be able to find him at that hour of the night and she gave me the name of several bars, then asked wistfully, "Are you sure you can't help with my little problem?"

When I refused, she pouted—a gesture that might have looked appealing on the face of a pretty twenty-year-old, but looked ridiculous on a sagging woman of over thirty.

I shook my head, made my excuses and left. I had a lot more to do that night.

CHAPTER 3

I MET UP WITH NIAMOR EVEN SOONER than I had expected. He was lounging in the shadows of one of the port's ramshackle wooden buildings and confronted me just a hundred paces down the street from the fish-and-swillie bar. Perhaps he'd even been looking for me. It would have been a safe assumption to make that I would be out and about at night, since that was the time when most of my sort of business was done. The port wasn't so large that it would have been impossible to find an acquaintance, if you knew the kind of places they'd be frequenting.

When Niamor materialized out of the shadows, I was leaning against a post so that I could scrape clean the sole of my boot with my sword blade (the woman who'd forged the weapon for me would have been appalled). I had apparently stepped on the slime trail of a sea-pony and the glue-like mucous had created a gall of sand and fish scales in my instep.

"Evening, Blaze," he said. He took my hand and raised it to his lips in a gesture that had gone out of style in high society fifty years before. "Time for some conversation?"

I slid the sword over my shoulder and back into its scabbard. "Certainly." I looked up and down the street. The lesser moon was already up and shedding a soft light. There was no one in sight, no one to overhear us, so I added, "Especially if the company doesn't mind imparting information."

"Information has a price in Gorthan Spit." He grinned at me and pulled me gently into the darkest shadows. I went willingly enough and didn't object when he put his arms around me (so much for my intended caution), although I raised a disbelieving eyebrow when he added, "You are the most magnificent creature that's come to Gorthan Spit in a year or two."

"Try again, Niamor. Or have you already forgotten that Cirkasian lovely we saw in The Drunken Plaice this afternoon?"

"Milksop. I like fire, I do."

"People who play with fire get burned."

The kiss was long and thorough and very satisfying—as far as kisses alone can ever be satisfying.

"Mmm," he murmured. "Sometimes I like to burn my fingers."

I buttoned up the tunic buttons he had just undone. "This lady is in no hurry to do likewise."

He pulled a rueful face, but didn't protest. "So? I can wait. I confidently predict that you and I are destined to share more than information one day."

He was about to say something further but someone came down the street in a swirl of blue robes. I just had time to note that the newcomer was wearing a peculiar hat and walking as if he had a pebble in his shoe, before he swept past, deliberately banging my shoulder as he went. "Slut," he said, almost spitting out his loathing.

I blinked in surprize and looked back at Niamor. "*Who* was *that?*"

He grinned at me. "There are a couple of Fellih-worshiper missionaries from Mekaté here. He's one of them."

That explained the strange gait and the hat. Men who worshiped the god Fellih wore top hats with a tall narrow crown and a small brim, tied under the chin with a big black bow. They thought it was a sin to venture outside their houses without covering themselves in this rather ridiculous and inconvenient headgear. In addition, they wore shoes with raised soles and heels that sometimes made them clumsy pedestrians. You probably haven't heard of them. They were a strange sect that sprang up on Mekaté, a combination of pagan superstitions and Menod ideas of a single God. They've largely disappeared now, swept away by mainstream Menod doctrine, and no great loss to humanity either. They were an unpleasant bunch while they lasted, and powerful too, in some places.

"Not going to go after him with that sword of yours to pay him back for the insult?"

"Come off it, Niamor. If I stuck my sword into everyone who ever insulted me, I'd be the worst mass murderer the Isles have ever known. So tell me, Fellih-worshipers are sending *missionaries* here?"

"Yep. Been trying to convert sinners to their peculiar brand of religious zealotry for the past couple of months."

I was incredulous. I had been to Mekaté. I'd heard the Fellih-worshipers preach. They muddled justice and judgment, sex and sin, vaginas and vice—the end result was the mix of ignorance, bigotry, and fear of death that they called their religion. They didn't impose the same rigid dress code on their women as they did on the men, but the moral code was similar for both sexes. Then, with odd logic, most of what was banned to their followers on earth was promised to them in heaven as a reward for their abstinence, which seemed ridiculous to me, but I had little patience with religious philosophy at the best of times.

I thought of Fellih-worshipers trying to preach salvation and their brand of puritanical morality to the people of Gorthan Spit and started to laugh. Niamor evidently didn't need to be told what was so funny, because he said, "I'd *love* to see them take on the whores down along Bonesetters Street."

"I'd like to see them telling the brothel owners on the dock-side to close shop."

"Can you imagine what would happen if they castigated Irma Goldwood for having dyed hair?" We both giggled like a couple of kids. Irma I remembered; she had tried to recruit me as one of her girls once. She was the rather large and foul-mouthed madam of the largest brothel, a formidable lady as unstoppable as a great white shark, and almost as scary.

Niamor was still smiling as he leaned forward, ran a thumb over my bottom lip in a gesture of intimacy and, lowering his voice, asked, "Just what *is* your interest in a Cirkasian slave, Blaze?"

I sobered up. *Careful, Blaze.* He's no fool, and you could like him far too much. "I have a mandate to buy one. It's that simple. But you can tell me something much more interesting: just what is going on here, Niamor?"

"You came in from Cirkase on a fishing boat this morning, right? And you already know that there's something going on? Who the hell are you, my lovely one?"

Laughter forgotten, we were sniffing one another out like a couple of cautious dogs and that could have gone on all night, with neither of us actually saying anything. One of us had to break the deadlock. I grinned. "Someone very like you, I think. I'm doing this for money, which I am very much in need of. Most of all I want to keep my skin intact. I don't like treading on toes, Niamor, especially toes that belong to people who are a lot bigger—figuratively—than I am. I would very much like to know where not to tread."

He nodded as if he accepted that much as truth. "Then we do have a lot in common. I thought I recognized a kindred spirit. Blaze, take my advice and leave. For all that you're a halfbreed and, I'll wager, a citizenless one too"—he reached up to brush curls away from my left ear, confirming that my lobe was indeed unmarked—"and therefore unwelcome just about everywhere else, you'd be better off looking for your slave on some other island. It'd be safer."

"Come on, Niamor, where else am I going to find a Cirkasian slave woman, especially one that's young and pretty? Most islands have banned the slave traffic, if not the slavery of criminals. You know that. The Keepers won't have it any other way. That ship from Cirkase is calling their cargo 'indentured servants,' would you believe."

"You should have taken up my offer to get you that woman at the inn. It'd be much simpler. She doesn't have a hope of leaving Gorthan Spit in one piece anyway, not her." He sounded cheerfully unconcerned about her fate.

I said, "Whoever tangles with that blue-eyed charmer will find her about as easy to deal with as a handful of lugworms in a rainstorm."

That interested him, but he didn't press the matter. He probably sensed I wasn't going to tell him any more. He reverted to my original question instead. "Blaze, I don't *know* what's going on. And that's a terrible admission for someone like me to make. Up until now, I've survived and prospered here because I knew what was happening. I knew the people. Not anymore. I'm seriously thinking of emptying Gorthan Spit's fish scales out of my shoes for good, and I advise you to do the same. Half of Gorthan Docks is scared hairless, and no one's talking. They're too frightened."

I caught his faint uncertainty. He was still none too sure whether he could trust me, any more than I was sure if I could trust him. I didn't think he had been the source of the dunmagic, but there was no way I could be positive. No smell of it clung to him now. I cursed the unexpected limitations of my Awareness. I had only my instincts . . . I took a gamble.

"Dunmagic?" I asked.

He gave me a sharp look with those dark eyes of his and lowered his voice even more. "I don't know. I don't have Awareness."

"I do." The admission was enough to kill me if he was a dunmaster. "There's dunmagic in the air, Niamor. I've been smelling it ever since I arrived."

"Shit." He looked at me with new respect. "You've taken a risk in telling me. I suppose you'd know if I was a dunmagicker, but what if I worked for one?"

I shrugged. "Then I'm as good as dead. Life's full of risks. What if I'm the one who's lying?"

He gave a reluctant chuckle. "Life's shit, isn't it? Hell, Blaze, you and I ought to team up. We could go a long way together, we could."

"I'm a loner, Niamor. Always have been. However, if you can find me a Cirkasian slave, I'll pay the percentage. And I'll owe you a favor. In the meantime, have you no idea who's behind this dunmagic?"

"Well—no. Until now I wasn't even certain there *was* dunmagic, although there have been a helluva lot of strange deaths lately. And most of them very nasty as well. There's been talk of people tortured to death or just rotting away, that sort of thing. And there's a village up the coast that's become a very bad place to visit. In fact, those who go there don't seem to come back. Creed, it's called. I used to bed a girl who lived in Creed, and she hasn't turned up in the Docks for weeks.

"I don't *know* who's behind it all," he added.

"But . . ."

"But I can have a good guess as to who his chief henchmen are."

"You interest me. Go on."

"There're four of them. Four bastards known for their unpleasant habits. A big redheaded Breth Islander called Mord—a killer, Mord is. Got to be with a name like that. Doesn't it mean death in Brethian crim argot? He's an ex slave-handler. Then there's his brother, Teffel. You'll recognize him by his nose: it's the size of a large sea-potato and about as attractive. He's just a cliché. All muscle, no brain, is Teffel. Then there's a small wiry halfbreed called Sickle, a torturer by profession until torture was outlawed just about everywhere. Didn't stop the likes of him, though, or the kind that employ his type—just made them more circumspect. He hangs around The Drunken Plaice a lot. Rumor has it he likes one of the backroom girls there, poor bint. The fourth one's the most dangerous of the lot: a Fen Islander with a chip on his shoulder about his short stature. His name's Domino and he's the one with the brains."

"But you don't think any of these attractive fellows meddles with dunmagic? Were any of them in The Drunken Plaice at lunch today?"

"Sickle the torturer was. But I've known the four of them for years, including Sickle. I've had business with them all, at one time or another. If any of them practices dunmagic, then I'm a lot more dense than I thought. No, this dunmagic business—if that's what it is that's got everyone so scared—started only about four months back."

"Then maybe you could give a thought to remembering who arrived on Gorthan Spit about four months back. Someone who has contact with at least one of those four. And who was in The Drunken Plaice at lunch."

He gave me an uneasy glance. "Offhand I can't think of anyone, but I'll give it some thought. Why?"

"Because someone cast a dunspell."

"At lunch? In front of everyone?"

"Yes. Not aimed at either of us, though, don't worry. But it was too powerful for me to say who was responsible."

"A dunmaster, then. That's a dangerous brew to stir, Blaze."

"If I know what's in the brew, then I'll know how to avoid agitating those ingredients that would give me trouble. I don't *want* trouble, Niamor. And neither do you."

"How to avoid it—that's the problem. There's just too much happening. And I haven't told you the half of it. For example, I haven't told you about all the people who have become interested in Gorthan Spit in the past few months. We even had a Keeper ship in here—Keepers! They've never concerned themselves with the Spit before. And there's a ghemph in town. Why would one of those thumb-fumbling web-foots come *here*? In addition, I've seen more patriarchs of the Menod in the last

couple of months than I've seen in thirty years of sinful living."
He shook his head in bewilderment. At a guess, Niamor had
never had much to do with the Men of God patriarchs, or any
other priest, for that matter.

A ghemph, however, now *that* interested me. I fingered my
empty earlobe instinctively. Ghemphs were citizenship tattooists.
Niamor's remark about thumb-fumbling was a gross calumny;
ghemphs were skilled artisans. But they weren't human. "The
ghemph. Is it still around?" I asked casually.

"Yeah, as far as I know. But don't get your hopes up, Blaze.
It's not doing any unlawful business."

I changed the subject. "Do you know anything about a Strag-
gler citizen called Tor Ryder? Or about a good-looking young
man who calls himself Noviss?"

He shook his head. "I know the two you mean, but God only
knows where they fit in. Neither of them are in the common line
of visitor, any more than the Cirkasian beauty is. And I don't
know where *you* fit in either. I wish you'd tell me more—"

"I've nothing to do with any of this. My only interest is in
the purchase of a slave." At least, that was what I'd thought
when I arrived. I was no longer quite so sure.

He looked at me doubtfully. "Ah—you're probably right not
to trust me too far. I have a reputation for keeping secrets, for
being reliable, but faced with dunmagic, I'd sell my soul to the
Devil, my mother to a brothel, and my friends into slavery, you
along with them." He shrugged. "Niamor always comes first
with Niamor."

I believed him. "Wise man."

"Look out, there's someone coming." He bent down to kiss
me again, shielding me with his body so that whoever it was
wouldn't be able to see me. I would have laughed if I'd been in
a position to do so; he was obviously very anxious not to be
seen consorting with a halfbreed who might later be recognized
as one of the Awarefolk.

A couple of drunken sailors walked by. When we surfaced
for air some time later, he said, "Lord, Blaze, you're almost
enough to make a man think of settling down—"

"Almost," I repeated dryly, and he had the grace to laugh.

"Be careful, firebrand," he said. "I'd hate something to happen to you, I would." He smiled a farewell and disappeared into
the darkness.

The rest of that night was spent in a succession of bars and shabby holes where the swillie was barely drinkable, the company barely tolerable, and the information nonexistent. No one knew where I could buy a Cirkasian slave. The slavers themselves, usually so very eager to make a sale, simply shrugged and said they had no such merchandise. When I tracked down a few of the seamen from the slaver ship that had come in from Cirkase the day before, hoping they would open up now that they were away from the ships' officers, not one of them admitted to having had a Cirkasian female on board, alive or otherwise. I tried bribery, I tried making them drunk, I tried tricking them into saying what they didn't want to say—and got nowhere. Maybe they were too scared to talk. Maybe they'd had a dunmagic seal on the subject placed on their lips. Probably the latter because around every single one of them I caught the sickening whiff of the red magic and that hadn't been there earlier in the day . . .

I set off for The Drunken Plaice before dawn, and almost didn't get there at all. Of course, having made it quite clear that I had enough money to pay for a prime quality slave (a lie), I suppose I must have looked like a plump sea-trout for the gutting. Few men expected a woman to be able to fight, and fewer still expected anyone at all to be able to stave off six armed thugs.

However, I didn't carry a sword for nothing. I was well trained, and experienced in the art of street skirmishing, and I had the advantage of carrying a Calmenter blade.

A Calmenter sword is at least a handspan longer than an ordinary sword and you have to be tall to be able to wear it, let alone fight with it. Even someone as tall as I was had to wear it in a harness on the back and reach for it across the shoulder. If it had been forged from ordinary steel, it would have been too heavy to wield properly, but Calmenter steel was actually a secret alloy as light and as sharp as the double-edged shaft of a horned-marlin, and even more deadly. I could make it sing when I put my mind to it . . .

And being attacked by six men on a darkened street put my mind to it.

They came at me out of a side alley with their swords already drawn, all six of them together, which was their first mistake. I could see from the clumsy way they crowded themselves that they lacked training. I half turned as if to run, which enticed the nearest of them into a lunging attack. Then, instead of fleeing as he expected, I sidestepped his thrusting blade and brought the heel of my left hand up into his nose—hard. Before the others had time to react, I had my sword in my right hand and was driving it past the body of this first assailant and into the chest of the second. With his view blocked by his friend, the second man never saw it coming and died on the spot. I hadn't really expected to kill him, as the thrust had been more or less blind, but he was undoubtedly dead.

I stepped back, and so did the others. The first man was clutching at his face, his eyes blurred with tears, blood pouring out from beneath his fingers. He reeled, half stunned, and was out of the fight. The other four hesitated, more cautious now. I demoralized them still further with a showy display of swordplay, weaving the blade back and forth through the air, smiling ferociously as I did so. It was all playacting, but in the dim light I hoped it looked formidable; if the sword had been made of Souther steel, I would hardly have been able to lift it in one hand, let alone make it dance. At the same time, I maneuvered myself so that I had the wall of the building at my back and they couldn't approach me from behind.

When they attacked again, it was halfhearted. They were still getting in one another's way, and their inept hacking was easily countered by my long Calmenter blade. Inevitably one of them made a mistake, a clumsy attack that I first turned aside, then followed up by tucking the point of my sword between his sword hilt and his fingers. His sword sprang from his hand and his fingers ran with blood. It was hardly a major wound, but the sight of more blood was all it took to end the fight.

"I'm off," one of them growled. "You didn't blasted tell me she could blasted *fight*!"

There was a murmur of agreement from two of the others, and the three of them retreated into the gloom of the side alley. The fellow with the bloodied nose had long since gone.

The remaining man glared at me. I made a move with my sword in his direction and he backed off some more, trying to look as if he wasn't hurrying. A moment later he too disappeared into the alley. When I looked around the corner there was no sign of any of them.

I might have continued to think that it had been just another ordinary robbery attempt if I hadn't seen the nose on that last man: it was as large and as squashily knobbled as a sea-potato. Teffel, the brawn without brain.

There was nothing in the dead man's pockets and I left him cluttering up the street, showing a lack of civic consciousness that was not unusual in Gorthan Spit. It was a rare night when the streets weren't decorated with a body or two. In fact, they had a sort of unwritten rule: only scavengers who stripped a body of its clothes were obliged to dispose of it, which usually meant throwing it into the ocean on an outgoing tide. Incoming tides sometimes washed the bones back, but not much else.

Back in my room, I went to bed thinking of sleep, only to find that my young neighbor had evidently made a fine recovery from the dunmagic with the aid of his sylvmagicking friend. By the sound of it, patient and healer had embarked on a night of lovemaking to remember for all time. They had endurance, I'll say that for them. They were still at it at dawn, which was when I finally fell asleep.

CHAPTER 4

THE NEXT DAY I WENT TO THE MAIN
wharf where the slaver ship from Cirkase was still docked. I
wanted to see if it was possible to sneak on board and search it.
Not a brilliant idea, but my only other one was worse: break
into the Gorthan Spit slaveholding house and have a look at
the merchandise, without an official guide—who might not have
shown me all there was to be seen. It was just as well that in the
end events overtook me and I never got around to doing either
of these foolhardy things.

When I arrived at the dock, it was clear that something was
happening. The place was crowded with onlookers. I saw Tunn
the tapboy and Janko the waiter from The Drunken Plaice, not
to mention the sylv Cirkasian beauty, all in my first glance
around. A moment later, I spotted two of the Fellih-worshipers
Niamor had mentioned; it was hard to mistake them with those
ridiculous hats and oversized bows tied under their chins. Besides, they towered over most people because the heels and
soles of their shoes were a handspan high. I'd been told when I
was on Mekaté that they wore them because the being they worshiped, Fellih, required his followers to be clean. They thought
shoes like that raised them above the dirt of the world and kept
them pure.

Call it religion, and people will believe the most ridiculous things. Why, I remember that on Fen Island there were marsh dwellers who made human sacrifices to will-o'-the-wisps, believing they were ancestral gods who had to be placated. So I went to have a look for myself, and you know what they were, those will-o'-the-wisp lights? Marsh gases! Stamp on the ground, the bog shivers, and out leaks the gas, glowing in the dark. And people were *dying* for that. But I digress.

There were also quite a few of Gorthan Docks' more respectable inhabitants on the wharf, as well as the usual pickpockets, crazies and beggars who haunted every crowd that ever gathered anywhere on the Spit. I had some trouble shaking off a halfwit who, for no logical reason that I could see, grabbed the scabbard of my sword and then wouldn't let go. A little later I glimpsed Niamor; he was talking to a man I knew to be a paid assassin wanted in at least four islandoms for murder. I wondered if Niamor's negotiating skills included arranging assassinations. I wouldn't have put it past him.

The cause of the crowd was obvious: a ship was on its way in. There wasn't all that much normal traffic through Gorthan Docks (any sane mariner with legitimate business avoided the place with the same dedication they devoted to avoiding a whirlstorm), so I supposed any off-island ship would have excited some attention. However, I had an idea that this one attracted more interest than usual.

I didn't need to see the flag, or the name, *Keeper Fair,* to know whose ship it was. I recognized the vessel from its design: the high poop deck, the raked masts, the cut-off stern—only Keepers built ships like that. The red flag, with its sleek, white horned-marlin, and Keeper motto, "Equality, Liberty and Right," was an unnecessary confirmation.

"Now what the spitting-fish are those meddling sods doing here again so soon?" a voice said in my ear.

I didn't turn around or acknowledge him; I knew Niamor wouldn't appreciate having everyone see us talking to one another again so soon. "Their job, I suppose," I murmured, bristling as I always did when people criticized the Keepers.

"Job? What job? Why can't they mind their own damn business? Bloody self-appointed lawmen of the Isles of Glory, pretending they're here for our own good. We don't want them. The rest of the world doesn't want them. Or need them. Keepers of equality? *Them?* Of reaction, perhaps! Liberty and right? Insensitivity and might, more like. Arrogant brass-lovers." He sounded both bitter and impassioned. I was so astonished that I did turn to look at him. He shrugged sheepishly, embarrassed at being caught showing that he did, in fact, care about something other than his own well-being. "Oh well," he added, laughing, "what does it matter? As long as they don't interfere with me, why should I worry?"

I didn't reply, but I knew his comments on Keepers were typical of common-folk attitudes. The powerful were always hated, no matter how much they did for others. And the Keepers had done much. They had wiped out most of the piracy and much of the slave trade that had once been so prevalent throughout the Isles of Glory; they had regulated trade and licensed the flow of commodities, and they now patrolled the tradeways between the island nations to prevent smuggling; they had enforced obedience to certain laws throughout the islands, laws that covered everything from shipping safety to the ban on cross-island marriage and breeding. I didn't agree with all they did, but it should have been clear to even the most shrimp-brained that the Isles of Glory had become less chaotic, that there was more personal security, more safety, since the Keeper Isles had extended their economic and legal dominance so widely.

The ship came in under sail and bumped against the dock as gently as a rowboat on a jetty. A typical piece of Keeper seamanship. There was very little the Keepers did badly. Just a look at the vessel was enough to know that they were special: the woodwork gleamed, the sails were unpatched, the ropes were neatly coiled, the brass shone, there were rat-barriers on the hawsers. A greater contrast to the shabby, fetid slaver tied up beside them couldn't have been imagined. And then there were the Keepers themselves: men and women in about equal numbers, tall and proud, ignoring ordinary mortals like the rest of us. And as always, my heart hurt just to look at them. Those pale golden skins, the rich auburn hair, the violet eyes . . . how many times had I ached to look like that, to be one of them. To wear the red cape they called a chasuble, with its white horned-marlin motif, as did all those on official service to the Keeper Council. To be a Keeper. To have sylvmagic, as a quarter of all Keeper citizens did.

Damn those unknown parents of mine who'd dumped their crying toddler in a cemetery in The Hub, the Keeper capital. Dumped their forbidden halfbreed in the one land that would inspire envy in her, to be raised, ultimately, among people she could never aspire to emulate. *Damn you both, Mama and Papa, whoever you were.*

A Keeper woman threw out the first of the lines. It came coiling down into the waiting hands of a dockside brat who ran to throw the loop over the bollard. She was about as pregnant as a woman can be without actually giving birth: her belly thrust tightly against her chasuble. I'd met her once before, and remembered that there was some sort of scandal about her marriage, but I couldn't recall the details. I was still trying to dredge up the memory when my attention was diverted to the middle-aged man who came up onto the poop deck and leaned against the railing to watch the final docking. His auburn hair had grayed along the sides, making him seem more distinguished, at least superficially, than his companions. His eyebrows arched steeply to give him a perpetually cynical expression, which somehow added to his aura of authority. The chasuble he wore was gold-edged and proclaimed his rank in the Keeper hierarchy: Councilor, one of the elected governing council. That was about as high as you could go in the Keeper Isles, unless you were elected Keeperlord. The Keeperlord ruled the Isles, but not with absolute power or by hereditary right as other Island lords did elsewhere. The Keeperlord had to be elected to the Keeper Council by Keeper citizens, and then to the post by Council members. Once elected, he was answerable to the Council.

The Councilor's glance drifted out over the crowd and met mine. His expression did not change one iota, and I thought—with shock—that he had known I would be there. I doubted that my expression was as static; he was the last person I had expected to see and doubtless my face betrayed my surprise. Someone of Syr-sylv Duthrick's status did not normally leave The Hub, let alone the Keeper Isles.

I turned abruptly and left the dock. I went straight back to The Drunken Plaice. Oddly enough, just as I reached the top of the inn stairs, I saw the Cirkasian go into her room. She must have left the wharf in about as much of a hurry as I had. I wondered what had sent her scurrying back. She, as both a practitioner of sylvmagic and a purebred Cirkasian, could at least have met the Keepers as equals. Unlike me, nameless halfbred Fen-cum-Souther brat. No pedigree, no sylvmagic, nothing to recommend me but Awareness, the one thing that had bought me a precarious semi-respectability, the one thing that had ensured I wasn't thrown out of the Keeper Isles the day I was old enough to fend for myself.

I lay down on my bed and waited. I knew they'd find me if they wanted me. After all, in Gorthan Docks there was only one inn that was anywhere near bearable.

And while I waited, I thought about Syr-sylv Duthrick.

WE'D FIRST COME ACROSS ONE ANOTHER when I was about eight. Duthrick wasn't a Councilor then; he was just a Keeper in Council service, a fairly lowly secretary, but with large ambitions. I was living on the streets of The Hub with a group of other outcasts, mainly children of varying ages. Our home was the old graveyard on Duskset Hill, where once upon a time the wealthy of the city had buried their dead in tombs above the ground. The place was ancient, the tombs neglected. They made good hiding places, fine homes for a pack of feral street kids with no money and no respectability and, at least in my case, no history or citizenship. There were a couple of adults living there as well: an old crazy-crone who collected rubbish to sell, and an elderly beggarman who couldn't, or wouldn't, speak. We kids worked for them. It was the only way we had to survive. If we worked, we were fed, it was as simple as that.

My earliest memories were of that place, the cemetery . . . of being passed from one person to another, of being neglected, of being cold and hungry and alone. I soon learned that the best person to look after me was me.

The day I met Duthrick, I was out in the streets with a couple of boys from Duskset Hill, earning some extra coppers scraping sea-pony slime from the roadway in front of some fancy Hub houses. A party of Keeper sylvs came past on foot, on their way to visit one of the residents. I had long since realized that I saw the world differently from other people: the silver-blue of sylv-magic and the illusions woven by sylvs were as obvious to me as a rainbow in the sky is to most people. I didn't know what my ability was called and was totally unaware that there were other people in the world who could view sylvmagic the same way I did. Up until then, I had no idea I could also see dunmagic, although I had heard about the red magic. Like everyone else, we had grown up fearing it, fearing those who practiced it, scared that one day we'd actually come face to face with it, even though we never did. Dunmagic was the bogeyman . . . feared, but also somewhat unreal.

Until that day, when a dunmaster attacked the sylv group. He was probably after a particular one of them, most likely the Councilor who ran the Keeper Guard at the time. As the dunmaster walked past, he cast his spells . . . I saw them, horrible, reeking, brown-red things crawling along the ground toward the unsuspecting group. I may not have ever seen dunmagic before, but I *knew* what it must be. Nothing else could have smelled so . . . so *wrong.* I screamed out a warning because, of course, none of the sylvs could see it.

I yelled, "Dunmagic! Dunmagic!" Wards of sylvmagic went up instantly all over the place, shimmering and beautiful, drawing strength from one another. They were like sheets of semi-translucent glass spun between bluish poles of twisting light, always shifting, always dancing with silver sparkles, just as sunlight dances on water. Brownish-red flared into crimson against the first of the silver-blue walls, but was unable to penetrate. In fury, the dunmaster flung a spell at me, which didn't have any effect—except that I threw up. At the same time, one of the sylvs suddenly doubled up, hit by a dunmagic sore that had managed to seep through an incomplete ward. *That* they could all see. There was bedlam for a while as sylvs panicked, and the dunmaster might have been able to flee, except for Duthrick. He'd been one of the group around the Councilor Guard, and he grabbed my arm, twisted it painfully and said, "*Who's sending it,* you snotty-nosed grub?"

I pointed at the man and the sylvs dealt with him en masse, while I stood rigid with shock, watching. You can't harm someone with sylvmagic, but you can bewilder him with illusion. And then you can stab him to death as he lies there on the road, trying desperately to ward off attacks by monsters that don't exist and guardsmen who aren't real. It wasn't a pleasant sight.

The Councilor, unhurt, came across to speak to Duthrick and me. He pressed a coin into my hand, thanked me for what I had done, and said to Duthrick, "A splendid example of what I have been saying for years: we need the services of Awarefolk." Ignoring Duthrick's scowl, he added, "Child, you are now in the service of the Keeper Council. Duthrick—see to it." He strode away, leaving Duthrick and me looking at each other with mutual distaste.

I didn't have any choice in what happened next.

Duthrick gave the orders; I obeyed.

In the end, he sent me off to a Menod brotherhood school for the poor, run by a few elderly patriarchs on the outskirts of The Hub. It wasn't much of an establishment. The first thing the brothers did was bathe me—and, of course, found out I was female, a fact that Duthrick had failed to ascertain. I was promptly packed off to their female counterparts at the Menod sisterhood school. It was a humorless place in a dark, grim building, run by women who seemed more interested in cleanliness than happiness. I hated it, and ran away several times. Each time, Duthrick was dispatched to bring me back, and our antipathy for each other grew. The sisters tried to teach me to sit down, sit still, shut up and do things like sew. Eventually they—and Duthrick—gave up and sent me back to the brotherhood school.

There I was more or less content. I learned to read, and write too (at least a little), and sport was a strong part of the day's activities. I was taught rudimentary sword skills, learned how to swim, how to draw a bow—all the so-called "manly" pursuits—along with less interesting stuff like how to cobble shoes, chop wood and wash stew pots. These latter activities were the sort of thing that was supposed to ensure gainful employment for students when they left the establishment, unless, of course, they wanted to enter the patriarchy.

Whatever I learned of morality, of decency, of gentleness, of kindness, of learning, I learned there, from those unworldly but decent men. They weren't particularly scholarly, but they did know children. Moreover, they understood poverty and how to alleviate the poverty of the spirit that all too frequently goes hand in hand with unlined pockets. They changed me from a child who believed in nothing, to someone who believed in herself. I will always be grateful for that, although in the end their doctrines were not enough for me.

Occasionally Duthrick would come and take me away for a while to perform some task or other: tell them if a child was sylv or not, testify in a court case as to whether a man had dunmagic or not.

I should have been happy. For the first time in my life I had enough to eat, I had enough blankets on a cold night, and no one was cuffing me over the head or stealing my bread. My life was not, however, all carefree. I was a halfbreed, and subject to the kind of taunts that most people could never even guess at. The Menod were kindly; the children were not. And always there was the threat that I would be sent off to Gorthan Spit when I was twelve because I did not have a citizen's earlobe tattoo . . .

"Hairy, hairy, halfbreed brat!" the boys would taunt, knowing I hated having to wear my hair long. "Watch your back, hairy tits, 'cos one day they'll come for you and drag you off to the Spits."

"You're only here because we allow it," Duthrick would say. "Put a foot wrong, and we'll pack you off to that sandy blight of flea-ridden hell. Halfbreeds are Spitters at heart . . ."

Sometimes I would sneak away and go back to the cemetery for a while, but it was pointless. That life had nothing to offer me anymore; even its freedoms were sham. Most of the children there never lived long enough to grow up.

When I was older, I tried again to escape the Keeper's clutches. What happened to me then was worse than anything that had gone before. In the end I came back because there were worse people than Duthrick in the world, and worse things than being teased in a schoolyard. But I don't want to talk about that now. Let's just say I was tied to the Keepers, bound to their service because the alternatives were unthinkable. I was a halfbreed, after all.

TWO HOURS AFTER I RETURNED TO THE Drunken Plaice, Syr-sylv Duthrick walked in.

My mouth was as dry as desiccated squid even as I faced him across the room. He was the one who had given me this assignment. His ruthless efficiency intimidated at the best of times, and now the thought that this task of mine was important enough for the Keepers to have sent someone like him after me almost scared the curls out of my hair. Or was it really just one of those absurd coincidences that people say happen all the time? I was no great believer in them.

He glanced around the room, set up four shining sylv ward pillars with a gesture of his hand, then linked them together in a lacy square around us so that we wouldn't be overheard. Only then did he condescend to incline his graying head, to smile in my direction. Over the years we had developed a way of dealing with each other: generally civilized and polite. Threats were always blurred with good manners; dislike was smothered in smiles. There was no point in behaving otherwise. Of course, even while he smiled, those deep violet eyes of his remained remote. I was used to that too.

"Blaze, Punt said you'd probably be in Gorthan Docks." (Punt, the fellow he had sent with me to Cirkase, had been as much use as a hole in a fishnet and I'd rid myself of him as soon as possible.) "Where's the Castlemaid?"

I felt sick. I could see my chance of fortune disappearing as fast as sea water into dry sand, and with it, the chance of earning citizenship of the Keeper Isles by my twenty years of service. I'd served Duthrick and his ilk most of my life, but they'd only started counting the years when I had finally woken up to how I was being used. I'd been about fifteen at the time, and finally brave enough to demand payment. Money, and the possibility of citizenship . . .

Duthrick had made a promise. I even had it in writing. But I also knew if I failed once too often, then my usefulness to him would be at an end; failure would become the excuse to turn down my application.

"Where's the Castlemaid?" he asked again.

I swallowed and said, evenly enough, "I don't know. Yet."

He raised an eyebrow into an even sharper arch than usual. I was thirty years old then, yet he could make me feel fifteen again . . . "It has become a matter of urgency."

"Why? Does the Bastionlord of Breth grow impatient for his bride?"

He was shocked that I knew. Then—Great Trench below—embarrassed. Duthrick was actually embarrassed that I knew the royalties of Breth and Cirkase were planning a cross-island marriage. I hadn't thought he had that much sensitivity. Or perhaps it wasn't sensitivity as all, but just discomposure because I knew the Keepers were facilitating something that they were supposed to despise. And, in truth, I couldn't help the bitter thought that it was all right for royalty to interbreed; *their* offspring were never citizenless, never cast off and despised as halfbreeds . . .

It was nothing new. There had always been one law for the Islandlords and another for us ordinary mortals. What was new was Keeper involvement. The Keeper Isles had no royalty and promoted themselves as the guardians of equality. They alone of all the Isles of Glory *elected* their rulers and they were prouder of that fact than all their other accomplishments put together. I had just shown Duthrick that I knew he and his kind had double standards after all, and he was a proud man. No wonder he was embarrassed.

"How did you know the Bastionlord was after the Castle-maid?" he asked sharply.

I shrugged. "I keep my ears open. I'm not stupid, Syr-sylv." Neither were the more prosperous villains of the back streets in the town of Cirkasecastle, which was where I'd heard the rumors.

He recovered his equilibrium. "There are political necessities which have to be observed at times, Blaze, whether we like them or not. This is one of them. The Bastionlord wants his bride. And you apparently haven't found her. Explain."

"I traced her to the Cirkasian port of Lem," I said, knowing he must be aware of all this if he had spoken to Punt. He was just determined to make me suffer. He didn't like inefficiency, and my failure to uncover the whereabouts of the Castlemaid of Cirkase was definitely inefficient. "She was brought on board a Gorthan Spit slaver ship just an hour or two before I reached Lem. Four quite unconnected people told me they had seen a Cirkasian girl wearing a slave collar taken on board. Two of them actually saw the coming-of-age tattoos on the backs of her hands. They thought she must have been some minor royalty who had displeased the Castlelord and was being sold into slavery. In the past, he's not been above doing something like that, apparently, at least to male relatives."

"These people didn't recognize their own Castlemaid, the Castleheir?"

I hid the smile that threatened to twist my lips up in a superior smirk. It wasn't often that I knew something Duthrick didn't. "Royal women *never* go unveiled in public in Cirkase. Not from the time they are five years old. In fact, they rarely go out in public at all. Castlemaid Lyssal was allowed out of the palace once a year—veiled—to attend the fleet festival. There's not a citizen of Cirkase, outside of the female palace staff and her own family, who knows what she looks like." I gave a sarcastic smile. "For all you know, the Bastionlord might be chasing a bride who looks like a sea-slug in spawning purple." (In actual fact she had been described to me by female palace staff as "truly lovely" and a "perfect vision," although one patently jealous maid had added "colorless" and "as skinny as a garfish." Her father, the Castlelord, had remarked nastily that, "She was good enough for the most expensive whorehouse, which is where I am tempted to place the disobedient bitch when you find her!" All of which had left me curious to meet the lady.)

Duthrick ignored my remark about sea-slugs. "You're sure it really was her on board the slaver?"

I shrugged again. "As certain as anyone can be under the circumstances. I traced her from the palace. She left of her own volition, by the way—ran away, in effect. But she was an innocent; how could she have been otherwise with an upbringing like that? She was captured by criminals on the outskirts of the capital. I don't think they knew what they had; maybe she told them, but who was going to believe she was the Castlemaid? The palace never publicly acknowledged she was missing. She was taken to Lem, kept there for weeks, waiting for a slaver. Then she was apparently sold. It was just bad luck that I didn't find her in time. As I said, I missed her by a matter of hours. I managed to find a fishing vessel that was about to sail to Gorthan Spit, and I came after her. I thought the Spit was the logical place to look, because it is the only place that openly trades in slaves, even if they do call them indentured servants or some other sweet-smelling thing. I told Punt to go back to The Hub and let you know what was happening, but I assume to get here so soon you must have caught up with him in Lem before he left."

He nodded. "I had business there. How far were you behind the slaver?"

"I arrived here a day after it did."

"So, where is she?"

"The captain and the crew of the slaver deny she ever existed. And I haven't found a trace of her. There is a Cirkasian woman of about the same age, who is said to have come in on the same ship—which the sailors also deny—but she can't possibly be the Castlemaid."

"Why not?"

"She has no royal coming-of-age tattoos. She's not a slave and never could have been. She has sylvmagic."

He frowned, disbelieving. "That's unlikely. Who's ever heard of a sylvtalent from Cirkase?"

"Why not? Anomalies do sometimes turn up in any breeding line. And we both know Cirkasians sometimes interbreed with off-islanders, don't we?" I added with sardonic sweetness. I wanted him to squirm.

He came as close to gnashing his teeth as anyone I'd ever seen. "This is just the sort of thing that the breeding laws were designed to prevent. The random spread of sylvmagic is just as dangerous as the occurrence of dunmagic."

"Pity people don't always obey the breeding laws as they should, isn't it?" I replied, still sugary. "She's skilled, this lass. Someone taught her how to handle her talent."

"*Not* a Keeper," he said with distaste, showing the usual Keeper disapproval of anyone but a Keeper having sylvmagic. They couldn't *do* anything about it, of course, but they didn't like it. And as far as Keepers like Duthrick were concerned, it happened far too often.

He still sounded sour as he said, "If she's the Castlemaid and she has sylvmagic, she could be hiding her tattoos under an illusion."

I was exasperated but I swallowed the insult. Keepers hated to acknowledge that there were some things that Awarefolk could do that sylvtalents could not. "She couldn't hide them from me," I said equably. "She has no tattoos. She has *never* had them. I saw the backs of both her hands quite clearly. And it's just as certain that Castlemaid Lyssal was tattooed on both hands in accordance with royal Cirkasian tradition. I checked. Besides, in the unlikely event that a Castlemaid did have sylvmagic, there's no way she could ever have become adept in its use. No one would have dreamed of teaching her, not in Cirkase. But this woman is skilled enough to cure a dunmagic sore."

"Then what happened to the Castlemaid?"

"I haven't the faintest idea—yet. It's possible that for some reason she never got here. They couldn't have landed her anywhere else—there was no time—so perhaps she was killed or died on board the ship for some reason, and was thrown overboard. Or maybe they transferred her to another vessel."

He looked even more appalled. "She's got to be found. And soon. I expect results."

"It might help if you tell me what is going on in Gorthan Spit. As you lack Awareness, it *might* have escaped your notice that the place reeks of dunmagic, but I doubt that you're entirely unaware of the problem."

"There's no need for you to concern yourself with that," he said stiffly. "We are keeping an eye on the situation. It is why we are here."

Of course. My problem with the Castlemaid was unlikely to

have brought them all the way to the Spit. When Duthrick gave me a task, he expected it to be performed without his help. I wondered why he had gone to Lem in the first place, but didn't dwell on it: maybe he had felt the need to placate the Castlelord for some reason or another. It wasn't my business.

His eyes glittered at me unforgivingly. "Why haven't you questioned the Cirkasian?"

"Because I can't be sure she's not part of some Cirkasian plot to dispose of the Castlemaid."

He was scornful. "Cirkasian plot? *What* plot?"

"You haven't been listening, Syr-sylv. No sooner had the Castlemaid escaped the palace than she was captured and sold into slavery. In a land that purports, in theory, to have outlawed slave sales—sorry, outlawed *indenturing* anyone who is not a criminal—she was sold to a ship that had dealings with the Castlelord's own agents. The whole thing stinks. My guess is that she was encouraged to escape and then betrayed. I'd like to know why."

He saw what I was hinting at immediately. "Believe me, the Castlelord is not involved in the disappearance of his own daughter."

"Perhaps not," I admitted. "But someone is. There's a lot more to this than you're saying."

"I am not at liberty to discuss politics with a non-Keeper. You were given enough information to deal with the situation. You have handled it badly. A full report on this will be made to the Council if you don't find the Castlemaid soon." He nodded abruptly, closed down the wards and left the room. I suspected he'd use his sylvmagic to hide his departure in the same way I guessed him to have blurred his arrival.

He left me with my anger, my frustration.

Five more years service, then if my application for citizenship was granted, I'd be able to look him in the eye as a person of worth. Then he and his fellows would have to address me as Syr-aware, then I would be able to own property in the Keeper Isles, then I would have a country. Five more years and I might just have that precious earlobe tattoo, the horned-marlin with the inlaid diamond splinter for a horn, the tattoo that would prove that I too had what most people automatically had at birth: citizenship of a nation, a place of belonging. Until then I was a halfbreed, welcome nowhere but a middenheap like Gorthan Spit, unable to own property anywhere else, or legally work anywhere else. Five more years . . . but only if I pleased the Keeper Council. Fail them, and my application had about as much chance as a tree had of growing in Gorthan Spits sand dunes.

CHAPTER 5

I WENT TO SPEAK TO THE CIRKASIAN, OF course. Syr-sylv Duthrick was right enough to question why I hadn't done it already. She was a lead, and anyone who practiced sylvmagic couldn't be all bad.

She wasn't in her own room, so I knocked on Noviss's door, and sure enough she was there. She was standing by the window, feeding some small dark birds on the sill. Noviss was lounging on the bed and the look on his face when he saw me was enough to sour whale milk.

"Sorry to interrupt," I said to him and turned to her. "I'd like to speak to you privately, if I may."

"She doesn't speak to slavers," Noviss said primly. He hadn't added the adjective "halfbreed" but I heard it nonetheless.

I almost sighed. The lad might look like an innocent but his self-righteous tongue was about as subtle as a sea-wasp sting.

"She can also speak for herself," the Cirkasian reproved him mildly. She left the window and came across the room toward me. "My room?"

I nodded and she led the way, without even glancing at Noviss. She might have been young, but she already knew how to put a possessive man in his place.

There was nowhere to sit in her room except on the bed, but

she had managed to procure decent brandy and a couple of whale-tooth mugs, so I was glad she'd suggested her room rather than mine. I was a little puzzled at her hospitality. On Gorthan Spit, gossip traveled as swiftly as a bore tide, so she had doubtless heard by now what I was after and I would have thought she'd be as touchy as her uptight friend, but she actually smiled as she handed me the drink. (I immediately wondered if it was poisoned and switched mugs when she put hers down and turned her back for a moment. I always made a point of being a suspicious bitch; it kept me alive.)

"Well?" she asked as she seated herself beside me and retrieved her mug from the wall ledge. "What do you want?"

"I want to know what happened to the Cirkasian slave who sailed from Lem in the same ship that brought you here." I had a feeling that it paid to be blunt with this lady.

"And can you think of a single reason why I should tell you?"

"You do know?"

"Perhaps."

"I want to buy her."

"We heard you were a pimp buying for a brothel."

"I did tell someone that, yes. It sounded a likely tale."

"And what's the real reason?"

"I was offered two thousand setus by her father to return her to her home." Substitute "Keepers" in place of "her father" and that was the truth.

"Ah. Then you know who she is." She sipped her drink.

"Certainly."

"The lady in question doesn't want to go home. She is free and safe, and she will stay that way. You may as well say goodbye to your two thousand setus."

"She's an innocent. How long will she last without protection?"

"She's not without protection. And what would happen to her if she went back would be worse." She took another swallow of her drink—without any ill-effect, of course. She was no poisoner. She continued, "The Castlemaid was to be married off to the Bastionlord of Breth, a fat, boy-loving tyrant twice her age."

"So?" I drawled indifferently. "I'm told such alliances are sometimes necessary. A cross-island royal marriage brings certain advantages: international accords, trade treaties. An internal one often leads to feuds between noble families. So, the Castle-maid has to marry the Bastionlord. That's the penalty of her birth. There are plenty of compensations."

The Cirkasian didn't move a muscle in her face, yet her eyes changed. They flattened; the irises became solid discs of steel. Not for the first time I had to revise my opinion of her. There was a core of hardness there that I hadn't been aware of before. She said harshly, "Doesn't that kind of double standard bother you? *You* especially? Why should Islandlords put themselves above the breeding laws?"

I shrugged. "It's always been that way." Still, I thought of my mother, trapped by passion or rape or ignorance into bearing a halfbreed, forced to abandon me so as to escape the punishment that would have been hers had anyone known of her crime. I fingered my bare earlobe bitterly. No one kept an Islandlord's child from his citizenship because of *his* mixed blood. No one hounded *him* from island to island.

I thought of Syr-sylv Duthrick. He and his fellow Councilors connived to break breeding laws for Islandlords even as they upheld it for people like my unknown parents. Like me. For a moment I was thirteen again, lying on the table in the Physicians' Hall in The Hub, knowing what was about to be done to me . . . *knowing* it, yet not really understanding. Not then. *Bastards all.*

But I didn't want to think about that. My future depended on Keeper goodwill.

"It's the Keepers who are to blame for this proposed marriage," she said suddenly, as if she had read my mind.

I pretended ignorance. "What have the Keepers got to do with a dynastic marriage?"

"Is there anything in the Middling Islands that the Keepers *aren't* involved in? The royal families of Cirkase and Breth only exist because the Keepers prop them up. The Keepers *like* royal dictatorships. Dictators are easily manipulated—and they keep the lower classes in their place. Keepers aim for unity of the Middling Islands under their leadership, with everyone bowing down to them because they are the ones with the power: with the sylvmagic. They tell us that without their protection, we'll fall to the dunmagickers. And people like the Bastionlord and the Castlelord jump to do their bidding, partly because they believe in the danger, but mostly because they know where the sauce for their fish comes from. The Keepers have bought them, just as they have bought everyone in the Middling Isles. We have become so dependent on them we can no longer stand alone . . .

"And in the meantime, people like the Castlemaid Lyssal get caught in the middle. Nobody cares, least of all people like you." She looked at me bitterly. "All you care about is your two thousand setus."

Her tirade had caught me utterly by surprise. Everything she said was true up to a point, and she couldn't have found a better way of making me feel about as low as a lugworm. But I needed my two thousand setus. Money was the only thing that kept me from joining the pox-ridden whores in some back street somewhere, and that two thousand setus was a small fortune. Without money, I had nothing except an unguaranteed hope I might earn Keeper citizenship with twenty years of service. Without an ear tattoo, earning a living was difficult. I couldn't legally live anywhere for more than three days at a time, except on Gorthan Spit; I could be legally harried across the Isles of Glory like a criminal—and had been, often enough. Even my services to the Keeper Council were unofficial and I couldn't claim exemption from the law because of them. At least with money I could buy some peace. I could bribe a landlord to turn a blind eye to his tenant's lack of citizenship. I could live well.

There had been a time when I'd thought money would also buy me a black-labor tattooist, a man or woman who could etch an island symbol and insert the precious stone within the tattoo, illegally, for a price. I had eventually discovered my mistake. The only artists who knew the secret of how to inlay the stone so that it did not fall out, so that the skin never grew over it, so that there was no scarring, so that its authenticity would never be questioned, were ghemphs—and ghemphs were incorruptible. They always had been and always would be, damn them. You couldn't buy beings who apparently wanted nothing more than what they already had.

The Cirkasian put down her drink and reached across to me to touch my hair. I jerked away, but she was only pushing back my curls to look for a tattoo. When she didn't find it, she withdrew her hand and looked at me with something like pity in her eyes. "You poor bloody isle-hopper. You don't have much sodding choice, do you?"

I blinked. "Er, not much," She'd surprised me again, this

time by her sudden lapse into earthy vulgarity; it was so at variance with her normal speech, with her aura of high-class style.

She poured some more brandy into my mug and reverted to her usual language without missing a beat. "Cut your losses on this one. You'll never find the Castlemaid Lyssal."

"Who the hell *are* you? A friend of the Castlemaid's?"

She shrugged. "What does it matter? I have Cirkasian citizenship, but otherwise, like you, I'm a renegade. My name's Flame, by the way."

I knocked my mug against hers in salute and started to chuckle.

"What's so funny about that? It's not my real name, of course. It's because of the color of my hair—"

"It's beautiful hair," I said diplomatically. It was yellow rather than red, so I assumed whoever had called her that must have been thinking of candle flame rather than a kitchen fire. "The name suits you."

"So? What's so funny?"

"My name's Blaze. Because I had a bit of a temper in my younger days. Together—" I grinned—"we're a conflagration."

We stared at one another and then simultaneously burst out laughing.

I hadn't wanted to like her. She was everything I wasn't: petite and lovely and purebred. And she had sylvmagic—which would have bought her Keeper citizenship if she had lacked a citizenship of her own. She had everything I'd ever wanted . . . Yet I liked her. I liked the intelligent humor in those lovely blue eyes, I liked the compassion I read there. I liked the way she came straight out and said what she thought; it may have been dangerously naive, but after the deviousness I'd had to deal with, it was a draft of sweet water. I said, "You'd better watch your step, Flame. Did you know that no one who sailed in to the Docks on that slaver from Cirkase would tell me you were on board?"

She shrugged. "They were well paid to keep quiet."

Did she really think money would buy the silence of dregs like that? Her strange mix of naiveté and shrewdness was puzzling.

I said, "I suggested that I would pay them more. Normally that would be enough to have such men show an interest, at least, but they were scared. Or dunmagicked. You didn't threaten them with sylvmagic, did you?"

She accepted without comment that I knew she had sylvtalent, but her frown deepened. "You don't *threaten* people with sylv-magic." She had a point. Sylvmagic could do lots of things as far as people who had no Awareness were concerned. It could deceive the senses, cloud the truth, blur reality, create limited illusions, promote healing—but you couldn't *hurt* anyone with it, not physically. Not like dunmagic. "What are you trying to say?" she asked.

"That someone didn't want me—or anyone—to know that you or the Castlemaid Lyssal came in on that vessel. And they were either willing to make some pretty dire threats or they used a dunmagic seal to make sure no one talked. I'd watch my back if I were you. People like that usually have rather nasty motives. Maybe they think they can earn a ransom from the Castlelord if they can return his daughter. Maybe they think they can find out from you where she is. Watch your back, Flame."

"I have the sylvmagic." She said it confidently enough, but there was a moment's doubt in her eyes, a flash of fear.

"That may not help you against dunmagic." That also was true; when dunmagic and sylvmagic clashed, it depended on which practitioner was the most skilled, and from what I had smelled around Gorthan Spit, the someone with dunmagic was very skilled indeed. In that one respect, I had an advantage over her: neither dunmagic nor sylvmagic worked against one of the Awarefolk. It wasn't dunmagic itself that frightened me. It was the fact that, because we Awarefolk could usually spot a dunmagicker as if he were a shark in a shoal of minnows, and because we were impervious to their spells, dunmagickers hated us enough to want us dead. And there was always an abundance of hideous non-magical ways to kill people . . .

Flame paled a little. "You have Awareness, don't you? You and that Tor Ryder both. I saw your faces when you opened the door while I was healing Noviss. That's how you know I have sylvmagic. You smelled it then. Neither of you could hide your surprise at seeing a Cirkasian sylv."

"They *are* rather rare," I said. "But you're not nearly sharp enough for Gorthan Spit. Didn't it occur to you that it might be dunmagic that we had? The dunmagicker who created that spell would have seen the healing of your sylvmagic spell just as you were able to see the damage that a dunmagic spell did to Noviss. Don't trust anyone, Flame. Not me, not Ryder, not even that pretty boyfriend of yours." Another thought struck me. "You don't *know* who this dunmagicker is, do you?"

She shook her head.

"Or why Noviss was the victim?"

She shook her head again. "Even Noviss doesn't know."

I sighed. "It doesn't take much to upset a dunmagicker. Perhaps Noviss was rude to him, not knowing who he was . . . that's all it would take. If he sees Noviss is still up and about, and if he realizes you're the one who cured him, then you could be in real trouble. I'd get off Gorthan Spit as soon as I could, if I were you."

"I want to. But I can't. I never bargained for what has actually happened: it's that time of the year when the two-moon double ebb tides combine with certain currents. Ships can come in from the north, the fishing vessels can potter around the coast, but no ship can hope to leave coastal waters for at least another week, perhaps longer. If they tried, they'd be swept south for days, weeks even." She gave a slight smile. "Thanks for the advice anyway."

I drained the last of my brandy and made for the door. Just before I left, she said, "You're still going to search for her, aren't you? What I said—it didn't make you change your mind."

I looked back at her and smiled faintly. "You're learning, Flame, you're learning."

Two thousand setus was a lot of money.

I hadn't given up yet.

THAT NIGHT I ATE IN THE TAPROOM.

Janko leered at me and deliberately brushed his clawed hand over my breast when he delivered my food; Tunn the tapboy grinned at me when he thought no one was looking; Tor Ryder of the Stragglers, still dressed in black, looked as serious as ever. Noviss glared in my direction whenever he wasn't staring moodily into Flame's eyes; I couldn't believe that the Bethanic idiot had been so stupid as to put in an appearance in the taproom, thus showing himself to be cured of the dunmagic sore. Was he really so confident that the dunmaster wouldn't try again? Or that Flame could save him next time?

While I was still wondering what made such a young man so arrogantly sure of himself, Niamor the Negotiator breezed in with some friends for a drink, winked at me, and breezed out again. The usual mob of slavers and reprobates were, however, missing and the reason was obvious: ten or so crew from the Keeper ship, all sylvs, had honored the place with their presence. They had used sylvmagic illusion to improve on their looks, a common and utterly frivolous practice that never failed to irritate me. The faint sweet scent of it drifted through the room from their tables. The trimming on their chasubles told me that not only were they all in Council service but every single one of them was a graduate of the exclusive Hub Academy, which meant they were the best the Keeper Isles had to offer.

They ignored me totally, of course, although I was damned sure there wasn't one of them who didn't know exactly who I was and what I was doing there. What I *didn't* know was just why *they* were there. Was the presence of a dunmaster on Gorthan Spit really enough to send a Keeper Councilor of Duthrick's stature scurrying across the ocean? Enough to make Academy graduates eat in a place like The Drunken Plaice? Of course, Keepers loathed anything that threatened their sylvmagic and were therefore dedicated to wiping dunmagic off the face of the islands (they still had a long way to go, mind you!) but they didn't usually send a Councilor and a shipload of their top officers to deal with one dunmaster. They normally sent someone like me, together with a few young Keeper sylvs who wanted to prove themselves. I wondered idly just how this lot thought they were going to find the dunmaster without the aid of one of the Awarefolk. I stared at them, exasperated by their arrogance and confidence, envious of their easy camaraderie—yet appreciative of their courage and all that well-trained, lightly sheathed energy.

Anyway, their presence certainly put a damper on the atmosphere in the taproom. Even Janko tiptoed around them. Noviss glowered in their direction as often as he glowered in mine; the boy was as transparent as a jellyfish. I wondered why the Keepers annoyed him so, and I wondered just how long Flame would put up with him. She had ten times his good sense.

However, it was Tor Ryder who interested me more that evening. His expression didn't change (did it ever?) but he was as tense as a sea-pony too long out of the water. I came to the conclusion that he didn't like the Keepers one little bit either. Interesting.

I ate my dinner quickly and went back upstairs. As I'd expected, Flame had locked both her room and Noviss's with sylvmagic, but that meant nothing to me. I just opened the doors and walked through the magic as if it wasn't there. I searched her room first and found nothing of interest. There were a few clothes, a bar of perfumed soap and a comb and brush, all of a quality that indicated she wasn't short of money, but there was nothing that gave me a clue to her true identity, or to the whereabouts of the Castlemaid.

Halfway through the search I had that funny prickling feeling you get sometimes when you're being watched; my heart lurched like a rowboat in a storm. I looked up, and found a line of birds roosting on the windowsill in the darkness, on the *inside* of the shutters. They were awake and were looking at me with bright, curious eyes. I decided I must be a poor burglar; my nervousness made me so sensitive that even the stare of a bird seemed sinister.

I moved on to Noviss's room, and there I had more luck.

I found a breviary in among his belongings.

And that could only mean one thing. He was a Menod. A Man of God. My jaw dropped about as far as it could go—that naive, immature boy was a lay brother of the Menod? He didn't fit with my image of the sect at all. I'd been schooled by Menod, after all. As a child I had sometimes loathed their discipline and their rules and their constant attempts to mold me into someone they thought I should be, mainly because I had never been a soft-shelled hermit crab, willing to shape myself to fit another's shell. I had respected their goodness, however. Later, as an adult, I had come to know a few of them, lay members of both sexes as well as patriarchs, and I had a sneaking admiration for their earnest dedication to Good with a capital G. I had learned to respect them all over again, mostly because they were so pragmatic. They did things rather than talked about what ought to be done. They didn't bother too much with public prayer or proselytizing like the Fellih priests. They certainly didn't hate anything that was fun, as the Fellih did. They may have been prompted to good works by their belief that such would take them to heaven, but nonetheless I had always found them genuine in their kindness and charity.

The relationship between Menod and Keeper was often strange, which might have explained why Noviss had glowered at the Keepers downstairs. Most non-sylv citizens of the Keeper Isles were in fact Menod, worshiping the Menod God and subscribing to the idea of a single all-powerful, all-loving deity.

There were more Menod patriarchs and worship-houses in The Hub than in any other city in any islandom. The Menod Patriarchy itself was centered on Tenkor, which was one of the Keeper Isles. In spite of all this, or perhaps because of it, the Keeper Council of The Hub and the Menod Council of Tenkor often squabbled, sometimes quite acrimoniously. The Keeper Council did not like the growing power of the Menod, nor did they appreciate the directives given to the faithful about the way they should behave if they were in administrative positions of power. The Menod criticized Keeper sylv morality and preached against the use of sylvmagic, calling it the temptation of the Great Trench. Worse still, at least from the Keeper Council's point of view, the Menod faithful were growing in numbers as many of the smaller religious sects in other islandoms, impressed by Menod charity and education, were being converted. And greater numbers meant more power . . .

At home in the Keeper Isles, anomalous situations were frequent. Many atheist Keeper Councilors sent their children to Menod schools, for example, because of their superior teachers. Some of the Keeper Council sylvs even attended services, seeking salvation as assiduously as any patriarch—indeed many sylvs managed to reconcile their faith and their use of magic. "Ethical Sylvs," they called themselves. Their catchphrase was "Sylv power with responsibility and Menod morality." As a consequence, the Patriarchy often turned a blind eye to what their sylv flock was doing in their spare time. I might have called them hypocrites, except that they had a strong aversion to injustice, such as the injustice done to obvious halfbreeds like me. Oddly enough, many of them, particularly many of their patriarchy, were Awarefolk, which gave me another affinity with them.

Well, Noviss had no Awareness, that's for sure, any more than he had compassion for the halfbred. If he was a Menod, he was a poor specimen.

I thumbed through the breviary and found a name on the flyleaf: Ransom Holswood. Holswood. A Bethany Isles name, if I remembered correctly, and Noviss had a ruby-shelled crab tattoo, the mark of Bethany Isles citizenship. Curiously, I was fairly sure I'd heard Holswood linked to the personal name of Ransom somewhere before. I'd have to think about it.

I didn't find anything else of interest and I left the room as unobtrusively as I'd entered, the sylvmagic locks seemingly untouched.

I WENT OUT INTO THE TOWN AGAIN THAT
night.

As usual, the day had cooled with the arrival of the afternoon Doctor, but the wind had dropped since and the evening was unpleasantly warm. A snatch of conversation I heard as I passed a group of middle-aged men loitering on a street corner told me I wasn't the only one to notice the heat. "Damn weather," one of them was saying. He scratched himself vigorously and I saw that his skin was covered with a scabbing rash; there wasn't a piece of him bigger than a fingernail that was free of it. I didn't know what disease it was that he had, but I guessed he'd been hounded out of his home islandom because of it. He continued, "I feel like a lobster on the boil. Must be three months since it rained last."

"Yeah," another agreed, "we'll be back to buying water from bastards with deeper wells."

I walked on out of earshot as one of the others began bemoaning the extortionate price of well water during a drought. It wasn't my problem, thank God. With any luck, I'd be off-island before any wells dried up.

I hadn't gone much farther before I saw the two Fellih-worshipers again. Not surprising really, as Gorthan Docks was not that big a town. They'd set up a raised stand, hung up a couple of lanterns, and were haranguing the passersby from this makeshift stage, exhorting them to change their ways or face eternal damnation. If they thought to make converts that way on Gorthan Spit, they were about as stupid as crayfish trying to find their way out of a craypot. It's hard to threaten people with hell when they already live there, and it is equally hard to entice them with a vision of paradise when in order to get there you had to abstain from anything even remotely enjoyable along the way. The inhabitants of Gorthan Spit, of course, gave as good as they got, and heckled the speaker unmercifully. I stopped to listen.

"Eternal life will be yours," one of the preachers shouted with impassioned sincerity as he wagged his finger at a drunk who could barely walk straight, "if you change your ways. Swillie is the instrument of the Devil, leading you down the whirlpool to eternal drowning in the Great Trench, choking and struggling for air as the demons of the Deep attack from the abyss . . ."

"Never mind, old Ike there'll drown happy as long as he's got his swillie," someone interjected.

"A nasty sort of fella, Fellih," someone else said loudly. "Drownin' people like that."

The speaker ignored them and turned his attention to me, singling me out with his waggling forefinger. "And you, you heathen woman, how dare you flaunt your sex in a man's clothing! How dare you proclaim your sins to the world by your wanton dressing! Do you not feel shame? You entice men to the sin of fornication that will block their way to paradise. You turn their thoughts away from Fellih toward lust of the basest kind—repent your evil. Cover your body in skirts and go forth with modesty, eyes downcast, to serve only your husband, lest you drown in the waters of hell . . ."

"Why, Blaze, I think he fancies you," a voice murmured in my ear.

It was Tor Ryder, of all people, standing right behind me. I had not thought to find that he had a sense of humor, and wondered if he was just being sarcastic.

Uncertain of how to take it, I ended up being entirely graceless. "Oh, shut up."

"Sorry," he said lightly. "They are somewhat repulsive, aren't they, with their absolute surety that they speak for a higher power."

"Not to mention their certainty that anything pleasurable has to be wicked," I said with a smile, trying to make up for being needlessly rude. The preacher was even then blasting forth about singing being the Devil's tool, and dancing the Devil's trap. "I think I'll be off to do some more sinning. It's more fun than listening to this." I said this loud enough for everyone to hear, and there was a ripple of laughter through the listeners. I nodded to Tor and went on my way.

I dropped by a couple of bars, drank a couple of mugs of watered-down swillie and asked some questions. About an hour later, as a result of the answers, I headed for a rooming house on the other side of the docks, a place that was renowned for the quality of both its whores and its swillie, either of which could be found in its cellar bar. I was looking for the ghemph that Niamor had mentioned—my own business this time, nothing to do with Keeper affairs.

The place was quite pleasant, as far as bars in Gorthan Spit went. It was clean and it was quiet. The woman who presided over the cash desk was as huge as a whale calf—and as intimidating as the calf's sire when it came to dealing with troublesome customers. I nodded to her and the narrowing of her eyes indicated that she recognized me. She had a good memory; it had been five years since I'd had a drink there. I gave the place a quick survey as I came down the steps. It didn't seem to have changed much and I couldn't see anything that looked dangerous: no armed drunks, drugged crazies or rowdies looking for a fight. The bar was the same block of hammered-down coral, the furniture could have been the same unmatched assortment of driftwood tables and chairs, the candles were still of the best spermaceti wax. The whores and the clientele might have changed, but the former were just as blatantly bored as their predecessors and the clientele looked just as harmless. Several Keepers from the ship were there. And Tor Ryder had evidently tired of the Fellih-worshipers, because there he was too, sitting with a man who was wearing a Keeper-style artisan's tunic that had seen better days, a poorly dressed fellow who certainly wasn't one of those from the *Keeper Fair*. I couldn't see the slightest touch of sylvmagic around him and I would not have been surprised if he was talentless. He lacked the air of confidence that Keeper sylvs always had about them.

Illogically annoyed that Tor had arrived before me, I gave him the faintest of nods and made my way to the customer who really interested me: the ghemph. It was sitting alone with an untouched glass of swillie in front of it. There was a circle of empty tables all around; people tended to give ghemphs a wide berth, although I couldn't have explained why. I'd never heard of one of them ever hurting a human, nor did they smell so very bad. In fact, if you saw one from a distance, you'd think it was an ugly human: tall, gangly, clumsy, but human. It was only when you approached that you saw the difference. Ghemphs were hairless, for a start. And their skin color was gray, at least on the face, darkening steadily the lower it went, until their feet were a sort of charcoal black. Their features were rather unattractive, with the nose and the ears flattened and the eyes lacking lashes or brows. Their sex was not obvious from the face or build, and as both sexes dressed alike and sounded alike, it was impossible to say whether a ghemph was male or female.

There were other differences as well. They had four thumbs,

one on either side of each palm. The hands differed from one to the other. The left hand had squat fingers with a grip strong enough to shatter a clam shell; the right had long dextrous digits capable of finicky work. Their feet were never shod and their long thin toes were webbed and clawed with retractable talons. I'd always assumed the webbing meant that they were fine swimmers, yet I can't say that I'd ever actually seen one in the water.

My knowledge of them was really rather superficial; like most people, I'd very little to do with them. In those days, there was usually only one ghemphic family in each town, although in the larger cities there would be a small community. There couldn't have been more than twenty or thirty thousand adults in the whole of the Isles of Glory before the Change. They were long-lived and slow to breed, and they usually had only one or two children.

They kept to themselves and were for the most part ignored by the rest of us, except when one of our newborns was due to receive a citizenship tattoo. Then, once the parents had obtained the prerequisite citizenship papers from a citizenship office, they took papers and baby to the nearest ghemph. For the payment of a fee, the ghemph made the tattoo and inserted that particular islandom's emblematic jewel—but not before it had made extensive checks that the citizenship papers were authentic. Ghemphs did, in fact, act as a check on any corruption of citizenship officials. They were so thorough that it was considered impossible for a child who wasn't entitled to a tattoo to receive one. And they never, never, accepted a bribe themselves, even though none of them was rich. As far as I know, their only income was from payments for tattoos. Funnily enough, they didn't bother with citizenship tattoos for themselves and no authority, not even the Keepers, questioned their right to come and go and live as they pleased.

No one knew when or how or why they became tattooists; it had just always been so. Because of what they did, because no one else knew how to do it so well, because they were incorruptible, they were indispensable. So they were tolerated, even respected, because they were necessary. Yet they were not liked, nor were they understood.

Like most people, I found them rather ugly. Unlike most, I disliked them for their rigidity in applying citizenship laws. Had ghemphs been more flexible or more corruptible, the whole system might have been bearable, or, better still, unworkable, and people like me might not have been regarded as outcasts, as less than human.

It was puzzling to see one of these creatures in Gorthan Docks. There was no such thing as citizenship of Gorthan Spit and therefore no work for a citizenship tattooist, although I suppose there might have been the odd sailor wanting to have a naked lady etched on his forearm.

As I've said, the Spit was the place you went if you had nowhere else to go. It wasn't even recognized as a nation. There was no government, no law, no order except what came from your own individual strength. So why would a ghemph go there? The only reason I could think of was that it too was an outcast, a renegade. *And renegades could be bought* . . .

I walked across to its table and stood there. "May I join you?" I asked, smothering my distaste for its kind.

The creature looked up, its face expressionless. As far as I knew, ghemphs never showed any emotion that was discernible to humans. It inclined its head in what I took to be a gesture of consent, so I seated myself. In answer to my raised hand, the waiter came across, and reluctantly dumped a mug of swillie in front of me.

I couldn't speak the ghemphic tongue, of course; no one could except they themselves. However, it didn't matter; all ghemphs understood the language the Isles of Glory and they could speak it, if they had to. Mind you, most of the time they said nothing. That was their way.

"I call myself Blaze Halfbreed," I said, speaking softly.

It inclined its head again, but didn't give a name to itself. As far as I knew, ghemphs had no names.

Knowing their dislike of conversation, I went right to the point. I unobtrusively pulled my hair away from my ear and said, "As you can see, I am citizenless."

It knew immediately what I wanted and it didn't wait for me to frame the question before it gave the answer: "No." The single word was brutally uncompromising.

I ran my tongue over dry lips. "Not for any price?"

It shook its head.

"Ah." I made a gesture of surrender with my hands and smiled ruefully. "It was worth a try." I raised my mug in salute and it did likewise, but it didn't smile. I was none too sure that ghemphs *could* smile.

I don't know why I didn't get up and walk away right then. There was no reason for me to stay. I think it might have been because I glimpsed something after all on that flat gray face, and it struck a chord within me. I could have sworn that I saw the ache of loneliness . . .

"Not much of a place, Gorthan Spit, is it?" I asked easily.

It regarded me with slate-gray eyes. Then it glanced around as if to test the truth of my remark, looked back at me and shook its head by way of agreement.

"Been here long?" I didn't really expect an answer, and I didn't get one. The ghemph drained its mug, stood up and bowed deeply, a respectful gesture they made to humans often enough. Then it said, "Earlobe tattoos are a symbol. Some people do not require symbols."

My eyebrows must have disappeared off my forehead in surprise at that. It was undoubtedly the longest and most articulate statement I'd ever heard from a ghemph. It was also somewhat obscure, but I didn't have time to ask the creature to elucidate. It was already heading for the door with its clumsy, loping walk.

I was still looking wryly after it when Tor Ryder came up, his companion having evidently also abandoned him. "May I join you?" he asked politely.

"Be my guest." I sat up a little straighter. For all his seriousness, Ryder was a *very* good-looking man and my body was very much aware of him. "We seem fated to bump into one another tonight."

"I thought you were following me."

I blinked, completely unable to judge whether he was joking or whether he was genuinely paranoid. It wasn't often that someone could throw me off-stride the way he did. I finally managed a noncommittal smile that could have meant anything.

"Tor Ryder," he added as he sat. "Of the Stragglers."

"Blaze Halfbreed. Of nowhere in particular."

"And so you remain, I think. I could have told you you'd never get anywhere with a ghemph." So he had guessed why I had approached the creature. I suppose the reason was obvious enough.

"How do you know I didn't?" I asked a little belligerently.

"I was watching the expression on your face."

"It was worth a try," I said again with a shrug. "However, it seems the ghemph was not a renegade after all. Have you any idea why it is here?"

"None at all. Blaze, did you see that man I was talking to when you came in?"

"The Keeper?" I nodded.

"I'd like you to meet him. He lives in a room upstairs and he's there now. Would you consider coming up to see him with me?"

A whole string of questions rushed through my head, not the least of which was: is this a trap of some kind? I was none too sure what to make of Ryder. The only reason I might have had some small trust of him was that he was one of the Awarefolk and Awarefolk tended to be slightly more trustworthy than common folk, especially when dealing with their own kind.

In the end I shrugged and said, "Why not?" But as I rose to follow Ryder, I felt uneasy, as if I was going to regret having said yes. And I had no idea why.

Letter from Researcher (Special Class) S. iso Fabold, National Department of Exploration, Federal Ministry of Trade, Kells, to Masterman M. iso Kipswon, President of the National Society for the Scientific, Anthropological and Ethnographical Study of non-Kellish Peoples.

Dated this day 6/1st Single/1793.

Dear Uncle,
Thank you for your inquiry as to my condition. It is a relief to be able to tell you that the fever contracted in the Isles of Glory has vanished, and I am now in excellent health. I hope you will apprise Aunt Rosris of this and tell her to stop worrying! Doubtless she will be convinced of the efficacy of the posset ingredients she sent so regularly. I shall come and see you both soon.

Who is this Anyara isi Teron that Aunt is so determined I should meet? Her last letter was full of it! I suspect she is trying to match-make for me again. I keep telling her that no young lady in her right mind would want to look at a man who is forever sailing away for years at a time, but I suppose an aunt's hope for her only nephew dies hard, even when it concerns incorrigible bachelors such as myself.

To return to less personal matters: I do not perceive any problem with my lecture to our august National Society next month and I look forward to presenting the findings of my research. Of course, I am a little nervous as well, as my methodology may be considered unorthodox—based as it is on interviews, rather than observation of behavior and the study of artifacts, which has been the preferred scientific method for most of my predecessors.

In answer to your question concerning the ghemphs: no, we personally saw none of the creatures, nor anything like them. However, the mythology about ghemphs seemed remarkably consistent on all the islandoms we visited. Everyone questioned agreed that there had been such an alien species once, living throughout the Glory Isles, and that they had been responsible for the insertion of citizenship tattoos, until they had all mysteriously disappeared, within recent memory. As far as we could as-

certain, this supposed "Exodus of Ghemphs" occurred at different times on different islands throughout the period known as "the Change." The Change started some time around 1742 (which is the time frame for the events recounted by Blaze) and continued for a number of years. It was over, and all ghemphs had vanished, by the time our first Kellish explorers and traders discovered the Isles in 1780.

Most people we saw who were more than ten or twelve years old had citizenship tattoos, apparently given to them shortly after birth, and they all agreed that these had been made by ghemphs. No children under this age had such tattoos—none.

We did not, however, find any pictorial representations of ghemphs, neither in any artwork nor in texts. We were hampered in our research of written records by our inability (with the exception of Nathan) to read the language of the Glory Isles, but we employed some of our own Kellish traders as translators and it seems that there are no records of ghemphs in tax archives, property ownership files, court files for both litigation and criminal matters, or in legal agreements filed with the registrar of records. In short, if they ever existed, ghemphs were never taxed, never legally owned property, never owed anyone money, never committed a crime, never signed an agreement, never registered a birth or death—and more intriguingly, were virtually never mentioned in other people's records. If they were real people, then they were almost invisible!

Glorians usually kept extensive written records of daily transactions throughout the islandoms, especially where these concerned citizenship, so we were led to the conclusion that ghemphs must have been more mythological than real. Moreover, when we tried to trace ghemphic skeletal remains, we were told they consigned their dead to the sea. When we investigated areas where they were said to have lived, we found no artifacts.

This discrepancy between oral history and tangible evidence is one of the most intriguing mysteries we have encountered on the Glory Isles and is worthy of further research. It will be difficult work, as there is a marked reluctance on the part of many people in the Isles to even mention ghemphs. Why there was a necessity to invent mythological creatures in the first place is unknown. I suspect that it has something to do with the shame people feel over the old citizenship laws, which were apparently draconian. It may have been a socially acceptable device that allowed Keeper officials to enforce these laws, while maintaining a myth that it was an alien race who was really responsible for them. I might add that when we did find citizens ready to talk, such as the elderly woman Blaze Halfbreed, their belief in ghemphs was so deep-rooted as to be ineradicable. Perhaps for such people, memory and time has blurred the line between myth and reality.

The present people of the Glory Isles are, of course, deeply superstitious and gullible, as their belief in old magic indicates. Do not be fooled by the level of their material development. That may be well above any other indigenous peoples we Kells have found on our voyages of discovery during the past century or more, but they still have not reached a level of philosophical sophistication anywhere near our own! When I saw the sailing vessels they possess, and observed their weaponry, I was at first fooled too, but they are still barbarians, holding barbarian beliefs. Their religion, while monotheist, is not the true faith of the Kells. They do not, for example, acknowledge that God still reveals himself in person to deserving individuals; nor do they believe that God once walked among us, in all his magnificence, to teach us the Rules for a Godly Life. I became so fond of my Glorian subjects, I was constantly having to remind myself of this basic flaw in their cultural character.

But I digress. Perhaps I should point out that there is another theory being bandied about here in the Department, postulating that there were indeed ghemphs and that they simply died out as native peoples often do after contact with more advanced civilizations—in this case the more advanced people being not the Kells but the Glorians. This theory hypothesizes that the ghemphs were human, of course, but with some racial characteristics that gave rise to numerous myths about their physiology. It doesn't explain all the anomalies, but it is an attractive theory, nonetheless, and obviously more un-

derstandable to us than the idea that they were a figment
of the imagination of islanders. I am still assessing the
problem.

You sound quite fascinated with Blaze. She is the most
amazing old lady, and I wish I could have persuaded her
to return with me to Kell. She would have made a wonderful exhibit at a public exposition. I have finished edit-
ing the translation of another packet of my conversations
with the sword-wielding lady, which I enclose for your ed-
ification. The translator, by the way, is again Scribe
Nathan. I cannot even begin to say how much I owe to
him. Although my knowledge of the language of the
Glory Isles is comprehensive, thanks to my studies of papers brought back by the first traders and explorers, without Nathan I would not have achieved nearly so much.
He is the son of the legendary trader, Vadim i. Pellis, and
as a boy in 1780 he was aboard the first Kellish ship to
sight the Isles of Glory. He subsequently lived for five
years in The Hub, and I am indeed lucky that he elected
to return there with us on the Seadrift. He has been working on the translation of the conversations into Kellish
ever since we returned here. I will bring him along to the
presentation.

I remain,
Your dutiful nephew,
Shor iso Fabold

"The trial?" I prompted, when he fell silent.

He drew his hair back and showed his left earlobe. It had been cut away. "Had my citizenship revoked. I was found guilty of treachery." I was beginning to find Wantage interesting after all. A citizen could be exiled for any number of things, but treachery to one's islandom was the only crime for which citizenship could be permanently revoked, and it rarely happened.

"I always looked up to those with sylvmagic," he said. "Always thought that they were our protectors, keeping us safe from dunmagickers, ordering our world for our benefit, and all. Never begrudged them what they had; thought it was justice that they were richer than us ordinary folk. Mind you, fellows like me didn't meet them all that often. I made boots for working folk mostly, not their fancy kind of slippers, not kidskin pumps and all.

"When I was a nipper in my father's shop I saw my first sylvtalents. They were just walking down the street, and they seemed to glow with silver-blue. I thought they were the most beautiful people in all the Isles. That was when I found out that not everyone saw them the same way I did—there were no Awarefolk around our parts. You know how rare Awarefolk are among the Keeper-born. So I shut up 'bout what I could see. Never did talk to no one about it much; only my family and my closest friends ever knew I had Awareness.

"Well, in time my Da died and I took over the business. I had a friend who owned the shop next door. A tailor he was, and as fine a man as you ever did come across. But he was a complainer, and he didn't like the way we was taxed. We always seemed to be paying over money for some reason or another. For me, there was a tax on leather, a tax on thread, a tax on the number of lasts in my shop, a tax because I owned a shop, a tax on the food we bought, a school tax 'cos I sent my youngest brother to the dame-school—tax on every darn thing you could think of. Well, I reckoned it weren't so very bad. After all, there was roads to be paid for, and the docks to be repaired and all those other things the people in The Hub did for us, like anti-pirate patrols. They had to have taxes to pay for them, right?

"But Glock—the tailor, you know—he didn't feel that way. He thought there was too many of them taxes and too many rich sylv folk, and so when there was an election for Townmaster of Margreg, he decided he was going to stand. It was unheard of for someone who wasn't a sylv to be Townmaster, you know.

No non-sylv had ever tried. But that didn't stop Glock. And he had lots of friends, and lots of people felt the same way he did. So, before you know it, it looked as though he might win, and Froctor, the sylvtalent who was standing agin him, was hopping mad.

"Don't know whether you know this, but they always invite the candidates in to have a look at the way the votes is counted—to make sure there's no fiddling, you see. And the counting men, they are well-known men of the town: burghers and such. Respectable folk. Well, Glock asked me to come along with him to watch the count. Do you know how you cast a vote in the Keeper Isles? Each candidate is represented by a color and when you go along to vote you are given shells of different colors. You drop the shell that matches the color of the candidate of your choice into the voting box and discard the shells you don't want into the remainder box.

"Well, when I went along to see the count, that's when things went all wrong for me. You see, I could see what was happening. The sylvs, they were changing the shells. With magic. There were two candidates for this election: Glock, who had purple winkles, and Froctor, with pink cockles. The counting men, they'd empty out the shell box on to the table in front of them, and to them, most of the shells were cockles—pink cockles to match Froctor's color. But I knew they weren't really—they were purple winkles, cast for Glock. What I *could* see was that they were all tinged silver. It was magic that made them look like pink cockles to everyone else. Even I could see a bit of pink, although they still looked like winkles to me. Them sylvs were standing there watching the count with smirks on their faces. They never dreamed that there was one of the Awarefolk anywhere in Margreg to see the truth.

"Even then, you know, I thought it was just Froctor and maybe a couple of his pals who was to blame. I thought the others couldn't have known—after all, sylvs see the results of anyone else's magic as reality, don't they? I mean, to them, them winkles of Glock's really would have looked like cockles. Well, to make the story shorter, I made a fuss. I complained to the outgoing Townmaster, and he told me I was a liar. And something in the way he said it told me that he had known all along . . . But there were common folk who did believe me, and there was trouble, although nothing came of it. There wasn't even an inquiry. So I went to The Hub. I was stupid, I suppose,

but I felt betrayed. They were *sylvs*. They were supposed to be
better than the rest of us. They were the people we looked up to,
our heroes. They shouldn't have behaved like that.

"I was . . . *ashamed* for them. Can you understand that? I
thought I had to go to The Hub, to tell the Keeper Council what
sort of people had power in Margreg. Thought it was my duty as
a citizen.

"But they said I was a liar, an—an inciter of riots. Told me to
go home and keep my mouth shut. But I wouldn't. They tried to
bribe me, and I flung the money back in their faces. I was horrified. Everything that I had thought to be true was a lie . . ."

He shook his head sorrowfully, and his voice was so choked
he couldn't continue. It was Tor who said, "In the end the only
way they could silence him was to have him stand trial as a trai-
tor, to blacken him as a liar and an agitator. They used false evidence. False witnesses—all sylvs. His citizenship was revoked,
his business taken from him. He was permanently exiled from
the Keeper Isles. Made a non-Keeper for telling the truth."

Tor Ryder was watching me closely as he spoke, as if wanting to see my reaction. I still had no idea why he had wanted me
to hear the story. I said, addressing Ryder, "He would have been
killed for less on some islandoms."

"Yes," Wantage agreed sadly. "But we are supposed to be
better. We are Keepers." He hunched up over his drink and
didn't look at me again.

Tor Ryder and I left together shortly afterward, and we
walked back to The Drunken Plaice. My hand hovered close to
my sword hilt all the way back. Ryder, the shrimp-brained idiot,
still wasn't wearing a sword, but we were a formidable couple
anyway, too formidable for the petty criminals of the Docks to
want to touch. The only person who dared to approach us was a
beggar, a man who obviously hadn't washed his body or his
clothes in a year or two. He was drooling in a halfwitted way
and I suspected that he was another victim of the policy—followed by most of the islandoms of the Isles of Glory—of
dumping the mad and the incurably sick on the Spit. Ryder
dropped some money into his outstretched palm and he sidled
away, giggling.

Somewhere along the way I asked Ryder why he'd wanted
me to meet Wantage.

"I thought it might make you think," he said obscurely.

I was still more puzzled. "Why should it make me think? He didn't tell me anything I didn't know already, at least in general."

I glanced across at him as I spoke and caught a look of sadness on his face. He asked, "Doesn't that kind of duplicity worry you?"

"Why should it? They can't deceive *me*! Besides, for the most part sylvs are better qualified to rule than people like Glock the tailor anyway. Dunmagickers have never gained control of the Keeper Isles as they have from time to time elsewhere, and it's only because sylvs rule there. So what if sylv methods are underhand—their skills are put to good use once they are in power. There are rules governing the use of sylv-magic, and they are usually obeyed. If Froctor had acted alone, he would have been found out and severely disciplined. He must have acted with the approval of the Council."

He stared at me, expressionless. I felt rather than saw his disappointment, and didn't particularly care. I hadn't asked for his approval.

He changed the subject and started to talk about his home, the Stragglers. It turned out that I had once passed through the small town that was his birthplace and we chatted about that, swapping tales of the delicious grilled lobsters they sold in the marketplace, and the way the hills tumbled down to the sea . . .

We said goodnight in the dark passage outside my room. I couldn't see him, but I was very much aware of him, of his maleness. I half expected him to touch me, to give some sign that he was not averse to sharing my bed, but he neither said nor did anything. I didn't know whether I was disappointed, or merely piqued. Part of me was a little afraid of him, of the edge to his humor, of the dark brooding quality in those sea-blue eyes of his.

He was an enigma, and enigmas are dangerous.

I WOKE TO THE SOUND OF POUNDING AT my door a mere half an hour or so after I'd fallen asleep.

I unsheathed my sword, went to unbar the door—and found the last person I had expected: Noviss. Or maybe more accurately, Ransom Holswood. He tumbled into my room, flapping like a stranded fish. "Please, you've got to do something," he said. "It's Flame—she's disappeared. Something *terrible's* happened."

I sheathed the sword; I couldn't believe this wild-eyed youth was any kind of danger to me. "Suppose you start at the beginning?" I suggested, and closed the door behind him.

"She went to—" he began, then blushed, stammered and finally mumbled something I couldn't catch.

"She what?" I asked, making no attempt to hide my exasperation. There was something about Noviss-Ransom that brought out the worst in me.

"She, er, went outside. To the, er, privy. And she didn't come back. I, um, waited. She had been, um, in my room. We were, er, talking, you know."

"Yes, I know." The dryness of my tone went right above his head.

"I went down to look for her, but she's not there. She's not anywhere! You've *got* to do something."

"Great Trench below, I don't *have* to do anything. I'm not her nursemaid! Maybe she just felt like going for a stroll. She'll be back in the morning."

"But she *said* she was coming straight back." He clutched at my arm. "Please, I don't know what to do."

I sighed and refrained from asking why he didn't look for her himself. The answer was obvious: he was scared silly of being the target of another dunmagic attack. It was also obvious I wasn't going to be allowed to sleep until I had made an attempt to find the errant lovergirl, so I said, "All right, all right. I'll go downstairs and have a look. Stay here until I come back." I buckled on my sword, put on my boots and left him there. He was still flapping in agitation.

The stink of dunmagic hit me the moment I stepped out of the back door of the inn. I would rather have shoved my nose in a case of rotting fish than have breathed in that vileness, but I had a look around. There were unpleasant tongues of red fluttering across the dirty grit of the yard. I'd almost decided I was not going to find anything that would tell me what had happened, when I heard what sounded like a snuffle from the fuel shed where the dried seaweed for burning was stored. I went in, sword drawn.

Tunn and his mangy pet were lying on top of the weed, wrapped in a blanket that was more hole than cloth. He had his hand clamped over the beast's nose, but its tail was thumping hard.

"It's only me, Tunn," I said. "Blaze. I'm looking for the Cirkasian woman. Have you seen her?"

His eyes were wide with fear. He nodded and the rush of words that followed was close to gibberish. Once I'd slowed him down, it was slightly more intelligible. The story was not, however, one that I enjoyed hearing.

The dog-cum-lurger had heard Flame and had woken Tunn—the shed evidently doubled as the tapboy's bedroom. The boy had pressed his eye to a crack in the shed wall and had seen her doubled up in the yard as if in terrible pain ("lik she git pokt middet in wit spittin' hot roastin' spit" was the way Tunn put it). She had been rolling on the ground clutching her middle. Tunn had been about to go and see what was the matter when he'd realized there was someone else there, standing off in the shadows by the wall. It had been too dark to see properly, but he'd thought it was a man. Whoever it was, they hadn't done anything except watch as Flame writhed in agony. Tunn, understandably, had been scared and had decided to stay put. Flame had finally stopped moving and had just lain there on the ground, whereupon the man had dragged her into the shadows. He'd spent some time there, but it was too dark for Tunn to see what he did to Flame, which, I guessed from his account, was probably just as well. A few minutes later the fellow had left the yard and gone out into the street.

Tunn had waited a while, trying to make up his mind what to do, but just when he'd plucked up enough courage to go and see if Flame was all right, several more men had come into the yard, bundled her up and carted her off. A minute or two later Ransom ("Noviss—t'pritty mun wit brums t'sweep t'eyes") had come down with a candle. He'd visited the privy, then he'd gone back inside, without looking in the fuel shed.

I wasn't particularly happy as I went back up to Ransom.

He jumped up off my bed as soon as I entered.

"Did you find her?" He sounded worried sick, and had good reason to be, I thought. Without Flame's protection, he was wide open to further dunmagic attack—next time there wouldn't be anyone around to heal him. But perhaps I maligned him. He did seem genuinely worried about her. "Something's happened to her, hasn't it?" he moaned, clutching at my arm again. "You must do something."

"You can say goodbye to Flame," I said bluntly. "Forget her, and get off the island as soon as you can."

"I *want* to leave, but there are no ships sailing out now. We were both going—but, please—*find* her. You have a sword, you're a fighter. You don't have to be scared of anything. *Help* her."

"Why in the name of all the islands should I? I scarcely know the woman." And she hadn't been in a great hurry to help me.

"You're a woman too, aren't you? Don't you want to help her? She's so good, and so beautiful! Nothing must happen to her—she saved my life."

I blinked at the extraordinary logic. "So? Maybe you should start praying."

"How can you be so hardhearted? She said all you cared about was money, and she was right! And you're probably a thief as well; she said you searched our rooms." (Now how the Devil had she known that? I could have sworn I'd left no traces.) "How can you just stand there and let her be kidnaped or whatever it is that they've done to her? That dunmagicking bastard has got hold of her, hasn't he?" He gulped and tearfully added a final shot: "Why shouldn't you help her? She's worth six of *you*!" He really knew how to endear himself to a girl, did Ransom Holswood.

I tried to tug my arm out of his grip.

"All right then!" he cried, releasing me to dig into his money belt. "If it's money you want, you can have it! Find her and bring her back to me safely and I'll pay you."

Now *that* interested me. "How much?"

He stopped digging around in his belt. "A hundred setus."

"Not enough. Not when dunmagic is involved. And it is."

He swallowed sickly, then looked down at his belt, calculating. He might have been infatuated with Flame, but he wasn't going to beggar himself over her. "Er, two hundred. That's all I've got." It was a palpable lie, but I accepted the terms. I was already thinking it might pay to have Flame in my debt: she was my only lead to the Castlemaid.

"All right. Two hundred it is." I plucked a fifty-setu coin out of his purse. "Fifty in advance, non-refundable. Now go back to your room," I said, "and stick your nose into that breviary of yours. I'll do my best, but prayers are about the only thing that's going to save your bed-mate."

Heaven help me if he didn't blush. It was then that I remembered that the brothers—and sisters—of the Menod were supposed to be chaste and confine their lusts to marriage. It's one of their sillier rules.

Ransom Holswood had certainly slipped from grace on that one.

CHAPTER 7

I PAID TUNN TO SHOW ME WHERE THE
dunmaster's four henchmen lived. Fortunately, the boy had
heard of Mord and the others and knew where they stayed. He
took me to a ramshackle place on the waterfront some distance
past the main docks.

There weren't all that many people in the streets at that hour,
although there was enough noise issuing from behind the doors
of bars, gambling dens and other such establishments to indicate that Gorthan Docks was far from asleep. Once we even had
to flatten ourselves against a wall to avoid being run over by a
couple of boisterous drunks riding sea-ponies. The huge animals slithered past at top speed, their segments clanking and
their airholes whistling with exertion. Looming up like that out
of the darkness, almost out of control, they were as frightening
as sea-dragons.

Once Tunn had indicated the house, I sent him back to The
Drunken Plaice and he was quick to obey. Mord's reputation as
a killer was well known.

The building was typical of what passed for a house in
Gorthan Docks: an untidy collection of rooms stacked on top of
one another like a child's cardhouse. It leaned drunkenly into its
neighbor on one side, and projected out over the water on stilts
on another. Buildings weren't erected in one single flurry of

construction; they just grew as their owners accumulated more building materials. Gorthan Spit, remember, had no trees. However, the island *was* in the path of the Great Summer Drift, the ocean current that came down from the Middling and Norther Islands for five months of every year, bringing with it all the flotsam from those more hospitable places. And every bit of wood that ended up on Gorthan Spit's shores was carefully collected and used. Planks from a wrecked ship, a piece of a Calmenter jetty, a whole tree washed down a Cirkasian river, a broken tiller from a Fen canal barge—who cared. If it was wood, on Gorthan Spit it was precious.

There was one thing that made Mord's place different from the equally haphazardly built neighboring dwellings: the odor of dunmagic clung to it like the smell of a long-dead whale.

I concentrated my Awareness, sought out the most recent traces of power and found them in the form of a dulled red glow around one of the upper floor windows. I had no idea whether Flame was there, of course, but I didn't know where else to look.

There didn't seem to be anyone around the building itself, but occasionally someone would stagger out of a nearby bar and vomit or belch or giggle their way down the street. I waited for quiet and then shinned up a wall to the roof of the veranda that ran around at first floor level. The uneven planks made it an easy climb for someone as sure-footed as I was.

The tiles of the sloping roof were made of cuttlefish skeletons, which definitely weren't supposed to support the weight of a person; they cracked and crumbled under me, but at least the beams beneath held. I disturbed a huddle of small birds sleeping under the shelter of some guttering and they burst into agitated chattering, even louder than the sounds I had made breaking the tiles. Fear lurched inside me. I hissed at them angrily, "Shut up! You want the bastards to hear?" A silly thing to do, because my voice only added to the racket, but then, it worked. The birds miraculously quietened. They continued to huddle together, their sharp eyes just black glitters in the moonlight, and my skin crawled. Their silence in response to my request was uncanny.

Just as strange was the fact that one of them then flew out of the huddle and up to the open window I had been aiming for and disappeared inside the building.

I dithered. A bird? Did dunmasters have traffic with birds? It seemed ridiculous. My fear was making me fanciful . . .

I climbed on.

The window, when I reached it, was shrouded with that savage redness of dunmagic. I loathed the look and feel of it, even though I knew it could not hurt me. A bird—the same one?—was sitting on the sill, a dark-colored creature hardly larger than a street-sparrow. In the moonlight it seemed utterly without feature: just a blackish bundle of feathers without anything to recommend it.

I hauled myself into the room and drew my sword. The bird didn't even move as I passed it.

Flame was there, standing in the dark. Behind me, the bird chittered. *"Blaze?"* she asked as if she couldn't credit it was me. I didn't blame her for being surprised, although I did wonder how she knew it was me. It *was* rather dark. "What in perdition are you doing here?"

"Oh, I was just passing and thought I'd drop in. See how you were getting on, you know. Can't you produce a sylvlight? I can't see a damn thing."

She obliged, and a round silver glow hovered in the middle of the room. One of the handier sylvtalents, I've always thought. I looked around. The place was filthy. There was no furniture and you couldn't have scraped the dirt off the floor with anything less that an ox and plow. Unidentifiable vermin scuttled away from the light.

Then I looked at her. As I expected, she'd been raped; all the signs were there. She stood still, eyes bruised, hands hanging by her sides, clothes torn and bloodied. The physical damage she would already have repaired with her magic, but there are some things that are not so easy to fix. "Oh shit," I said softly.

Her eyes dropped. "Yeah."

I suddenly felt very much a woman. I wanted to hold her, comfort her, but I sensed that it was the wrong moment. I wanted her strong, not emotional. "What happened?" I asked.

"Someone jumped me with dunmagic when I went to the privy. I don't know who it was. I still don't know. He blurred himself, even when he—" She swallowed. "He got his bastards to bring me back here. I was knocked silly with dunmagic; I couldn't do anything. He's so goddamned *powerful,* Blaze."

"Mm. I know. What does he want with you?" Besides the obvious.

She held out her left arm. On the bare skin, between elbow and wrist on the inner side, there was a mark. I took her hand in mine and frowned as I looked at it. The smell was appalling: not just rotten, but evil. Yet it didn't look like the usual dunmagic death sore. This was red, not suppurating. Even through the blurring of my Awareness it looked swollen and unpleasantly inflamed. It filled me with inexpressible dread.

"What is it?" I whispered, afraid of the answer.

"It's a contamination. A dunspell of subversion."

I looked at her, uncomprehending, trying to remember why the expression sounded familiar.

"It's going to change my sylvpowers to dunmagic. It's going to make me his willing acolyte, his spawn. But part of me, deep inside, will always know what I was, even as I live his hell. Do you understand, Blaze?" She looked up and I noticed the wildness of her eyes. "Gradually this poison is going to spread through my body until I'm like *him.* And there's nothing I can do about it. *He* is going to use me to do unspeakable things for him, with him . . ."

I felt sick, physically ill. I wanted to vomit, as if by emptying my stomach I could reject the horror of what she said. Not her. She didn't deserve that. I remembered now: another time, another place . . . some sylv children, kidnapped. There had been rumors of a similar intended fate for them, but on that occasion I had been in time. I heard my voice saying coldly, "Fight it."

"Do you think I'm not trying? But I can't. My sylvmagic is nothing in the face of this. Within a few days or so, you won't know me, Blaze. Oh, I'll look the same. But I could kill you—slowly—and laugh while I did it. Yet underneath I'd know what I was doing, and be unable to do anything to stop myself . . ."

"I'll get you out of here, somehow—"

"How? I can't pass the dunmagic wards. Believe me, I've tried. And what difference would it make anyway? What's happening to me will happen, whether I'm a prisoner here or free, out there." She clutched at my shirt. "Blaze, you've got to kill me. Now."

"I—"

"You must. Don't you see? You *must. Please.* Before it spreads."

I swallowed, still sick.

"If you can't do it, then give me your sword. I'll do it myself."

I stared at her. She was so beautiful, so young. I felt a hundred years old in comparison. I'd never admired anyone as much as I admired her then. I'd never hated dunmagic more.

I found my voice. "No. *No,* damn it. They won't win this one. I won't let it happen. Listen, Flame, there's a whole shipload of Keepers down there in the port. That's enough sylvmagic to fill the Great Trench. Together they might put an end to this—" I indicated her arm.

"But would they?" Her voice was bitter. "They don't much like sylvtalents who aren't Keepers."

"They hate dunmagickers more. Of course they will want to stop you becoming one. Anyway, there's another way out for you as well. If the dunmaster dies, so do his spells."

"And who would kill him for me?" she asked simply.

I wasn't about to make any rash promises; I wasn't *that* stupid. "The Keepers are after him for a start," I said. "Cheer up, Flame, there's hope yet. But first I have to get you out of here." I looked around some more, tracing the remnants of the dunmagic warding that kept her imprisoned in an unlocked room.

"How did you find me?" she asked curiously as I examined the walls. I could almost feel the effort she made to speak normally.

"Your boyfriend told me you were in trouble."

"My boyfr—? Oh, Noviss. And you came after me, just like that?" She was politely disbelieving.

"Well, no. Not exactly. He offered to pay me."

She put her head on one side. "How much did you take him for?"

"Two hundred setus. Do you think I let him off too cheap?"

She considered. "That's a lot of money. But then he has quite a lot."

"What in all the islands do you see in him anyway?"

She grinned knowingly, not a bad effort for someone who had just landed in hell and hadn't yet found a way out.

I stared. "*Really?* Isn't he a little young for, er, sufficient experience?"

She was offhand. "Oh, they have a curious custom among the nobility of the Bethany Isles. When young men, or women, turn sixteen years old, they are put in the care of a professional love-teacher of the opposite sex. For a couple of months they are taught, by an expert, how to please a partner."

I was interested. "Is that so? I shall have to try a Bethany noble some time."

She smiled faintly. "Noviss was my first lover, you know. And it looks like he's going to be my last." At least she wasn't thinking of the bastard—or bastards—who had raped her. She was made of extraordinarily strong stuff, this Cirkasian. And she was puzzling. How had someone so ravishingly desirable managed to hang on to her virginity so long? Had she perhaps been one of Cirkase's veiled, cosseted and closeted noble ladies? And why did I get this curiously mixed feeling when I spoke to her? Sometimes she seemed so worldly wise; at other times she was almost childlike.

I finished my circuit of the room just as the bird on the sill flew across to land on her shoulder. In the sylv light, it shimmered with iridescence and I recognized it as the same species—the same individual?—as had sat next to me in the taproom of the The Drunken Plaice that first day. She absent-mindedly raised her hand to stroke it under the chin with her forefinger, but it was the bird's action that stilled me. It reached out with the tip of a wing and touched her cheek.

It was such a *human* gesture, so unbirdlike, a gesture of comfort, of love. I think I must have gaped, because the expression on Flame's face changed, challenging me, *daring* me to mention it. And I couldn't. Not then, not when she was stretched so thin that only a superhuman effort on her part was keeping her together, keeping her from madness.

I said calmly. "Our dunmagicking bastard has forgotten to ward the ceiling."

She forced interest. "Has he? But it's too high for me to reach."

"Yes. I'll break in from above and pull you out. That'd be the easiest way, I think. All right?"

She nodded.

I left via the window and made the further climb to the top roof. More cuttlefish tiles. Easy to pull them away and make a hole. I climbed through into the dark of the ceiling space where the rafters sagged under my weight. I kicked through the thin ceiling in one corner and looked down on Flame's upturned face. Then the rafter cracked and I tumbled into the room, landing on the floor just ahead of half the ceiling.

"It'll never take the weight of us both," I said, a little unnecessarily. "The best thing is for you to climb through from my shoulders, and I'll go out through the window again."

She nodded. And then we heard sounds: the unmistakable noise of someone climbing the stairs. Perhaps I *had* been a mite noisy with my ceiling demolition. I grabbed Flame by the neck of her tunic and jerked her sharply toward me. "Now listen to me, and listen well, Flame. If I have to worry about you being dunmagicked again, we're both dead. You've got to get out of here. Don't kill me by being noble. I can look after myself, I promise you. Understand?"

She hesitated only a fraction of a second. Then she nodded.

"Go back to The Drunken Plaice. The obvious will be the last place they look, I hope. Wait for me there. Tell Noviss to make a nuisance of himself asking everyone where you are, as if you haven't come back." She put her foot into my hand even as I spoke and was up on to my shoulders as surely as an acrobat. She reached up, had hold of the rafters and was gone just seconds before the door burst open.

I recognized Mord from Niamor's description: a red-haired killer. His brother Teffel—with the sea-potato nose—I'd met before. Killers with the hearts of sharks, both of them. They didn't seem distressed to find Flame gone; I supposed they thought that with the dunspell on her arm she was as good as their master's property already. They were much more interested in the fact that they had me, believing, no doubt, that I had come in through the ceiling, helped Flame leave the same way and was now trapped by the wards. By the smirk on Teffel's face, he appeared to have forgotten my skill with a sword. Or perhaps he just felt more secure in the company of his brother.

They were armed with both swords and knives. Teffel reversed his hold on his knife and threw it. He knew what he was doing; only his stupidity in trying to maim rather than kill me gave me time to flick myself sideways. Even so, he nicked me in the arm. A minor wound, but it tore the upper muscle enough to hinder the effectiveness of my sword arm. I had no time to think before Mord followed up with a throw of his own. Another sideways flick, another wound. The knife went into my side, but it did more damage to my clothes than my hide. It bled copiously, though, and looked a great deal worse than it was. I pulled out the knife and flung it through the window, an action that was designed to disconcert them. Knives were a valuable commodity on the Spit and not usually thrown away, especially not in the middle of a fight. After that, I hammed it up a little in the best Hub theatrical tradition. I looked as though I was dying on my feet. The sword in my hand dropped weakly.

Teffel, the fool, fell for it. Even as his brother shouted a warning to stop him, he came at me like a charging bull and I carved up his belly like raw beef. He died with a surprised expression on his face and a lot of his innards steaming on the floor. Then I, like an utter idiot, put my foot in the mess and slipped, going down almost under Mord's feet. Enraged, he forgot I was a woman and put his boot where he thought it would do the most damage. It did hurt, but not enough to be incapacitating. I grabbed his foot and he went down into the blood and muck as well. I rolled clear then; it wouldn't do me any good to indulge in wrestling with a man of his size. I counted myself strong, but I'd always found it was unwise to assume anything other than the fact that most men have the edge when it comes to brute strength.

I managed to slice open his leg as I scrambled up, but it didn't seem to worry him. The angrier he became, the less he seemed to feel. He erupted off the floor, sword sweeping at me as he came. I fended him off and sparks flew from the clash of blades. He didn't have any finesse, but he was a strong man and agile too. I knew I'd win this one eventually, but I wasn't sure how much time I had. We were making more noise than a couple of scrapping sea-lions and Mord's fall must have shaken the whole house.

He kicked me in the shins. I came in under his guard and nicked his wrist but he didn't drop his weapon. He circled me warily, and put his back to the window. I thought of the dunmagic. It still glowed around the window frame. I came at him with a flurry of lunges, one after the other, none quite carried through, all designed to force him back. He hit the wall—and felt the dunmagic. It jerked him forward, toward my weapon. His face changed subtly; he felt the trap.

My blade wove patterns in the air in front of his nose and he fought me off with a desperation that didn't improve his swordplay. Still, he hadn't lost all his caution like his foolish brother.

Then the unexpected happened. A dark shadow rose up in the window behind Mord, an arm snaked around his neck and pulled his head back sharply, right into the dunmagic wards. He dropped his sword and screamed, but the sound was choked off by his attacker. Red light played along Mord's skin, rather a pretty effect really. A faint smell of burning reached my nostrils.

"I think you're roasting him," I said mildly. I couldn't see who was there but I didn't need to. I knew. And I knew that dunmagic wards meant as little to him as they did to me.

"Probably," he said and sure enough I recognized the honey-smooth voice. "It's just that you seemed to be taking so long about disposing of him, I thought I may as well join in."

God, the man *did* have a sense of humor. "Do you mind if I put him out of his misery?"

"Be my guest," Tor Ryder said politely.

I killed Mord, and his body collapsed on to the floor. Ryder, who had been balancing himself somewhat precariously with one hand on the windowsill, pulled himself into the frame and sat there. "You look a bit bloody," he said conversationally. "Is any of that yours?"

"Not a significant amount." I wasn't about to dally. "We've got company," I added. "Of a rather nasty kind." I could hear someone else clattering up the stairs and the stink of dunmagic had suddenly doubled. The company was very dubious indeed and, by the noise, there was more than one person. One part of me would have liked to have stayed, to have had a look at just who was going to run through that door, to have tried to solve Flame's problem there and then. The saner part of me prevailed. It always did. I was tired, my wounds ached, and Ryder—damn him—wasn't wearing a sword. I sheathed my weapon, vaulted past him across the sill, hung for a moment by my fingertips, and then let myself drop on to the veranda roof below. More cuttle-fish tiles disintegrated. The landlord was going to have a real problem with leaks by the time I'd finished with this building.

Ryder landed beside me and before I could move he had grabbed me by the hand and pulled me farther across the lower roof, around the side of the building. "This way," he said. "We'll go into the water." He gave me no time to object. A second later we were plunging into the sea.

I came up spluttering. The salt stung my cuts and I tried to remember if there were any blood-hungry fish found in Gorthan Spit waters.

"You *can* swim, I suppose?" he asked at my elbow.

"You picked a fine time to ask, Tor Ryder," I replied, a little on the sarcastic side.

He grinned at me in the moonlight, and I thought to myself that this was the first time I'd ever seen him smile. He moved forward toward me and kissed me full on the lips, a brief rather saltily damp kiss that was as tantalizing as it was unexpected. I raised an eyebrow and stared mutely as we trod water. Somehow I had not thought of Ryder as being a man given to flirtations at serious moments, and several seconds later it was clear that this was a very serious moment indeed.

A bolt of dunmagic, red and malignant, sizzled into the water next to us.

It didn't seem to worry Ryder too much. He said casually, "You see that boat over there? The closest one?" He nodded out to sea. "Think you can swim that far under water?"

I looked. There were several small boats anchored there. Beyond them, farther out still, there was a line of lanterns shining like pearls on the black velvet of the sea: the night fishing boats. "Sure."

"Next bolt, we play dead. Dive and swim for the other side of the boat."

My thoughts followed his. The dunmaster hadn't seen us go out through the window. He probably thought that we'd come in and gone out through the ceiling, where there were no wards, so he had no reason to think we weren't vulnerable to dunmagic. With a little bit of luck, he would even think that one of us was Flame. It was reasonably dark and from that distance, it might be impossible to tell the difference.

I nodded my agreement, and the next moment the bolt came, evil and compelling. It hit us and I sank, only starting to swim once I was submerged.

Strangely enough, it was on that long and exhausting swim to the boat that I recalled where I had heard the name Ransom Holswood before. It all came back to me, prompted, I think, by Flame's remark about the customs of the Bethany Isles nobility. Holswood was the family name of the ruling house of Bethany; it was the Holdlord's name.

I thought back to what I had heard, not so very long ago, about the family. The Holdlord, I remembered, had been the father of two sons: Tagrus and Ransom. Tagrus had been the heir, Ransom the younger son. Ransom had elected to join the Menod, hoping one day to belong to the patriarchy, but when Tagrus had died in an accident, the Holdlord immediately asked his younger son to forget his Menod ambitions in order to take up the position of Holdheir—and Ransom had refused.

Obviously the young man had still not obeyed his father's request. He was now on Gorthan Spit, masquerading under the name of Noviss, unless I was very much mistaken. I wondered what the Keepers would make of that.

CHAPTER 8

NOW, WHERE WAS I . . . ? AH YES, I WAS telling you about our escape from the dunmaster's house. We were in the water . . . I came up on the far side of the boat. Ryder was already there, clinging to the gunwale. The vessel was a small one-man fisher, with a front cabin, a single mast and a stern tiller.

"Ah, there you are. I was beginning to think I'd lost you—you hold your breath like a seal."

"Now what?" I asked. Taking to the water had been his idea. Let him get us out of this one.

He gestured to me to be silent and we listened for any sounds of pursuit. Sound carried in the still air; from somewhere along the shore we could hear the sound of a fiddle, the thump of dancing feet and the whoops of enthusiastic drunken dancers. I half expected there to be more bolts flying after us, but there was nothing.

"We'd better stay here in the water for a bit nonetheless," he said. "Luckily these waters aren't known for their sharks . . . We'll climb into the boat later. Are you all right?"

I pushed my dripping hair away from my face and hooked an arm through a loop of rope that hung over the gunwale. "Fine. Curious though. Were you looking for me? Or Flame? And if so, why? And how did you know where to find us? And who the hell are you anyway?"

"You already know my name, and you know I'm a Stragglerman. What else is there? As for tonight, well, I was woken up by the din that young fool Noviss was making when he banged on your door. I eavesdropped and then I followed you."

"But why? And why did you intervene when you did?"

"Why not?"

"I can think of twenty reasons why not without drawing breath. All of them would have been perfectly adequate for me, had I been in your shoes."

He shifted his hold on the boat and reached out to touch my face, running the back of his hand down my wet cheek. "Call it lust then. A desire to see that you survived the night, for purely selfish reasons."

"You've got to be joking."

He shook his head. "No. Making love to you would be one thing I would never joke about . . . that cut of yours has started bleeding again. Let me tie it up for you." Using one hand, he pulled a black kerchief from around his neck and wrapped it around my upper arm, his movements deft and gentle. I was still trying to fathom him, and not having much success. The blanks in his story gaped like bottomless holes.

"Don't look so worried, Blaze," he said. "Just accept that I have an entirely personal interest in keeping you alive and well."

"I was managing quite well without you," I pointed out. I thought to myself that life in Gorthan Spit was becoming tedious; I doubted that I had met a single person who was quite what they claimed to be. Everyone had their secrets . . .

"Have you had any luck finding your Cirkasian slave?" he asked, changing the subject. In the dim light, it was hard to see how he had taken my rebuff, but he sounded unfazed.

"Not yet."

"You're actually after a particular slave, aren't you. The Castlelord's daughter? I did hear she'd vanished. And you think Flame might be her—or know something about her."

"How in the sweet hell did you know that? Castlemaid Lyssal's disappearance is supposed to be a well-kept secret! And she's only been gone two months. Less—"

"Oh, I get about," he said vaguely. "I was in the Keeper Isles before I came here and I know a few people there. Blaze, the girl probably ran away, you know. She had reason. Those god-less Keeper hypocrites were selling her off to that pile of lard, the Bastionlord of Breth. He's cruel and amoral, a pervert—a man who seeks out children, boys not old enough to know what's happening to them until it's too late. He's also fifty years old if he's a day."

By this time my surprise had me spluttering like an idiot. How come everyone seemed to know the politics of the Island-lords all of a sudden? It was one thing to hear a few whispers along a back lane in Cirkasecastle, quite another to have it openly discussed in other nations. I said, "Nobody's supposed to know all this. Who *are* you?"

"Nobody special. I just keep my ears open. I have an interest in knowing what the Keepers are up to. And they are the ones who pressed the Castlelord for this match. I'd love to know why. You don't happen—"

"No, I don't! I'm not privy to Keeper secrets." And I knew that not even what Flame had said entirely explained why the Keepers were interested in furthering a cross-island marriage.

He shook his head sadly. "That poor girl—is it any wonder that she wanted to run away? The wonder of it is that she had the guts."

Something was nibbling curiously at my toes. I wriggled my feet in irritation and hoped it was nothing larger than a minnow. I said, "She was stupid. She fell into the hands of slavers almost immediately. She would have been better off staying home."

"If you find her, are you really going to return her to those bastards?"

"It means two thousand setus to me. Of course I'll return her."

"You're still working for the Keepers, aren't you?"

"What if I am?" I asked belligerently. I was rattled, or I wouldn't have been so gauche. Then I winced and wondered where my wits had gone. "How did you know that? And what do you mean, *still*?"

"I've heard of you before. The Keepers sent you to Calment Minor ten years back to help put down the rebellion there. You were the Council agent who saved the son of the Governor of Calment Minor when the convoy he was traveling in was at-tacked. I heard the Governor offered you citizenship as a reward, and you turned him down."

Blood rushed to my head. That was something I preferred not to think about too much. I had come so close to a precious tattoo, only to find there was a price I would not pay for it after all.

"There were . . . strings attached to the offer," I said tightly. I shivered slightly. The water had seemed warm enough at first but now I was beginning to feel the chill.

He nodded, sympathetic. "He was a very nasty piece of corruption, Governor Kilp. You were on the wrong side in that affair, you know."

"You knew me then?"

He seemed amused. "Not *quite*. I almost ran up against you several times, though. Saw you from a distance once or twice. Do you remember Gilly's Scarp? That was me."

I remembered all right. It had been one of the most frustrating moments of my career. I'd been told to find and capture a guerrilla scout nicknamed the Lance of Calment, a young man who was running supplies and messages and arms between one of their rebel mountain strongholds and supporters in the city of Tanta. I'd thought I had my quarry snared, but I'd been neatly outwitted. I'd climbed onto a ridge with a couple of men assigned to me by Duthrick, expecting to have the rebel I was after trapped in the gully below—only to find him outlined on the top of Gilly's Scarp opposite, out of arrow range. He had waved at us cheekily before heading off to safety.

"Great Trench below! That was *you*? And you admit to it? You could still be hanged for taking part in that rebellion, you know!"

"Only in the Calments. And I suppose the Keepers would send me back to the hangman in Calment Minor if they knew who I was. But they don't. They never did."

"And you calmly tell me this? I could turn you in! Are you crazy?" I was already wondering if there was a reward for his capture. I'd made money turning in fugitives before.

"I have that reputation."

He was giving me surprise after surprise. That serious, unsmiling man I remembered from earlier in the day was a great deal more complex than I had first assumed.

"Are you cold yet?" he asked. "Do you want to get in the boat?"

"I can wait a while longer if you think it's better."

I thought of the Calments, remembering wild days of danger and challenge when I'd pitted my wits and my sword against the desperation of a peasant uprising that had come to within a breath of success. I'd been only twenty years old, and this man could hardly have been more than three or four years older. "What was your rebel name? I don't remember hearing of a Tor Ryder. And I always thought that the man who got away at Gilly's Scarp was—"

"The Lance of Calment? Yes, it was." He sounded a little shamefaced. "I was young then and had a hankering for the theatrical. Tor Ryder is my real name, the one I was born with."

"*You* were the Lance?" I was incredulous, at a loss for further words. The Lance had been both an irritation and a challenge to me in the excitement of that year in Calment Minor. I'd lost count of the number of times I'd thought I had him trapped, only to find he'd managed to slip away. It had become almost a game to me, and it had been a game I'd lost. I'd helped to put down the rebellion, but the escape of the Lance had been one of my failures. Oddly enough, in the end it had been a game I was glad enough to lose; the Governor and his cohorts had proved to be very nasty indeed and I'd developed a sneaking admiration for the rebel scout I'd chased from one side of the Calments to the other but never managed to catch . . . or meet.

He caught my half-smile at the memories. "It was a strange sort of fun, wasn't it? We were younger in those days."

He'd changed in more than his age though. The Lance of Calment would never have gone anywhere without a sword in his belt and a bow and quiver on his shoulder. Now Tor Ryder walked some of the most dangerous streets in the Isles of Glory without a weapon in sight.

He swam down to the end of the boat and peered around the stern. "He can't still be waiting for us to come up," he said, referring to the dunmaster. "Let's get in the boat before we get too cold." He pulled himself out and then helped me over the gunwale. The boat rocked alarmingly, but there was no reaction from the shore.

The vessel was actually quite a pleasant one. There was shelter in the small cabin, and a comfortable pallet. Tor Ryder set about untying the painter from the buoy that anchored us, then raised the sail.

"We're stealing this?" I asked.

"A petty larceny. I thought sailing back to the fishermen's wharf might be safer than walking through the streets. We can leave the boat there and I'll pay the wharfmaster to keep an eye on it until the real owner turns up. Always assuming that's where you want to go."

I thought of Flame and that contagion spreading through her body . . . "Yes, I do."

He raised his eyes to the sail, now hanging loosely above our heads. "I'm afraid we're not going anywhere just yet, though. There's no wind." He looked back at me. The greater moon had risen, and I could see him better now. Those blue eyes of his were still serious, but I wondered how I had missed seeing the crinkles at the corners. He might not have had Niamor's light-hearted view of life, but he was far from being a humorless man.

"You had better get out of those wet clothes," he said. "Wrap yourself in the blanket there. It looks clean enough."

I nodded, but I didn't move. "What makes you so certain that I won't betray you to the Keepers?"

"After all this time? You may do a lot for money, Blaze, but unless you've changed a great deal over the years, you would never do anything quite so petty."

"Petty? Perhaps there is still a price on your head that is beyond merely 'petty.'"

"Perhaps. I've never bothered to inquire. But I still don't think you would try to collect it. Not you."

"You sound as though you think you know me quite well."

"I do—or I did. It pays to know the enemy. The only thing I didn't know about you in those days was how beautiful you are close up."

"Flame is beautiful. I'm just big."

"You are magnificent," he said simply. "And I like big women. I'm rather large myself."

Niamor had used the same word: magnificent. Somehow, I liked it better the way Tor said it. "You're a fool, Tor Ryder. People change."

I was sitting amidships, dripping wet. When I shivered, he came forward and started to unbutton my tunic. I didn't move. He peeled the wet cloth back over my shoulders, eased out the injured arm first, then the other so that I sat naked to the waist. The wound in my side had stopped bleeding. Fortunately, the knife had penetrated only the fleshy part of my hip, doing little damage. He pulled the blanket up over my shoulders, then knelt at my feet, his hands on my knees. "Yes, people change. But you haven't, not that much. Back in Calment Minor I felt a strange sort of kinship with you, as though we were two of a kind, for all that we fought on opposite sides. I felt it again, that night we bumped into each other in front of Noviss's door."

He placed his right hand palm to palm with mine. Awareness recognizing Awareness. Kinship. I recalled the way I had felt about the Lance of Calment . . . Yes, there had been a strange sort of comradeship there, for all that we had done our best to kill one another. But it had nothing to do with being two of a kind. Tor Ryder and I were sea-trout and lake-salmon: kin that swam in different waters.

He laced his fingers into mine. "Be warned, Blaze. If we take the natural step forward from here, you'll never be able to walk away without a backward glance. Not the way you could walk away from someone like Niamor." (Great Trench, was there *anything* he didn't know?) "Love me now and there'll be ties between us that will last forever."

I knew he was right.

I shivered, afraid, desiring. I think I saw the beginnings of grief then, just as he did. "It would be madness," I said.

"Yes," he agreed.

The boat was still, fixed in a sea so smooth it could have been oil in a bowl. The pearldrop lights of the fishing boats radiated pathways of gold across the surface of the water, seemingly solid enough to walk upon. I couldn't believe we were having this conversation.

I reached out and began to unbutton his shirt. My eyes misted—and I *never* cried. "It won't be worth the pain it brings," I said.

"Yes, it will," he promised.

And it was.

A HINT OF A BREEZE SHIVERED THE SAIL, puffing it out a little, and I stirred in the arms that held me. Strong, gentle, loving arms. Tor Ryder's arms. I tried out the name, to see how it would sound, to revel in the rich tones of it . . .

"Mmm?" His murmur was a caress.

"Nothing. I just wanted to hear your name." In the space of a single night I had become another person. I hadn't fallen in love—not quite, but I had learned to love. I, who had never loved anyone in thirty years of living.

Tor Ryder of the Stragglers, one-time rebel Enemy. Syr-aware. Lover. A man far too upright for me . . .

And Flame of Cirkase, sister-woman, Syr-sylv. Someone I wanted to call friend. A woman whose courage made me ache with admiration. Whose courage shamed me. Whose actions made me look at myself and see things I didn't want to see.

I felt a wave of sick suspense wash over me. What was I doing? Neither of these still-embryonic loves would be easy to bear. And why Tor? Why not Niamor, who was surely more like me? I thought of the dark-eyed Quillerman: a self-serving man, kind and caring—but only when it suited him. A man more inclined to laugh at life than to be inspired to change it for the betterment of others. With Niamor I could have laughed, had fun, forgotten my troubles for a while, as I had done with others before him . . . so why not him?

In my heart I knew the answer, of course; with Niamor there would have been something lacking. For all our similarities, with him I could never have felt any link of kinship. With him, there would never have been any depth. As there never had been in the past with all those others. But Tor . . . Tor was offering me something wondrously new and profound . . .

Even so, part of me was a reluctant lover. Something fundamental within me was being challenged by this love, and I wasn't sure I wanted to acknowledge it. In fact, all of this was far too sudden.

I drifted off to sleep rather than think about it.

When I awoke, Tor was gone from my side. I raised my head to find him sitting in the stern, motionless, staring out over the sea with sightless eyes, all his senses turned inward to a place where I could not follow. He was gone from me as surely as if he'd left the boat.

I felt as cold as Calmenter snows.

I looked away from him toward the shore. We had drifted farther out to sea and were in among the fisher fleet. Their lanterns gleamed only dimly now as the sky lightened. The golden paths across the water had gone. I could hear the sound of voices and laughter coming from the fishermen as they hauled up lines, pulled in nets. I lay back, to look up at the mast just visible in the pre-dawn light. A bird was sitting on the crosstree, a creature too small to be one of the usual seabirds. I eyed it uneasily; it looked like that pet of Flame's. I wondered how long it had been perched there. It cocked its head to one side and I suddenly felt very naked. I pulled the blanket up over my body. "Scram," I said. "Go tell her I'm all right."

If I hadn't known better, I would have said it laughed as it flew away.

Tor surfaced, his face still a mask, but his voice was a meld of curiosity and amusement. "Do you always talk to birds?"

"No. Only some. What's odd is that they seem to under-stand—sometimes. Tor?"

"Yes, my love?"

God, the shiver at those words! "Who are you?"

"A wanderer of no particular address and no particular wealth. Presently employed as a baby-sitter." He moved back to my side, to slip an arm around me, to become mine again.

"Baby-sitter?"

"Of a kind. Although the baby doesn't realize he's being sat."

"Ransom Holswood?"

"Ah, you know his real label? Yes, that's the lad. Holdheir of Bethany. And a real shrimp-brain at times. I still can't imagine what he thought he was doing coming to Gorthan Spit. I think he must have seen himself as a Menod hero going off to give succor to the godless of Gorthan Docks. Only thing is, after a couple of initial traumatic forays, he's been too scared to do anything except sit in The Drunken Plaice and feel sorry for himself. By the time there's a ship out of here, I just may be able to persuade him it's time to go home."

"You're working for the Holdlord?"

"In a manner of speaking," he said casually. Too casually. "His father doesn't want to *force* him home; that would make him resentful. On the other hand, he doesn't want him to come to any harm either, so I was sent to keep an eye on him. That was easily enough done when he went to the Keeper Isles, but it's not so easy here."

He was lying, or at least not telling the whole truth, and I knew it. I knew him too well . . . We'd only just met, but there were parts of him I knew as well as I knew myself . . .

Now that Tor had jogged my memory, I seemed to recall hearing that the Holdlord had ranted quite forcefully about how his son was going to be dragged back to do his royal duty. The Holdlord of Bethany was no more a kindhearted father than the Castlelord of Cirkase.

I suppose I should have been upset that Tor lied to me, but

somehow I wasn't disturbed. I, who had never entirely trusted anyone in my life, trusted him. The lie didn't seem to matter. It seemed that love could change a lifetime of wariness into reckless disregard for even elementary caution.

Love makes fools of us all.

I said, "Unjust, Tor. You want to take the errant Bethany Holdheir home, but you don't want me to do the same thing to my errant Cirkasian Castlemaid, who is also an Islandlord's heir."

He rolled over and nuzzled my breast. "There's a difference. She'd go back to become a pawn of Keepers and wife-prisoner of a foul pervert. Ransom's another story. He wanted to be a Menod patriarch. But it was palpably obvious to everyone except himself that he wasn't suited to the job. I've high hopes that he's realized that, now that he's seen how the godless live in Gorthan Spit." He chuckled. "Gorthan Docks has been a terrible shock to Holdheir Ransom."

"I didn't think you'd be interested in restoring a royal heir to his hereditary position. Wasn't that what the Calmenter revolution was all about: the peasantry ruling the land instead of royalty?"

"An over-simplification and you know it. However, I've mellowed since those days. I don't think rebellion is the answer anymore. Change will come naturally if only the Keepers would stop propping up the corrupt in the name of liberty, and using their damned sylvmagic to do it. Ransom's a Menod. Menod don't like Keepers and their reactionary ways—once he's Holdlord, there'll be hope for Bethany at least, especially if he has a Menod teacher of caliber to straighten out the kinks in his thinking."

I stirred uncomfortably. "Do you hate the Keepers that much?"

"I don't hate them at all. I just think there are better ways of living than under the system they promote. In Bethany's case, a Menod ruler would be a change for the better."

He sounded almost disinterested, but there was still something in what he said—or perhaps in what he had not said—that touched me with cold. I changed the subject; there were some trails that were best not followed. Cowardly, I supposed, but I didn't want to start arguing about politics when we'd only just made a beginning. "Why the dunmagic attack on Ransom?"

"I don't know for sure. It could be simply because he is one of the Menod. It could be because he's a tactless idiot who says the first thing that comes into his head without considering the feelings of those he's speaking to. It could be because this dunmaster is a nasty piece of work. I think he enjoys giving pain. And who better to give pain to than a Menod? Ransom was too obvious with his prayers, at least before the lovely Flame entered his life." He smiled faintly. "Since then, the prayers have been relegated to a position of lesser importance. As for Flame's kidnapping, that may have been in revenge for her cure of Ransom. Dunmagickers don't like their work thwarted and I imagine he worked out who was to blame."

"Have you any idea who the dunmagicker is?"

"No. He's too clever. The Keepers are looking for him too, I suppose?"

"I suppose so. Anyone that strong must be a danger to them. But they don't take me into their confidence."

He rolled over on to his stomach and propped himself up to look at me. "Why do you work for them, Blaze?" I heard the seriousness in his voice. This was the man I had seen in the taproom; the man who sometimes found little humor in the realities of life. "They aren't worthy of your service. They are so damned *arrogant*. They have appointed themselves the guardians of the Isles of Glory, but who told them we wanted a guardian? They think their way of life is the ultimate in living and it never occurs to them that it's flawed. You must have lived in the Keeper Isles, you know what it's like. If you're a sylvtalent and Keeper-born, then you're rich and powerful. But God help you if you're peasant-born with no sylvtalents. Oh, I know that they say anyone can rule in the Keeper Isles, and they have elections to prove it, but you heard Wantage's story. And have you ever met a Councilor who wasn't a sylvmaster? You can't even be elected a village headman unless you have sylvtalent. Whenever a non-sylv tries to be elected to anything, he loses, just as Wantage's friend lost. And he never realizes why. But we do, don't we, Blaze? You and I and Wantage know because we can see their spells . . . We can see the magic they use—to ensure an election victory, a good sale, an advantageous deal. Sylvtalents rule and grow rich; common folk grow poorer and more impotent day by day. That's the system the Keeper sylvs would have the rest of the Glory Isles believe is so wonderful. *That's* the system they tout as being the epitome of equality and liberty and right. Huh!" He was almost spitting his contempt.

"That's only half the story," I protested. "You don't mention what they have achieved on the Keeper Isles: the great cities, the coastal and riverine transport systems, the paved tradeways, the schools, the printing of books, the hospitals. The way the arts have flourished under the patronage of the rich: the literature, the drama, the poetry, the artworks. The sheer wonder of living in a place like The Hub—"

"Try being poor in The Hub," he said tartly.

"I have," I replied, even more tartly. "But if you have drive, you can climb out. I did."

"Only because you had Awareness. Without that, you might well still be starving in a gutter because they wouldn't *let* you climb out. And you've hardly joined the elite of the Keeper Isles even now. Blaze, can't you see what they are like? Can't you see how they try to manipulate us all? Oh, I'm sure you'll start talking about what they've done for the stability of the Isles of Glory—but what is the cost? We're all becoming dependent on them. And then, if one of us steps out of line, they tread on us like we were bladder wrack on the beach to be popped underfoot.

"When Xolchas Stacks dared to buy grain from Bethany where it was cheaper, instead of from the Keeper Isles, the Keepers stockpiled the guano that was the Stacks' main export— bought up all the stocks for three whole years—then released it all on to the market at once so that prices plummeted and the Stacks were bankrupted because they couldn't sell their own guano. Then the Keepers moved in and bought the place up. The people of Xolchas Stacks are economic slaves to The Hub now. That's just one example of what happens to people who go against the Keeper Isles. Blaze," he repeated, "such people aren't worthy of your service."

"Tor," I said quietly, "I don't serve them because they are worthy. Or because their causes are worthy either. I serve them because they offer me a chance of citizenship. Because the Keeper Isles are the only place—besides Gorthan Spit and similar hellholes—where I can find semi-legitimate employment. You don't know what it's like to be a non-person. To be a—a nothing, simply because of an accident of birth. Despised and despoiled because you're a halfbreed, not one thing nor another. I've been spat on and raped and beaten and robbed because I was a halfbreed. I've been starved and reviled. Besides Keepers, the only people who ever offered me friendship were

Menod, but they also told me to suffer this world with dignity because I'd find reward in the next. That's not good enough for me.

"The only people to offer me a way out in *this* world—to offer me anything at all that was real—were Keepers. Oh, I know it wasn't any kindness of heart that made them make the offer. It was because they find Awareness a useful talent sometimes, and there are very, very few Keepers with Awareness. It was because it's handy for them to have a non-Keeper agent they can send to other islandoms on Keeper business. If I make a mess of things, no one can blame Keepers: it's all the fault of a citizenless halfbreed. I know they need me, I know they use me, but I take money from them for my services. So the Calmenter rebellion might have been a mistake on my part (not that I had much choice in those days), but much of what I've done for the Keepers has been worthwhile. I helped to clean up Fis on the Bethany Isles, where there was a dunmagic enclave, you may remember. I assassinated the dunmaster who ruled Forth in Mekaté. Five years back I was one of those who stopped the dunmagickers who ran slaves from Gorthan Spit to the Spatts. It was I who uncovered that school for dunmagickers in Mekaté. I was the agent who tracked two kidnappers from The Hub to Fentower and returned the Keeper sylv children they probably intended to subvert to dunmagickers.

"While I work for the Keeper Council, I can—at least unofficially—live in the Keeper Isles. I can buy a decent life. With money, with my Calmenter sword, with my Awareness, I've finally earned respect. It may be grudgingly given, but at least no one spits on me anymore. Don't ask me to turn my back on the Keepers and be noble, Tor. I can't do it. I'd lose everything I have worked so hard to gain."

"You think I'm a self-righteous bastard."

"Something like that."

"Yeah. Sorry. It's easy for someone like me to preach; I had it simpler. I just hate to see you working for Keeper sylvs. They are cold-eyed sharks."

"They're not so very bad."

"They're a lot more dangerous than you know. Blaze—marry me."

"What?" The word was half laugh, half incredulity.

"Marry me. I have well-placed friends in the Stragglers. Perhaps I could get you citizenship there by virtue of marriage. You are obviously half-Souther anyway. It's worth a try."

I didn't know whether to laugh or cry. It was hardly a romantic proposal, but he meant it, and not just because he wanted me to have citizenship either. I shook my head. "Tor Ryder, where have you been all your life. No one *ever* marries a halfbreed."

"It's not actually illegal."

"No, but it's damn foolish. A halfbreed spouse is a heavy liability. And you must know that—that there are . . . other reasons why a halfbreed makes a poor wife. And an even worse husband."

"Shit." The expression on his face was one of black rage. "The bastards made you barren?"

By way of answer, I slid the blanket down and showed him the savage brand on my shoulder blade, the mark that told what had been done to me. The deep scar had puckered in the years since I had received it, but the symbol was still clear enough: an empty triangle, a sign of barrenness, of infertility.

"Keepers did that to you?" he asked, his voice thick with loathing.

I nodded. "If it hadn't been them, it would have been someone else." How many times over the years—in how many islandoms—had I been forced to show the brand, to show the proof that I was no longer whole, no longer capable of having children? It'd happened so often it had come not to matter. It was just part of being a halfbreed. Few people tried it with me anymore anyway; a Calmenter sword and the look in my eye made the question seem unwise. I shrugged and added, "There's not a nation in the Isles of Glory that will tolerate fertile halfbreeds. Unless they are royal-born, of course."

Thirteen years old and held down on the physician's table by Keeper doctors. Half-conscious, crazed with pain, ripped apart by their hands as they inserted the cet leaves that would cauterize my insides, make me less than I had been. Many girls didn't survive. Perhaps male halfbreeds were luckier; their operation might have been more drastic, but few of them died of it.

And then, just when I thought I'd had all I could bear, they rolled me over on to my stomach with their foul hands, they held me down, they took up the branding iron—I still remember the sight of it—the dull red of the triangle just out of the coals. I still remember the smell of my own flesh burning. I still remember.

"The Menod have been trying to have that practice outlawed for years," Tor said tightly. "I thought it was dying out."

"Officially perhaps. But there will always be fanatics around to perform the operation, even if it is ever made illegal." I shrugged. "At least I lived. And I don't have to worry about bringing another halfbreed into the world to suffer as I did . . . But I couldn't let you marry me, Tor."

"I wasn't asking you to marry me because I want your children. I asked you because I love you."

I gaped. We hadn't spoken of love; the idea was ridiculous—far too soon, too rash. I wasn't that kind of person. Neither was he. Finally I said, "You've only known me a day. Not even that really. Just an hour or two."

"I've known you my whole life. You are the other half of myself." He had never been more serious—and I could never love him more than I did at that moment.

"Think about it. Promise me you'll think about it."

"Yes," I whispered. "Yes . . . I will . . . think about it." The promise of a lifetime with him was a tantalizing feast displayed to the habitually famished. *Impossible.* How could it have been otherwise?

The sail billowed as the wind returned at last. Tor rose to dress and steer the boat toward the fishing harbor.

CHAPTER 9

IT WAS DAYLIGHT BY THE TIME WE
climbed the stairs of The Drunken Plaice. I thought we'd made
it back without being seen, but who knew for sure?

Tor slipped into Ransom's room to check on the lad; he was
asleep, his breviary in his hand. I went on alone to see Flame.
She was awake, lying on her back staring at the ceiling. A quick
flicker of relief was the only indication she gave that she might
have been worried for my sake. I appreciated her reticence. I
hated people who made a fuss. I knew she had been worried; I
knew she was grateful. I didn't need telling.

She hadn't slept and wasn't likely to, not for quite a while if
I read the signs rightly. I came and sat beside her and took her
hand. "Are you all right?"

"I try not to mind about what they did to my body. That, I
will conquer. And I can heal the physical hurts . . . but not this."
She indicated the arm. "A few days, Blaze. And then it'll be too
far gone to cure."

"I'll go and see the Keepers as soon as I've cleaned up." In
truth, it had been a long night, and I would have liked to have
gone to bed.

Her expression was bleak. "Take care, Firebrand. He's
vicious. Inhuman. He enjoyed what he did to me. He likes to
hurt. He enjoyed watching what the others did to me." She was

silent for a moment, her eyes wells of dark memory. Then a whispered, "You've been raped too, haven't you?"

I nodded.

"I saw it in your eyes when you looked at me in that room. You *knew.* You read my soul with understanding . . . it helped. You didn't say anything, but somehow you showed me something: *that it didn't matter.*"

"It doesn't, not once it's over and you have survived. *You* didn't do it—they did. I don't know whether this will help too, but two of his henchmen are dead. The redhead and his brother, the one with the nose." The Menod would say that true justice for such crimes should come from God, not Man, and that revenge damages he who wreaks it. They are wrong. I knew firsthand how cathartic a killing could be. I'd shed the last of my innocence as I drove the knife into the man who'd raped the child I was on Breth—but I'd never dreamed of him thereafter. He was dead, and I still lived.

Flame understood. She smiled grimly. "I'm glad. But I already knew. Ruarth told me."

I looked across at the window. It was open and, sure enough, there were several of the dark birds just sitting there on the sill. They were preening themselves and in the morning light they were actually quite handsome. The iridescence gleamed and each had a red band across the purple patina of the breast, rather like the ceremonial sashes bestowed on honored courtiers in Brethbastion or Bethany Hold. I swallowed my disbelief. "Er, which one is he?"

Her smile was genuine this time; a reminder of the person she had been yesterday. She turned her head to the window. "The one on the left."

"I can't tell the difference between them. Can you talk to them all?"

She dragged her focus away from her fears to concentrate on me, then nodded. "That particular species, yes. Not birds in general. These understand us, you know. But their language is a mixture of everything: movement, chirps, stance, song. You could learn it, if you have the patience."

I looked at them dubiously. "Would they mind?"

"You are my friend," she said, as if that explained all.

Her breathing had steadied now and I wanted to keep her from thinking about what had happened to her, so I said, "Tell me about them."

She didn't answer immediately. Instead, she looked across at the birds. She didn't say anything aloud, but her expression made it clear she was asking for permission to talk to me. Apparently she received it, because after a minute or two she said, "They are Dustel Islanders. Their descendants anyway. You know the story?"

I nodded. To the south of the Stragglers were long lines of rocks now called the Reefs of Deep-Sea. Once, they had been a string of stony islands called the Dustel Isles, inhabited by typical Souther people: brown-skinned, dark-haired farmers and fishermen, with dark blue eyes. There had been a war over royal succession, and then they'd fallen foul of a dunmaster called Morthred the Mad. They had tried to block his attempt to turn the islands into his own personal domain of enslaved subjects. Because there was an unusual number of Awarefolk and sylvtalents among them, they had managed to resist him—for a time. However, according to the tale, in vengeful rage and madness, Morthred had sunk the islands under the waves, drowning the inhabitants and obliterating the fishing villages and towns and city of Dustelrampart. All that remained now were a few reefs where the fishing was good but the waters treacherous. Morthred himself had disappeared. It was rumored at the time that in his madness he had overextended himself and as a result his powers had dissipated.

The story wasn't entirely a seadream; there were still plenty of elderly people alive whose parents had known those southmost islands well. The Dustel Isles had existed, of that there could be no doubt. There were even small communities of Dustel people on the Stragglers, descendants of Dustel citizens who had been elsewhere when the islands had disappeared. No one questioned that the Dustel Isles had existed, but whether their disappearance was due to dunmagic or just to some natural disaster was more hotly debated.

"I thought the only Dustel Islanders were those who now live on the Stragglers," I said doubtfully. "And they are human." It was *very* hard to believe in those birds.

"No. At the time of the submergence, Morthred turned those who were on the islands into birds. Birds like these. And he contrived the spell so that they would have normal human lifespans, and a human intelligence. He thought to torture them with their memories of what they had been, of what they had lost. To Morthred, death comes as a release for the tormented, therefore he prefers to keep his victims alive.

"With the Dustel Islanders he erred. They learned to accept their fate. Their descendants may dream of being human again, but they do not live in despair. They think that one day Morthred will reappear, and they will find a way of forcing him to retract his spell."

I was startled. "Reappear? Wouldn't he be a trifle *old* by now?"

"If he had died, wouldn't his dunspell have vanished? The Dustel Isles would have reappeared, a little worse for having been submerged, perhaps, but they'd be there. The Dustel birds would have become human once more. That has never happened because Morthred is still *alive*. There are many stories that say the really powerful dunmagickers don't age like normal men. The Dustels believe that one day all Morthred's magic will return to him, and he will try to seize power somewhere in the Isles of Glory once again. And then they'll find him." She let that sink in, then added thoughtfully, "Morthred was very powerful. His spell against the Dustels has lasted almost a hundred years. That's a long time for a spell."

We exchanged glances, and she really did not have to add her next words for me to know what she was thinking. "The dunmaster who did this to me is also very powerful."

"Great Trench below, Flame. Even in the unlikely event that they are one and the same—and I don't believe it for a minute—what could anyone do about it? Least of all a flock of—forgive me, Ruarth—mere birds?"

"There are more than just a flock. And many of them have sylvtalent. Or Awareness. Didn't you notice how Ruarth could fly through the dun-warded window?" That point had escaped me at the time. Stupid. I sat there on the edge of the bed, doubtless looking as though I'd been slapped in the face with a wet fish. Until then I hadn't *really* believed in birds with human intelligence, human abilities. Not really. But I couldn't deny the proof: no living creature would have been able to pass that dunmagic ward, unless they had Awareness. And birds and animals didn't have Awareness. Only humans did . . .

"No," I protested, confused. "Wait a moment, if Ruarth has Awareness, he wouldn't *be* a bird. Dunmagic doesn't affect Awarefolk."

She gave a bitter smile. "When Morthred cast the original dunspell, all the Dustel Awarefolk on the islands died. Every one. They were drowned because they couldn't fly away. *They* didn't become birds. Their very protection against dunspells was what killed them. Ordinary islanders and sylvtalents, however, were transformed into birds. Ruarth, and the others like him today, are their descendants. Ruarth's parents are birds, as were his grandparents. But *their* parents were birds who were once human. Dustel Awarefolk are impervious to present spells, just as you are, but they are powerless against a dunspell which has been part of them since they were embryos in their eggs, long before their Awareness developed."

"So there are still Awarefolk and sylvs born to Dustel birds."

She nodded. "You know what Awareness is like. It just pops up every now and then, even in families without any Awareness. And being sylv often runs in families. It makes no difference that the families are now avian, rather than human."

I nodded, understanding, and capitulated. "You had better introduce me, Flame."

She beckoned and one of the birds flew from the windowsill to land on her hand. "Blaze, this is Syr-aware Ruarth Windrider. Ruarth, this is Syr-aware Blaze." (The citizenless weren't entitled to the Syr prefix, but I appreciated her bestowal of it on me anyway.) Ruarth nodded solemnly and looked at me with a dark blue eye, his head cocked on one side. The blue of his shoulders shimmered in the light.

"How do you do?" I said politely. "I'm sorry I cannot understand your language." I looked at Flame. "Perhaps, if Ruarth agrees, you could tell me a little about him?"

She nodded. "He is twenty-two years old. He is a member of the royal house of Dustelrampart and is one of the great-grandsons of the last human Rampartlord of Dustel. We more or less grew up together. He was born in a nest in a wall niche outside the window of my room; that's how I came to know him. His mother has sylvtalent. She was like a mother to me when I was growing up . . ." She looked down unhappily. "Ruarth is very upset over what happened to me today. He feels . . . impotent, and it is hard for him to deal with."

Her words hinted at emotions too unbearable for me to want to think about. I could see how much she cared about him, but the depth of the attachment seemed weird to me. It made me feel uncomfortable. I asked, "Does Noviss know about him?"

She shook her head. "No one knows but you. No one, ever.

We pretend he's a pet. Lots of people know the Dustel Islanders became birds, but very few people know that they were *intelligent* birds. Still fewer know that they had intelligent descendants."

And I was one of the very few. I inclined my head toward Ruarth and his companion, acknowledging the compliment that they had paid me. Ruarth bowed back. "*Was* that you on the boat, Ruarth?" I asked.

He nodded.

I blushed.

And I learned what a Dustel looks like when he grins.

BEFORE GOING TO MY ROOM, I SPOKE TO Tor and Ransom; I wanted to work out a way of concealing Flame's presence in The Drunken Plaice. We decided that Ransom was to continue to pretend he was upset by Flame's disappearance, and all of us were to smuggle food to her. Ransom, of course, was close to total panic. With the dunmagic beginning to work its evil in Flame's system, it was unlikely that she would be able to help him if he was attacked again. I had to admire the way that Tor soothed the boy. This lover of mine had three times my patience. He coaxed Ransom into calm, encouraged him to turn to his religion, quoted liberally from breviary prayers, and soon had Ransom hanging on his every word. The Holdheir was as gullible as ever; it never occurred to him to question just why Tor should be so helpful. I almost felt sorry for the boy—Tor Ryder could be every bit as devious as I.

I then hurried back to my room, where one glance at my reflection in my hand mirror made me decide to wash my hair before visiting the Keeper ship. Duthrick valued appearances and he would be neither pleased, nor inclined to listen to me, if I rolled up at the *Keeper Fair* looking like a shipwrecked mariner. The clam shell washbowl didn't hold much water, and the pitcher contained well water that was so hard it made the soap curdle—and I was expected to make the one pitcher last three days, or so the drudge had told me. However, I couldn't bear the feel of salty hair, so I did my best with a couple of clam shells full.

Of course, there was no question of washing my clothes. The only time that anyone did any laundry on Gorthan Spit was when it rained, which wasn't very often at this time of the year.

I changed into a set of clean clothes and hung the salty and blood-soaked ones out of the window to dry. I used the remainder of the water in the pitcher to wash my cuts, and then smeared them with some ointment I had brought with me from The Hub. It was expensive stuff, imported from Mekaté, and reputedly made of a special type of fungus mixed with honey from a particular type of flower, plus the ash of medicinal tree bark. Whatever it was, it worked. I always carried some and had done so since I once discovered just how dangerous a septic wound could be. To remind me, I had a large scar on my leg that had started as a small wound I'd received when thrown against a marlin spike during a storm on a ship.

I was slipping into my sword harness, ready to leave, when there was a knock at the door. I expected it to be Tor and called out for him to come in—but it wasn't Tor. It was the pregnant Keeper woman from the *Keeper Fair.*

I groped around in my mind and came up with a name. "Syrsylv Mallani. This is a surprise."

She looked a little sheepish, which meant she wasn't a messenger from Duthrick: she wanted something for herself. "Blaze. I was wondering if you would remember me."

"Why ever not?" There was actually quite a good reason: we had not had much to do with each other in the past. Mallani had once helped me out on one of the tasks Duthrick had set for me. She had been polite, helpful and distant—not traits that were particularly memorable. Perhaps the most interesting thing about her had been that she did not use magic to improve on her looks. Nor did she now: there was not the slightest trace of sylv blue playing on her skin. That intrigued me, because she was not a beautiful woman, although there was plenty of character in her face. She was about thirty, lean and spare and energetic. She carried herself like a sail filled with the wind—taut and eager, yet prone to tear if there was too much pressure.

I finished buckling on the scabbard and picked up my money belt. "I was just about to go to the *Keeper Fair* to see Duthrick. How may I help you, Syr-sylv?"

"Um . . . I don't know how to say this."

I put down the money belt. This was going to take time.

"I want you to use your Awareness to tell me if my baby has sylvtalent."

I was relieved. A nice simple task. No catches, no dangers—easy money. "Certainly. There will be a fee, of course. Send someone to fetch me once your baby is born, which, by the look of it, is any time now."

I expected her to ask the price. Instead she said, "We might be sailing at any time, or you might have to go—you can't tell now?"

I hesitated, staring at the bulge of her pregnancy. "I don't know . . . In fact, even *you* don't look like a sylv at the moment. You haven't used any magic in a long time."

"No. Some women say it's not good to use magic while carrying a baby. It weakens us, and that would hurt the child." She looked away, almost on the verge of crying.

I hid a sigh. "Suppose you tell me what all this is about. What's the hurry to know? And why are you worried anyway? Every Keeper sylv woman I've ever known has had sylv children." Thinking of Ruarth's mother, I amended that slightly, but not aloud: *Or Aware children.*

"Yes, because they have sylv husbands. My husband is a non-sylv."

That was when I remembered the circumstances of her supposedly scandalous marriage. She had been the first of the Keeper Council's sylv agents to defy convention and marry a non-sylv. There was no law against it, but sylvs who wanted to work for the Keeper Council *never* married away from their own kind.

She said, stumbling over the words, "Some people say that could mean my child will be a non-sylv. I've never heard of that happening, but it worries me . . . And I've been told that if the baby is not a sylv, I will have to give it up if I want to continue in Council service."

"That seems a little extreme."

"It is," she wailed, momentarily losing her fragile hold on her equilibrium. "It's Syr-sylv Duthrick's idea. He says I'd be so preoccupied with the baby if it's not a sylv, that I won't be able to do my work."

I snorted. "He's just punishing you for betraying your own kind and marrying elsewhere." I always thought the worst of Duthrick's motives.

She didn't quite dare to agree with me, and said instead, "The waiting is killing me . . . I have to know, and I don't know when I'll see another of the Awarefolk."

"There are plenty of other Awarefolk."

"Perhaps, but how would I know? They don't make a habit of telling sylvs who they are. Blaze, can't you try? I've been told that babies leak magic . . ."

"That's true. All small sylv children do. But I've never tried with one still tucked up in the womb."

"Please."

I shrugged. "All right. But I can't promise anything. First, let's discuss the price." I gestured at the wall to indicate the room next door. "There is a young woman in there with a dunmagic sore of subversion; she needs help."

Her eyes widened. "You want me to help her? I—I can't. I can't risk going anywhere near dunmagic, not when I am carrying." She looked terrified and edged away from the wall, a useless endeavor considering my whole bedroom was as small as a ship's brig. "Anyway, one sylv isn't strong enough to do that. You'd need several."

I sighed. I had expected as much. "Five setus then."

I expected her to bargain (it was an outrageous sum to ask for such a small service) but she dug in her purse, produced the money, and placed it next to the clam shell washbowl. "How are you going to do this?"

"Perhaps it would be best if you untie your tunic and lie down." She did as I asked, baring her abdomen, and I ran an unskilled eye over the swell of her body. She really was enormous. "When are you due?"

"Soon. A few days."

I moved around her, studying her from all angles. Then I touched her skin. The baby kicked, and I felt it—a small bump against my hand, pushing upward as though he was ready to escape his prison. I felt a rush of tenderness, of wonderment. I had always resented the fact that the choice to have a child had been taken away from me, but that feeling was just part of the blend of anger inside, an anger that was always there, all part of being a halfbreed. Part of me. Now, however, for the first time in my life, I felt something else—an ache. A regret. *This would never be mine.*

I hurriedly took my hand away, appalled by my own vulnerability.

She looked up at me, her eyes pleading, desperate. Having a child was not enough for her—it had to be a sylv child. I said evenly, "I am sorry, Syr-sylv, I simply can't tell. I cannot feel or see any sylvmagic, but that may just be because your own tissue blocks the way. You must wait for the baby to be born. Send me a message and I will come."

Something died in her eyes and she nodded, rolling off the bed and buttoning her tunic. "Thank you for trying."

I almost didn't say anything. I almost let the moment pass; it wasn't my business, but something made me say, "There are worse things than having a non-sylv child."

She looked back at me then, and a split second later her eyes widened in understanding. "You're sterile," she said. "They made you sterile."

I nodded.

"That's—that's—" She stopped, aware that there was nothing she could say. And perhaps in her heart she did not think that halfbreeds should have children.

"What's it like to be sylv?" I asked suddenly. I'd always wanted to be one, but that was more because sylvtalent would have brought citizenship with it. I'd never really considered what it was like to *be* sylv. To have that kind of power. It was impossible of course; you were either born sylv, or not.

She took my question seriously. "It's wondrous. I love having the power to heal. I help out in the hospice when we are back in The Hub, in the children's ward . . ."

"You make people pay for your services."

She looked surprised. "No one works for free, Blaze. *You* don't."

"Not everyone can afford to pay for sylv healing."

"We can't be responsible for that. I do my best, but I've got to eat too."

"And the other powers: the illusions? The ability to confuse people, make them believe things that aren't true?"

She was on the defensive now. "To have that kind of power is an awesome responsibility, and only those who accept that responsibility can be allowed to use sylvtalent. There are laws to govern the use of our powers. Strict laws. And the penalty for misuse is very harsh: you have your powers rendered inert."

I quoted a sailor's proverb to her: "The captain rules the ship, but who rules the captain?" but she didn't understand what I was trying to say. It never occurred to her that the Keeper Council itself may have needed controlling. I gave an internal sigh, and wondered what I was doing. A short time earlier I had been defending Keepers to Tor Ryder; now I was giving his arguments back to a Keeper. "Forget it," said. "It doesn't matter."

We walked downstairs, talking niceties. She promised to speak to Duthrick on Flame's behalf if he raised objections to my request for help. I promised to tell her the magic status of her baby, once it was born, without further payment. We parted outside the inn. She had an errand or two to do before returning to the ship, and I wanted to speak to Tunn. Secretly, I hoped I wouldn't see her again. I was almost positive that if her unborn child had been a sylv, I would already know it—and I didn't want to be the one to have to tell her what she did not want to hear.

IT WASN'T VERY FAR FROM THE DRUNKEN Plaice to the main harbor where the Keeper ship was still tied up at the wharf. I didn't think I would be in any danger; I was still hoping that my part in Ransom and Flame's affairs was obscure. I still hoped that the dunmaster did not know I was one of the Awarefolk, and did not know that I was the one who had rescued Flame.

I had no premonitions. I was even happy. If it hadn't been for Flame's predicament I would even have been joyful, but I was confident that I could enlist Keeper help with her problem, that the Keepers would in fact be able to help. In fact, I—who so prided myself on my shrewd cunning—was uncharacteristically short-sighted. Maybe I can blame fatigue; I had not slept much that night.

I didn't go straight to the docks. First, I asked Tunn where Niamor lived. Fortunately, he knew. For someone who rarely spoke, Tunn was surprisingly well informed. He told me Niamor's rooms were on the second floor of a dockside building.

The shops were open when I set out; in Gorthan Docks morning was the time for buying fish. There was plenty of the fresh catch to be had because the night boats had come in. Even better, as far as I was concerned, were the temporary stalls erected along the laneways, where sweetfish threaded on fishbone sticks were grilled over seaweed fires. I bought two sticks and ate the smoke-flavored flesh as I walked down to the harbor docks, my feet scrunching in the fish scales of the laneway.

Following Tunn's directions, I found Niamor's house easily

enough, and he was at home. In fact, he was still in bed when I knocked on his door; people like him slept late in Gorthan Docks.

His grumbling changed to cheerful hospitality when he saw who had woken him up. He waved me in with every indication of pleasure, and loped about getting me a drink while I looked around. His rooms were the closest I'd ever seen to comfortable living on Gorthan Spit. They were spacious, clean and well appointed. Niamor knew how to look after himself.

"Any luck with your slave?" he asked as he handed me a drink that steamed in a carved whalebone mug; a potent seaweed brew that I knew from previous visits to Gorthan Spit. Non-alcoholic, but it carried a punch that sprang the eyelids apart nonetheless.

I quelled my impatience. When dealing with Duthrick I needed every bit of information I could obtain to use as leverage, or incentive, or payment. I shook my head in answer to his question. "I was about to ask you the same thing."

He shook his head in turn. "I've asked everyone I know, and they all say there isn't a Cirkasian slave woman on the Spit. If anyone told you different, then they didn't know what they were talking about."

I sighed. "Ah. Oh well. Too bad, eh? And what about the dunmaster? Have you had any luck figuring out who he might be?"

"I made out a list of everyone in The Drunken Plaice at lunch that day, and I've eliminated most of them. I'm still checking out the remainder, finding out how long they have been on the island. But you know what Gorthan Spit is like. People come and go like smelts on spawning runs and nobody notices. I'll let you know when I've come to a conclusion, but the name will cost you dear, Blaze my sweet. Although you can pay in kind, if you like. In advance too, if you want."

He put his head on one side and gave me that charming smile of his. A day back I would have said yes, but not any longer. My initial attraction had faded as quickly as the color of a starfish left in the sun. Tor's doing, of course.

Embarrassed, I cleared my throat, all too aware that up until now my signals to Niamor had told a different story. "Sorry. I'm . . . er, busy just now. And, Niamor, be very, very careful. If that bastard has the slightest hint of what you're doing—"

"Don't worry, this Quillerman here is very good at looking

after his own skin . . . Did you hear what happened last night, by the way?"

"About the Cirkasian disappearing? Yes." I finished the drink and stood up. "Her pretty friend has been telling everyone. Ridiculous boy—he woke me up in the middle of the night, and now he's asking everyone to send out a search party. He thinks he's back on one of the law-abiding Middling Islands."

"I told you she wouldn't last long on Gorthan Spit," he said as he took me to the door. "But that wasn't what I meant. I hadn't heard about her. I came across Domino in a rage in the early hours of this morning—apparently someone killed both Mord *and* Teffel last night. With a sword. Domino is not at *all* happy. He tends to take such things very personally, Domino does. Perhaps it's not me who should be careful." He bent his head slightly to kiss me on the cheek. "Take care, my lovely firebrand."

He opened the door for me and I went out.

But I never did get to the Keeper ship.

They were waiting for me outside Niamor's house. And this time they never gave me a chance to draw my sword. All I heard was a soft footfall behind me; all I saw was an upraised hand holding a cudgel as I half turned, my hand groping for my sword hilt too late.

CHAPTER 10

I WOKE TO PAIN.

I was staked out like a rayfish drying in the sun: arms and feet spread-eagled and pinioned at wrist and ankle; a thong around my neck that was also staked into the ground on either side so that I could not lift my head without choking myself. I was, in fact, in the sun with compacted sand and dried seaweed under my body. The sea, now at high tide, lapped a pace or two away from my feet. I was naked and my head ached abominably. I also had a fair idea that worse was yet to come.

"She's waking up."

The words were softly spoken, said with pleasure, and they froze me with their malice. I did not know the voice. I could not see the speaker; he stood somewhere above me, behind my head. Although I could move my head a little from side to side, there was no way I could glimpse anyone behind me. I knew it had to be the dunmaster; the stink of dunmagic was so thick it furred my throat as I breathed.

"Just as well for you. I would have been *most* unhappy had she died. Hitting people on the head is a risky way to immobilize them—please remember that in the future."

I could see the other two men, the ones he had addressed. They were both short. One I remembered seeing that first day in The Drunken Plaice: a wiry fellow with lined skin. Sickle the

torturer. A halfbreed, with an impossible combination of Calmenter honey-brown eyes and Souther brown skin. No earlobe
tattoo. And he was no eunuch either—which meant that he was
either a lot smarter than most of his kind, or he had lived out
most of his life on Gorthan Spit, where no one worried too
much about interbreeding.

The other was even shorter, a fair-skinned Fen Islander with
green eyes and brown hair. He looked at me with fervent hatred:
Domino, who had an obsession about his short stature, who
hated the tall, who looked at me now—and smiled.

"Syr-master," said Sickle deferentially. "What are
th'orders?"

The dunmagic stirred as its originator moved; it whirled
around my head, raging at its impotence against me. The smell
of it contaminated the air, so intense that I could feel its
strength. Its *increased* strength. It was growing stronger, day by
day. The Keepers had better find this man before he was too
strong for them . . .

"I want to know who helped her free the Castlemaid, that's
all," the voice purred from behind my head. "The Cirkasian will
return to me of her own free will shortly. I don't need to track
her down. But I don't like not knowing who the other one was;
such Awarefolk are dangerous to me. Find out, then dispose of
her however you please. The longer you take over it, the happier
it will make you, eh? A week, a month, a year. There's no need
to hurry. Perhaps chained to the wall in our whorehouse as a final destination? But just get that name first. And make sure it's
the right one, you understand? Don't let her fool you."

He didn't wait for an answer. I heard him move away over
the sand, taking his dunmagic with him.

I could breathe again. I could puzzle over why they thought
Flame was the Castlemaid. I could recall silly things like Ruarth's mother had sylvtalent. I could meditate on what fools Tor
and I had been to think that we could deceive a dunmagicker
like this one.

I looked around as best I could, searching for any hope.
However small.

As far as I could see, staked out as I was, I was on a deserted
beach. There were no houses, no buildings, no boats out on the
ocean. The only things in sight were a couple of sea-ponies, tethered to stakes at the edge of the water. They were cavorting in
the sea, keeping themselves cool, their glistening coils winding

in and out of the waves like a thread following a needle. A dried-
out sea-pony is a dead one. They're not much use as mounts, except on a place like Gorthan Spit where the sea is never more
than an hour or two's slither away.

They were my first hope: they represented a way of escape,
if only I could free myself.

The second hope was just out of reach: my sword. It lay on
the pile of clothing beside me, tantalizingly close.

The third hope was in the sand itself. Stakes might not hold,
even in hard, compacted sand, if I was free to work at them. But
I doubted Domino or Sickle would leave me here alone. Still,
there was a lot I could do under the guise of writhing in pain.

Guise? It wouldn't be guise. Pain was inevitable where these
two were concerned.

I looked up at the cloudless sky: the sun was almost over-
head. Close enough to midday—but what day? I had no idea
how long I had been unconscious. I had a thirst that stuck
tongue and lips together as if they'd been smeared with sea-
pony slime. My head ached and ached without end.

Flame. Shards of memory scored my mind. How long did
she have left?

Domino leaned over me. "This is going to be very slow,
lady-bitch. But I make you a promise, huh? Give me the name
he wants and I make sure you're dead by tomorrow night, 'stead
of some time next year. That's your choice, my sweet. Think
about it, eh?"

I gave a hollow laugh. "Tomorrow night? In this heat I'll be
dead without water in a matter of hours."

He didn't take the hint. He nodded to Sickle. The torturer
came forward with a gutting knife in his hand. "This stretch of
coast here is known for its blood-demons," Domino continued.

I didn't react. I'd never heard of blood-demons.

He read my mind. "Maybe you never seen one. Lemme
show you what they look like." He walked down to the water's
edge, picked up something and walked back. He held up a
seashell of some kind for me to have a look at. It was about the
size of a man's thumb; an upper hard purple shell covered a
softer body underneath, like a limpet. He turned the creature
over to show me the underside: it was spongy and pulsated gently. There didn't seem to be any claws or mouthparts, nothing
that seemed lethal or horrible.

Domino smiled down at me, his green Fen eyes so like mine.

They have beautiful eyes, the Fenlanders. Have you noticed? The color of clear seawater over coastal sand. I used to wonder whether I inherited mine from my mother or my father . . . but I digress. Deliberately, I suppose. Even after all these years I find it hard to talk about what happened next.

Domino said, "Still wondering, eh?" He put the creature on his arm, soft part down. "It don't hurt. 'Less it finds an open wound and tastes blood. Then it hunkers down into the gash, turns its stomach inside out and sucks. I been told—by those who've felt it—that it's a very painful thing, 'cos of the poisonous gastric juices. Mind you, I only got their screams to go by. None of them were able to actually *speak*."

He looked at the blood-demon with affection. "They can go months without food. Then, when they do find a wounded fish or animal, they go into a sort of feeding frenzy. A small school of them can guzzle a whole whale in a week . . . Oh yeah, they have to crap as they eat, of course, and what they crap is mostly pure acid. It adds to the pain, I'm told, though I always doubted that it was possible to feel more under the circumstances. Still, you'll find out shortly, eh? Perhaps you could tell me; for future ref'rence, you understand."

"Let me get on with it," Sickle growled at him. "*He* wants that sodding information today, not next week." Casually he bent down and slashed at my breast with his knife. The wound wasn't particularly deep or serious; he didn't want me to bleed to death. He wanted it slow . . .

Domino dropped the blood-demon into the cut. For a moment nothing happened. Sickle grinned at me, and opened up another slice on my stomach, and yet another on my thigh. The creature on my breast wriggled a little, settling into the wound as if it belonged there. Sickle disappeared from my vision and then returned with another couple of blood-demons. He ran his hand insolently over my body before placing them into the other cuts. Then he loosened the thong around my neck. "We wouldn't want you to choke, would we?" he asked.

A moment later pain ripped my body apart. There is no other way to describe it.

I hadn't been going to scream. I hadn't been going to give them the satisfaction.

I started to scream and went on screaming. Yet I heard nothing. The pain would not allow me to hear. Or see. Or think. Only to feel . . .

If it had been enough to want to die, I would have died in the first five seconds.

Time has no meaning to the tortured. Thirty seconds of agony seems like a lifetime. When the torture doesn't stop, there is no concept even of the length of a lifetime—there is only a longing for death. Death is the vision that keeps madness at bay; the knowledge that it will come is the sole salve for endless pain. I thought I was going to die with pain and I was glad.

I do not know how long I lay there with the blood-demons in me. When they took them away, I would have thanked them, had I had the strength. The sun was still in the sky; a flock of small birds chattered away in the murram grass; seabirds squabbled over the waves; everything was as it should be on an ordinary day.

A water-filled sponge was pressed to my lips and I drank eagerly, separating parched tongue from the roof of my mouth, glorying in the sweetness of the moisture, in the cessation of an unreal agony. Now it was merely painful. Worse was the knowledge that sooner or later I would tell them anything they wanted to know. The stakes they had used to anchor my bonds had been loosened by my struggles; they hammered them in, deeper this time.

Domino's voice whispered in my ear. "The name, bitch. The bastard who was with you when you took the Castlemaid. Quick now, or there's a week of this in store for you."

I opened my eyes and saw Sickle, impassive-faced. He was less obvious about his enjoyment of my pain. Sickle, fellow halfbreed, professional torturer. Professional . . . I gambled with the life of the one man I had ever loved.

"Tor Ryder. Tor Ryder—at The Drunken Plaice." I stumbled over the name. *Beloved. Forgive me.*

The silence seemed to last too long.

Then Domino asked, "Well?"

And Sickle shook his head. "Nah. She's too good for that. *He* reckons she's in Keeper service. They only employ the best. And she's a halfbreed." He gave a cynical laugh. "You wouldn't know what that means, Dom, but I do. Abandoned at birth. Left to die in some gutter somewhere. Nine in ten halfbreeds never make it to adulthood on islandoms other than this one; only the tough ones get as far as she and I have. For some reason she wants us to go after this Ryder—it's either a trap of some kind, or it's a false trail. A lover who spurned her, maybe. She wouldn't give up the correct name after one bout with the blood-demons. Not this lass." He grinned at me and dropped the blood-demons he had been holding into the wounds on my body.

I floated in pain, shouting out for everyone I had ever known, whimpering for forgiveness, calling on a God I had never believed in. The colors came: reds and oranges, burning my eyeballs. I was dismembered, my pieces lying in the sun to be desiccated and sold. I was scrabbling for food thrown in the backways of The Hub when I was five; resisting the sexual advances of an older boy when I was six; fighting the delusions of fever in a vermin-infested tomb in a cemetery when I was seven; having my womb irreparably scarred when I was thirteen; stabbing the man who had raped me in Bethany when I was fourteen; earning my passage to Fen Island by sleeping with a stinking captain of a fisher a few days later; selling my soul to the Keepers in order to keep my body alive when I was fifteen . . .

You were right, Niamor. Life's shit.

Flame, sweet Flame, can you survive a little longer . . .

I have to die.

No one can live with this pain.

I don't want life on these terms.

That water's good . . .

I'll give you the name, just kill me.

Syr-aware Duthrick. (God, how he'd hate the downgrading!) The Keeper Syr-councilor. Tell the dunmaster, I don't care. (He probably won't believe in an Awarefolk Councilor anyway, but who knows.) Just kill me.

"No, you big bitch, not yet. We haven't finished . . ."

Beloved . . .

AN ETERNITY OF PAIN IS A LONG TIME.

Long enough to bore even those who enjoy the watching of it.

They tired of their game, especially when I drifted in and out of consciousness, robbing them of their triumph, especially when they had to refix my bonds again and again as I struggled. They threw away the blood-demons and began to taunt me with descriptions of other tortures they had in store for me, agonies so vile I couldn't conceive that it would be possible to endure them. For them, half the enjoyment was to savor the victim's dread.

I wasn't sure whether it was the same day, but anyway, the sun was setting over the dunes. The tethered sea-ponies came out of the water to lie intertwined on the sand, licking each other and enjoying the rest now that the heat had gone from the sun. Their green hides were tinged with the pink of sunset. Sickle threw a bucket of seawater over me, washing away the sand and blood. The sting of it in my wounds might almost have been pleasant after the hell of the blood-demons, if I hadn't known that it was just the prelude to more pain.

I dreaded all right, but I was lucky. They never did get around to the next installment they'd had in mind.

Domino bent to check my bonds—and took an arrow in his rump. The feathered shaft stuck out like a make-believe tail for a make-believe animal in a strolling players' masque, but the arrow was real enough to have him howling with outrage and pain, even while it seemed an absurdity. He bucked through the haze of my pain, a pantomime ass, braying to the audience ... Then Sickle, still gaping at Domino, went down with an arrow in his shoulder and I stopped lying there passively as if I'd been lightning-struck, and began wrenching at the already loosened bonds and stakes.

Another arrow, in the thigh this time, had Sickle rolling on the sand screaming. Domino was scrabbling away on all fours, a second arrow in his backside waggling beside the first in an even more ridiculous caricature of a tail. I had my right arm free, stake still attached, and was fumbling for my sword where it lay, just out of reach, with my clothes.

"I'm here, love," someone said in my ear. "It's all over."

His voice was heaven.

I closed my eyes and stopped fighting, stopped hurting, stopped the desperate struggle to look after myself. For the first time in my life I gave myself over to another's care.

He cut the bonds and raised me gently against his chest. "How badly are you hurt?" he asked, and his voice ached for me.

"Lucky ... I don't get sunburned easily. I'm a little ... tattered ... here and there ... but it's not as bad as it looks." Or feels. Not anymore.

"Do you want me to stake these fellows out and feed them to the blood-demons?" His tone, coldly clinical, made it clear that he had recognized the wounds on my body—and knew what they signified.

I opened my eyes and looked around. Domino had vanished, but he couldn't have gone all that far. Sickle was trying to drag himself toward the sea-ponies, but his injuries were severe and he wasn't making a very efficient exit.

"That would be . . . a sort of poetic justice, Tor. But . . . no. I don't think it's . . . quite your style. You don't have to do that for . . . me."

He hesitated. "My style? No, I wouldn't have said so . . . but it's tempting, Blaze, very tempting. I would if it would help you. I would do anything."

"Just kill them, Tor. People like that shouldn't be allowed to exist."

He left me briefly to execute Sickle with my sword, knocking him out and then slitting his throat with ruthless efficiency. When he turned his back on the body as if he didn't want to acknowledge what he had done, the look on his face jagged at me like sharp coral.

I held out my hand and stayed him as he moved to go after Domino. "No, Tor. Leave the other one."

He couldn't bring himself to hide his relief, although he tried. Something didn't quite match up with what I knew of him, but I was in no state to mull over it just then.

He was back at my side, lifting a drinkskin to my lips, tending the wounds, helping me to dress, chafing my wrists and ankles to restore circulation, touching me with gentle care, concealing his pain.

"Flame?" I asked, finally giving voice to the fear in me.

"She was still hanging on when I saw her last, about four hours ago. It was she who told me where to find you. When you didn't come back this morning she was worried. She sent a flock of Dustels out looking for you all over Gorthan Spit. One of them saw you and returned to tell her. You *do* know about the Dustel Islander birds?"

"I do," I said, and added talking Dustel birds to my growing list of things he ought not to have known about, but did. "The dunmaster's bastards were waiting for me, Tor. Outside Niamor's house. They knew I was the one who had saved Flame. I don't know how they knew. And I don't know how they knew where to find me this morning."

"We found the tapboy with marks of a dunmagic whipping. Could that have had anything to do with it?"

"*Shit.* Oh yes. That could have everything to do with it. My fault—I asked him the way to Niamor's. And he knew Flame was back; he told me he saw her come in. And he knew I went after her last night. *Damn.* The poor boy."

"He's still alive. Do you know who the dunmaster is yet?"

I shook my head. "Perhaps we should have waited in that prison of Flame's, seen who it was coming up those stairs."

"And if he'd had enough company, maybe we'd be dead by now."

"Perhaps. I think he must have seen us go out through the window after all, Tor. He knew we were Awarefolk. The dunmagic bolts he sent after us were sent in anger, not with any real hope of killing us. But I must get back. Flame."

"Ransom went to ask the Keepers for help. Perhaps they have done something by now."

Gently he helped me to my feet. I looked around; Domino had disappeared into the sand dunes. "You came alone?"

"Yes. I hired a sea-pony."

"The Lance of Calment strikes again . . . You fire a mean arrow, Tor." He still wasn't wearing a sword, but at least he did have a knife in his belt as well as the bow and arrows.

He smiled slightly. "On the contrary. I meant to kill them. All I managed to do was stick them full of shafts like spicesticks in a pomander. I'm out of practice. I haven't shot an arrow since—since those days in Calment Minor." Come to think of it, he had probably loosed a few in my direction back in those days. Perhaps the same thought occurred to him, because there was suddenly something remote about him, a withdrawal.

I touched his arm in question. "What's the matter, Tor?"

He turned stark eyes to me. "I was too late to help you. I don't know how to help you now."

It was only half the truth, and I knew it. Something else troubled him, but I let it ride and dealt with the problem he had mentioned. "You saved my life. You stopped my torture. What more could a lady in trouble want? As for now, you can go on loving me. That's all I ask. I'm as tough as dried rayfish, Tor. I was born a halfbreed, and there's nothing much anyone can teach me about survival. But to have someone love me—that is a joy I've never known before." I quelled the pain that standing up had aggravated and told him the truth: "Just to have you look at me the way you do is to make life worth anything fate throws my way, even a torture or two."

I took a deep breath, as if that would bring order to jumbled thoughts and chaotic emotions. I let my hand fall away from his arm.

"But we don't have time for this—I must get to Flame."

He was back to his efficient self. "Can you ride a sea-pony?"

"Of course. How far are we from Gorthan Docks?"

"Three hours ride along the beach. Are you sure?"

I forced a grin. "Stop playing mother, Tor. I'm not used to it."

He smiled reluctantly and took my hand.

I DON'T KNOW WHY THOSE ANIMALS are called sea-ponies; they don't resemble the real meadow ponies I've seen on the Keeper Isles. Those are shaggy things hardly bigger than a dog. Sea-ponies swim better than they gallop. They have fins along their sides and a fin for a tail—and no legs at all. They're rare outside Gorthan Spit nowadays. People prefer those animals you introduced us to: horses. You haven't seen a sea-pony yet? Well, they resemble oversized earthworms as much as anything, I suppose, but even there the resemblance is only partial. Earthworms don't have necks, and sea-ponies do. They have long bodies with many segments, each one covered with a hard shell that conceals body tissue; the necks rear up from the ground to a height well above that of a tall man, and the head is very little different to the neck below it. The stalked eyes, feelers and mouth parts are there on the front side; the breathing apparatus is on the same segment but on the other side, facing the rider. Or riders. One sea-pony can carry five or six people—more than your horses can!

Anyway, I was grateful for the use of a sea-pony that day, I can tell you. Tor settled me in front of him, both of us sharing the same body segment. He knew how weak I was and wanted to give me support on the ride: the rhythm of a sea-pony can be tricky. On land they move by contracting their segments from the rear and then shooting their front half forward; if you aren't careful, you could end up with a snapped neck when they reach top speed. Riding one is an art, but I'd ridden every animal there was to ride in the Isles of Glory, including sea-ponies, and mastered them all. I hooked my feet into the man-made hollows on the segments and leaned back against Tor's chest.

He gathered up the reins that fitted on to a halter around the head.

"Ready?" he asked.

I turned back to assent, and drew a sharp breath instead. From where we were then, at the top of the dune, I could see what hadn't been visible from where I'd been staked out at the water's edge: a village. Its outline against the sky was just discernible in the crepuscular light of dusk. But it wasn't the realization of its existence that made me gasp; it was the angry red glow that seemed to hang over it. I heard Niamor's words echo in my head: *those who go there don't seem to come back . . .*

"In the name of all the islands," I whispered, "what abomination is that?" I knew it was dunmagic, of course. What appalled me was the extent of it. Surely no one dunmaster had caused all of that.

Tor urged the animal forward by poking it in the soft skin between the segments with a riding-prod. "There's more than one dunmaster here," he said, "that's obvious."

"The Keepers must be told—"

"I imagine they know."

"There's something you're not telling me." I hadn't meant to say that. I hadn't wanted to force him to tell me his secrets, but my fear had overridden my respect for his privacy.

"There have been many disappearances of sylvtalents over the past year or so," he said with an oblique neutrality.

I thought of Flame. Sylvtalent under a spell of subversion. To be forged by dunmagic into a perversion of herself.

I glanced back once more at the village and my stomach tightened with nausea. The red was more than the contamination of dunmagic; it was a disease eating at what had once been true, evil forged from good, a cancer wrought from healthy flesh and healthy minds.

"Oh sweet God—" The words jerked out of me. In my horror, I turned on him. "And you would condemn the Keepers? They are the only people who can stop this."

He shook his head, implacable. "No, Blaze. Only Awarefolk can stop this. Sylvtalents can be corrupted, just as Flame is being corrupted." He prodded the sea-pony again and its pace quickened.

I couldn't think of anything to say. Every thought I had appalled me.

Letter from Researcher (Special Class) S. iso Fabold, National Department of Exploration, Federal Ministry of Trade, Kells, to Masterman M. iso Kipswon, President of the National Society for the Scientific, Anthropological and Ethnographical Study of non-Kellish Peoples.

Dated this day 13/1st Double/1793

Dear Uncle,
Yes, I would be delighted to stay with you and Aunt Rosris before and after my presentation to the Society. And I have taken note of your warning about the charming Miss Anyara isi Teron, and shall be on my guard against her smile. My aunt always has impeccable taste and I am sure it will take all my powers of resistance! I was, by the way, delighted to hear that Aunt has had her first religious aetherial. I know how hard she has prayed over the years that she would be one of those blessed to have such a transcendence at the holy Menara festival. Cousin Edgerl writes that Aunt's face was quite transformed by the wonder of her visual experience. I live in hope that one day I will be blessed in a similar fashion and that my face too will shine with the miracle of seeing God before me.

As to the anomalies in the conversations I have sent you so far, you are quite right, of course. It has been a source of considerable puzzlement, not only to us researchers aboard the RV Seadrift, but to numerous Kellish traders and missionaries who have been dealing with the islanders much longer than we have. What are we to make of people who talk of magic as though it was something with which they themselves have had intimate contact; what are we to believe when people speak of the Dustel Islands existing and then not existing; what are we to make of people who all say that the tattoos in their ears were made by a race of alien people that none of Kellish origins has ever seen?

Are Blaze Halfbreed and others of her ilk just congenital liars, who love to weave improbable stories? Or do they believe what they tell us, no matter how unlikely it seems to our ears? Herewith is another packet of conversations; yet more tales of intrigue and, I hope, an insight into a culture that—alas—no longer exists in quite the same form. Partly the fault of Kellish contact, partly the fault of this weird episode in their history, the period they call the Change.

Yes, I have tried so hard to keep an open mind, and not to let my own cultural leanings influence the oral history we have recorded here, but God knows, it is difficult sometimes.

I remain,
Your dutiful nephew,
Shor iso Fabold

CHAPTER II

ONE LOOK AT FLAME DROVE ALL THOUGHT of my own pain out of my mind. She was fighting what was happening to her, but she was losing the battle. Her arm was a vicious red, swollen as far as the elbow, the skin stretched hot and taut. And yet it lacked any signs of putrefaction that a dunmagic death sore would have caused by then, and she did not seem to be suffering much pain. It was fear her eyes held, not pain; so much fear I could hardly bear to meet them.

Ransom clutched at my arm the moment I entered the room; the wretched man always seemed to be clinging to me. "Where have you *been*? Don't you *know* how she's been suffering? Why weren't you *here*? The Keepers wouldn't listen to me! How could you go off and leave her?"

It was Tor who soothed him, leaving me free to go to Flame. She did not reproach me but her muttered words seared anyway. "The bad grows inside me," she said. "I begin to hate . . . I think awful things about everyone." She looked down at her arm. "It's like this because I'm trying to fight it. Once I've given in, the swelling will go away. But inside . . . Oh God, Blaze, the inside of me! Blaze, don't let me live like this. *Promise me*. If the Keepers fail . . ."

I scarcely recognized my voice as I gave her the promise. "I'll see you dead before I see you succumb to dunmagic. I swear it."

"You kill her and you'll have *me* to contend with," Ransom spat in my direction.

Tor interrupted, voice smooth. "We have a sea-pony downstairs. Can you carry Flame down, Noviss? We'll take her to the *Keeper Fair*." He touched me on the arm, acknowledging my slim hold over my emotions. Too much had happened that day. I wanted a bath to wash away the contamination, I wanted to be held and cosseted, I wanted to feel safe.

Instead we took Flame to the Keeper ship.

When Tor and I had returned to The Drunken Plaice from the beach, I had insisted that he not be seen with me. Once we had reached the first of Gorthan Docks' houses, I had made him walk back to the inn by himself. Now, too, he slipped away by himself to the docks. It was the only way I knew to keep him safe, but we both knew it was a fragile safety at best. I hadn't wanted him to go to the *Keeper Fair* with us at all, but he insisted, probably because he knew how close to collapse I was, how much in need of his support. He arranged to meet us at the ship while the Holdheir helped me with Flame.

THE KEEPER ON SHIPWATCH WAS A woman with a hooked nose that spoiled the balance of her face. She had woven a sylvspell to replace the offending beak with a cute retroussé and she didn't like meeting me face-to-face one little bit. The retroussé was just a silver shadow to my Aware eyes; in fact, if anything, it drew attention to her flaw. And she knew it. She knew who I was and she knew I saw her exactly as nature had made her and she hated it. She was surly and didn't want to let us on board.

I insisted Syr-sylv Duthrick be consulted, and finally we were allowed up the gangplank. However, the moment we all stood on the deck, Tor and I exchanged startled glances and began to wonder if the Keeper woman had had another reason for keeping us off. Somewhere below us, deep in the ship, something reeked with sylvmagic warding. The amount of effort that must have gone into the raising of such wards was extraordinary, and for the life of me I couldn't think what the ship could be carrying that could possibly warrant such a tangle of protection spells.

We were all shown into the wardroom: Ransom, Flame, Tor and myself. Flame was on her feet, but had to be heavily supported by Ransom. While we waited, the two of them sat down in adjacent chairs. Ransom could hardly keep his eyes off Flame's arm, which did little to reassure her. Tor stood gazing out of the porthole, thoughtful and unobtrusive. I strolled around to examine the room. It was wood-paneled throughout, with intricately carved cornices on the ceiling, and patterned inlay on the floor. The walls were decorated with oil paintings of Keeper Isles scenery: bucolic scenes of gamboling children, red-cheeked milkmaids and neat haystacks inhabited by impossibly cute mice; or clean cobbled streets filled with impeccably dressed men and their smiling wives, going about their business while their children in spotless pinafores rolled hoops and played with dogs. Somehow it left me with the same feeling I would have had if I had eaten a whole jar of honey at one sitting.

Some ten minutes later Duthrick entered, alone, his violet eyes flashing his annoyance. He glanced at Tor and dismissed him from his consideration almost immediately. He had no way of knowing that Tor was one of the Awarefolk, and apparently found nothing in the way the Stragglerman dressed or held himself that might interest a Keeper Councilor. He nodded to Ransom, prepared to be marginally more polite, perhaps because the expensive cloth of Ransom's coat proclaimed him to have the status of the rich, if nothing else.

I explained what had happened to Flame and he glanced down at her, indifferent to both her fear and her beauty. He cut me short with a brusque, "I can see what the matter is, Blaze. I am not blind. And this young man was here earlier today telling it all at great length, although a little incoherently. But as I explained to him, to treat her would require more power than that of any one Keeper."

"You have more than one," I snapped. "Consult them."

He arched an eyebrow in that intimidating way of his, but after a measured moment of thought, he left us to do as I asked and did not come back for almost an hour. I spent most of that time wondering why I was making an enemy of Duthrick. Was I saltwater mad? What possessed me to be rude to the one person I depended on for so much?

When he returned he was more urbane, but he was still alone.

"We have discussed the matter at length," he said. He looked at Flame, not me. "We wish you to know that your cure would cost us dearly. We need our sylvpowers to deal with the dunmagic here. To treat you would be to deplete ourselves, at least temporarily. Nonetheless, we are willing to do it. There is, however, a payment to be made."

"I'll pay it," Ransom said in immediate reaction, and then added hurriedly, "if the sum is reasonable."

"The price is not one you can pay," Duthrick told him. He turned his attention back to Flame. "We wish to know where the Castlemaid can be found. That is our price."

I held my breath. I was sure she would tell, and I could see any chance I had of benefiting from the situation vanishing.

Flame was silent so long that Ransom could not restrain himself. "If you know, *tell* him, Flame. He won't hurt her."

Flame ignored him and addressed Duthrick. "You would have me sell her to you for all time."

"We want only what is best for her. She, or her children, will be in a position one day to inherit Cirkase *and* Breth—most people would hardly consider that a burden."

"You already have both islandoms under your sway: she would be your pawn forever." Sweat beaded along her forehead. Her voice was weak but her resolve held.

"Even if she were never found, we'd still be in a position to influence those islands."

"No," she said quietly. "You need her. If the Bastionlord can't have her, he'll not have anyone. And he might blame you for not bringing him the Castlemaid. He has craved her alone of all women, ever since he glimpsed her without her veil at Cirkasecastle last year. She's the only one he could ever bring himself to breed from; his interests normally lie in other directions. Besides, if he has no heir of his own get, the line will fall to his much younger cousin—and his cousin does not favor Keepers. Without the Castlemaid, you'll definitely lose influence over Breth Island eventually. With her, you'll have the Bastionlord's gratitude and cooperation for as long as he lives."

Was that enough to explain Keeper interest in the Castlemaid? I doubted it. Besides, there was a tenseness underneath Duthrick's bland urbanity that told me there was more to it than that.

Duthrick continued, still addressing Flame, "All that can hardly matter to you. Anyway, you are a sylvtalent. You know us—you are of our kind. We do not use our talents for evil as the dunmagickers do. Our influence is not to be *dreaded*." He managed to sound both hurt and bewildered.

Flame, however, was implacable. "Castlemaid Lyssal matters

to me. She does not want to wed the Bastionlord. She also glimpsed *him,* you see, and he wasn't veiled either."

God, I thought, she can still joke.

Duthrick looked amazed. "You would rather be subverted to dunmagic than tell me where she is?"

She looked him straight in the eye with unself-conscious dignity. "No. That I will never allow." I tried to intervene, to stop the words I knew she was going to utter, the words that would condemn her, but she continued to hold Duthrick's gaze and never saw the warning look I threw her. She said, "But I *would* rather die."

Duthrick pulled himself up, as regal and forbidding as only he knew how to be. "Then die."

His callousness made me draw breath sharply, even though I had sensed it was coming. If he thought he would eventually have to deal with yet another dunmaster, he might have considered curing her before she succumbed, but if she was going to kill herself, then he had nothing to lose by refusing her. She hadn't seen the trap; she lacked my guile and understanding of what other people could be.

Duthrick didn't leave the matter there either. He said, "Don't think the death of the dunmaster will free you from the subversion spell. It won't. Not unless he dies very soon indeed. Once you are a dunmagicker, you will be a dunmagicker for all time. Of your own volition."

I wondered if he was lying, but then decided he was not. It made sense; subverted sylvs would not want to change back to what they had been because they would now *be* dunmagickers, and dunmagickers hated sylvs. So, if the dunmaster died, they would use their own dunmagic to make sure they stayed the way they were. A self-perpetuating perversion. That subversion spell was diabolical.

Ransom, for once, was silenced. It was Tor who spoke. "There is nothing to be gained here," he said softly to me. "Neither Flame nor the Syr-sylv will ever change their minds." He nodded at Ransom. "Help Flame out."

Dumbly, Ransom obeyed and Tor followed. Just before he left, he turned to look at me. "Some prices are too high," he said. I couldn't decide whether he was offering me the words as an explanation or a warning.

I stayed behind. I felt flayed. My heart had contracted into a hard and painful gall in the middle of my chest. I knew how to save Flame—but she didn't want to be saved at that price. Haven't I had enough pain for today? I raged to myself. Must it go on and on?

"How can you do this?" I asked Duthrick, in my pain unable to do more than whisper. The feeling of betrayal was almost more than I could bear. "It is inhuman."

He shrugged. "It's your fault. You should have had the Castlemaid in your hands by now."

"And if I had, you would have cured Flame without a price?"

He shrugged. "Perhaps. But what I said was true. We do not want to deplete our powers just now."

Bitterness twisted in me, tightening the gall. I knew I'd never be the same again after this day; the guilt would last forever. I made my decision, and blanked out the alternative so that I could go on living with what I did. I didn't tell him what I knew, and Flame paid a terrible price.

I changed the subject. "Do you know about the village of dunmasters to the west of here?"

"Of course."

"Ah, yes. Of course. And—don't tell me—you will deal with it."

"That's right."

"There's enough power there to turn the lot of you into creatures like Flame, the corruption corroding your souls and your bodies until you either kill yourselves or succumb."

"We will prevail."

"I hope you are right, Syr-sylv. I really do. But let me give you a warning: the dunmaster, the one who is responsible for all this, has put you at the top of his list of people to be dealt with first."

Of course, it was unlikely that the dunmaster would take my naming of Duthrick too seriously when he heard it from Domino. I had only done it because the Syr-sylv was the one person I could think of who might just have sufficient protection to keep himself safe—reasonably safe, anyway—from a powerful dunmaster. From Morthred, if it was Morthred.

Duthrick looked at me uneasily. "How do you know that?"

I grinned. "I told him to. More or less."

It was as good an exit line as any and I turned to walk out of the cabin—but he had to have the last word.

"Blaze," he called after me. "What we have warded below: it is physically guarded as well."

I stopped and looked back. He'd read my next move as if I were an open book, and had aborted it before I could even plan it. "Damn you, Duthrick," I said quietly. "Damn you to the Trench below."

THE OTHERS WERE WAITING FOR ME ON the dock.

I looked at Flame and took her hand. "I have one more card to play."

Fear ignited in her eyes. "Don't go after the dunmaster—"

"I doubt if I could find him in time. I was thinking of something else. Will you trust me a little longer?"

She focused her eyes on me with an effort. "I trust you." She wasn't talking about the hope I offered her; she didn't believe in it. She trusted me to kill her.

I turned to Ransom. "You owe me one hundred and fifty setus."

He was outraged. "How can you think of money at a time like this?"

"Easily. Pay me."

"I said two hundred if she was returned alive and well. Look at her! She's not well!"

Tor said softly, dangerously, "Pay the lady, Noviss."

"But—"

"Pay her."

He dug into his purse and begrudgingly handed over the money. "Now take Flame back to the inn," I said.

"The inn?" he protested. "It's not safe there!"

"No, it's not," Tor agreed. "Not for any of us." He looked at Ransom with compassion. "I'm afraid it's not safe anywhere. But the dunmaster is not going to bother Flame for a while yet. He thinks he already has her in his power and all he has to do is wait for her to come to him. So the inn is as good as anywhere else. Come, Noviss, help Flame up onto the sea-pony. The creature is fretting; it needs to get back in the ocean soon."

When the two of them had ridden off, Tor asked softly, "Are you thinking of what the Keepers have hidden? Of finding out what it is and then somehow using the knowledge as a bargaining point?"

I shook my head. "No. Duthrick has anticipated that. He knows me too well—it's guarded with more than sylvmagic and

I haven't quite come to the stage where I can kill Keeper sylvs just to see what they are hiding. I have another way out for her, I hope . . . Go back to the inn, Tor. I'll be all right."

He accepted the dismissal, knowing his Awareness was needed by Flame and Ransom, but not liking the role I had assigned him. I suspected that it was more his duty to Ransom that made him decide to accede to my request, not any desire to oblige me. Had the circumstances been different, he would have come with me no matter what I said. Instead, he jammed on his hat, pulled the brim low, and slipped away across the wharf.

Once he was gone, I went to Niamor's house. I had to pick my way through sleeping vagrants littering his doorway, and felt a stab of sharp emotion: a mixture of pity, shame, anger—and relief that it wasn't me there. The odor of unwashed poverty was familiar and childhood memories welled up; I had to push them away, not to think, not to remember.

I was lucky to find Niamor home; normally he would have been out at that time of night, but these were not normal times.

He wasn't quite as enthusiastic about seeing me as he had been that morning, but he invited me in and gave me a drink. It was a drink I needed; I hadn't had nearly enough liquid that day, and I hadn't eaten since the grilled fish that morning. I choked on the potent alcohol, which prompted him to offer me water as well. It was equally welcome, although Gorthan Spit well water always tasted faintly of salt and fish.

"What's up?" he asked. He was uneasy, although he hid it well. "I still haven't singled out a name for you." He waved a hand toward his desk where a few sheets of cheap paper were scattered haphazardly, as if to say "I've been working on it."

My last real hope of extracting Flame entirely unscathed from the mess she was in died within me. I took a deep breath and wished the day would end. "I came to warn you," I said. "The dunmaster knows I came to see you this morning."

"So?" he drawled. "He can't know I'm helping you to identify him. Believe me, Blaze, I've been *very* careful on this one."

"Even if he doesn't have the faintest suspicion about that, you could still be in trouble. Niamor, the dunmaster had the Cirkasian, and I played a part in her rescue. He knows it. He's vengeful: dunmagickers are like that. Anyone who has had contact with me could be in danger. It's time for you to move out. I hope it will only be temporary—the Keepers are working on the demise of this fellow."

"*Damn.* You fool, Blaze. Couldn't you leave well enough alone?" He gave a quick glance around the room as though regretting what he saw. "Damn you, you firebrand. I might have known anyone as splendid as you spelled trouble—"

"Halfbreeds are always trouble, Niamor, splendid or not. You'd do well to remember that."

"Yeah. My mistake." He sighed. "I'll send a message to you in a day or so. I'm close to working out who this fellow is. In the meantime, I will move out."

I didn't doubt that he had a bolthole already planned for just such an emergency. I said, "There's one other thing you can help me with."

He threw up his hands. "Sheesh. She's just wrecked my life and now she wants to poke at the remains."

"I just want to know who's the best doctor in Gorthan Docks. And where to find him. Or her."

He laughed. "Now I know you're joking, right? The only good doctor in Gorthan Docks is the afternoon sea breeze, love. There's a good herbalist, though."

"I need a surgeon."

"If you need an operation—and I must say you don't look half as good as you did this morning—then I advise you to take the next ship out and get it done elsewhere."

"There must be someone."

"If you want to die, sure. Believe me, sweetheart, you're better off without Gorthan Docks' only doctor. He's a drunken butcher, he is."

I stared at him. "Well, maybe that's what I want. A butcher."

"That was only a manner of speaking. I wouldn't even trust this fellow to carve up a festive dinner. He's a *drunk,* Blaze, the good doctor is. Got the shakes. Memory failing. Halfway through delivering a baby he thought he was amputating a leg. The result was not pretty. Forget him."

"All right then. What about a real butcher?"

"Come off it, love. We eat fish on Gorthan Spit. You can't tell me you've forgotten that. Fish-gutters are a setu a score, though," he added helpfully.

"There must be *somebody.*" I sounded desperate. I *was* desperate.

He thought for a moment. "Well, maybe there is someone. Fellow named Bloyd. I did hear tell he was a butcher by trade, although he sells fish now. I heard he had to leave the Norther

Islands because he carved up his wife one day and sold her to his customers as prime pork."

"You joking?"

He shook his head. "That's the story I heard."

"Where would I find him?"

"At this hour? He'll be in that wretched little cantina where the fish-gutters hang out. It doesn't have a name but you'll find it by the fishmarket. It doubles as a brothel, and you'll recognize it by the bouncer who decorates the doorway. Size of a whale, he is." He shook his head as if exasperated by my foolhardiness. "If you really want to use a butcher when you actually need a surgeon—which has to be the height of insanity—then you had better get yourself an herbalist as well. There's a very good one on the island at the moment, believe it or not. You can find him down in Chandlers' Row. He's rooming with a family of halfbreeds—fellow called Wuk and his wife and kids. His name—the herbalist's, I mean—is Garrowyn Gilfeather. A Mekaté man. Quite a character."

I touched his cheek, more grateful than he could possibly know. It almost seemed that things were beginning to go right at last. "Thanks, Niamor. Take care—"

He kissed me, without passion, on the lips. "Only a temporary good-bye, I hope, my lovely firebrand. I'm still hoping we'll share a bed one day. Take care yourself, huh?"

I BORROWED A LANTERN FROM NIAMOR and went to find the herbalist first.

He wasn't too hard to find. A man selling rancid tallow from a tub on the sidewalk in Chandlers' Row told me which place was Wuk's. "The one with all the people outside," he said, pointing a greasy finger down the street.

"Why the crowd?" I asked. There must have been about thirty people in a line outside the house. It was a narrow building, two stories high, made of rocks cemented together with shell-lime in a haphazard mosaic, its solidness topped by seaweed thatching.

He shrugged indifferently, but gave me a reply anyway. "The herbalist that lives with 'em. Sells medicine that works, would you believe? One of those Mekaté medicinemen."

That sounded promising. Only trouble was, I didn't have time to wait in line. I nodded my thanks and walked up to the building with a purposeful stride. Once there, I saw that the queue led up to a wooden lean-to built on the side of the house. I bypassed the waiting people as though I knew exactly what I was doing, opened the door to the lean-to without knocking, and closed it behind me.

The interior was unprepossessing—the usual hotchpotch of materials put together to fashion walls and simple furniture. A seal-oil lantern illuminated the herbalist who sat cross-legged on the floor next to a huge sea chest, and his customer, an old woman, who sat on a stool in front of him. They both stared at me, then the man turned his attention back to the woman. "Follow the directions exactly, d'ye understand? Nary a change."

She nodded seriously as he folded up some leaves and seeds into a parcel with seaweed wrapping. "And the cost, Syr?"

"Nay, no Syr," he said with a laugh. "Not this mun. I'm no more than a humble selver-herder from a distant land. Pay what ye will, gentle lady, no more, no less."

Shyly, she dropped some coins into his hand and bobbed a curtsey. On her way out, she skirted me without a word and closed the door behind her.

The herbalist met my gaze and we took each other's measure. He was on the wrong side of middle age, this Garrowyn Gilfeather, and I had never seen anyone like him, ever—for all that I thought I had met representatives of all the nations of the Glory Isles. He was from Mekaté, all right; the lantern light shimmered on the pearl inserted into the tattoo of a rabbit on his earlobe. However, he bore no resemblance to the Mekaté people I had encountered before. They had all been dark Souther folk, like the top-hatted Fellih-worshipers. High-nosed, clean-shaven aristocratic-looking people with deep black eyes. This man was red. And hairy. Broad at the shoulder but not, I guessed, very tall. His hair was red, a sort of gingery color I'd never seen before, and all crinkled. It surrounded his head like a wild array of fleece, worthy of a Calment mountain ram. He had a red beard to match, although that was streaked with gray. A large long nose peaked into a sharp red end that seemed strangely mobile. The tip wriggled at me like that of a dog picking up an interesting scent in the air.

His skin was white, but it was blotched with red freckles, except where hair grew thick and curly on his arms and what I could see of his chest. He truly was a red man.

The clothes he wore suited his wild appearance, although

they seemed inappropriate for Gorthan Spit's suffocating heat.
They were made of some kind of rough wool woven in a twilled
pattern that confused the eye, and looked all the more startling
because the fabric was tucked into haphazard folds around his
body rather than sewn, or tied, or buttoned.

I looked back at his face. His eyes were flecked, and I could
not quite decide what was the predominant color. A deep slate
gray? Or the dark red-black of freshly spilled blood perhaps . . .

They regarded me with an amused skepticism, I do know
that.

"Well, wee bittie lady?" he asked finally. "Have ye looked
your fill?"

"My pardon," I said, hastily gathering my wits. "Are you
Garrowyn Gilfeather, herbalist?"

"Physician," he corrected. "At your service. And ye, I think,
did not wait y'turn." His accent had a lilt to it that was all charm
and music and it was easy to ignore the bite to the words.

"No. It is a matter of urgency."

"Ye look healthy enough."

"A friend needs a surgeon, immediately, or she'll die."

"Ah, lass, I'm no surgeon. I don't like blood."

I shifted my gaze to the sea chest. It had hinged top and
sides, all of them swung wide so that it opened out into a cabi-
net. One side was filled with square drawers, labeled with writing I could not read, the other with shelves of stoppered bottles
and corked ceramic pots. On the floor in front was a small mor-
tar and pestle and next to that a brass brazier, no larger than a
chamber pot, which glowed with hot coals.

I looked back at him. "Can you drug her, though? So as
she'll sleep through it? I've heard that Mekaté medicinemen
have the secret of that . . . And you have the salves to prevent
infection afterward."

"Ay. Possibly." He shrugged. "Naught is certain, know ye."

"I'll pay you ten setus, if you come to The Drunken Plaice in
half an hour. I'll have the surgeon."

"And m'patients?" he asked, waving a hand at the door.

"She's doomed if we wait."

Those eyes looked at me from under wooly eyebrows that
grew every which way, and the look skewered me with its acuity; the nose wriggled some more. I tried not to look at it.

"I'll be there. Who should I ask for?"

"Blaze. Blaze Halfbreed."

He nodded. "In half an hour."

I MADE MY WAY TO THE FISHMARKET, every sense alert, but I smelled nothing of dunmagic. I didn't have any trouble finding the cantina Niamor had described. It was about as sleazy a place as I'd ever seen in all the Isles of Glory, and it stank worse than any. The large bouncer on the door didn't want to let me in. I was the wrong sex, it seemed. Only males went in by the front door. The females used the back, and those that did all belonged to the local pimp.

If it came to that, I didn't particularly want to go in anyway.

I raised one hand to my shoulder to finger the swordhilt on my back, and held up a coin with the other. "Is there a man named Bloyd inside?" I asked.

The bouncer guffawed. "Yeah. He's here." He plucked the coin out of my fingers. "You wanna talk to him? I'll call him out; this I gotta see."

Bloyd proved to be a huge man with an impressive combination of fat and muscle that normally marks a wrestler. He looked clean enough, but he smelled of fish. He looked me up and down in disbelief. "I don't have nuttin' to do with halfbreed muck," he said.

"Aw, come on," the bouncer protested. "She's just about your size, Bloyd."

"I want your service as a butcher," I said. "And I'll pay. You are a butcher?"

"The best in Calment Major—once."

Just then, some more customers arrived and the bouncer's attention was diverted. I drew Bloyd away. "You got your tools still?"

"What's a butcher without his choppers?"

"Do you know how to joint and truss a sorgret carcass for Calmenter stuffed roast?" It was one of the most complex things I could think of that would ever be asked of a Calmenter butcher, and it involved both deboning and some delicate stitchery.

"Sure."

"I'll pay you twenty setus for a special job. But it's got to be good."

"Twenty setus? What in all the island do you want me to butcher—a sea-pony?"

I told him.

HALF AN HOUR LATER WE WERE AT THE Drunken Plaice, having called at Bloyd's house for his butchering equipment first. I had glanced inside his master-butcher's case. His knives and choppers and saws were Calment-made, and that meant quality. He looked after them well too: they all had an edge that could have split a sea-urchin's spine lengthways.

Garrowyn Gilfeather was already at the inn, and the three of us went upstairs together. Halfway up the steps, Garrowyn grabbed my elbow. I turned to look at him. In the dim lantern light, I could see that his nose tip was twitching in agitation. "What is this," he hissed. "What are ye playing at, girl?"

"Pardon?"

"I can smell it," he said. "The *wrongness*."

"You're Syr-aware?" But even as I said it, I knew it wasn't true. If he was one of the Aware, I would have sensed it.

"Charnels, no. This is *dunmagic* I smell?"

"It is." I was muddled. How could he smell dunmagic, yet not be Aware?

Now I had the two of them glaring at me. I said quickly, "A dunmagic sore that needs removing, that's all. There's no dunmagicker here."

They were only partially mollified. I went to Flame's room first, leaving the both of them outside the door, eyeing each other; a mindless shark and a scheming octopus sizing one another up even as they wondered what was going on.

Tor and Ransom were both in the room. Flame was lying on the bed. The swelling in her arm had started to go down but her eyes were beginning to glaze; she could hardly focus them at all now. "I've brought a doctor," I said without preamble.

"A doctor? No doctor can help me." She gave a gesture of defeat. "Surely you know that. Not even a halfbreed is that dumb." She turned her face to the wall.

A Dustel on the bedpost, presumably Ruarth, glared at her and snapped its beak.

"It's the dunmagic talking," I told him. I jerked my head at Tor, and he took the hint, ushering Ransom out of the room with him. "Flame," I said, "the poison's still mostly in your arm. If we could get rid of it, then you have a chance of destroying what's got into your system, of destroying it with your sylvmagic."

She twisted back to me, eyes widening. "You sadistic bitch! You want to *amputate* my arm?"

"Why not? Flame, with your sylvmagic, you have a chance. Most people who die after amputations, die because of infection. But your sylvmagic can deal with that. And just to make certain, I've brought a Mekaté medicineman along as well."

She was silent.

"Would you rather be dead?"

There was an agitated chatter from the bedpost. Ruarth hopped from foot to foot and flapped his wings.

She listened, the dunmagic temporarily subdued, and tears rolled down her face. "He says I must."

"The Mekaté man will drug you so that you don't feel anything while the doctor does it. At least for a while."

She nodded, trusting still. "All right. After all, what's an arm or two?" She gave a ferocious smile. "Ruarth says *he* does without."

I blinked hurriedly.

It seemed that every day in this place was bringing me closer to shedding tears I'd once thought I didn't have within me anywhere.

CHAPTER 12

BLOYD PLAYED UP TO THE DOCTOR ROLE with a lofty dignity that was only spoiled when he opened his mouth: his accent was pure artisan. He spread his equipment out on a table we had brought up from downstairs, laying out each implement on its own white cloth, while I carefully blocked Flame's view. Four knives of varying sizes. A whetstone. Thread of several thicknesses. Four curved needles of different lengths. A bottle of whiskey. Two saws with differing teeth sizes. A number of clamps. A pile of muslin cloths. Everything reassuringly clean and sharp . . . Ruarth, however, showed considerable agitation until I frowned at him. Ransom, who had come back in with Tor, wasn't much calmer. Garrowyn's hedgerow eyebrows shot up to meet his thatch of hair when he saw the array of butchering tools. The look he gave me was one of both amusement and mockery. "Are we dining, lass, or amputating? Are ye wanting herbs then, not drugs?"

"Do your job," I snapped at him. He grinned, then opened up the pack he had brought with him and took out his pots and bottles.

We dosed Flame with Garrowyn's pain-killing herbs and sleeping drafts, while Bloyd rubbed his hands together. "Well, now, lass," he said cheerily. "The last arm I chopped off was

actually me wife's. And I promise you, she niver felt a thing.
Niver missed it neither . . . Now let's see the problem."

We lifted Flame up onto the table and he examined the arm
distastefully as she began to drift off. Then he looked at me.
"Thirty setus, and not a copper less." His voice was as hard as the
muscles of his arm. He knew what he was looking at and he knew
how much trouble interfering with a dunmaster could bring him.

I made a show of quibbling, but my heart wasn't in it.

My heart wasn't in what followed either.

The drugs dulled Flame's pain, but she wasn't entirely unconscious. We had her strapped down, but each slice into her
flesh made her thrash about and give vent to moans that had me
wincing as if I were the one being operated on. It was awful.

"Be quick," I told Bloyd. "And you *do* realize that this is *not*
a carcass. She can bleed to death."

His relish for the job was undisguised. He had made the first
cut even while I was still adjusting the last of the ties and thereafter kept up a running commentary on what he was doing and
why, directing Tor and myself to do this, hand him that, put
pressure there, press here. For reasons which I didn't quite understand, he said he had to take the arm off just above the elbow, not at the joint. He made the first cut in her skin much
lower down so he would have sufficient to fold over the stump
later. Ransom fainted while he was explaining that bit.

I couldn't afford the luxury of passing out. I had to watch
every move Bloyd made, scared all the while that he'd forget he
was dealing with living flesh. When Flame began to groan and
surface to a waking state, Garrowyn dropped a cloth over her
face that was wet with one of his bottled concoctions. The smell
of it was sweet and nauseating. Even so, Flame screamed when
Bloyd took the saw to the bones, but then, mercifully, she
seemed to sink deeper into unconsciousness. Garrowyn felt for
her pulse, but gave me a reassuring nod. "The beat's strong," he
said. "She may be bonny but she's as strong as Sindur's Crags."
I'd never heard of the place, so it wasn't a particularly reassuring remark.

Bloyd was a good butcher, I'll grant him that, and his blithe
callousness was possibly an advantage, because it meant he
wasn't nervous. The fresh blood didn't faze him in the least and
he tied knots in blood vessels with casual calm, as though he
knew exactly what he was doing; even his sewing up afterward

was deft. Garrowyn watched him with sharp eyes and gave a running commentary of his own. "Well now, that must be the main tube for the blood. Hadn't ye better staunch that flow then, mun? Hey, wee fella, I wouldn't touch that, if I were you—rather tie that one off there, there's a wee laddie. Eh, now that's a neat stitch, sure it is." I wanted to scream at him to shut up. It wasn't until much later that I realized the success of the operation probably owed much to his suggestions.

I paid Bloyd his money, warned him to keep his mouth shut (I had no fears that he wouldn't; he knew what was at stake if the dunmaster found out what he had done), and ushered him to the door. Then I turned back to help Garrowyn and Tor bandage the stump and return Flame to the bed. She was already surfacing, and pain was making her draw breath in shuddering moans. Yet she needed to be conscious. She had to rid her system of the residue of the dunmagic and she had to banish any infection from the operation itself, so when Garrowyn suggested some more sleep medicine, I shook my head. "Not yet—she has to deal with her own healing first. Mix some pain-reliever instead."

I spared a glance for Ruarth on the end of her bed. Birds were just birds to me and little ones all looked alike anyway, or they did until I met the Dustels, but I would have had to be blind not to see the utter dejection felt by this one. Poor Ruarth. He sat huddled, his wings hunched, his iridescence muted, his head drooping, those deep blue eyes so filled with misery I wanted to comfort him—but I didn't know how to go about it.

Flame moaned again and vomited. We cleaned her up and I took her right hand, the only one she had now. "It's over," I said, "but now you have to fight some more."

Her eyes opened and the pain hit her, almost sending her back where she had been. I watched as she fought it—and won, as I had known she would. She even managed a smile of a kind. She was quite a woman.

Garrowyn gave her the pain-reducing draft from his medicine kit and went to stand near the window. My place by Flame's side was taken by Ransom, now conscious and eager to make up for his earlier display of squeamishness.

"You need to rest," Tor said quietly to me. "You too have wounds. I'll look after things here." He waved a hand around as if to encompass everything: the blood, the amputated arm, Ransom, Flame.

I nodded. "Thanks, Tor."

"Are you sure you'll be all right?"

I nodded again and touched his arm in gratitude.

Then I looked across at Garrowyn where he was propped against the wall, watching us all with those calculating eyes of his. His nose still twitched. I couldn't help thinking of rabbits; they had noses that always seemed to be quivering. "I *really* don't like blood," he said.

"We owe you our thanks," I said as I counted out the money I had promised him, and I added gravely, "Especially if you don't like blood." In truth, I was inclined to believe him. He looked quite pale.

He took the coins, saying, "I'll leave the bottle of painmask. Give her two spoonfuls every two hours."

"Will you come back tomorrow?" Ransom asked.

He shook his head. "Nay, not me. I've too much respect for me own safety." He hefted his pack and made for the door. I picked up my lantern and followed on his heels.

Tor thought I was going to my room, but I had one more thing to do before I could allow myself to rest, so I walked downstairs with Garrowyn.

"No frets," he said. "She'll be bonnie."

"I don't know what we would have done without you. Tell me, why is it that Mekaté medicines are so much better than those of other islands?" I'd seen a man have his leg cut off without the benefit of such drugs; it was not a scene I liked to remember, and that had been in one of The Hub's best hospitals.

"Because selver-herders think with their skulls instead of their superstitions."

It was the second time he had used that expression, selver-herders, and it meant nothing to me. "Who are they?"

"The people of the Sky Plains. The Roof of Mekaté. Ye ever been to Mekaté?"

I nodded.

"And yet ye've never heard of us. Ye visited the dross, Blaze, and missed the gold."

"If it's so wonderful, then why did you leave?"

"The trouble with paradise is that there's no room for devils."

"You weren't a devil to us tonight."

"Ask any man about his devil and ye'll get a different answer. Ask a Fellih-worshiper, and he may tell you 'tis a woman who speaks her mind. Ask yon young mun upstairs, and he may tell you 'tis the dirty beggar in the gutter who would gut you as soon as plead your charity. Ask you, Blaze Halfbreed, and ye may say 'tis the man who denies you a birthright."

He was far too sharp to be a comfortable companion, Garrowyn. In petty revenge, I asked: "And if I were to ask your fellow selver-herders who their devils were, what would they say?"

"They'd say a man who is different. No more, no less. Paradise must have rules, y'see. And one man's paradise can be another man's hell." We had reached the outer door to the inn, and he turned to me, the lines of his aging face furrowed into a mocking smile. "If ever ye find what ye're looking for, ye'll probably hate it. Life's made of ironies like that. All I ever wanted to be was a chirurgeon, and then I found the smell of blood makes me want to chuck up."

I changed the subject. "How can you smell dunmagic and not be Aware?"

He smiled, mocking me still. "I have an excellent nose, lass."

He signaled a lantern boy to come and light his way, and then he was gone, swinging down the street, clad in that strange garment that seemed to have no form, his hair a circle around his head like a clump of unruly dune grass.

Once he was around the corner, he threw up. I heard him.

I TURNED MY ATTENTION TO THE REASON I had come downstairs: I had to find Tunn. I had not forgotten what Tor had told me of the tapboy's dunmagic whipping.

He wasn't in the fuel shed.

I found him huddled with his dog behind the fish boxes. It was the smell that led me there, the smell of a dunmagic whipping that conquered even the stench of fish. He cowered away when he saw me, and his speech—if he was indeed trying to speak—had degenerated into utter gibberish. What I saw by the light of the lantern made me want to retch.

He had weals all over his body as if he had been beaten. But I knew that physically he hadn't been touched; those welts had been raised by spells and were designed both to give maximum pain and to heal slowly. What had been done to his skin was sick. The effect it'd had on his trust and on his mind was worse. I tried to reach him but he wouldn't let me near. Every time I extended a hand to him, or even spoke, he cringed in fear. The only living thing he was going to trust was his canine pet. He wouldn't take the ointment I had brought for him. In the end I left it there on the ground, hoping he would make use of it. It wouldn't heal the wounds any faster, but it would deaden some of the pain, as I tried to tell him.

Then I went back to my room to suffer my guilt. I ought never to have involved the lad in the affairs of a dunmagicker.

That's enough for today, if you don't mind. Some things hurt to remember, even after all this time . . .

CHAPTER 13

I KNEW I SHOULD NEVER HAVE COME BACK to Gorthan Spit.

There I was, not only with no prospect of ever earning my two thousand setus, but also unpopular with my paymasters, in danger of being further mangled by the dunmaster's henchmen—and possibly, by association, putting Tor Ryder in a similar mess.

Even a few hours' exhausted sleep followed by a real bath, achieved by bribing the drudge (two buckets full of brackish water instead of two clam shells), did nothing to make me feel any happier.

Further inquiries at the dock the next day confirmed that there was still no chance of a passage out of Gorthan Spit, not that Flame could have been moved yet anyway. She spent the day, attended by either Ransom or myself, marshaling all her power against the dunmagic that her system had absorbed. The effort left her drenched in sweat, close to collapse, and with no energy to talk.

Every time I encountered Ransom, he glared at me. He evidently blamed me for everything that had happened, and was quite sure that my interest in Flame was purely mercenary anyway. He thought I stood by her only in the hope that she would tell me where the Castlemaid was to be found. He did me an injustice. For a start, I was fairly certain by this time that I knew exactly where the Castlemaid was. In addition, it was quite clear to me that if Flame would rather die than tell the Keepers what they wanted to know, she certainly wasn't going to tell me. However, I'd already noticed that Ransom was about as short on logic as he was on charm.

When he wasn't with Flame, he was talking to Tor in his room. Fortunately, he was always a little calmer, a little more rational, after such conversations. Somehow Tor, with his quiet composure and soft humor, had a therapeutic effect on the Holdheir's uncertain temper and childish sulks.

The effect Tor had on me was just as therapeutic, if less calming. I forgot my fears in his arms and I learned how to give of myself and, even more importantly, how to accept from another. I was in a constant state of wonder, it was all so new. Not even the tension of knowing that any interlude of peace and safety was no more than that—an interlude—could take away the joy.

There were many things about Tor that still puzzled me. For example, his paymaster: just who had asked him to keep a protective eye on Ransom? And why, when I approached him unexpectedly, did he sometimes seem so . . . remote? He would sit so still, so divorced from the world around him, concentrating so hard on something deep inside himself, that he had no time for anything, or any person, in the real world. At those times I didn't seem to count.

There were other things that puzzled me too—about the Keepers. What was it that they had so well protected in the deepest holds of their ship? Why did pleasing the Bastionlord of Breth mean so much to them? Why did they need Breth so much? I'd been to the place, and I'd seen nothing about it to indicate it was vital to The Hub's sphere of interest.

Toward the end of the second day after the amputation, it became clear that Flame was not progressing as well as we had first thought. A visual check of her body showed me that it wasn't the dunmagic that was the problem; she had that almost beaten. Garrowyn's unguent seemed to have stopped any infection of the wound, more proof of the efficacy of Mekatéen medications. However, with all her talents turned to defeating the remnants of dunmagic, Flame had nothing left for herself. She had lost an enormous amount of blood and her stump was not healing; it oozed fluid. She had no reserves of sylvtalent to draw on to deal with it. She had exhausted herself and her magic. Only rest and health would return her to her former sylv strength; rest she had, but health was quite another question.

I went out on the streets again, to fetch Garrowyn back. I thought he might have some restoratives, or just advice. Anything. But I couldn't find him. When I spoke to Wuk the Chandler, the man who had been his landlord, he told me that Garrowyn had come back late at night on the day before last (evidently immediately after the operation), had packed his things up, and gone. I asked around, but the only person who seemed to have seen him was a ship's captain. Garrowyn had come to his ship to ask about a passage out of Gorthan Spit. On being told that no departures were possible until the winds and tides changed, he had simply disappeared.

I sighed. Garrowyn had obviously taken the mention of dunmagic very seriously indeed, and had gone into hiding. I can't say I blamed him, although I'll admit I uttered some choice words of abuse under my breath when I realized just how thoroughly he had managed to vanish.

As a last resort, I went to see Addie Leks in the fish-and-swillie bar. She was busy in the kitchen, grilling fish innards over the seaweed fire. It was hot in there, and sweat ran down her arms to mix with the food. She had a nasty black eye, and the look she gave her husband, the manager who doubled as the waiter, was somewhere between fulminating and just plain scared.

"Garrowyn?" she said. "Sure I know him. He scarpered night before last. Everyone's talking about it. He was a godsend to the sick in this pizzling dump and if he's gone—" She shook her head and fingered the swelling along her brow. "But it seems some huge chappie with a huge sword came to get him on that evening. Wanted him to treat his wife. Well, Garrowyn did, but she died, and now the husband is mad enough to deck Garrowyn and flatten 'im to a flounder. So Garrowyn did a flit."

I hardly recognized the story. In twenty-four hours, Gorthan Docks had not only changed my marital status, they had also managed to change my gender.

Addie flipped the last of the fish offal from grill to plate, decorated it with crispy-fried salted fish scales, and yelled for her husband to come and get it.

"Where do you think he is?" I asked.

"Oh, hiding out with his girlfriend, of course."

"He has a girlfriend?"

"How should I know? But that's what I would do if I was a chappie on the run." She leaned blowsily over the kitchen counter. "They say he's actually a clan-noble from the wilds of Mekaté, a prince, in fact, from a place they call the Sky Plains. Ran away for daring to kiss his older brother's wife . . ."

Addie the romantic again. I hid a sigh and gave up. As I left for The Drunken Plaice, she jerked a thumb in her husband's direction and whispered: "Blaze, we'll split the cash box if you'll deal with *him* for me . . ."

I felt tired and oddly dirty. Was that how people viewed me now? Someone who would kill for a few coins?

SOMEWHERE TOWARD THE END OF THE next day I had to face the fact that Flame was going to die. And face the fact that I, who could have saved her from ever having to go through all this, had chosen not to do so. It was useless to tell myself that it was the way she wanted it; I still felt wretchedly guilty.

ANOTHER NIGHT. A HOT ONE. I HAD THE window open and the Dustels were arranged along the sill with their heads tucked under their wings. Doubtless, Ruarth was one of them. Flame was groaning softly in an uneasy sleep. Tor and Ransom had long since gone to their rooms.

I heard someone come up the stairs (the treads creaked so badly that they were audible even over the noise from the taproom) and I stiffened automatically; fear and tension were a continuous part of my life by then. I opened the door a crack and looked out.

It was Syr-sylv Duthrick.

He'd lit a sylv light, a dim one, and stood on the landing looking about, as if uncertain of which room he wanted.

"Are you looking for me?" I asked. I said it softly enough, so as not to disturb Flame, but he would have had to be as insensitive as a rock-clamped limpet not to hear the resentment in my voice.

He nodded and doused the light with a gesture. "Yes. May I come in?"

I stood back and motioned him inside. He glanced over at

the bed, saw Flame and stepped over to have a look. There was only a single candle burning but it was enough for him to see her bandaged arm and poor color.

"Ah. So that's what you did," he said. "But she's not doing well." He hesitated, frowning. "The dunmagic is gone, though."

"Yes. She's just too weak."

He nodded. "Blood loss. Shock. It happens sometimes with surgery."

"You could save her still, and without undue expenditure of power now that dunmagic is not involved."

He nodded again. "I could."

The bastard wanted me to beg. "Will you?"

He turned his back on her indifferently. "She knows the price."

I just stared, silent.

He hesitated, but the pause seemed artificial. He had not come expecting her to have changed her mind. "I need your help," he said at last.

"To do what?"

"This dunmaster—he's too strong. We need someone with Awareness to see his spells for us, and to identify him for us."

"Tell me, Syr-sylv, since when have Keepers been so concerned with what happens on a sordid stretch of sand and fish scales like Gorthan Spit? This place is a human garbage dump. It has no assets, except the fishing grounds to the south. Why worry your heads at all about a dunmagicking bastard on Gorthan Spit?" I thought that, thanks to Tor, I already knew the answer to that one, but I wanted confirmation.

He debated momentarily whether there was anything to be gained by explaining, and apparently decided there was, because he said, "We wouldn't concern ourselves if we thought he was going to stay on Gorthan Spit. But he's been moving through the Middling Islands in secret, gathering and subverting sylvtalents, just as he tried to subvert this Cirkasian. He's apparently brought them all to Gorthan Spit, but we doubt that he intends to remain here. He just needs a place to stay for a while, to consolidate himself perhaps—we don't know why. But you can rest assured that he doesn't intend to remain in a place like this." He looked around the room with distaste as if it symbolized all he disliked about Gorthan Spit.

"You've been following him for some time?"

He nodded. "Always a few steps behind. We don't even

know what he looks like, thanks to his habit of changing his appearance at every stop with his dunillusions. He's very, very clever. We believe his purpose is to eventually challenge Keeper power in the Middling Islands. Hence our interest. We've lost a lot of sylvs, Blaze. Some of them Councilors."

I hadn't known that, and I stared at him in shock. "You've kept that very quiet," I said.

"We didn't want to start a panic."

Or didn't want to admit their failure to protect fellow sylvs? And, as a consequence, how many had been taken simply because they hadn't been warned? I opened my mouth to say as much, and then thought better of it. As they say, quarrel with the well, and you die of thirst . . . Instead, I asked in all seriousness, "Syr-sylv, how are dunmagickers made? I've always assumed that they were just born, in the same way that sylvs are born, but is that so? Or are they all subverted sylvs?"

"Both. A dunmagicker with a sylv partner has dunmagicker children. Always."

"And if a dunmagicker mates with a non-sylv?"

"There are no records of *any* dunmagicker progeny in such cases. God knows, the bastards have raped enough women over the years for us to be fairly certain of that." He seethed with loathing, and I warmed to him a little. He didn't like rapists.

"You had better tell me everything you do know. I don't like walking about half-blind with ignorance."

"There's not much to tell. We first became aware that there was something afoot about three years ago, when we heard rumors that there had been a lot of Menod deaths and many disappearances of sylvs. But they weren't *Keeper* sylvs. They were just scattered people from all islandoms—a healer here, a family there . . . Nothing much to go on, and it didn't seem to be our business. And then eight months ago Angiesta vanished. And she *was* one of ours. You remember the case. I sent you and Syr-sylv Ralph to investigate. You found traces of dunmagic at her house. That was the first indication we had that a dunmaster was involved."

I remembered the incident all too well; it had affected me badly because from all accounts Syr-sylv Angiesta had been a lovely woman, a mother of three violet-eyed daughters, a much loved wife. Her husband had been shattered. I had traced the dunmagic trail to the nearest port and there the trail disappeared. Which boat had been boarded, where it had gone and whether Angiesta had been on board were all unanswered questions. One of my failures.

"After that there were other cases on the Keeper Isles," Duthrick said. "He subverts our sylvs, and then gets them to subvert their friends. In the past two months we've lost ninety-two people, Blaze."

I was aghast. "*Ninety-two?* You should have told me, Duthrick. Why send me off on a piddling mission to find a Castlemaid who doesn't want to be found, when there was something as terrible as this happening? You needed one of the Awarefolk."

"Finding the Castlemaid is not a piddling mission!" he snapped. "And we have other Awarefolk who work for us."

That was news to me, but it could have been true. I didn't say anything, I couldn't. Ninety-two people lost . . .

"He was diabolically clever. He sent subverted sylvs in small groups to attack single sylvs—our people didn't have a chance. Once they felt the attack, they'd try to raise the wards, but against the combined power of three or four people, what hope had they?"

I said thoughtfully, "He may be clever, but he's also vengeful. And both impulsive and cruel too, where his antipathies are concerned. I would say he has an almost pathological hatred of Awarefolk. Those are all traits that may bring him down in the end."

He considered that. "We have noticed that many of the people he has killed were those with Menod ties. We thought he must dislike the Menod—but perhaps it was the Awarefolk among them that he was after. He has murdered a great many Menod patriarchs and there are a disproportionate number of Awarefolk in their patriarchy, as I am sure you know."

"Rans— Noviss . . . he gave Noviss a dunmagic sore, and he's a lay Menod, but not one of the Awarefolk."

"Maybe Noviss was rude to him."

I grunted. It was quite likely. "So what are you planning here?"

"An offensive on the village where these subverted sylvtalents live."

"Beware, Syr-sylv. I've glimpsed that place. It shimmers with the raw hell of dunmagic. If you and your friends have the sort of power to rid Gorthan Spit of that dunmagic sore, then you've been hiding it from me."

"You think we will fail?" He raised a disbelieving eyebrow. "Keepers are not in the habit of failing. However, there is something we must do first—we must identify this dunmaster. Destroying the village and those in it will not help in the long run, if the original dunmaster escapes. He must be eliminated, preferably beforehand."

"If you mean killed, say so, Syr-sylv. Your propensity to cloak unpleasantness in soft words is one of your less endearing traits. And is it really necessary to wipe out the people in the village? Can't you *save* them?"

"Not the subverted sylvs, no. What I said to Flame was the truth. They are dunmagickers now, make no mistake about that. What they were is irrelevant. They don't *want* to revert to their original sylvmagic, except perhaps in their deepest souls. And if they don't want to, they won't. They have enough power of their own to prevent it happening."

I glanced at Flame, glad at least that I had saved her from that. "If I knew who the dunmaster was, I would have given you that information already. I don't know who he is. I know we have been in the same room on at least one occasion, and I have spoken to him another time, but without seeing his face or recognizing the voice. I have felt his spells, but I can't identify him."

"Why not? Surely that is what your talent is—"

"Awarefolk sense sylvs or dunmagickers because we see or smell their magic. Each spell leaves traces of itself behind on the person who cast it, and that residue usually lasts a week or two, even several months sometimes, depending on the strength of the spell. But if a sylv doesn't cast a spell for a few weeks then he looks like everyone else to us. The same with dunmagickers."

"This man has been casting a few spells, wouldn't you say?"

I ignored his sarcasm. "The problem here is actually the opposite. This man's dunmagic is simply too strong. I've been smelling and seeing the residue of his spells ever since I arrived on Gorthan Spit. The stink of dunmagic is *everywhere*. Even when he actually cast a spell in the same room as me, there was so much evil I couldn't pinpoint its origin.

"However, I have someone investigating for me who may have some information that will be useful. You cure Flame's illness and pay me the two thousand setus I would have got for the Castlemaid, and I'll find out who the dunmaster is."

He looked across at the bed, his violet eyes now a velvety purple in the dim light. They reminded me of smooth, potent Bethany portwine. After some hesitation, he said, "All right, I'll help her. I will build up her sylv magic so that she has the strength she needs. It will take a mere hour or two. But there'll be no money, except expenses, and there shouldn't be much of those. If you want your money, you'll have to produce the Castlemaid."

He looked back at me, and we held the stare. I suspected my face was as unreadable as his. He had me where he wanted me, of course. He knew me well enough to sense that I wasn't my usual disinterested self around Flame. He knew I cared, and he guessed that there was very little I would not do to save her. He might not have shown anything on his face but I knew what he was thinking. He thought she was my lover and he was conservative enough to despise me for that, just as he despised me for being a halfbreed. I could almost feel his contempt. For some absurd reason, that hurt. After all these years of his indifference, why should I care? But somehow he still had the power to hurt me.

"Start now," I said. I picked up my cloak from where I had thrown it over a chair. "I'll look for my friend."

CHAPTER 14

MORE ABOUT ME? IS IT RELEVANT? IT'S not a particularly pretty tale. I'm not proud of the way I grew up. True, I've not been ashamed of it either . . . when you're a child, you can only act within the boundaries of what you know. I did my best, I made mistakes, but I *survived*. Not many half-breeds do, when they have no support of a family. I was lucky, because I had Awareness. Awareness . . . and Duthrick.

I tried to escape him once, you know.

I ran away from The Hub, in fact from the Keeper Isles, when I was fourteen. I intended to be free, to go my own way, never again to have to do what I was told in order to stay alive.

The rebellion had always been there, I suppose, but it became more focused when I was removed from the Menod boys' school. I must have been around twelve, and I'd just had my first menses. The patriarch teachers, somewhat embarrassed and at a loss, decided that an adolescent girl was definitely a distraction to adolescent boys, not to mention to mostly celibate patriarchs, so they informed Duthrick that they would no longer teach me. Duthrick had me placed in a sylv girls' school, not the original one I had been in, but another.

He could not have chosen anywhere more inappropriate.

It was an elite school for children who would one day work for the Council in one way or another. Everyone else there had sylvtalent and they were just learning to make the most of their skills. The place was awash with illusions, shams, spells and sylv sophistry . . . every one of which was as transparent to me as a glass jellyfish. Being a tough twelve-year-old with a chip on my shoulder the size of a whale jawbone, I was scornful of their games and their sylv lies, and I showed it. Small wonder, then, that everyone loathed me. And a schoolful of adolescent schoolgirls, I quickly discovered, could be enormously innovative in their revenge . . .

I was in a constant state of war with everyone and could never relax for a minute.

I actually did not attend all that many classes because most were geared toward the use and development of sylvtalent. But I did have to learn, by rote, all about Glorian politics and geography and history. And, as it was clear by then just how tall and large I was going to be, Duthrick ordered that I be trained as an athlete: swordplay, archery, swimming, rock climbing. He had his own vision for me, I can see that now. An instrument with Awareness, someone who could do his bidding and yet who was strong enough to look after herself.

I kept looking for some sign of concern, for some sign that he cared about me as a person—and I kept on being disappointed. And yet I kept looking. I was only a child, after all . . .

They made use of me just as they had before. Duthrick, or one of his staff, would occasionally come and I'd be taken off to perform some task or another that involved the use of Awareness.

I hadn't been long in the school when I had my first taste of travel to another islandom. Duthrick sent me to act as page to Syr-sylv Arnado, a wealthy middle-aged man in Keeper Council service. He was one of the Council's foremost guards, a famous sword fighter whom every young practitioner dreamed of emulating, including myself. At first I was in utter awe and could hardly string two sentences together in his company. He put up with that for the first day, but on the second, as the Keeper ship we were on scudded through the straits between Hub Island and the Spokes on our way to Bethany, he suggested we do some sparring. Of course, it wasn't really sparring—what he was doing was teaching me—and fortunately the awe was soon replaced by a desire to learn as much as possible. We ended the outward journey the best of friends. I made him laugh with my graceless manners and forthright way of putting things.

I thought he was quite the most patient and kind man I'd ever met. Of course, I did my best to imitate him and doubtless it was laughable, but I like to think that some rudiments of his polish rubbed off on me. I never learned to be the suave courtier, but I could put up a passable imitation for a while if need be, and I owe that to Arnado. Perhaps the greatest service he ever did for me was that he took the vague beginnings of self-worth that the Menod had planted within me, and built on it. "Good soil," he used to say, "even if it falls into the sea, becomes an island. You are good soil, Blaze, and don't let anyone else ever tell you otherwise."

Our assignment in Bethany, Arnado explained, was to see if there was any truth to the rumor that one of the Holdlord's chief advisors was a dunmagicker, and if it was true, to do something about it. I was so naive, I didn't even think about what the second part of the assignment meant. I followed in Arnado's wake, enjoying every bit of the experience, delighted to be away from that horrible school and my schoolgirl nemeses.

Arnado had letters of introduction that gave him entry to the court of the Holdlord, and I tagged along as his page. It was my first introduction to how the nobility lived, and I was torn in all directions—between laughter and horror and sheer fascination. The rich, I found, could be so absurd. They could spend hours each day seated in front of a mirror preening themselves like sea-mewlers straightening their feathers. They'd rather dress uncomfortably than be unfashionable, which I found incomprehensible. In fact, I found their self-absorption disturbing: how could they live in such wasteful luxury, while others could not even afford a roof over their heads? I suppose I moved around in a daze, a sand-eel that's just found a coral reef for the first time and can't close its mouth at the wonder of it all.

It took over a month for me to pick up the stench and trails of dunmagic, mostly because it took us that long to be invited into the top echelon of Bethany society. However, within a few days of being sent an invitation to the Holdlord's personal functions, I came across the dunmagicker: not the Bethanylord's advisor, but the advisor's new wife. She had the old man so befuddled with spells he just said whatever she wanted him to. There was even evidence of dun color about the Holdlord himself: she must have cast a spell or two in his direction as well.

I told Arnado what I'd found out. He ruffled my hair with a smile. "Are you sure, my little firebrand? Remember, I will act on your word, and if you are wrong, then the wrong people could die."

Even then, I didn't fully understand. I said indignantly, "Yes, of course I'm sure. She's a dunmagicker, and her husband's so drowning in crimson I don't think he has a single thought of his own anymore."

"Good. Then your job is done." He pressed some money into my hand. "I want you to pack up all your things, and mine, and go down to the river wharfs and book us two seats on the next boat down-river to the sea. Take the baggage with you. Wait for me at the wharf. Think you can do that?"

I nodded. He had already shown me where the wharves were and how to buy the tickets. I ran off happily, did as he asked, and sat down to wait.

When he arrived he seemed rather somber and disinclined to talk. We boarded the riverboat and he stood in the bows, watching the water slide past, as we were poled downstream. When he finally spoke, what he said shocked me out of any complacency I had about my role in Keeper strategies. "I killed them both, Blaze," he said, "on your say-so. I thought about sparing him, but if he was that much sunk into the red-shit, his mind would never have been the same even after she died—so I killed him too."

I stared at him in utmost shock. Stupid, of course: whatever had I expected?

"The Bethany Holdlord?" I asked finally. "He asked you to do this?"

He gave a harsh laugh. "No, child. That's the whole point: to go in quickly, kill the dunmagicker and leave without the Bethany Holdlord ever finding out that Keepers have been interfering in Bethany politics . . ." He sighed. "We do the Keeper Council's bidding, Blaze. Never forget that. We don't ask anyone else's permission, because ultimately it is *our* safety—Keeper safety—that will be compromised by dunmagickers."

I sat there on the hatch of the riverboat and watched the land slide silently by. "We are running away," I said. "They could be hunting us."

"Yes. But unlikely. Don't worry, I was very careful."

"You killed two people because of what I said."

"Not people, Blaze. A dunmagicker and her husband."

"But no one else knows that. If they catch us, they'll think

we just murdered a man—a very important man of Bethany—
and his wife."

"Yes."

"And because it was a dunmagicker it makes it all right?"

That surprised him. "Of course. We can't treat them like ordinary folk—while we were waiting for them to show their true
natures, they'd be laying spells of confusion and illusion, or
seeding us all with dunmagic sores. We have to hit them first. It
doesn't *bother* you, does it, Blaze?"

"No," I said, "Of course not." And it didn't, not then. In fact,
the killing never bothered me at all, until I had to kill a Quillerman who meant something to me. Until I had to kill dunmagickers who were subverted sylvs . . . But that was more than
seventeen years later.

I CONTINUED TO DO SIMILAR TASKS FOR
Duthrick and the Council, not all of them so simple. Sometimes
I accompanied Arnado, sometimes other sylvs. I was attacked
by dunmagickers on several occasions and once in Spattshield I
was arrested for murder by the island's guards. I was all of thirteen, and I had not actually done the killing. That was done by
the sylv I had accompanied on that occasion, a nasty piece of
work called Fiesta. The moment I was caught, she made off
back to the Keeper ship leaving me to fend for myself. I might
still be languishing there if it hadn't been for the Keeper ship's
captain, who insisted that Fiesta go back for me and sent a couple of sailors along to make sure she did. I'd sailed with him before, and he had a soft spot for me, you see.

With sylv magic it was not all that difficult to free me: illusions to mystify the guards while Fiesta blurred her entry to the
building and stole the key to my cell, more magic to blur us
both on the way out . . . Yet she sulked all the way home, furious that the captain had humiliated her by insisting she go back
for me, furious because I had allowed myself to be caught in the
first place. Furious that her reputation was sullied because of a
halfbreed brat.

She had her revenge when we landed back in The Hub. She
told some of the old Keeper sylv fanatics about a halfbreed girl
whose future fertility would threaten island purity if they didn't
do something about it . . .

I told her I'd kill her one day for that. (She must have believed me because shortly afterward she asked for a transfer out of The Hub and went to live on Segorn in the Spokes. It has been my fervent wish that she spent the rest of her life looking over her shoulder, looking for me.) Still bleeding from the cet leaf cauterization, still in pain from the branding, I went to Duthrick in outrage. I don't know what I expected. Regret? Sympathy? Great Trench, but I was naive! All I received was the knowledge that he himself had fully intended that I be sterilized soon anyway. Perhaps he had intended it to be done more humanely, with sylv healing to take away the pain, but he had never intended that I wander the Glory Isles with the potential to have children.

The last vestiges of my childhood died that day, without me ever having really *been* a child.

A week later, I ran away, intending to leave the Keeper Isles and Keeper service for good. I certainly never wanted to see Duthrick again.

I stowed away on a coastal hopper carrying coal from The Hub to Xolchas Stacks. Of course I was soon found and an irate captain had me working like a slave to pay my passage. I was put ashore on one of the stacks—the rocky columns rising up from the sea like pockmarked phallic symbols—and immediately found out just how hard it is for a halfbreed with no money and no Keeper backing.

I went from stack to stack, begging passage, always hoping the next island would be better than the last. It never was.

In the capital, Xolchasbarbican, they finally ordered me off the islands and forced me on to a tramp sailing for Breth. On Breth, things went from bad to worse. For a time only my sword kept me safe, but in the end even that was stolen while I slept. Desperate and starving, I became a thief myself, sinking lower and lower into the underbelly of life in Brethbastion, always having to dodge the authorities, hide, slink away, live a life of stealth. The nadir came the night I was attacked while I was asleep, and raped. I killed the man responsible when he made the mistake of falling asleep beside me. He was the first person I ever slew, and I looked upon it as an execution. I don't even know who he was.

I took his purse, and fled the city. A few days later, on the coast, I bargained with the stinking captain of a fisher to get to Fen Island; the price was high but I paid it. I slept with him all the way to Fen. I felt as dirty as a lugworm buried in tidal mud, dirty inside and out, as if I'd never be clean again.

Life in Fen was marginally better. I had green Fenlander eyes, so it wasn't always immediately clear that I was a half-breed, a situation I fostered by growing my hair long so that it covered my ears and staying out of the sun to lighten my skin. I sometimes managed to find legitimate work, at least for a day or two. In addition, I kept growing. I was becoming a large woman, a little less obviously a victim. Still, it was no kind of life, and deep in my heart I knew it.

When I saw a Keeper Council ship in port, staffed by those tall, violet-eyed people with their numerous talents and learning, it was like a revelation. *This* was what I wanted. To be one of them—not to be a second-rate woman sleeping and clawing her way to equality. All right, so I could never be a sylv, but I could be a Keeper. I could be a respected human being of stature. Or so I thought.

When the ship sailed for The Hub, I was on board.

I went back to Duthrick, who was now a Councilor, but I was a hardened, more determined and tougher person. I expected, at the very most, for him to offer me little more than I had before. I expected him to look on me as merely an Aware henchwoman working in exchange for my keep and the chance not to be hounded from place to place as a noncitizen with no rights. I was prepared to fight for more than that.

To my amazement, we hadn't exchanged more than a few words before I realized he was as desperate as I was: he needed me. He wasn't wearing the smug I-knew-you'd-be-back expression I'd expected. Instead he was polite and smiled way too much. I sensed that, for once, I was the fiddler crab with the bigger claw in the confrontation . . .

It was some time before I realized what had happened: Duthrick had earned his reputation for acuity and success because he'd had me to help him, me and my Awareness. On the strength of his successes, he had been able to win one of the elected Councilor posts—only to find that he was fast losing his ability to succeed at the tasks he was given now that he didn't have a tame Awarewoman to help out.

In the end I had the promise of regular pay, tacit permission to live in The Hub, and an agreement that twenty years of service would buy me citizenship. I had sold my soul to the Keepers for the next twenty years . . .

I was just fifteen years old.

Letter from Researcher (Special Class) S. iso Fabold, National Department of Exploration, Federal Ministry of Trade, Kells, to Masterman M. iso Kipswon, President of the National Society for the Scientific, Anthropological and Ethnographical Study of non-Kellish Peoples.

Dated this day 43/1st Double/1793

Dear Uncle,
Thank you for your kind words after the presentation. I was not certain whether it was well received, as it generated such heated discussion—but you are right. Such debate can only be good for the Society and the future of ethnographical studies.

Did I tell you that Lecturer Vescon iso Mattin approached me afterward to say how shocked he was that I had made such an unprincipled hussy as Blaze Halfbreed the subject of my studies? It just goes to show that there are still Kellish scientists who do not understand the true function of a field anthropologist. Little does he know how much I left out about the sexual mores of Blaze and Flame! One of the disadvantages of having ladies in the audience: one has to be so much more circumspect.

Do tell Aunt Rosris that I appreciated her kindness to me, as always. I am sending her a separate note to this effect, and do tell her that I found Miss Anyara to be an exceptional young lady. It is gratifying to meet one of the feminine gender with such a lively mind and a deep interest in ethnography. If she was shocked by the subject of my talk, she certainly did not show it, although she admitted afterward that she found the idea that a woman would talk to a man about her life in such a frank way quite disconcerting.

I have undertaken to visit her and the Teron family next weekend at their country estate, not far from here.

I remain,
Your obedient nephew,
Shor iso Fabold

CHAPTER 15

SO THERE, YOU KNOW A LITTLE MORE about me. It's odd: I haven't spoken of that part of my life for years, and now that I have, it is to someone who disbelieves half of what I tell him. Oh, don't apologize. It really doesn't matter. I find I am quite enjoying the reminiscence.

Anyway, to return to Gorthan Spit . . . I'd just left Duthrick to heal Flame while I went to find Niamor.

It was only when I was on my way downstairs that I remembered I didn't have the first idea of where the Quillerman would be. Then I started to worry. Why hadn't he been in touch with me? Over two days had passed, and I'd heard nothing.

I passed though the taproom, noting the group of silent Keepers sitting at a table; doubtless Duthrick's bodyguards. On seeing me come down alone, one of them hurried for the stairs to check that his master was safe. I smiled sourly, acknowledging that at least Duthrick wasn't fool enough to venture out alone. I glanced around to see if Tunn was well enough to be working, but it was Janko who was doing all the serving. He leered when he saw me—I seemed to stimulate that reaction in him just as the sight of food starts a dog dribbling—and I ignored him.

It was only once I was out in the street again that I began to feel puzzled. There had been something that wasn't quite as it had been. Something about Janko. His feet—I tried to visualize the change, but I couldn't catch hold of it. It didn't seem important so I made a mental note to take a good look at his feet next time, then went on toward the docks.

I decided to try Niamor's old place first, just on the off-chance that he had not moved.

It wasn't a totally uneventful walk; a stroll in Gorthan Docks rarely was. A few hundred paces from the inn I was propositioned by a rather fleshy young man with no earlobe tattoo. He was drunk and I suspected that what he proposed was more wishful thinking than practical possibility—it was likely that he bore a brand like mine on his shoulder. I declined his offer and he promptly slumped down against a wall and went to sleep. If he did have the money he'd offered me, it would be missing by morning.

A little farther on I had to make a detour to avoid a fight that involved ten or fifteen people wielding diverse weapons, all set to murder each other over some trivial matter, no doubt.

At Niamor's place the vagrants were cluttering up the entrance again, their pitiful belongings clutched tight to their chests even in sleep. They ignored my banging on the downstairs door. No one answered from inside, but it didn't matter much as the door wasn't locked anyhow. I went in, groping in the darkness, feeling my way upstairs to the entrance of Niamor's apartment. Even before I reached it, I could feel the dunmagic. I was glad I had warned Niamor.

His door wasn't locked either.

I pushed it open and the wave of fetid badness hit me, making me recoil instinctively.

Then I heard faint sounds of movement: a soft rustle, a grunt. There was something alive in the darkness beyond the main room.

Dunmagic flickered aimlessly across the floor and furniture. By its light I found a lamp and fumbled in my belt pouch for a handflint. It seemed an age before I had it lit and was targeted by its yellow glow.

There appeared to be nothing untoward—and no one—in that first room. I carried the lamp into the next. I had my sword out in the other hand, and walked on the balls of my feet, ready for anything. The next room was Niamor's bedroom.

At first glance there seemed to be nothing wrong. Nothing was disturbed. The smell, however, was vile. A stench of rottenness that was so strong it teared my eyes and rasped my throat as I inhaled.

And then I saw the cause.

Niamor was there, lying on the bed. Another victim of a magic so foul it ought to have been shunned into extinction by every living creature . . .

He was alive, if that can be called living. The only thing recognizable about him was the gold "Q" in his earlobe, and that was because there was a small section of skin surrounding the tattoo that was clear and uninfected. The rest of him was a swollen mass of green rottenness, so engorged with corruption that his arms and legs and neck were mired in gross rolls of it. His agony was a tangible thing, streaking out to meet me, slamming into me with the power to take my breath.

"Oh God—" My gasped words were an appeal to a being I really didn't believe in.

I knelt by his side and laid a hand on his bloated cheek. He had once been so handsome. My hand shook. I wanted to do something, end this, make it all go away, stop his pain; I wanted to stop *my* pain. The grief hurt—badly. First Tunn, now Niamor. *Because of me.*

It took all my control just to speak in a whisper. "Niamor, it's me. Blaze."

He looked at me with smudged, hopeless eyes framed by lids so swollen he could barely lever them apart. "Kill me," he said. I only heard him because my face was so close to his lips.

"Yes." I swallowed. He was already long beyond saving. "Who is he, Niamor?"

He tried to tell me, but I couldn't understand the sounds that came from his distorted throat. His eyes left me to look into the main room.

I guessed at what he was trying to say. "On the desk?"

There was the faintest of nods.

"Is there anyone I should inform? Any message?"

This time there was a slight movement of negation. Thirty-five or so years of living, and he had no one to care whether he lived or died. The tragedy of that touched me; it was too much mine. Outcasts, making the best of our world, and in the end we died alone.

I said, "I'll make you a promise, Niamor—one day I'll kill him, for you."

I could barely hear his whispered, "Yes." I bent my head to

hear him better. "Firebrand . . . a pity." There was the tiniest up-turn of his lips that could have been a regretful smile. Under different circumstances, we would have had time to be friends. He hadn't deserved this.

I kept my voice and my hand steady only with an effort. "Now Niamor?"

His mouth formed the àssent, but this time there was no sound. I kissed his cheek and the foulness of his decay seared my lips. His neck was so bloated I couldn't find the right place to stop his arterial blood flow and render him unconscious. I had to kill him while his eyes still looked at me, begging, re-proachful . . . It was almost beyond my capacity.

I put the tip of my sword against his breast and thrust it in at an upward angle, hard, so that it would slip under his lowest rib and enter his heart. Then I twisted it. He arched, bursting over-stretched skin, spilling green rottenness, and died.

I withdrew the blade, wiped it clean and didn't look at him again. I couldn't. I vomited over the mat and lurched toward the main room. I was staggering, drunk on horror and pain, as I turned to his desk. I huddled into the chair, my head in my hands, the smell of death in my nostrils.

I have been forced to kill two people in my life whose deaths have seared me, and the memories of those deaths have contin-ued to ravage me through the years. Niamor's was the first. Even now I sometimes wake in the night, sweating, and the smell of that room is as strong in my nostrils as it was then . . .

It was a long time before I could bring my revulsion under control enough to enable me to look at the papers scattered on the desk.

I blessed those Menod patriarchs who had instructed me in the rudiments of reading, then aroused in me a passion for the written word that had made me interested enough to read any-thing I could get my hands on. I had no problem with Niamor's precise script.

The first sheet was a rough plan of the taproom of The Drunken Plaice, with all the tables and chairs sketched in. Be-side most of the chairs there was a name. Some of them I rec-ognized: Niamor himself, Sickle, Flame, Tor, Noviss, and Blaze. This was how everyone had been seated at lunch that first day, and one of these people must be the dunmaster.

The next sheet I looked at listed the same names in no par-ticular order. Every single one of them had been crossed out.

Beside most of them there were notations of some sort, usually indicating the length of time the person had been on Gorthan Spit. *"Houch the Hulk,"* I read, *"slaver, Breth, been coming Gorthan S. 18 yrs. Tom Gessler, fishmonger, Gorthan D. resident 6 yrs. Tor Ryder, Stragglers, profession unknown, 1 week, on trader from Keeper Isles."* And so on. There wasn't a single person who matched the criteria I wanted: an arrival on Gorthan Spit that coincided with the beginnings of the dunmagic troubles. Yet Niamor, dying and in agony, had indicated the desk. He had expected something on these papers to mean something to me. The answer was there somewhere, if only I could see it.

Half an hour later I did. And when I did, I wished I hadn't.

I LEFT FOR THE INN IN A HURRY. I DIDN'T even ransack Niamor's room to take whatever he had of value. Perhaps I wouldn't have done that anyway; the manner of his death had scored me deep, and I might never have been able to bring myself to stay there longer than I did. Later, when the horror had faded, I regretted my haste to be gone. I could always have done with more money and I don't think he would have minded. Besides, I have nothing to remember him by, nothing but my memory of the way he looked before he died . . . and that's a memory I never wanted.

I left his things for the scavengers and strode off to the inn, my heart beating uncomfortably fast. Fear was beginning to replace the revulsion within me as I thought this through. Somehow I didn't think that Niamor had been killed because he knew the identity of the dunmaster, for how could the dunmaster have guessed Niamor knew? And if he had guessed, he would have searched the Quillerman's rooms, destroyed his papers—but that hadn't happened.

In fact, I didn't even think the dunmaster had been in his rooms. All those traces of dunspell color had not been left by him; they had spilled from the excess within Niamor's body. The bastard had probably placed his dunspell without Niamor even being aware it had been done, while he was in a bar somewhere, or walking down a street. Niamor had probably just felt a little sick, returned to his rooms, and by the time he'd realized just what had been done to him, he'd been too ill to move.

And why? I thought I knew. Niamor had died simply because

the dunmaster was playing with us—with me, with Ransom and
Flame, perhaps with Tor (for now that I knew the identity of the
dunmaster, I had little reason to believe he was unaware of Tor's
involvement) and, indirectly, with Duthrick too. We represented
all the things he would hate most: the Menod, sylvs, Awarefolk,
a Keeper agent, the Keeper Council. The dunmaster enjoyed
seeing us squirm on his hook. Enjoyed having us know that
anyone who helped us was doomed. What was it Flame had said
about Morthred? *He prefers to keep his victims alive.* We were
his real victims. Niamor was merely a tool to hurt us. To hurt
me. *Morthred.* I felt sick.

THE INNKEEPER WAS SERVING IN THE TAP-
room, in a foul temper because he hadn't seen Tunn for three
days and now Janko had disappeared—again. It seemed Janko
was not renowned for his reliability. Duthrick's Keeper bodyguards were still there, still coldly sober and still sending suspicious looks my way.

I ignored them, asked the innkeeper for some swillie, and
while he was filling the mug from the barrel, I inquired how
long Janko had been working for him. "How in all the islands
should I know?" came the bad-tempered reply. "A few months,
I guess. Too frigging long. That palsied cripple's *never* here
when he should be."

I realized then what had been different about Janko's foot. I
felt even sicker. I gulped down the drink, which I really needed,
and went on up to Flame's room.

Flame, it seemed, was entertaining guests, even though it
must have been two in the morning by then. Her room seemed
full of people. Duthrick was still there and Tor and Ransom had
joined him. A rather unkempt and sleepy Dustel, presumably
Ruarth Windrider, was perched on the inner windowsill. I
glanced at Flame who smiled wanly in my direction and I saw
to my relief how much better she was. She might have been tired
and weak, but her color was normal. I flickered my eyes toward
Ruarth, then looked at Duthrick and returned my glance to her.
My unspoken message was barely discernible, yet she caught it;
she might not have understood the full implications of my worry,
but she saw straightaway that I was concerned that Duthrick
might know Ruarth was sentient. She gave a faint shake of her
head and I allowed her to see the relief in my eyes. I wanted her

to appreciate how important I thought it was that Duthrick did not know about Ruarth, and I blessed the ease with which we seemed to be able to communicate without words.

I turned my attention back to the others. Duthrick was bristling irately, as tense as a beached pufferfish, although not everyone could have read the signals as well as I did. He stood rigidly straight, the arch of his eyebrows almost hitting his hairline, his eyes now the cloudy indigo of an angered sea-star. Ransom was flushed red and his fists were clenched. Ruarth had his head cocked so that one deep blue eye stared at the Syr-sylv. Tor was leaning against the windowsill next to the Dustel, arms folded, a cynical smile playing at the edges of his mouth but never quite breaking out. He at least looked composed—until he noticed the expression on my face.

"Blaze, what is it?"

"Niamor's dead. The dunmagicker got to him." I turned to Duthrick. "Niamor was the friend I spoke of. I think he found out who it is we're after, though. It's—"

Duthrick raised a hand to stop me. "Let's have this conversation in private, Blaze."

I looked around at the others. "No. Why? Flame and Noviss have both suffered at the hands of this man, and Tor is a friend of mine." To my surprise, it was Tor that Duthrick was looking at. I had thought it must have been Ransom who had upset the Keeper. Now I realized my mistake. It was Tor that Duthrick objected to—even hated. Something had happened between them that had changed Duthrick's initial indifference at their first meeting on the ship to an intense dislike and mistrust now. I shrugged and continued. "It is Janko the waiter who's the dunmaster."

Ransom digested that, then looked appalled. For a moment I thought he was going to faint. Tor frowned, Flame stared, Duthrick looked bewildered. "Do you mean the deformed potboy downstairs?" he asked. I nodded. He shook his head. "How can that be? I don't have your abilities, Blaze, but surely that crippling of his is the result of a dunmagic spell. It doesn't look natural. No dunmagicker would allow himself to be so deformed, least of all one as powerful as this. And I can't believe it's just another one of his dunspelled disguises. And you'd see through that anyway."

I shook my head. "No, it's not a disguise. That's his real self, for the moment anyhow. I rather think he fell victim to his own magic. Sometime in the past, he raised a spell of such power that he was unable to control it—part of it whipped back on him. He was turned into a twisted deformity, far worse than what we see now, and he was left powerless. All he could do was wait. Time restores power to its normal levels, as you well know. I suspect that he has had to wait decades. Now, however, he is recovering his power quite fast and is using part of it to restore his body. In the time I have been here his left foot has straightened and his dunmagic is noticeably stronger." I sighed. "I always did smell dunmagic on him; I just thought it wasn't his. My Awareness didn't let me down after all. I jumped to the wrong conclusions."

While I was speaking, Ruarth, over on the windowsill, had been doing a fine imitation of an agitated hen, hopping from foot to foot and flapping his wings, chattering all the while. Duthrick ignored him; I doubt that he even noticed the bird. Even so, I stepped across so that I blocked his view of Ruarth and I gave Flame a signal behind my back, hoping she would guess that I wanted her to shut the wretched Dustel up.

Flame hastily translated the essence of what I guessed was exciting Ruarth so much. "Morthred the Mad perhaps—"

"Oh, beach pebbles!" Duthrick interrupted, mocking. "Morthred's been dead a hundred years."

"I've heard skilled dunmasters can be very long-lived," I said mildly. I had come around to Ruarth's way of thinking as far as Morthred being alive and well was concerned. "That dunmagicker I killed in Porth—there were people of eighty living there who swore he'd been old when they were toddlers. And there is—" I broke off and stiffened. I looked automatically at Tor to find he was looking at me, alarmed. Ruarth was poised on the sill, head raised, as if listening. Three Awarefolk, and we'd all smelled and felt the same thing.

Ransom was the first of the others to realize something was wrong. His eyes widened and his head swung up like a frightened seal pup's. "What is it? What's wrong?"

"Dunmagic," Tor said tersely. "Our friend is very close. He just let loose a spell."

Ransom began to shake.

Duthrick acted. Fast. He had the room warded in a flash. Four pillars of light undulated in the corners like silver sea-snakes and power flowed between them to form walls of light. Poor Ransom couldn't see any of it; not knowing we were protected, he continued to tremble. As it turned out, he was the wisest among us. We were far from protected.

Ruby magic met silver-blue head on. Ruarth, Tor and I could see the dunmagic as a ball of dull red, its potency veiled, just as dying embers conceal their power to burn; Duthrick saw only that the sylv wall shivered and then began to crack; Ransom and Flame saw nothing except our horrified faces, although I'm sure Flame must have known enough about sylvmagic to realize what Duthrick had done.

The crack spread, shooting out in all directions like explosive ruptures in sheet ice, then the wards shattered with the inrush of unbridled power. *That,* even Ransom felt. The room was filled with wind, Ruarth was blown right out of the open window and everything loose went flying. Air was sucked out of my lungs and I found myself gasping and in pain as I dragged in a breath.

By the time we had all recovered from the blast of sylvmagic, the red ball was in the center of the room, hovering between Duthrick and Ransom. The stench curled my toes.

Duthrick looked at me. His golden skin was suddenly an unhealthy sallow shade. "Where is it?"

"About an arm's length to your right, at waist height," Tor drawled. "I wouldn't move if I were you."

Nobody budged. The seconds dragged. I felt mesmerized, unable to drag my eyes away from the floating sphere. Even though it could hardly threaten me, I was afraid of its malevolence and I ached for Flame. What must she have been feeling?

"Is it directed at me?" she asked, and her voice was steady enough. I noticed, though, that sweat shimmered the skin at the sides of her eyes and that the hair in front of her ears curled wetly. "Could he have sensed that I am no longer suffering from his spell of subversion and sent another?"

"It's not likely," Duthrick replied. "I doubt he knows you have rid yourself of his spell."

She wasn't reassured. "Then who?"

"Well, it's not for Blaze," Tor said calmly, his voice soft, "that's obvious. It could be for me, as Janko may not know I have Awareness, but then I doubt that he knows I'm here in this room. Which leaves Noviss and Duthrick. There's always a good possibility Noviss would be in your room, Flame, as I'm sure all the inn's servants know, so it could well be aimed at him. Presumably everyone downstairs knows Duthrick is here somewhere because he came in through the taproom." He looked at the Keeper. "Or did you conceal your entry with a spell?"

Duthrick shook his head regretfully.

"What—what will it do?" Ransom stammered. He was staring around wildly, trying to see what was not visible to him. Nobody answered for the simple reason that nobody knew.

Duthrick, to do him justice, was now icily contained. Those violet eyes of his were flatly unemotional. He was also busy, warding just himself this time. Strands of silver wrapped around him until he was encased in a glowing cocoon. A moment later he conjured up another spell, aimed at blurring his outline at the same time as giving reality to illusory versions of himself. There were suddenly six Duthricks in the room, all clearly visible to everyone. It was perfectly obvious to Tor and I which was the real Duthrick, of course, because we could see the spells that made the illusions as well as the illusions themselves. I looked across at Flame, but she shook her head to indicate that she was too weak to try any warding of herself.

"I doubt whether that will do much good, Syr-sylv," Tor said, and his voice quivered with amusement. Then before any of us could stop him, he stepped forward and plunged his hand into the middle of the red ball of light. He winced as he touched it, there was a wave of putrefaction, and the ball disintegrated in myriad red wisps, none strong enough to do much damage alone. But still the smell continued to burn away at my nasal passages. It was hard to believe at times like this that the un-Aware could not *smell* dunmagic.

My laconic "It's gone" was a cover for the stomach-churning fear that Tor's action had only managed to increase.

"There's no need," Tor added, as Duthrick and Flame started to look around to see if they could see any damage resulting from the dunmagic attack. "It has dissipated. There was no specific ill intent there. And I can't smell magic outside anymore either."

"What the bloody hell is he up to, then?" Flame asked, her face regaining its color.

Ransom's eyes widened; it seemed he had never heard her swear before and he didn't like it.

"He's toying with us all," Tor said. "He enjoyed that. He wants us to know he can have any of us any time he wants, the Syr-sylv included."

Ransom went as white as wave tops in the wind. "God help

me." Then he changed. He drew himself up to his not inconsiderable height and turned to Duthrick. The transformation from a confused and frightened youth to regal Holdheir was startling. "Syr-sylv," he said, "my name is not Noviss as you have been led to believe. I am Ransom Holswood, Bethany Holdheir." Flame's head jerked up in surprise, which surprised me in turn. Evidently, for all that she knew he was noble, he had not told her just *how* royal. "I ask protection of you and your ship for myself and for Syr-sylv Flame Windrider of Cirkase."

Windrider? I raised a quizzical eyebrow at Flame when I heard the name, and she returned a defiant look. My heart grieved to think how much pain she was storing up for herself there. As they say in the Spatts about unlikely couplings, "when you marry the wind to the clouds, you should expect it to rain."

Ransom continued: "I wish to return to the Bethany Isles as soon as possible on board your vessel. I believe my father will reimburse you handsomely."

Duthrick's eyebrows had also shot up. He obviously hadn't known Ransom's identity either. He looked at me. "Is this true, Blaze?"

It was a compliment, I suppose, his assumption that I would have known. I shrugged. "I believe so."

Now it was Ransom's turn to look astonished. "How did *you* know?"

He knew I had searched his room—Ruarth had told Flame, and Flame had told him—yet it had never occurred to him that I might have read the flyleaf of his breviary. I smiled at him, but didn't explain.

"Blaze," said Duthrick, "makes a point of knowing things. However, young man, last I heard, Bethany Isles *had* no Holdheir."

Ransom flushed. "I am certain that the rift between my father and me will be healed as soon as I return."

Duthrick bowed politely. There was a touch of irony in his next words, indicating he had also heard about the Holdlord's ire, but I doubt if Ransom caught it. "Ah well, in that case, I will be delighted to return you to Bethanyhold, as soon as possible. However, we do have business in Gorthan Spit that may take some days to complete. You are welcome on board the *Keeper Fair* in the meantime. As I am sure you know, it will be impossible for us to sail out for several days anyway; the currents and winds and tides do not allow it."

"And Syr-sylv Flame?"

Duthrick turned toward the bed. "I have helped her healing at considerable inconvenience to myself. If she wishes any other service from me, then she knows what to do to obtain it."

For a moment Ransom struggled with himself, torn between seeking sanctuary with the Keepers, or staying with Flame, whose power was obviously insufficient to protect him. Flame, bless her kind heart, made it easy for him. *I* wouldn't have. "Go, Noviss—um, Syr-holdheir," she said. "I would rest easier if I didn't have your safety to worry about too."

There ensued a short argument, with her saying go, and him saying, no, I can't leave you like this, an argument which Flame, of course, won. Then there was a tearful good-bye (from Ransom) and a much more prosaic farewell (from Flame), followed by a passionate kiss (bestowed by Ransom, received matter-of-factly by Flame). I would have clobbered him.

I turned to look at Ruarth, now back on the windowsill. He was preening his feathers and apparently taking no notice, but I wondered.

Duthrick's parting shot was addressed to Flame. "You know what you have to do to receive Keeper protection." He nodded to me and ushered Ransom out.

"Hmph," said Tor, scathing. "As if his protection is so wonderful. Janko could make fish chowder out of Duthrick's spells."

"What," I asked him, "did you do to upset the Councilor?"

He looked injured. "Me? I was perfectly polite."

Flame grinned. "Duthrick didn't want Tor or Noviss in the room, so, not knowing Tor had Awareness, he tried to remove them with sylvmagic. Tor stopped him and told him what he could do with his spells. I'd never heard that expression before, but it was quite graphic. Something about using them in a way that would ensure constipation, wasn't it, Tor?"

"Something along those lines. I can't say I like the man. He has the hide of a leatherback turtle and about as much compassion. He doesn't like Awarefolk, Blaze."

I shrugged. "What Keeper sylv does? Tor, where do we go from here?"

It was his turn to shrug. "My baby's been sort of removed from my jurisdiction. I'll just wait around and see what happens next, I think. I suppose we can hope that Duthrick will deal with Janko—with all the other Keeper sylvs behind him he may manage something. Why don't I bring some bedding in here, and then you and I can take it in turns to keep a watch on Flame while the other sleeps?" He looked at Flame apologetically. "Not that we'd be able to do much if Janko decided to harm you again, I suppose."

"He must know just about all there is to know about us," I said gloomily, "seeing we've all been living right under his nose since we arrived in Gorthan Spit."

"Well, let's hope he doesn't know about the amputation yet," Tor remarked as he left the room to get the bedding.

I went to sit by Flame and took her hand.

She said, "I've no right to involve you at all. Either of you."

I ignored that. "How are you really?"

"Weak, but recovering." She looked at her stump. "I can feel it, you know. It's as though my arm is still there. I can move the fingers—everything. I have to keep looking at it to convince myself that it's really gone." She gave a small heartrending laugh. "I'll be able to make a new one with sylvmagic, you know. Then only you Awarefolk will know it's not real."

Us Awarefolk—and her. You couldn't hold anything, or feel anything with a sylvmagic replacement. Sylvmagic illusions were just that—illusions. It has always puzzled me, though, how other people could be so completely fooled by them to the extent of being able to touch and feel what wasn't there.

I changed the subject. "Flame, about Ruarth—be very careful to conceal your friendship. Especially from Keepers. It could be used against you," I added vaguely.

Fortunately, Tor returned before she could ask what I meant. He laid the bedding on the floor and smiled at me. "Who's first for sleep?"

"Me. I'm—" But I had no words to describe how I felt.

He reached out and touched my cheek. "I'm sorry about Niamor. Do you want to talk about it?"

I shook my head. "Never. Not ever." And I turned away from the comfort he offered.

CHAPTER 16

NOTHING MORE HAPPENED THAT NIGHT, except that I had enough bad dreams to supply a storyteller with a lifetime of horror tales. When I awoke to take over the watch, roused by my own nightmares, I didn't feel rested. Fortunately Flame seemed to have slept well in the first part of the night, and she only woke up again just before sunrise. I fetched her a glass of water and as she didn't seem to want to go back to sleep, we chatted for a while. She was uncomfortable, but there was no sign of fever, and what was left of Garrowyn's medication kept the pain to manageable levels.

As she seemed inclined to talk, I asked her about her life in Cirkasecastle. At first, she was evasive, but I persisted and she eventually opened up. "You've been to Cirkasecastle," she said, "you've seen how people live there. But maybe you don't know *why* the nobles live in the inner castle, right under the nose of the Castlelord? Because they live where the Castlelord says—and he prefers his nobles to be where he can keep an eye on them. Of course, they can go to their country estates in the summer, when the Cirkasecastle gets noisome and the summerfever starts up, but for the rest of the year, everyone lives right there within the castle walls. And everyone has a titular appointment: Keeper of the Seal, perhaps, or Mistress of the Chambermaids. You can refuse to conform, of course—but your country estate will be confiscated, and your appointment given to someone else, along with its income, and there's nothing you'll be able to do about it.

"And so aristocratic families stay in the inner castle. Every day, the men report to the Castlelord, the women to his consort, and they decide what everyone is going to do that day. Go hunting in the country, or play one of the court games. The men might go down into the city proper to carouse in the inns; the women may call their dressmakers or practice their dances. If there's someone the Castlelord doesn't particularly like, then he'll give them some work to do: maybe supervise the collection of taxes, or preside over the legal courts. And everyone is so scared of losing their position, of losing their income, they jump to his bidding. Even the children are caught up in the politics of it: 'No, dear, you can't play with Nasko today. That wouldn't be wise. The Castlelord doesn't like his father any more.' "

She shuddered. "You know what the worst thing is? Growing up thinking that all that is *normal*. That it's a good way to live. I would have accepted it all, been just as shallow as everyone else, just as cowed—if it hadn't been for Ruarth and his family." She glanced at the foot of the bed, where the Dustel slept, head tucked under his wing. "The Dustels of Cirkasecastle, they taught me that there was another world out there, where things were done differently. And that it was a better place."

I had to ask, of course; I'd spent an inordinate amount of time pondering about just how a young girl started talking to a bird. "Tell me how you and Ruarth—" I began.

She laughed softly. "To understand that, you have to understand the kind of life I had. I spent a lot of time in my personal rooms . . . Children don't mix with the adults in noble households, except for servants and dancemasters, fencing teachers and protocol tutors and such. They don't even see their own parents except in formal settings. In our family it was one dinner a week. I didn't see other children much either. There was an enormously complicated protocol involved when one noble child went to visit another, so those who looked after me couldn't be bothered with it. The result was I spent a lot of time alone in my own rooms.

"Ruarth and his family lived on my windowsill and in the niches around it. It was a large and very ornate sill: lots of crannies. One thing I used to do was put out food for them. I soon

found I could recognize one from another, and that there was
one that seemed to be especially friendly. Ruarth, of course. After a while he used to fly in to spend time with me. I was only
about four when this started. I used to talk to him as if he was a
person. Gradually I learned that he was actually talking back to
me, it was just a matter of understanding it . . . Some Dustel
language is obvious. Shakes of the head for no, or nods for yes,
just like everyone else. Other gestures are more subtle, but
fairly easily understood—things like wait, come, here, there. A
stamped foot means 'I'm angry,' shrugged shoulders means 'I
don't know,' and so on. As for the chirps and sounds, I learned
those the same way a child learns speech from the adults
around them: by repetition. We both learned to read at the same
time, and that helped. I'd write out the alphabet, and he would
peck at the letters . . ."

"Did you go to school?" I asked.

She shook her head. "No. None of the Cirkase nobility went
to school. It was the mark of the despised middle class to be educated—why learn to read and write when you can pay someone to do it for you? But I learned anyway. In a way, I was
lucky. My father was so busy he didn't have time to worry about
me, and my mother was neurotic and so often ill that I was left
to my own devices even more than most. Ruarth's mother said I
should learn, so I persuaded my father's accountant to teach me
to figure and his scribe to teach me to read and write." She
looked at Ruarth's sleeping form fondly. "Without the Dustels
and without those two men, my life would have been very different . . ."

"I didn't realize it was so bad," I said. "Is it true that Cirkase
is run by clerks and bookkeepers? This so-called middle class?"

"Absolutely true. In the past it worked because the
Castlelord kept a tight rein on his underlings. Now," she shook
her head ruefully, "it's all falling apart—and so it should. It's
no way to govern. The literate class is going to overthrow the
nobility one day, and they won't know how to stop it. Why
should they—the scribes and accountants and merchants—do
all the work, carry all the responsibility, for very little pay?
D'you know, Blaze, as a little girl growing up in the Castle, I
had seventeen personal servants. Seventeen. I never had to
brush my hair, or tie my own shoes. I never had to do anything.
Anything at all. And what did I do to *earn* that kind of service?
Nothing. If it hadn't been for the Dustels, I would have been the

world's most spoiled and unhappy child. It was boredom that made me take a second look at the birds on my window ledge; it was a child's inquiring mind imprisoned in a stultifying environment that led me to question what I saw . . . How many other inquiring minds has the Cirkasian system stifled?"

She looked down at her amputated arm. "I'm glad I left. I'd do it all over again, even if I knew beforehand the price I would have to pay."

In my heart, I knew she wasn't talking about just her arm.

"Yes," she said, answering my unspoken question. "Even that. If I'd stayed in Cirkasecastle, what would have happened to me would have been worse than rape. I would have been violated again and again, in subtle and degrading ways, every day of my life." She was silent for a while, then said, "A noble woman can't walk outside without being heavily veiled. Everything you look at, you see through a layer of cloth. Lower class people aren't supposed to see our faces. And yet our servants saw us—even bathed us. So where's the *logic*? It was just another way of keeping people in their 'place.' It was hell, Blaze. In the end I would have been married off without my consent, to bring prestige or commercial benefits to my family, as if I was a commodity."

She met my gaze. In the candlelight she looked lovely: the soft light muted her pain and blurred the edges of her beauty but, to me, it was her compassion that made her truly lovely. "I'm sorry. You who have had such a hard life must find my whining about the luxury of mine somewhat tasteless."

I shook my head. "We all have our prisons. We just have to transcend them."

"Yes. The Dustels showed me how. What about you, Blaze? How did you climb out?"

I thought about that. Was it the crazy crone, in the Duskset Hill cemetery, who taught me to rely on myself? Was it the Menod who started me on the right path with their unworldly charity? Arnado, who introduced me to elegance and his own brand of honor? Duthrick, who gave me something to aim for and a mission in life? Or was it just my anger—my rage—at the injustices my mixed birth had ordained for me.

She seemed to read my mind. "Don't tell me it was Duthrick. That man is poison. Keepers are all—"

"Oh don't you start. I hear that all the time from Tor."

"He's right. If it weren't for the Keepers, who prop up the

creaking aristocracy in Cirkase because they find it easier to
deal with tyrants, our islandom would be a better place. Keepers preach equality and the election of leaders, but in practice,
in other islandoms, they think it threatens stability and so they
make sure the tyrants remain."

"I think Ruarth must be an anarchist to have taught you all
these things," I growled. "You and Tor are a pair. Have you any
idea what sort of government you'd get if all the Islandlords
suddenly disappeared? There'd be chaos!"

She snorted, an unladylike sound, and we both retreated
from the subject for fear we would end up arguing. We chatted
a little more, but then she stirred restlessly, trying to get comfortable. I gave her more medicine and she drifted off to sleep,
holding my hand in hers.

I WOKE LATER TO FIND THAT I HAD SLEPT
sitting at her bedside, my head on her bed. She was still sound
asleep. Ruarth was nowhere about.

It was the sound of Tor moving around the room that had
awakened me. "Flame's fine," he said.

I stood up and groped for equilibrium. In retrospect, what
had happened during the night seemed unreal. "Tor," I said
slowly, taking care to keep my voice down, "why didn't either
you or I rush out of the room and run a sword through the bastard? We don't have to fear his magic."

"D'y'know, I think it might have been what he wanted us to
do? I think he's a little afraid of us—of you, anyway. How
much he knows about me is uncertain. Perhaps he thought you
would rush out of the room in search of him."

I thought about that. "You think it was a trap? Someone like
Domino—several of them—waiting with him, swords drawn."

"It's possible. I'm sure he must have been protected, but perhaps his main intent was just to tease us."

"But . . . I never thought of attacking." I was taken aback,
and oddly shamed. "He had me so frightened, I was almost paralyzed."

He gave a grim smile. "Ironic, isn't it? That he bothered, I
mean. He's more afraid of us than is warranted. He just doesn't
know what it's like to have Awareness."

I knew what he meant. We weren't just made *aware* of the
presence of dunmagic. We felt, and smelled, its *wrongness,* its

evil; we could sense its terrible capability. When faced with Janko's power, our senses were almost overwhelmed with the horror of what he was, of what he could do. The night before I hadn't the slightest doubt that he could have submerged a string of islands beneath the sea, and laughed while he was doing it. It was no wonder we had found it hard to act.

"Dunmagickers, Tor. Who—*what* are they?"

"Menod texts say they are manifestations of the Sea Devil."

I gave a grunt of dissatisfaction. "That tells us nothing. Are they born, or are they made?"

"You're wondering if they all start off life as sylvs, and are later subverted."

I nodded. I'd asked the same question of Duthrick; I just wanted confirmation.

He shook his head. "No. There are definitely cases of dunmagic babies born to sylv mothers who were raped or bedded by dunmagickers. Just as many non-sylv women have sylv children when the father is a sylv. And I rather think that dunmagicker women always tend to have babies contaminated with dunmagic."

"What makes them different? Why do they seem to feed on pain and the despair of others?"

"I don't know. The Menod belief is as good as any—that all evil comes from the Sea Devil."

"To believe in the Sea Devil, one has first to believe in God," I said.

He gave a faint smile. "Yes," he agreed. "But then, I do."

I didn't want to think about that. I changed the subject. "What do you know about the inundation of the Dustels, Tor?"

He pulled at his ear, as if that would help him to remember. "There are so many tales, it's hard to say what's rumor and what's fact. I must admit I always dismissed the idea that a single dunmagicker could drown a whole chain of islands as just plain popped bladder-wrack. Empty of substance . . . not proven. I do know that the Dustels had a lot of problems immediately before the islands disappeared. The usual sort of thing: the outer islands of the group thought they were badly treated, paid too much in taxes and didn't get enough in return. It's a common enough complaint, and we in the Stragglers have heard similar moans. A wise ruler does something about them before things get out of hand. From what I remember of my history, in the Dustels the ruling family ignored the complaints and there was a civil war. One of the Rampartlord's sons joined the rebels. Some terrible atrocities were committed by both sides. Worse still, outsiders got involved: the Keepers stuck their nose in as usual; the Menod patriarchy were somehow involved, because there was a big monastery complex on one of the outer islands; the Stragglers supported the ruling house. Just before the islands disappeared, the rebel islanders were defeated in a huge battle and many of those who remained were executed. The ruling army was, however, decimated as well, so it wasn't a happy victory. That's about all I know."

"Morthred? Dunmagic?"

"Lots of rumors *after* the fact. I once dug out some of the historical records on the period prior to the inundation, and there were some vague references to dunmagic use in the Dustels. Nothing much. Morthred was a name coined after the event, not before. It means 'red death' in island argot and people called him that because they said he was responsible. I'm sorry now I didn't poke around in the records a bit more."

I should have wondered about his scholarship and where he'd had access to records, but he pulled a rueful face and shrugged, and all logical thought fled in the face of his charm. My heart beat a little faster, but there was nothing I could do about it right then.

THERE WAS STILL A LINGERING SMELL OF dunmagic about as I went down the stairs, sword in hand, to the privy a few minutes later. Everywhere I looked there were stale traces of angry redness to confuse my Awareness. It clung to the stair, glowed dully in the doorways, rotted around the chair and table legs in the taproom.

There was a group of Keepers sitting at the table near the kitchen door having a late breakfast. They were casually dressed; not a chasuble in sight. In the face of so much dunmagic their sylvmagic seemed wholly subdued. One of them I recognized: she had been at the sylv girls' school at the same time as I had, but she did not react when our eyes met, so I let my gaze drift on as I walked through to the yard.

Coming back a few minutes later, I ran into Janko just inside the doorway. He was his familiar salivating self, only now when I looked at him he did not seem pitiable, but obscene.

And he thought I was still unaware of who he was. I knew I might never have such an opportunity again.

My sword was out and plunging at his chest almost before I gave a thought to what I was doing.

I would have succeeded in the murder—and changed the course of history—but for one of those perverse acts of fate that occur sometimes to throw even the best plans out of kilter. The cookboy, staggering under an armful of seaweed for the stove, chose that moment to enter the room behind me. As he brushed past, his view obscured by his burden, he joggled my arm and the lunge that should have skewered Janko through the heart merely removed two fingers from his left hand.

A number of things then happened at once. Janko let out a murderous yell and hurled a dunspell at my face. It didn't harm me, of course, but it exploded in my eyes in a foul shower of bloody light and sent me instinctively cringing back, gagging. The cookboy shrieked and threw the seaweed all over us in his panic. Real blood from Janko's hand sprayed into my face, and just when I should have been embarking on a follow-through attack, I had to spend time wiping it from my eyes. The innkeeper was in the kitchen doorway yelling, "Janko, what the piss-arse hell is going on?" Janko did not answer; he was too busy warding off my next attack with another explosion of power. Then I had company. The whole contingent from the Keeper table joined me.

I thought they had come to help. I thought they were Keepers from the *Keeper Fair*. I thought Janko was going to die. I thought I was about to become the Glory Isles' new hero . . .

But they weren't from the *Keeper Fair*.

They were dunmagickers. Subverted sylvtalents.

The shock of it—to see those tall golden people with dunmagic playing over their skins. To see the malevolence in those beautiful violet eyes, to see their hunger for my pain. Dunmagic Keeper sylvs! It was as if the sun had failed to rise . . .

I fought. Dear God, how I fought. I grabbed up a chair in one hand and positioned myself against the wall. Janko, of course, kept out of the way and left it all to his acolytes. They came at me with their swords and their Keeper training and their hate. And somewhere at the back of those glowing eyes I saw traces of what they had once been. It was as Flame had hinted . . . there was indeed a part of them that knew what they had been, and behind the hate there was black horror.

I had rarely had so little relish for a fight.

I warded off the first flurry of lunges with the chair, and then managed to kill one of my attackers with a quick thrust made through the chair legs. They showed no signs of distress at her death, but they were more cautious after that. They took it in turns, two at a time, to come at me in a series of fast slashing attacks, one immediately following another, knowing that sooner or later my concentration would flag when I tired. These weren't untrained street louts like Teffel and his ilk—these men and women had probably graduated from The Hub Academy and they knew how to fight in tandem. There are some odds that are just too great. I let out a bellow for Tor.

One of the Keepers used a chair to batter at mine. I managed to open up a deep disabling gash on his arm, but I lost the chair. Without it, I knew I was going to lose.

Then, just when I thought I was dead, the game changed again. Tor came down the stairs in a roaring fury, swinging a sword like an avenging angel, and lopped off a head in a remarkable two-handed stroke that had me wondering if he also had a Calmenter blade. It wasn't a bad effort for someone who had—at least over the past week—shown a marked reluctance to wear a sword, let alone use one.

The odds were a little better then.

I fought on, concentrating on defense, blocking and blocking again as they lunged and slashed. There was no elegance, no finesse. It was sheer hard work and strength; a fast, brutal fight that we would probably eventually lose, in spite of our skill and experience, because there were more of them.

Tor disabled another, a woman, and we were down to four opponents, plus Janko. I was vaguely aware of the innkeeper dancing around the room in a frenzy of worry, pleading with us not to break anything more, and would we *please* take the fight outside? Occasionally he added an agonized entreaty to Janko to tell him what the Great Trench was going on. Janko ignored him and shouted something about not killing either of us; he wanted us alive, turd-damn it, and then we had more company—more of his subverted sylvs—and it was all over.

I was lying on my stomach on the floor, my sword taken from me, a foot planted firmly in the small of my back to stop me rising while my hands and feet were tied with a piece of fish netting. It hurt. Somewhere off to my left, Tor was receiving similar treatment. I made a quick review of the damage: a raw graze along my cheek where I'd been hit by a chair leg, a cut across the back of my right hand that hurt like the sting of a devilfish but which didn't seem to be bleeding too copiously, a badly bruised side where I'd caught a blow from the flat (fortunately) of a blade. I'd live. Long enough to wish I hadn't, I supposed.

Once thoroughly trussed, I was rolled over on to my back. I felt like a king crab with its claws tied. Janko looked down at me, and for the first time I saw him as he truly was. No leer. The eyes that met mine were intelligent, and totally cold. The face was as twisted as ever, but the dribble was gone, and it was his good side I noticed now, not the deformed. It was the face of a handsome man, but one who had never been touched by compassion for anyone. Worse still was the icy hate that seethed there, especially for me. He would have personally ripped me apart, piece by piece, if he'd thought that was the worst punishment he could offer me.

"This time," he said, "you won't escape. And you won't die either. Remember that." The voice—that of a well-educated, well-bred man—was the one I'd heard when I'd been staked out on the sand, not the one I associated with whining Janko the waiter. He touched my face with his boot, digging the toe into the graze. A petty, pointless torture, except for its promise of a grim future for me. Then he crouched down, so that his face was close to mine. "You are going to wish you had never crossed me. Do you know what people used to call me, Blaze Halfbreed? Morthred the Mad. But they mistook: I was never mad. Everything I ever did was calculated, just as everything that will be done to you will be planned. To the last detail. Remember that too."

I looked away from him—and my heart almost stopped. From where I lay I could see the top of the stairs, and Flame was there, leaning weakly on the railing. Even as I watched, her outline blurred as she made herself indistinct. Sylvs couldn't quite render themselves invisible, but they could make themselves difficult to see. How she managed it in her weakened state I had no idea. I dragged my eyes away.

And my terror deepened with every thought. She would go to Duthrick. I almost groaned. She had suffered so much to conceal the Castlemaid's whereabouts. I couldn't bear that she would reveal it for me.

As for Tor, I didn't even want to think about what was in store for him.

We were carried out of the inn, passing the innkeeper on the way. His eyes were as large and as round as setu pieces and his chin wobbled in fear. Janko-Morthred, perhaps in revenge for some past maltreatment, lashed out with a dunspell as he passed and the hapless man writhed on the ground, screaming. I caught a glimpse of red welts across his face and a smashed and blood-ied nose. He might not have agreed, but I thought he had es-caped lightly.

Unbidden, the memory of Niamor's death returned to me.

To put it mildly, we were fish caught in a netful of trouble.

THEY TOOK US TO THEIR VILLAGE BY SEA-pony, strapped beside each other, head and legs dangling on ei-ther side of the beast, as if we were sacks of dried fish. My bonds were too tight and my head bumped against the animal's segmented carapace. The only good thing was that they had tied us so that our heads were almost together.

As we passed through the streets of the town, pedestrians gaped at us, their marketing momentarily forgotten. One or two people did ask our Keeper guards what we had done, but they weren't given a reply and no one protested. It took a brave man to question Keeper sylvs, and the inhabitants of the Docks were not renowned for either their bravery or their neighborly con-cern. They shrugged and got on with their business.

I edged closer to Tor so that my lips were almost against his neck. "Since when have you owned a Calmenter blade?" I asked in a whisper.

"Since I was that Calment Minor rebel with more youth than good sense," he replied. "Why in all the islands do you want to know that?"

I didn't want to know that at all, of course; what I really wanted to know was why someone who owned a Calmenter blade never wore the damn thing. I wanted to know why a man who had once been the Lance of Calment had changed so much—but I didn't know how to ask the question.

"Don't show them that we care about each other," he said.

I gave the faintest of nods in return. He was right. There was no point in giving Janko—no, *Morthred*—an added lever he could use to cause us pain. I thought it likely, however, that the dunmaster already knew of our friendship. The man had lived and worked alongside us for days, after all, and he hadn't done it for the fun of serving tables.

We bumped along uncomfortably. My cheek bled and the blood seeped into my eye, but there was nothing I could do about it. I kept my eyes open. I needed to see if Flame would send a Dustel after us. She did of course; a whole flock of them. I soon saw them, fluttering along, down low among the murram grass. The problem was I couldn't figure out how I was going to let them know that there was something I needed to say. As it turned out, I need not have worried; Ruarth Windrider had already thought of that. At least, I was fairly sure it was him. He came flying in from behind the sea-pony, so sneakily that even I didn't see him until he was perched on the back of the beast, not far from my face.

I said in a quick whisper, "Janko admitted he is Morthred. Be careful—he'll know you for what you are. *And don't let Flame bargain with Duthrick for his help*—he'll give it anyway." I hoped I was right about that. I didn't have any illusions about Duthrick's sense of public duty or his affection for me, but we did know he was intending some sort of attack on the dunmagickers.

The Dustel nodded and slipped away.

Tor said in my ear in a voice full of sadness rather than fear, "Ah, love . . . I wish it hadn't come to this."

So did I. And it was all my own sodding fault.

CHAPTER 17

MY PREVIOUS GLIMPSE OF THE VILLAGE of Creed had also been from the back of a sea-pony. This time I was considerably less comfortable and a great deal more fearful. The whole place reeked with dun power, and wherever I looked, there were flickers of red and scarlet and crimson. The village faced a beach and was sheltered by a semicircle of dunes. On the western edge, just beyond the last of the houses, the rocky area (the scab on the back of the Gorthan Spit sand-eel) began, sloping upward at first, then leveling off into an undulating plateau of no great elevation. On the seaward side, this plateau ended abruptly in a sheer wall that plunged straight into the sea. I'd once seen all this from the deck of a ship, but it wasn't what interested me now. It was the village itself, the houses.

In the four months or so that they had been there, Morthred and his cohorts had changed the rickety huddle of huts that had been a cockle-farming village, as I recalled from my earlier visits to the Spit, into a settlement that would have been worthy of a high-class suburb in The Hub. There were several streets paved with crushed blue shell and lined with white houses. At first glance I thought the buildings were constructed of some sort of white stone, but when I had a close look later, I saw that it wasn't stone at all. The blocks had been quarried all right, but quarried from the millions of tiny white seashells that had accumulated and become cemented, over hundreds of years, into a textured solid mass along some of the Gorthan Spit coastline. In the sunshine, the flat-roofed houses were a glare of white pristine beauty, aesthetically a vast improvement on normal Gorthan Spit architecture. I wondered why no one on the Spit had thought of using shell blocks before. I supposed it was just that no one had ever been quite as innovative as Morthred the Mad.

I was to discover that being innovative was a talent of his. There were a lot of things I saw in Creed that I'd never seen before.

I'd never seen people look the way they did there. They didn't seem human, none of them. Walking dead would have been a better way to describe many . . . most. At first I thought some were ghemphs because they seemed to be hairless and grayish. Later I discovered that it was just that their hair had fallen out and their skin had discolored after the months of poor treatment and starvation. Their heads all seemed huge, but perhaps that was just because their bodies were so emaciated. Skin was like parchment over an empty framework of bone . . . were they men or women? I couldn't tell. Most had probably been inhabitants of the original village before Morthred came along. One of them may once have been the girlfriend Niamor had mentioned. Now they were just slaves, to be used and discarded if they were no longer useful.

They were chained with dunmagic. It danced over their bodies in an almost pretty crimson color, draining their desire to escape, or their will to defy. Even more chilling was the fact that, although there were some children in the village, not one of them was under about ten; nor were their any elderly people. This had been a settlement of cockle farmers and their families once, people like Niamor's girlfriend. Now only the strong remained.

The second kind of people in Creed were just as pitiable, but in a different way: the subverted sylvtalents. They weren't all Keepers. I saw tattoos from Breth and Mekaté and the Spatts as well—in fact, from most of the islandoms. They weren't starved or ill-dressed or ill-treated and they themselves were as vicious and as cruel as Morthred himself, yet it tore my heart to see them. I could read their doomed struggle in their eyes. They could never be sylvs again and they knew it. Their new evil side rejoiced, but the inner flicker of what they had been stared out at us in despair and horror, unable to conquer the evil, begging for release, for death. Part of me wanted to kill them all, to put them out of their misery. Part of me wondered if, presented with the opportunity, I'd ever be ruthless enough. Niamor's death still haunted me.

The third group of people were genuine dunmagickers. They gathered around us as the sea-ponies came to a halt, doubtless to see what Morthred had dragged home. Judging by their tattoos, it was clear they came from all over the Isles of Glory. I think there were about fifteen of them. Their presence surprised me. Morthred had apparently done what no other dunmaster had ever done: he had *united* a group of dunmagickers. They were usually much more solitary. Even the dunmagickers' enclave on Fis that I had helped to destroy a few years earlier had been leaderless, a much looser association of dunmagickers than this.

When I thought of the amount of power Morthred had accumulated in one place, I shuddered.

Tor's thoughts ran on similar lines. "So *much* of it," he muttered when no one was looking. But he sounded interested as much as frightened. He was intrigued, as if dunmagickers and their power presented an intellectual problem to be solved. "Morthred must be aiming for control of the whole of the Isles of Glory. Otherwise, why so many of them?" He was right. My heart bottomed like a sunken ship.

Dunmagic chains had no effect on us, of course, so our chains were real. We were removed from the sea-pony and each of us had our feet shackled first, ankles so close together that we could do no more than shuffle. Then we each had a heavy pole, a palm-width in diameter, placed across our shoulders so that it extended more than an arm's length on either side. Our arms were forced behind the pole and our wrists fastened, also by means of shackles, toward the ends of it, so that we became ungainly top-heavy creatures with our arms outstretched and useless. It was excruciatingly uncomfortable.

Once we were thus disabled we were taken to a room and confronted with Morthred. He was not alone: Domino was there, reclining uncomfortably on a litter, and the look he directed at us was ferocious with hate. I almost groaned. Why in all the islands had I stopped Tor from killing the bastard? We were going to regret our magnanimity.

Morthred was seated and surrounded by subverted sylvtalents; his bodyguards, I supposed. His chair, a large one draped with an ornate cloth, was on a raised platform. The whole arrangement was a makeshift imitation of the Keeperlord's audience room back in The Hub, not to mention several other Islandlord throne rooms I'd visited on Keeper business at one time or another. It left me with no doubt as to how Morthred saw himself.

I had been constantly having to quell my desire to vomit ever since we'd arrived in the village: that terrible smell of dunmagic in such concentrations was almost more than I could bear. Now, in the presence of Morthred and so many other dunmagickers, it had an intensity which was physically painful. It dug, claw-like, into my body.

I forced myself to face him.

He had changed again. His left hand, now missing two fingers, was straighter than it had been when I had first seen him. The stumps were already largely healed, although it had only been a matter of hours since I'd lopped off the fingers. He was growing stronger by the hour.

And then I saw what was hanging on the wall above his head: two Calmenter swords. One, which I suspected was Tor's, was bare and still fouled with blood. Mine had been replaced in its scabbard and hung from a hook as though it was an ornament. He had intended it as an insult, I knew, but I found the gesture childish. I was not so easily roused to fruitless anger. I was just glad that I now knew where the weapon was. Hope died hard in me.

He smiled when he saw where my eyes had gone.

"Blaze," he said. "Keeper-servile. One of the Aware. Half-breed. Who lied to my servant Domino. All reasons to see you punished, and punished you will be. Eternally punished—at least until you die of old age. Don't look to death for release, halfbreed." He turned his head slightly, without taking his eyes from mine. "You hear that, Domino? She is not to die of her ill treatment: she is just to *want* to die."

"I hear, Syr-master."

He turned back to me. "Domino is a trifle incapacitated, as you can see. Doubtless he will see to it that one of the causes of this pain has reason to feel pain in return." He transferred his attention to Tor. "You, I believe, are Tor Ryder of the Stragglers. Another of the Aware. I don't know why you decided to involve yourself in my affairs, but it is a decision you will live to regret." He nodded at one of the Keeper dunmagickers who had brought us in. "Have both put in the oblivion until Domino is well enough to deal with them personally. Perhaps the Cirkasian can share with you the, er, *joys* of dealing with them, Dom, when she arrives. That would be a nice touch, I think."

I almost felt relief. I'd thought I'd have to face something like the blood-demons again; an oblivion seemed almost a luxury in comparison, especially when it didn't include solitary confinement. I didn't know then that there are different kinds of agonies.

I don't know whether you have yet come across an oblivion on your travels? They were an invention of a Barbicanlord of Xolchas Stacks some generations ago, I believe. It's a room, or a dungeon, or a hole in the ground—any place in which all light and external sound is blocked out so that the prisoner confined within has no idea of the time of day. Such a prisoner is supplied with food and water, irregular amounts at irregular intervals, so that he can never judge the passing of time and never know for sure when he will next be fed. That much I knew. What I didn't know was just how terrible such a place can be.

Our oblivion was an underground room, built, I believe, of shell blocks (although I never did see them). We were taken first into a darkened room that was lit only by the most meager of candles placed close to the door. There was a large trapdoor in the center of the floor. A rope was looped around me and I was lowered through the trapdoor into the oblivion below. It was so dark there I could see nothing, not even how far it was down to the floor. Once I was standing, the rope was pulled away. Tor followed me, there was a sound as the trapdoor was closed and we were left in a darkness that was so intense I felt that I could have sliced it with a knife.

I stood stock still, suddenly aware of how diabolical our punishment was to be, shackled and spread-eagled as we were. We could not touch each other, could not hold each other. We had no way of adjusting our clothes when we needed to rid ourselves of our own body wastes. We could not even scratch when we itched.

Then I realized that, although the darkness was absolute, the silence wasn't. There was someone else—or something else—there. I heard the faintest of rustles and barely perceptible breathing.

"We're not alone," Tor said unnecessarily.

"No." The voice that replied was male, and frail. "There are two of us here." A hacking cough came at us out of the darkness.

"Who are you?" I asked.

"Dear God—a woman?"

I nodded, forgetting no one could see. "My name is Blaze—" I began and then stopped. Why give information that wasn't needed? For once I would be judged by who I really was, not by my halfbreed looks and lack of ear tattoo.

Tor spoke into the silence: "And I'm Tor Ryder of the Stragglers."

More coughing, and then, "I'm Alain Jentel, Syr-aware Menod patriarch from the Spatts. I believe I know you, Tor Ryder." His tone, rich with irony, seemed to hint that he actually knew Tor quite well.

There was a long silence before Tor's dry reply. "Yes, we have met. I'm sorry to know that you are here, Alain. I had heard of your disappearance."

The frail voice quavered. "Dear boy, how long ago was that?"

Dear boy?

Tor cleared his throat. "Some three months, I believe. We are ten days into the second double-moon month."

"Ah. It—it has seemed longer . . ."

Tor, I knew, was very upset. I could read it in his voice and I was intrigued. Usually he was too self-contained to show emotion so openly.

"And your companion?" I asked the unseen Alain.

"You may call me Eylsa." The second voice that came out of the darkness puzzled me for a moment. I could not pin it down as masculine or feminine. And I thought I had heard it somewhere before. There was a hint of laughter in it as it added, "And I believe we also have met, Syr-aware Blaze Halfbreed."

So much for no one knowing my halfbreed status. But at least whoever it was had added a courtesy Syr title. "We have?" And then I knew. "The *ghemph?*"

"At your service."

"How did . . . ? What happened?"

Had I thought about it, I probably wouldn't have asked the question; one didn't expect to have a normal conversation with a ghemph. However, in this case the answer came back readily enough: "The dunmagicker, ah, took exception to my presence on Gorthan Spit."

"But—why?"

Once again the reply came unhesitatingly. "I was sent to find Morthred by my people, Syr-aware. By all the ghemphs in the Isles of Glory. To find out what was happening. We had all heard tales about this dunmaster subverting sylvtalents and the matter was of some indirect concern to us. Should dunmagickers control the Isles of Glory, for example, it would be unwise to assume that we would continue to live in a state of relative peace and prosperity, as we now do. It seemed provident to assess the situation, to ascertain if this Morthred was of some threat to our security. Morthred, alas, took exception to my asking questions."

I felt a rising desire to burst into hysterical laughter. Ghemphs hardly ever said more than a word or two, yet this one was as long-winded and as convoluted as an official proclamation. But then, this ghemph was different. It had once told me that some people did not require symbols . . . "I think," I said finally, "that you may have decided that he is indeed a threat to your security."

"That has been my conclusion, yes." Once again there was a suggestion of laughter in the words. The ghemph had a sense of humor.

"Perhaps," Tor interrupted, "it may be best if you told us about this place. And be careful if you move around us. We are shackled to poles placed across our shoulders."

Alain reached out and touched me, to feel the method of my confinement, and I jumped as his fingers brushed by my waist before they adjusted to the correct height. "Ah. That is one torture they neglected, happily, to impose on us." His fragile voice was threaded with distress. He took a deep breath and made an effort to control the quaver, and his cough. "You are in a square room just four paces by four. In one corner, to your right, there is a hole for the disposal of . . . um . . . anything. Doubtless you can smell it. At irregular intervals, the trapdoor is opened—it makes no difference to the darkness down here—and some food and water is lowered in. The amount is . . . just adequate; the taste and variety is better not dwelled upon. We never know when the next meal will be delivered, so it is best not to eat or drink it all at once. There is nothing more to tell you. No one has ever come for me since I was put in here, which was at the beginning of my imprisonment. Three months, you said?" His voice trailed off. He sounded more than old: he was very sick.

"I've only been here a day or two," Eylsa added. "They have not shackled me either."

I went to sit with my back to one of the walls. I closed my eyes, although it made no difference. The darkness was so close I felt as though I was wrapped in it. Sound seemed to have intensified. With nothing audible from outside, even our breathing seemed loud. My shoulders ached, my wrists were already rubbing raw, the chains at my ankles dug into my flesh no matter which way I placed my legs. I had already begun to realize that small aches could become large ones. In the hours ahead I was to learn that it didn't take blood-demons to make agony real.

"One of you is going to have to help us," I said. "We can't even feed ourselves."

"Of course," Alain said quietly, his distress still palpable. "Would you like a drink now? We have water."

We both drank; it was the first liquid either of us had had all day. I'm ashamed to say that we finished all the water they had.

"You must try to rid yourselves of those poles," the ghemph said suddenly. It came across to Tor and I heard it rustling about, presumably examining the way in which he was manacled. There was a muffled bump and a ghemphic exclamation I didn't understand. Then it said, "Correct me if I'm wrong: there's an iron band around the pole about a handspan from either end. The pole seems to have been made narrower at this point so that each band is smaller in diameter than the rest of the pole. Each band is attached by a very short chain to a wrist manacle. The manacles have been locked on your wrists and are made to open with a key."

"Correct so far," I agreed. "I might add that the manacles are Mekaté-made which means that they are just about impossible to pick, even if we did have the right equipment. All the best locks come from Mekaté."

"Now that's something every well-brought up lady should know," Tor said dryly.

I pulled a face in his direction. He would sense it, I knew.

"If the pole could be whittled away, it could be pushed through the bands and you'd be free of it," Eylsa said.

"We have nothing that could do that," Tor replied.

"I have," said the ghemph. "I have the claws on my feet."

We absorbed that in silence. Then Tor said, "The wood is hard. How strong are your claws? It would take weeks!"

"You might have weeks," the creature replied with dry humor.
"Start with Blaze then," Tor said.
I didn't protest. I wanted to be free of that yoke too much.
"Very well," said the ghemph and began there and then.

CHAPTER 18

I DON'T KNOW HOW LONG WE WERE IN the oblivion. Days, certainly. But just how many, I don't know. When we finally got out of there I never did get around to asking anyone. I just wanted to forget the place. I never have, of course. You don't forget that kind of hell easily, that combination of pain and fear, hope and despair, all against a background of total blackness and reeking foulness.

The lack of any routine was harder to take than I had thought it would be. Our bodies seemed to find it difficult to cope with being without any kind of daily rhythm. I found it hard to sleep and would wake in wild panics that left me sweating and upset. I craved water or food when there was none; at other times there seemed to be too much, too often. We tried to ration ourselves, but the food went bad easily and if we still had water left when the next lot was delivered, it was wasted because the container was just topped up. If we tried to hurriedly drink it before attaching the lowered rope to the drinkskin so that it could be hauled up and refilled, then the rope would be quickly withdrawn and we would be left without replacement food or water.

At first I hardly noticed the smell. It was only later that the fetidness of the air became a choking burden. With four people using the privy—no more than the hole Alain had said it was—the stench worsened as the days went by. We had no water to spare for bathing, of course, so our own body smells became stronger as well.

Then there was the ache of muscles pulled into unnatural positions across shoulders and arms, the pain of sores rubbed into open ulcers on ankles and wrist and back—agony I had to learn to live with. But it was the lack of light, not the presence of pain, that threatened to crush my spirit. I knew that if ever I was free again, I would never be able to pass a blind beggar without putting something in his bowl, never. No matter how little money I had. I now knew too well what it was to be without sight. That sort of total darkness: it overwhelmed, dragged me down, made me wonder if the world really existed or if it was just all part of my mind, found only in my imagination . . . I hated it.

And yet the oblivion wasn't all horror, at least not in retrospect.

The three of them, Tor, Alain and Eylsa, they were the company that kept me sane.

Tor was my rock, my love. It was in the oblivion that I came to know him best—although, even then, he never told the whole truth. Perhaps, in the end, that was what made the difference . . .

I did learn about his childhood. About how he was born the son of a fisherman in the Stragglers but declined to follow a seapath after his father had drowned in a whirlstorm near the Reefs of Deep-Sea. "My father loved the sea; I feared its moods," he explained. "Funny, but in the end, I think I've seen more of the sea than my father ever did. From Calment Major to the Spatts, I seem to have been through every passage, visited every port, sailed past the lamp of every lighthouse, and survived a Trench full of storms along the way."

"What were you doing?" I asked. "Did you work as a sailor?"

"No. I just traveled a lot," he said vaguely. "Working. Seeing the world. Actually, when my father died, I apprenticed myself to a scribe. I was about fourteen then." Scribes were letter writers, petition drafters: an essential job in places where not everyone could read or write. "When I was sixteen, my mother died and my sister married, so I used my inheritance to buy the tools I needed: portable scribe's desk, pens, inks, parchment, seals. I added a sword and knife as a precaution, although I didn't know how to use either, and headed off to earn my living."

For eight or nine years he traveled the Isles of Glory, learning more about life and people in those years than in all the years prior. Finally he fetched up in the Calments just when Calment Minor, smarting under the rule of that bastard, Governor Kilp, was ripe for rebellion. More by accident than design he became a rebel. That was when he earned his Calmenter sword, made for him by a Calmenter metalsmith at the request of a man whose life he had saved. A gift in return for a blood-debt, just as my blade had been.

After the rebellion was all over, he found himself on the run from both the Keepers—who had given Governor Kilp aid— and Calmenter troops. He was without money and no longer had his scribing tools. It was then that he decided he had no real taste for war. He had seen too much of the sickening slaughter that followed the collapse of the rebellion, when Kilp's troops ran berserk through the islands raping women and children, killing anyone who didn't give the right answer to their questions.

I knew what he was talking about: I'd been there too. Appalled, I had walked away from Kilp's offer of citizenship and a place on his military staff. Tor's reaction was more radical. He'd sworn to himself that there had to be a better way of solving the problems of the downtrodden than resorting to the sword. He'd put away his Calmenter blade . . .

I had left Calment on a Keeper ship, my passage paid, money in my purse. Tor, penniless, finally managed to escape by working his passage to Quiller on a filthy whaler. In Quiller-harbor he chose to lie low for a while. He was afraid to resume his old profession, as the Keepers knew the Lance of Calment had once been a scribe. Instead he became a reading teacher for a Menod community just outside the port. Although he wasn't of their faith, they accepted him because they needed his skills. He lived with the Quiller Menod for three years before he moved on.

Things began to make sense to me when he told me that. I said, "That's why you were able to talk to Ransom on religious subjects so easily."

"Yes. I learned the breviary from start to finish. They used to read from it at mealtimes. And if you wanted dessert, you had to sit through a sermon as well. As I was usually hungry . . ." That deadpan dry humor of his again; I loved him for it. He added more seriously, "They were good people."

When I questioned him about what he'd done afterward, he became vague again. I thought he may not have wanted to detail his exploits in front of the other two, so I didn't press the matter. But I wondered: was he some sort of agent provocateur, working against the Keeper Isles? A spy for some rebellious assembly? A writer, perhaps? One of those who produced the seditious handbills that surfaced from time to time, the kind that preached freedom and something called "universal franchise." They often contained the sort of ideas that Tor gave voice to when he spoke with me, ideas that sounded all very fine, but I could not see them ever being put into practice, or indeed being successful if ever an islandom could be persuaded to try them out. My view of mankind was far more jaundiced than Tor's, I think. I thought that if everyone had a hand in government, we would end up with mindless anarchy. "Those with the loudest voices and the most memorable slogans would end up ruling," I said during the course of one discussion.

"Education is the key," he replied. "Giving people the truth."

Anyway, he never explained exactly what he did for a living. As far as I could see, he had worked in a number of different jobs in almost all of the islandoms at one time or another, and much of what he'd done had been aimed at lessening the influence of Keeper traders and sylvtalents. He'd even lived on the Keeper Isles for a time, which is when he had first come across Wantage the shoemaker.

I supposed that it was his connection with the Menod of Quiller that gave him an interest in Alain Jentel. He certainly spent hours in the oblivion talking to Alain. They spoke mainly of religious matters, usually in low voices at times when I was talking to the ghemph. Alain, I gathered, was trying to convert Tor to his way of thinking, and they had a number of long discussions on dogma where Tor's ideas and Alain's seemed vastly different, although Tor's knowledge of the Menod religion, as well as some of the older pagan beliefs, seemed to me to be the equal of Alain's, and rather unusual in a layman. Mostly their talk bored me; I didn't understand much of what was said, and all the quibbling on minor points of belief or behavior seemed a ridiculous waste of time. Of course, by this time I was wondering if Tor was a Menod. He certainly seemed to believe in God, and I was a little surprised at how seriously he seemed to take it, but then I also heard enough to know that he could be scathing about Menod beliefs as well. For instance, he laughed at their emphasis on chastity for the unmarried, calling it an artificial invention of Man; an invention that God, having given us all our desires, would Himself condemn as unnatural. This kind of argument seemed unimportant to me, however correct, and I couldn't understand why Tor's beliefs upset Alain so much, but they did.

At other times, Tor would withdraw into himself. He seemed perfectly content to spend hours in silence, thinking. He remained equable, even cheerful, and calm. I, on the other hand, was like a caged cat. I prowled (as much as one could prowl while wearing a six-foot yoke in a cell the size of a ship's cabin); I lost my temper; I railed against fate, against Morthred; I raged and shouted. Inevitably it was Tor who calmed me, who reduced my energy to more manageable levels. He had so much more inner strength than I did, yet he was careful never to shame me—although there were many times when I should have been shamed. I did not take my imprisonment well. Especially when I knew it would probably culminate in an endless hell of pain and torture.

"Tell me about yourself," Tor would say when it was obvious I was reaching the limits of frustration. "Tell me about your life. I want to know everything . . ."

"Do you remember anything about your parents?" he asked once.

The oblivion faded and for a moment I was back in another world—the immediacy of childhood. A fleeting touch with a memory: a perfume, a face, a feeling, a never-quite-to-be-forgotten sense of warmth and safety. And then devastating betrayal when all that had disappeared. "Sometimes," I said slowly, "sometimes I have a feeling that I remember, that there was someone . . . And then it's gone, and all I remember is being hungry and cold and frightened."

"Who looked after you?"

"A couple of crazies in the cemetery of Duskset Hill. In a desultory sort of way. And the older street children living there did their best, sometimes. We looked after one another . . . I was later told that I'd been dumped there one night, wrapped in a blanket, on top of one of the graves. I think I was probably less than two years old at the time." His question had raked the ashes of memories I had deliberately doused. Once they were rekindled, I had to go on remembering, talking. "I used to daydream all the time about how my parents would come for me, how it was all a terrible mistake. I'd obviously been stolen away from my true birthright . . . Silly, stupid dreams."

I paused and the silence lengthened until Tor ventured into the void. "It can't have been a safe environment for a child of your age. I am surprised you survived, let alone came through a strong and vibrant human being."

I hardly heard the compliment, I was so submerged in memory. "It was a close thing," I admitted. "I almost went under a number of times . . . When I was about six or seven, for instance, one of the older boys started to molest me. He threatened me with all kinds of unpleasantness if I told. At first I just tried to avoid him as much as possible . . . Then, when he persisted, the crone who lived there with us said something I've never forgotten: 'Child, you have to look after yourself. No one is going to do it for you.' After that, I stopped dreaming. I knew that there was only me, the halfbreed. I had to make my own life. Defend myself. And so I fought back. I made such a ruckus every time the boy came near me that the others started teasing him. In the end, he gave up and turned his attentions elsewhere. He was the one who started calling me Blaze; I think he wanted to mock me, but I delighted in the name. Up until then, I'd just been 'the halfbreed.' If ever I had a name, I'd long since forgotten it."

"Did you ever try to find your real parents?" Tor asked.

"Yes, I went to look through the birth archives in The Hub a few years ago. I looked for records of a halfbred Souther-cum-Fenlander. I never found anything. Possibly my mother never registered my birth. I suspect that she kept me for a while, but then, when I was old enough to run around and people could see that I was a halfbreed brat, she just abandoned me. Otherwise she could have been in trouble because of the laws on cross-breeding. They punish that with enforced sterility on the Keeper Isles."

"The Menod have worked for years to get rid of these antiquated ideas on island purity," Alain growled. It was the first time I'd heard him sound so irate. "It is iniquitous. We are all God's children."

"Yeah," I said.

Poor Alain. He wasted a lot of time trying to talk to me about God, to give me the faith to help me meet whatever it was that was in store for me, but I couldn't accept what he offered. I couldn't believe in his God of goodness or in his sky heaven for the faithful. I questioned everything. I couldn't take anything just on faith. I couldn't believe that, if there really was a God who wanted to be worshiped, who wanted us to live by certain rules, He would have made such a rotten job of telling us just how He wanted it all done, or just how He wanted us to behave.

I did like Alain, though. He was a gentle man. He was dying and he knew it, but he never lost his dignity or questioned his faith. He was always trying to give us most of his share of the food and water, saying it was wasted on a man who was coughing up his lungs. There were many times when he was greatly distressed by his inability to breathe properly, yet he always made light of it. If he was in pain, he never told us. He never seemed to resent or even be embarrassed by the personal tasks he and Eylsa had to do for Tor and me. He was everything a Menod patriarch should have been.

He was also a well-read, educated man with a fund of knowledge he was always willing to share. I learned much from him about history, politics, trade, treaties: there was no end to his store of facts. I took the opportunity to question him about the fate of the Dustel Islands, for example, and he told a story that I have never forgotten.

The last human Rampartlord of the Dustels had two sons and a quarrelsome archipelago of low-lying coral islands and atolls to rule. In order to maintain order, he sent his eldest son, the Rampartheir, to the farthest island to help with the governing. The heir was a sylv called Willrin, and the island, unusually fertile and beautiful for the Dustels, was called Skodart. It was inhabited by fiercely independent islanders who, unlike most Dustel Islanders, were farmers and herders rather than fishermen. They produced almost all that they needed and hated the taxes and restrictions imposed on them by Dustelrampart, which had laws that were more biased toward the welfare of fishermen, cockle farmers and seaweed growers.

Willrin was a young and impressionable man when he departed for Skodart. Within the first year, he had fallen in love with an islander, and married her without the royal consent that was mandatory for the heir. He then compounded the error by having twin sons, both in line for the throne, but unrecognized by his father back in Dustelrampart. In addition, he undermined his father's position by supporting the islanders in many of their causes. It was a situation with all the ingredients for tragedy even then, but as the years went by, it worsened.

The second eldest son, named Vincen, was kept by his father's side, and gradually came to think of himself as his father's favorite. The Rampartlord demanded Willrin's return to the capital; he refused and stayed where he was, gathering huge support in Skodart as a champion of the islanders' rights. In his anger, the Rampartlord tutored his second son in all the things that a Rampartlord needed to know about ruling . . .

Vincen may have been popular in Dustelrampart and the main island where people knew him, but on the outlying islands, people looked to Willrin. It was clear that no matter which son the Rampartlord favored, there would be trouble. Had he been a wiser man, he might have preempted revolt by good rule and diplomacy, but he was a tyrant with little idea of governance except absolute obedience to his rule.

The Keepers, of course, supported him. Tor and Flame were right: Keepers hated any thought of revolution or change, believing that such things were destabilizing. They sent Keeper sylvs as advisor-warriors and sold the Rampartlord the weapons he needed, turning the islandom into an armed camp. The Menod, on the other hand, had a vested interest in Skodart. They had a large monastery there that was the center of much of their intellectual life. There was a huge library, a seminary, and so forth. While they strove to give the appearance of remaining neutral, the patriarchs on the island actually had a good relationship with Willrin.

The Rampartlord declared Vincen his new heir and stripped Willrin of his title of Rampartheir. Willrin declared his island and the surrounding atolls free of Dustel Island rule and named them the independent Islandom of Skodart.

The Rampartlord declared war on his elder son, and sent his younger son Vincen to subdue Skodart Island. Vincen landed on a neighboring atoll and sent a conciliatory message to his brother, reminding him of their kinship, and telling him that he had no wish to harm his childhood playmate. Vincen was perfectly willing, he said, to consider a compromise. Perhaps they could discuss the matter. On the basis of this promise, they agreed to meet on a small island offshore from Skodart, just the two of them and a couple of personal pages.

However, unbeknownst to Willrin, Vincen was planning treachery. He sent some of his troops, led by Keeper sylvs, to capture Willrin's family while he himself was meeting his brother. Using magic, they were able to do just that—except they missed one of the twins, a sylv boy named Gethelred, then aged about thirteen. They took the rest of the family: Willrin's wife, the other of the twin boys and two younger daughters. As soon as Vincen received a message on the success of the kidnapping, he attacked and slew Willrin. He then took the rest of the family back to his father in Dustelrampart. The Rampartlord put out a proclamation saying that if the missing twin, Gethelred, turned himself in, then he would spare the rest of the family.

According to Alain, Gethelred, with the help of Menod patriarchs, tried to do just that, but the ship he was on was delayed by storms and he did not make it to Dustelrampart before the deadline. His mother, twin brother and two sisters were all brutally killed and their bodies nailed to the city walls. They were the first thing that Gethelred saw when his ship eventually reached the harbor and sailed up to Dustelrampart's docks.

"And how long after that did the Dustels sink?" I asked. I was thinking to myself that these people were all Ruarth's ancestors. Perhaps Vincen was his grandfather . . . or would it be his great-grandfather?

"About ten years," Alain replied. "Gethelred escaped, by the way. The Menod hustled him back on to the ship and took him straight to Skodart. They say he went mad with grief when he saw what was done to his family . . . The Keepers and the Rampartlord launched a punitive attack on Skodart and wiped out almost all the population. It was a particularly brutal war because so many of the people on both sides were sylvs."

"Sylvmagic can't be used to kill," I said, my defense automatic.

"No, but there are so many innovative things they can do while using normal weapons. Blur their presence, sneak into places and wreak havoc, confuse with illusions. It makes for a nasty war. In the end, the population of Skodart was decimated because the Rampartlord managed to enlist many Awarefolk."

"All wars are nasty," Tor said quietly. "What's the point of the story, Alain."

"I don't have one really. Blaze was asking, that's all. I suppose the odds are excellent that, if the Dustels really were submerged by the magic of one man, then it all had something to do with that war."

"Probably only because it provided the confusion that enabled a dunmagicker to take advantage of the situation," Tor pointed out.

CHAPTER 19

AND THEN THERE WAS EYLSA . . .

The ghemph and I spent a lot of time talking while it worked on my pole. I had to lie on the floor, or sometimes tilt myself into a semi-reclining position, depending on which side Eylsa decided to tackle. It was a long job. The wood of the yoke was hard. Eylsa's claws were stronger and sharper than fingernails, but they were hardly made for this kind of work. Worse still, when the wood did split, it came away only in tiny splinters. God knows what sort of wood it was, but from our point of view, it couldn't have been worse.

We talked while Eylsa worked and somehow at those times I was actually glad of the darkness. It made me less conscious of the physical differences between us.

In the darkness, I couldn't see the ugly flat face, the grayness, the hairlessness; in the darkness, even a ghemph seemed human. In the darkness even a halfbreed could have innate dignity. While we were both prisoners in that hell, it seemed important that I was aware of our similarities, not our differences.

I remember one of my first questions: I wanted to know Eylsa's gender.

That provoked a laugh. It paused in its clawing and answered, "At this precise time? I am in a period of transition. Neither one nor the other. We are all born female, Blaze, every one of us. Then, when we're about thirty, we commence to change. By forty we are wholly male. Of course, we put much less emphasis than you do on the importance of sexual differences. Young ghemphs can bear and feed young, older ones can father them and are more experienced workers, but otherwise we make no differentiation between the male and the female work tasks or lifestyle. Perhaps it would be better if you thought of me as female. It will be a few years yet before I can consider myself male."

It was just as well that Eylsa couldn't see my face. I said, finally, striving for neutrality: "That is not something that is generally known to us."

"No. We try as much as possible to disguise the differences between ghemph and human. We do not normally discuss such things with humans—it is not considered wise."

"Why not? And why is it that you are telling me?"

I did think she might refuse to answer that, but she didn't. After some consideration she said, "To begin with, I do not think you would tell others beyond the confines of this oblivion, if I were to request you to refrain from doing so—which I do. Moreover, perhaps our present unpleasant circumstances warrant a change of what is customary. And I would like you, specifically you, to have more knowledge of us. You were the first human who spoke to me as if—as if I were your equal. You wanted something from me, but you respected my refusal; you weren't even angry. You don't know how refreshing I found that."

I was assailed by guilt, remembering how unsympathetic I had felt toward all things ghemphic at the time. And I wondered about what it was like to be a ghemph, that normal politeness from a human could be so memorable.

She sighed. "It is not in ghemphic nature to be garrulous. Even now, I find it somehow *onerous* to state these things, although the darkness helps. You see, we ghemphs do not converse much even with one another. We have no need to do so. We *know*, without words. If a mother touches her young in passing, then the young one knows it is loved; it does not need to be apprised of the fact. If someone bestows something on me, I incline my head in thanks. A movement of the head, a fluttered finger: these things mean much more to us than they do to you. We leave conversation for only the most formal of occasions.

"And then, our lives are so very ordered that there is very little that needs to be discussed. We have an aversion to change. We hate uncertainties. We try to live as we have done for centuries: it is . . . necessary. We are so few, and humans are so many and despise us so much. We must be wholly predictable to survive. We must never present you humans with a threat. Thus we are unchanging, subservient, meek. Yet we must never be useless, for that could also lead to our demise as a race. And so we help to perpetuate the citizenship tattoo. We have steadfastly refused to show anyone the secret of the process, so we will never be redundant, and we have never made an illegal tattoo, not for anyone." She made a sound that might have passed for ghemphic laughter. "And that is definitely the lengthiest speech I have ever made in my life."

I considered what she had said, and the more I thought, the more appalled I was. I'd never given a thought to ghemphs before, except to resent their rigid support of the citizenship laws. Now I had a picture before me of creatures who had to live in a state of anxious uncertainty, knowing that we humans could wipe them out entirely—and that we were stupid and cruel enough to do so if we thought we'd been provoked.

I said politely, "I used to dislike you ghemphs. It always seemed to me that without you, the whole system of rigid citizenship would fall apart. Without you, people like me would find ways to circumvent the system. I still think that, but at least I know now why you do it. I can see that it isn't for some trivial reason of conservatism. I'm sorry now that I asked you for a tattoo. I didn't realize what such a request meant."

"And I'm sorry I couldn't give it to you. Could you turn your hand slightly? I want to twist the chain out of the way."

I moved, quelling a grunt of pain as she continued. "We ghemphs know exactly how iniquitous the citizenship laws are. But we lack the courage to change the system. It grieves us, it shames us, but I don't think we will ever change; you are right to despise us. In the presence of a halfbreed we can only be shamed.

"But *you* don't need the symbol of an ear tattoo to prove your worth, Blaze. You have the dignity of being the kind of person you are. No one can ever take that away from you."

Perhaps not. But citizenship laws could make it very difficult to live. I held the bitter words back. Eylsa had, after all, uttered what amounted to an apology for her whole kind and it would have been churlish to point out that an apology didn't alter anything as far as I was concerned. I changed the subject. "Where do you come from? Ghemphs I mean."

"Come from? Why, nowhere! We were here first. You humans are the ones who came from somewhere else. More than a thousand years ago . . ."

I gaped. *That* was a new concept. *We* were the interlopers, the strangers?

Tor and Alain had caught this last, and I was aware that they both turned to listen. It was a surprise to them, as well.

"How many people came?" Tor asked, fascinated. "And how did they arrive?"

"And from where?" Alain added.

"A place to the west, far, far to the west. Or should I say, from many places. There were many names . . . you would know some of them, because they named their new homes after the old: Cirkase and Breth, for example. And you came in waves . . . canoes, dhows, rafts. Fleeing what was behind you. Many of you were fiercely independent and didn't want to mix with those that came before or after. In the end, though, it was impossible not to have some contact, for trade, because each islandom is too small to produce all the things it needs.

"For many years you spoke of returning to your original homes once the Kelvish had gone . . . but you never did. It was one thing to sail east with the current, quite another to sail back again against it."

"Kelvish?"

She shrugged. "It meant nothing to us. We were sea people, not land people." That remark did not mean anything to me at the time; it was only many years later that I understood what she meant. But that's another story . . .

Alain gave a grunt of amazement. "Kelvish? Don't tell me all those old legends about the warrior demons of Kelvan were true? I was brought up on those! I had this old Fentower nursemaid who knew them all. 'Behave yourself, little Alain, or the Kelvish warriors will ride in on their beasts and give you bad dreams.'"

"It would explain much," Tor said softly. "I thought we started on one island and spread outward, so it always puzzled me how it developed that each island was so adamant about having its own citizenship, and not interbreeding. And I wondered too why there are physical differences, not to mention so many linguistic differences, even though we have always traded with one another."

"Linguistic differences?" I asked. "You mean things like calling porridge *muckie* in Mekaté and *scunge* in Quiller? And why the Fenlanders roll their r's and the Calmenters squeak?"

"Yes. And how all islands used different words for their walled cities: haven, fort, shield, castle, bastion, tower, citadel."

"Barbican, hold," I added. "Yeah. I never thought about all that before."

"It wasn't because we were the same and then developed differences. Just the opposite. We were originally different but are now slowly becoming the same . . ."

Alain said softly, thoughtfully, "And if there really are Kelvish who pushed people out of their original homes: how long before they come after us?"

There was a moment's still silence, then Tor gave a half-laugh. "Somehow, Alain, I think we're in enough trouble right here and now without thinking about that one! After all, it's been a thousand years."

My thoughts went off on another tangent. "Elysa, you said you were sent to find Morthred—who sent you? Do your people have some kind of central organization?"

She shook her head. I heard the movement, although I couldn't see it. "No. But if an important matter like this arises, then a message goes from community to community—a warning if you like. There has never been another such in all my lifetime. This one about Morthred is the first in over a generation.

"Once the message has been considered, those who desire to reply send suggestions back to the person who issued the original warning. It is up to that person to act on the most frequently mentioned course of action—in this case, that an attempt should be made to find Morthred, to keep an eye on what is happening, so that we would not be taken unawares by any change that he wrought. You see, we felt that a dunmagicker who ruled widely in the Isles of Glory would not care too much about citizenship laws, and even less about ghemphs."

"It was you who sent the original warning?"

"No. Ouch! Sorry—just a splinter in one of my toes. No, it

was not I. It was my grandfather, but he is too old for journeying, so I chose to go in his place."

"That must have been . . . difficult for you, if you do not like change."

She sighed. "It was. Home is always so much more comfortable. So much safer. We are staid creatures. Although, to be quite truthful, I have always been a shade more venturesome than most of my kind, a little more curious than most—all grave failings of character. And now I am finding I even have a liking for the sound of my own voice! It must be all this darkness . . . I am thirty-five years old, you know, and am coming to the end of my female years. In all that time, no male ever wanted to set up house with me. They thought I was too unpredictable. Perhaps they were right—look at where my adventuresome nature has landed me!"

"Why did Morthred have you put down here?"

"I learned too much, came too close . . . he found out and had me captured."

"But why not make a slave of you like the others?" Tor asked.

I heard the surprise in her voice as she replied. "Did you not know? He couldn't make a slave of me because ghemphs cannot be dunmagicked. We don't have Awareness quite like you Awarefolk, but no one can magick us. So he put me in here instead. The real wonder is that he didn't just kill me." She sighed again and sat back away from me. "Blaze, I am going to have to stop for a while. My claws are beginning to tear."

Still later, Eylsa told me something more about ghemphs. She said that although they were all given a name at birth, they didn't use it the way we use names. A name was only used by ghemphs to refer to others, to talk about others. They never used it to someone's face. Many ghemphs never, in fact, learned what their own name was! Eylsa had only learned hers by accident.

However, each ghemph also had what they called a spirit name. This they chose for themselves some time in their childhood. But they only ever told it to those they loved. It was a very secret name, to be used in only the closest of relationships.

There were other things Eylsa told me about the ghemphs too, but they have no bearing on this story and I don't intend to relate them now. They are secrets that are better kept.

* * *

OF COURSE, MOST OF THE TIME THAT WE
spent talking, all four of us contributed to the conversation. Our
most popular subject was the politics of the Isles of Glory, especially the relationships between the islandoms and the whole
question of Keeper influence.

Tor and Alain were united in their condemnation of the
Keeper greed, specifically Keeper sylv greed, for wealth and
power. Tor was particularly worried by what he called "increas-
ing Keeper sylv amorality." "Look at Duthrick," he said. "He's
a Councilor, one of the rulers of the Keeper Isles. As such, he's
supposed to uphold the essence of their motto 'Liberty, Equality and Right,' but what have we been watching him do just
lately? Try to find the Castlemaid so he can take her back to a
marriage she does not want. So much for liberty of choice.
Refuse to cure Flame until such time as it suited him. So much
for what is right. Be delighted to help Ransom, but only once he
found out who he really was. So much for equality." I knew he
was looking in my direction as he added, "Sylvtalent is perhaps
just as bad as dunmagic. Worse, in a way. Dunmagic at least
doesn't pretend to be anything but evil. Sylvmagic in the hands
of the Keeper ruling class is clothed in hypocrisy and is used to
put down the poor, to boost Keeper sylv wealth and power at the
expense of both their own sylv citizens and those of other islandoms as well—"

I interrupted. "You used to blame the Keepers for the ills of
the world; now you seem to be blaming the magic itself. Make
up your mind, Tor. What *is* to blame here?"

"Well . . . both. You can't separate the two. However, you
can't blame non-sylv Keepers for anything; they are just innocent pawns who suffer from Keeper sylv arrogance just as much
as people from other islandoms do. And it's not just Keeper
sylvs alone who misuse their power. All sylvs do, but there really aren't many non-Keeper ones. A few thousand I suppose,
scattered throughout all the islands—not as many as there are
ghemphs even. Deep down, I really think we Awarefolk should
aim for the end of all magic, not just dunmagic. It does more
harm than good. It is certainly what has made the Keeper Isles
and its rulers what they are."

I noted that he didn't have any suggestions as to just how we
would rid the world of something sylvs were born with—it
seemed to me you may as well decide to rid the world of big
noses, say, or buck teeth. I said, "I've never seen Flame misuse

her power. And I think this is where I should begin listing all the good things that have been done using sylvpower: the healing, the illusory dramatic arts, the—"

"Yes, yes, we know. But now that we know sylvtalent can also be subverted to dunmagic, can we be so complacent about it? There have been so many sylvtalents disappearing over the past year, only to reappear as dunmagickers."

Alain gave a grunt of assent. "He's right, Blaze. Besides, sylvmagic is power, and of latter years it seems to have become power without responsibility, power with a very dubious morality; an evil thing. At other times, it is misused in a frivolous way. I have seen sylvs change the color of their eyes to match their costumes! They fritter away their powers on such silliness, even as sylv healing is withheld from those who cannot afford to pay for it. And now, the very existence of sylvmagic is putting the whole of the Isles of Glory in danger because a dunmagicker is subverting every sylvtalent he comes across. We would be better off without it."

Eylsa, who had not said a word so far, now stopped her scraping at my yoke and gave voice to my earlier thought, "But how can you possibly aim for an end to all magic? No one knows how to rid the Isles of dunmagic—the sylvs have been trying for generations—let alone rid the Isles of sylvmagic."

"Perhaps if teaching the talented how to use their powers was made illegal—" Alain suggested.

I was scornful. "And drive it underground? Anyway, they'd never agree to that in the Keeper Isles."

Such conversations went on for hours, but of course we resolved nothing. I do remember Tor saying toward the end that, if he ever got out of this oblivion and free of Morthred, he was going to devote the rest of his life to finding a way to curb Keeper power and ridding the Isles of *all* magic. I thought it was a dream and said so.

Mind you, I *had* altered my views. There had been a time when I would have considered the very thought of curbing Keeper power not only impractical, but unjust. True, I'd never liked Duthrick, but I had admired sylvs since I'd first laid eyes on them around The Hub. And now, although I wasn't quite as adamantly anti-Keeper and anti-sylvmagic as Tor and Alain were, what had happened on Gorthan Spit up to that point had certainly wrought a change in my attitudes.

Tor, of course, had been aiming for such a change almost

from the moment he had first met me—and desired me. He was a far-sighted man, Tor Ryder.

And we all know now just who was right in the long run. That gutter-born cynic, Blaze Halfbreed, was not nearly as perceptive as she liked to think.

Letter from T. iso Tramin, Lecturer (Second Class), Mithodis Academy of Historical Studies, Yamindaton Crossways, Kells, to Researcher (Special Class) S. iso Fabold, National Department of Exploration, Federal Ministry of Trade, Kells.

Dated this day 47 /1st Double/1793

Thank you, Fabold, for letting me see these papers before publishing, and before what promises to be yet another fascinating presentation to the Society. I did so enjoy your first talk on the Isles of Glory. Don't be upset by some of the harsh remarks made by the old-school ethnographers who prefer looking at bones to hearing oral history! These fuddy-duddies will have to move over for the new schools of thought . . .

And what a fascinating subject you found for your first set of interviews! An extraordinary woman. May I say that your admiration for this old dame of the Dustels came through in every word. It is, however, just as well you censored some of what she said! The delicate ears of the ladies in the audience would have burned red had they been privy to all that went on in your conversations with the formidable firebrand. I sometimes think it was a mistake to allow the ladies to sit in on the Society's public meetings . . . But I digress.

Of course, you are right in what you surmise in the note you sent over with the papers. The Kells moved out of the Contranshan Plains from the year 302 to the year 719, in successive waves. This exodus was prompted by two factors: the need for arable well-watered land as the Contranshan Plains became progressively drier; and the opportunity provided when explorers opened up the passes across the Picard Mountains. The fertile, well-watered Picard coastal areas beyond were ideal for agrarian settlement. The fact that these numerous coastal valleys and off-shore islands were already inhabited by seagoing peoples of Picard did not, I'm afraid, count for much with our unpleasantly aggressive ancestors.

Because the Plains-born Kells were more technologically advanced, with better weapons (both the long bow and the crossbow had already been invented), and because they had horses and knew how to ride them, the coastal peoples—with none of these advantages—had little chance of resistance. Many of them laid down their arms and ended up as serfs. Over many, many generations the differences between original inhabitant and invader blurred, and if you ask someone like me who was born in Lower Picard, I can't for the life of me tell you whether my ancestors were Kells or Picards.

I am afraid that I am totally unaware of any stories about Picards who fled overseas and ended up half a world away in the Glory Isles. It seems a little farfetched . . . When I say they were seafaring people, it was more that they plied the coast, fishing mainly, and that they conducted some sea-trade between the different estuarine ports. They were not ocean-going explorers.

It is probably true, though, that there were many different racial or ethnic groupings among the Picards. Early Kellish commentaries seem to indicate that the people of one Picard coastal valley were often quite culturally and linguistically different from the next, and that the differences were sometimes accentuated by physical variations.

You ask about the words "Kelvan" and "Kelvish." They do occur in one early Kellish work of literature, The Annals of Tyn Weswinter. They seem to have been used interchangeably with Kells and Kellish. Coincidence? I don't know.

There are some other facts which would back the case for believing that Glory Isles people came from Picard. Firstly, the scattering of words familiar to us that crop up in your Isles of Glory. Our present Kellish language is a meld of the original Contranshan Plains' Kellish, which dominates, and Picard languages and dialects. If your theory is correct, then the language of the Glory Isles could well be an amalgamation of the original Picard tongues. We would therefore have many words in common, as you note in your letter to be the case. Secondly, there are indeed some place names which seem familiar . . . Mekaté for example. There is a Makatay in Valley Picard—I was born there! In truth, migrating peoples often give place names to their new homes that echo the places they have left behind.

And so, although it seems amazing that people, using small fishing boats, which was all that was available to them, should have launched themselves on to the Sol-witch Current and traveled across the Vast Sea, I am, reluctantly, coming to believe it. I shall write a paper on the matter.

But who in the hell were these ghemphs? And where are they now?

Do send me some more of these interviews. I am fascinated!

Yours,
Treff iso Tramin

P.S. Who was that stunning beauty on your arm at the presentation? If that's the attention you field ethnographers get, I am going to change my profession! I spoke to her briefly afterward, in the company of her parents, of course, and had the impression that she secretly admired Blaze's independent soul. She's not one of these outrageously liberated women who believes in female franchise, is she?

CHAPTER 20

IT SEEMED TO TAKE ABOUT THREE DAYS, as far as we could judge the passage of time, for Eylsa to whittle down my yoke enough for us to try to slip it through the bands. Even that wasn't an easy job. I had to ram one end of the pole against the wall, again and again, until finally it began to shift and the others could pull it free. It would be nice to say that with the removal of the yoke the relief was immense; in actual fact I was in agony. Alain tried to massage some normality back into my shoulders and arms, doing his best to dodge the sores that had been rubbed there, but I was in excruciating pain from cramp and tortured muscles for hours.

The bands now dangled from the manacles still around my wrists but I wasn't going to complain; those remaining irons were nothing compared to that hellish yoke.

Eylsa's claws must have been ragged and aching by then, but she never said anything. In fact no sooner was I free, than she turned her attention to Tor's pole.

Poor Tor. He had more days to endure, trussed up like that, not knowing all the while if we were going to get him free in time to attempt some sort of escape, or if Morthred would send for us first to find out what had happened to Flame. I know it was always in my mind that, if Flame had still been under than dunspell of subversion, she would have been fawning at

Morthred's feet by now. When she hadn't turned up on sched-
ule, what action had he taken? I'd thought he would haul me up
out of there to find out what was going on, but no one came near
us except to deliver the food. Then it occurred to me that perhaps not as much time had gone by as we had first thought. We
had no way of telling.

Tor must surely have had the same thoughts, but he remained
as calm as a rock-pool in the sun. Nothing ruffled his temper. He
must have been in terrible pain, yet he could still joke about his
situation. I had the same thoughts again and again. He was a very
special person. I didn't deserve him. Which made me about the
luckiest halfbreed on all the islandoms . . .

We did discuss the idea that I should escape first, of course,
and then return with tools to free Tor, but the risk of being
caught was high. Rightly or wrongly, we decided that Tor and I
had to make our escape together for the best chance of success.

I tried to help release him from the yoke. While Eylsa
worked on one end, I did a bit at the other, using the edge of a
band from my pole to rub away at the wood, but in the dark I
was never sure how much I was achieving.

We talked a lot about just how we were going to effect our
escape from the oblivion, tossing ideas around like children
toss the shell of a dead horseshoe crab in a game of catch. Just
how was it going to be possible to get out of the trapdoor, way
above our heads, right in the middle of the room? Alain insisted
that, however we did it, he was to be left behind. He was too
sick, he said, to escape anywhere. In our hearts we knew he was
right: his presence would have hindered us too much. If we
were successful, we would come back for him; if we weren't,
well, he wouldn't be much worse off than he was just then.

After Tor was free we waited another day or so for him to re-
cover, then we put the final plan we had agreed upon into operation. We waited until food and water had been delivered, then I
climbed into a sitting position on Tor's shoulders and felt for the
trapdoor, but, as we had expected, it was too high. The others
passed one of the poles up to me and I pushed upward with that.
The pole hit the ceiling, and with a little bit of maneuvering I
managed to push the trapdoor open with it. The fools had been
so confident of our helplessness they hadn't bothered to keep it
bolted. Opening it made no difference to the darkness, though.

I positioned the top of the pole against one corner of the trapdoor and steadied the other end against my shoulder, bracing it

as firmly as I could. The rest was up to Eylsa. She sheathed her claws and climbed up Tor and then onto my shoulders, where she supported herself for a moment by leaning on the pole. Poor Tor; with only minor help from Alain, he had to bear the weight of us all. It was fortunate that he was such a large man and that ghemphs are light-framed. Eylsa mounted the pole, using her claws this time. A few seconds later her whisper came back through the darkness; she had made it. She pulled the pole away from me and I jumped down. Tor collapsed in relief. I think both of us were shocked to realize how weak our imprisonment had made us.

Our original intention was that I should then try to follow Eylsa. If I stood up on Tor's shoulders and she reached down to help me, it should have been possible. However, when we tried it, Tor wobbled so much I couldn't get my balance—we were both hampered by the fact that our legs were still closely shackled. In the darkness, Eylsa could not find my outstretched hand and in the end we gave up. After some discussion it was agreed that Eylsa wait for the guard to bring the food, knock him out and then we could use his rope to climb out of our prison.

Eylsa—rather unhappily, I thought—closed the trapdoor on us.

It occurred to me that ghemphs had a long history of non-aggression toward humans, and I wondered aloud whether she would really be able to bring herself to attack whoever it was that brought us the food. Tor groped for me in the darkness and put an arm around my shoulders to give a squeeze of reassurance. Alain said, "Have faith. The cause is a just one, and God will help her."

I felt Tor tighten, as though the words annoyed him, but he didn't say anything. I thought cynically that what Alain had said was typical of the Menod; when they had made up their minds that they were right, they were sure that God was on their side and no amount of defeat and tragedy would change their thinking. You had to admire the sheer stubbornness of their faith, if nothing else.

I was so sure that Tor also found Alain's certainty exasperating, that I was startled when he said, "Would you give us your blessing, Syr-patriarch?" His request was formal and sincere, but still I couldn't believe that he thought a Menod blessing would make one whit of difference to our success. I guessed he must have requested it more for Alain's sake than ours. It would give the patriarch comfort to know that we, and our enterprise, had been blessed. Alain was the one who would have to sit in this hellish place and do nothing more than wait . . .

Tor pulled me down beside him so that Alain could place his hands on our heads. "In the name of the gentle one, God the Creator, we ask for a blessing . . ." he began. I can't remember exactly how it went; such prayers always bored me. They still do. I recall that it was long, and while Alain made his convoluted plea for divine intervention and salvation, I reflected on what a hypocrite I was, kneeling there. Still, if Tor thought it was going to help Alain, I was willing to go along with it. It did occur to me, though, that Alain was no fool. He must have known how I felt.

Those last few hours were hell. I felt all the frustration of a lobster trapped in a wickerpot. Tor, of course, seemed perfectly relaxed. He chatted and joked with Alain as though we were all sitting calmly in some tavern in the Stragglers. We were lucky, I suppose. It could have been several days before more food was delivered, but I rather think it was only a matter of hours later that the trapdoor was thrown open and the rope came snaking down. Ordinarily we were supposed to attach the drinkskin so that it could be pulled up and refilled, but before any of us could move, something heavy came hurtling down after the rope, to hit the floor with a rather nasty thud. Luckily the three of us had been sitting back around the edges of the room.

Alain groped with his hands to see what had fallen. "Oh, merciful God," he said.

This was followed by an anguished whisper from Eylsa, above us. "Great Whirlstorms . . . I didn't mean . . . That was the guard! I didn't know he'd fall in when I hit him. I couldn't really see—the light hurt my eyes."

"Bring the candle to the edge of the trapdoor," Tor told her calmly.

A single flame high above our heads was hardly Gorthan Spit at midday, yet it had us all blinking with pain. Alain bent over the man. "He's dead." He sounded bleak.

I looked up to the ghemph. "Don't worry about it. It's a subverted sylv, not a slave." I'd seen the sylv colors under the red dunmagic, both beginning to fade in death. I turned my attention to searching the body for anything we could use.

Alain glared at me. "He was human, and his death is deserving of your regret."

"No," I said harshly. "He was better dead." I added inanely, "And if he were himself, he would tell you that. Confound it, he wasn't carrying anything useful."

Alain looked shocked at my callousness. "How can you think of that now?" he asked and bent his head to murmur the prayers for the deceased, something I've always thought was a totally useless procedure. Even if there was a heaven, the man's soul was either there or it wasn't; no prayers from the living could possibly change its destination.

"Is the rope tied?" Tor asked.

"I'm doing it now," Eylsa replied. "I just hope it's strong enough to hold you."

"You go first," Tor said to me and I did as he asked. Once again my weakness shocked me. A simple rope climb, that would once have been child's play, had become an effort.

Tor didn't follow immediately. He stayed to say something to Alain and then the two men embraced. Not for the first time I had the feeling that the patriarch and the Stragglerman knew each other better than either of them had ever said.

I put a hand on Eylsa's arm. She was trembling. "Don't let it bother you."

"It is one of our strictest rules—no human may be harmed by any action of ours."

"Dunmagickers," I said practically, "are not human. They certainly do not practice humanity. Not even subverted sylv dunmagickers. The man he was has been long dead." I reached down to help Tor up through the trapdoor. "That man did not choose to be a dunmagicker, it's true, but he was no less evil than Morthred for all that. You have put him out of his misery, Eylsa. You did him a favor."

Tor, now standing beside me, nodded in agreement. "She's right."

"Great Trench below!" I exclaimed, getting a good look at him for the first time in days. He looked awful—bruised, dirty, wretched—and I'd never seen him with the beginnings of a beard before. "You look like one of those Breth Island hermits!"

"Probably smell like one too. Mind you, you should take a look at yourself some time." He grinned at me. "God, it's good to be out of that place!" He bent down to lower the food and water, and the candle, through the trapdoor. When we'd finished, Tor knelt at the edge of the hole and looked down on Alain's upturned face. "Good-bye, my friend. One of us shall be back for you—"

The frail voice came echoing up: "And may God walk with you, lad. With you all."

Tor closed the trapdoor and we were once more in the dark.

"Somehow," I said softly, "I have the feeling that Syrpatriarch Alain Jentel doesn't altogether approve of me."

I sensed Tor's grin. "You're too godless for him, my love. And he thinks you're a bad influence on me." He shrugged. "It's a failing of most patriarchs, alas. They are so damned good themselves that they manage to make us lesser mortals feel like eternal sinners without a hope of getting even a peek in heaven's door. Come, let's get out of here."

We felt our way across to the door and opened it up. There was light outside, dim daylight filtering in through windows somewhere ahead. We were playing it by ear from there on. We had no plan. It was just as well, because anything we'd contemplated would never have eventuated anyway.

We crept (Tor and I didn't have much choice about creeping, since we were still shackled about the ankles) down the passageway looking and smelling like three slum-dwelling rats. The room at the end was a torture chamber of some kind, built mostly underground, with the windows high up just under the ceiling. It was filled with all the despicable paraphernalia of torture, but there was no one there. At one end there was an open-hearth fireplace—at the moment unused—built at waist level, with a large chimney above. "The bastards," Tor muttered, looking around. "The utter bastards." He picked up a hammer and chisel. "Maybe we can remove these damn irons," he said. "Come here, Blaze, and let's have a try." I was only too happy to oblige. It took us a while, but eventually both of us were free of our manacles and shackles.

The relief was enormous. I began to feel human again as I flexed my arms and legs, feeling at last the returning strength.

"Weapons," I said and picked up a pair of long-handled pincers. Their purpose was probably to take hot coals out of the fire. Tor, with a little less enthusiasm, helped himself to something that looked like a cross between a roasting spit and a sword, and held on to the hammer as well. Eylsa looked with distaste at everything that was available, then went over to the fireplace where there were several long-handled pokers and morosely picked up one. She didn't say anything; being free seemed to have put an end to her loquacity.

I was still looking for something more useful than the pincers when the door swung open—not the one we had come through, but one on the other side of the room—and we were fairly caught.

I felt we were all frozen, like tadpoles caught in pond ice after a sudden cold snap. Although I suppose it didn't take more than several seconds before the room exploded into action, in that brief moment of stillness, I was aware of so much.

The first person into the room was Flame.

I felt as if I'd been hit in the throat and punched in the stomach at one and the same time. *Flame!* Morthred *did* have her. Why? *How?* She was as good as dead. No, worse. *Shit!*

She was accompanied by Domino, now able to walk, although he was dragging a leg. He had a proprietary hand on her arm and was laughing at something she'd said. And she—she was smiling down at him, those beautiful blue eyes of hers sparkling like sea-wet periwinkles glistening in the sun. There were four other dunmagickers with them, at least one of whom was the genuine article, but it was Flame who had all my attention.

She was dressed immaculately in clothes I hadn't seen her wear before. I've never been one for noticing what other women wear, but even I saw that the material matched her eyes perfectly. She looked lovely. Regal. As though she belonged in some royal court somewhere. Come to think of it, it was the first time I had seen her wear a dress of any kind. It had long sleeves and she had built herself a sylvmagic arm to replace the one she had lost. Dunmagic red whispered along her skin, mixed in with sylv silver-blue.

I was confused.

What in God's name had happened?

Thoughts rushed through my head, one hard after the other. (Fortunately, thinking on my feet had always been one of my talents. Sometimes it was when I had more time to mull things over that I made my worst mistakes.) My first thought was she couldn't have been subverted; we had cut off the spell along with her arm, and Duthrick, who could see the end result of a dunspell even better than I, had confirmed it was gone. Then: but Morthred's had time to subvert her again. Then: but she would have killed herself if that had happened. Then: not if he'd stopped her. Then: but if that was so, what in all the islands is that sylvmagic I can still see? None of the other subverted sylvtalents showed so much sylv color . . .

Then I knew what must have been the truth, and my heart dived. An anguished *"No!"* tore from me almost at the same time as we all moved.

Flame turned to Domino and drawled, "Why, it seems that your prisoners have escaped, my friend. How *can* you have been so careless?"

Domino's hand dropped to his sword, and the dunmagicker behind him sent a spell zipping across the room to splash harmlessly against my chest. One of the others tried something similar with Tor. He sent his hammer hurtling through the air just as Flame said, "Dunmagic is not going to hurt *them;* they are Awarefolk."

Tor's hammer smashed into the face of the dunmagicker and he died on the spot. It seemed the Lance of Calment had surfaced in Tor once again. I guessed that the torture chamber had upset him.

I was already into the fray with my pincers, holding them splayed open as I lunged forward. I brought up a foot against Flame and sent her tumbling against Domino, who now had his sword out. Then I was upon the dunmagicker behind him. He hadn't yet drawn his weapon when I snapped the pincers together on either side of his face—hard. He screamed and raised his hands to his head—a mistake, because it enabled me to go for his sword.

I had it out of its scabbard, but never did get to do anything constructive with it. The last of the subverted sylvs had been shouting for help and now help arrived in the form of nine or ten others. In the confined space I went down under an onslaught of clutching hands and striking fists. I was dimly aware of Domino shouting helpfully, "Don't kill them, don't kill them!" and didn't know whether to be glad or sorry. Then both Tor and I were on our backs on the floor, surrounded by a ring of sword blades, all pointing at us.

"This is becoming a habit," I muttered to Tor.

"One I'd break if I knew how," he said in a disgusted voice.

I heard Flame's drawl: "How very amusing, Domino! I had no idea that when you suggested we go and get the prisoners it would be so exciting!" The periwinkle-blue eyes that looked

down on me contained none of the bleakness of those of her fellow one-time sylvs. Hers were triumphant glitters, as hard as
the shells they resembled.

I didn't want to think of her.

Instead I thought: Where in all the islands is Eylsa?

CHAPTER 21

THEY TOOK US TO MORTHRED'S MOCK-UP of a throne room, really not much more than a dining hall.

There I was shackled once more, arms and legs spread-eagled against the wall at one end, while Tor was similarly chained at the other end. Fortunately they hadn't actually suspended us—we both had our feet on the floor. That was unintentional, I think; because both of us were above average height, the rivets for the shackles were too low on the wall for us to dangle from them.

It was growing dark and slaves lit torches on the side walls that stretched between us. Others stacked the long tables down the center of the room with food: no sign here of the unappetizing staples of smelly shrimp paste and seaweed that we'd had in the oblivion. There was fresh lobster and grilled ocean trout; crispy fried seahorse, sea-cucumber stuffed with crab meat, and cockles braised in oyster sauce. There was kelp-lettuce salad sprinkled with fish-roe, and squid stewed in its own ink and flavored with algae spices. I was hungry just looking at it all.

When all was ready, Morthred led his court into dinner. He'd used dunmagic to make his deformed left side match the rest of him. Through the blur of his dunspell I could just make out how he would appear to everyone else except Tor. His body was straight, his limbs normal, his face handsome but very ruggedly so—its angular planes were like pieces of sun-baked granite. He escorted Flame, his good right arm intertwined with her illusory left one. That was enough to tell me he didn't know her hand did not exist. He would not have held her that way had he known she could not feel his hold—indeed there *was* no hold. He gripped nothing but empty magic. For all his great powers, he lacked Awareness. He could not see the silver-blue of her magic, and the illusion was as real to him as her own flesh and blood.

She had changed her clothing. The dress she now wore was red and it was a little too large for her. The neckline plunged almost to her waist at the front and the way she played with the folds of it told me she was self-conscious about wearing it.

He led her before me, smugly triumphant. "You see?" he mocked. "All you strove for is now mine, Blaze Halfbreed." He dropped Flame's hand and stroked that lovely golden hair of hers instead. Then he let his hand trail down her body, touching her insolently and intimately. She shuddered with involuntary distaste and he laughed. "She doesn't like it, does she? She knows how I plan to enliven my nights. She knows it well, don't you my precious?" He turned his attention back to me. "She's a dunmagicker now, and she'll never be anything else. And because it's *my* dunmagic power that has subverted her, she will always be subservient to my will . . . she can only obey. You would have liked her to be your bedmate, wouldn't you? Perhaps if you're a good girl, I may let you watch one day."

I didn't know whether to be glad that he had mistaken my sexuality and therefore didn't know of my love for Tor, or to be appalled that I might have to watch what he did to Flame, or to be sickened even to contemplate what he had already done to her . . . How long had she been in Creed? What had she endured? It might have been better to have been the object of his attentions myself—but there was no likelihood of that. He did not desire me; I was too large and I was one of the Awarefolk. Come to think of it, when Janko had looked at me his leer had always been one of mocking insolence rather than lust.

He turned to Domino who was standing at his side. "You let this halfbreed escape again, and I'll feed *you* the blood-demons."

Domino gave me a hate-filled look. "What do you want done with her, Syr-master?"

"If you want her for the night, take her—but as she is, understand? She's not to be unchained." He looked at me, his twisted mouth vicious. "I think I know how best to hurt her kind.

Tomorrow morning put her in the blowhole and leave her there for a week or two. Alone. Lets give her time . . . to think about what we're going to do to her."

"And Ryder?"

"Cut out his tongue first and then his balls. Blind him and put him among the slaves. That should be enough to curb his activities, eh? Show him to Blaze when you've finished with him. I want her to see what happens to her friends."

Flame's eyes lit up and she ran the tip of her tongue over her lips in a sickening gesture of a dunmagicker's perverted lust. "Let me work on Ryder," she said. She turned to look at him where he was chained, not so far away that he couldn't hear every word that was spoken. "He used to be a friend of mine. I do so like to show my friends how I've changed."

Morthred roared with laughter. "Of course, of course!" he said. "Let that be your reward for the pleasure I shall have tonight." That wiped the smile off her face, as he had intended. Morthred wasn't a fellow who believed in his underlings becoming *too* happy.

He turned away and led his party of dunmagickers to the table.

The dinner seemed endless.

Tor and I were not, of course, fed at all. When the hall was emptied of its diners, Domino came to gloat. He stood facing me, staring up, his hands on his hips, looking like a belligerent crab. "You hear what the Syr-master said, eh?" he asked.

I returned his gaze calmly enough. I was fairly certain that he would not act on Morthred's suggestion: he found me too repulsive. I asked, "Are you going to get me down from here first?"

"Not likely, is it?"

"Then you had better get yourself a box to stand on, little man, because there's no way you're tall enough to reach what you want here. That would take a *real* man."

I thought he was going to run me through there and then. His sword was in his hand and his face was red with fury.

Tor hurriedly intervened. "You kill her, and Morthred will have you for breakfast. Toasted." Then he added in a flat voice that was deadly in its menace: "In fact, if you touch her at all, Dominic Scavil of Hethreg Cove, you'll have to watch your back for the rest of your life. No matter where you hide, no matter how far you go, I will find you." Domino looked shaken, whether because Tor knew his full name and his home town (*how,* for heavens sake?) or because of the nature of the threat, I couldn't tell.

I closed my eyes in annoyance. We had agreed not to show the bastards we cared too much about each other.

"Fat lot you'll be able to do 'bout it," Domino mocked, turning on him. "Tomorrow you'll have no balls, 'n no eyes, 'n no tongue even. You won't have nothing left to pleasure the ladies with, and even less to trouble me."

"Don't forget I'm Syr-aware, my little man," Tor said calmly. "We Awarefolk are not like others, and it doesn't do to forget it. Touch her, and one day I'll find you and carve you up into little pieces, even if I have to crawl on hands and knees and sniff you out like a dog to do it."

There was something about that tall Stragglerman of mine that could be deathly chilling; a hint of ruthless drive that he usually kept sheathed. I'd had glimpses of it from time to time whenever he had spoken of Keeper sylvs, but now it rimed both his stare and his voice. He looked and sounded dangerous. Even if Domino had originally had any desire for me, I think it would have vanished with Tor's words.

He turned away and shouted for guards. When two subverted sylvs, both males, came in answer to his summons, he gestured at us. "You are to guard them both tonight, understand?" Then he turned on his heel and limped out of the hall.

I eyed the two ex-sylvs, both Keepers, cautiously.

They looked at me without interest. They refused to be drawn into conversation but they did stay, and they did stay awake, so Tor and I were not free to speak. There was so much I wanted to say to him, and no way I could say it. I could only hope that he already knew all that I wanted to tell him . . .

I actually slept a little that night. I worked out a way to balance my body so that I was just comfortable enough to doze.

There was little else to do. I could worry about what had happened to Eylsa. I could worry about what hell Flame was enduring. I could worry about whether Alain was safe. I could worry about the blowhole. I could worry about what was going to happen to Tor the next day.

Tor. *Cut out his tongue first . . .*

It was easier to sleep than to think.

Dawn came far too soon.

* * *

I HAD NO CHANCE TO SAY GOOD-BYE TO
Tor. I was taken down first and led away. Neither Domino nor
Morthred was there, but presumably it was on their orders that I
was led outside. I was hungry, thirsty and in desperate need of a
privy, but no one took any of those needs into account.

They took no risks: I had my hands tied behind my back
with rope, and there were no fewer than eight subverted sylv
guards surrounding me, all with drawn swords. I was gaining a
reputation, it seemed. I even heard one of them mutter about the
only woman he'd ever come across who frightened the shit out
of Domino. It might have been funny, except I wasn't in a mood
to appreciate it.

They took me quite a long way from Creed village, up the
coast to the west where the plateau of rocks thrust out into the
sea, high above the water, far too high ever to be covered. The cliff
face was exposed though, and the sea thundered against it as if
it found the presence of stone on this otherwise flat and sandy
island a challenge to be conquered.

I wondered what the hell these bastards were intending to do
with me.

I'd seen blowholes before, in the Cirkase Islands. They have
a lot of rocky coast, and there is a place where the sea crashes
against a low platform of rock, driving water through underground passages with such a force that the ground trembles.
Then, with a great whoosh, the water shoots up through inland
holes so that you'd think there were whales beneath the
rocks . . .

Gorthan Spit's blowhole was a poor imitation. There was an
underground passage, it's true, but the blowhole itself—some
twenty paces or more wide—was far too broad and deep for the
water to "blow." It just welled up and then drained down again.
The lip of the hole was some ten paces or more above the high-
est level of the water. The hole itself was more or less circular
and the sides were sheer and slick with spray and green algae.
Anyone who had the misfortune to fall in would never be able
to climb out again.

I took one look and started to protest. "Hey, wait a moment—you're not supposed to kill me." I tried to back off from
the edge, but one of the men grabbed my arm. "Put me in there,
and I'll die of thirst and starvation, not to mention being battered to death on the rocks."

One of the guards laughed without mirth. "You? Not you!

Last man we put down there lasted six weeks, and he couldn't even swim. You'll get fed, every low tide. Water too." He lifted his sword, slashed the rope that tied my hands and gave me a shove from behind.

I clutched his coat with both hands. I curled my fingers into the weave and dug in. For a moment the two of us teetered on the edge, my feet slipping, his arms flailing. Then one of the others grabbed him to stop him following me over the edge. Still I wouldn't let go. Yet another guard tried to uncurl my fingers and another, not so sensible, gave me a further shove toward the edge. Then, suddenly, I was flying through the air clutching an empty coat.

I hit the water, back first, the shock driving the air from my lungs. I came up whooping.

When I could breathe again, I shook a fist up at them while they stared at me over the rim of the hole. If they had been true dunmagickers they would have laughed. Perhaps that was the most horrible thing of all; they didn't do anything. They just looked, and my anger turned to pity. I think it was then that I was, for the first time in my life, glad that I had not been born a sylvtalent. Nothing at all was worth the risk of being like one of those poor subverted sylvs with their lack of passion and their almost puzzled cruelty. They were like children doing wrong but too young to understand the iniquity of what they did.

They went away without another word.

I turned my attention to my predicament.

It wasn't as bad as I'd thought it was going to be. I found I could actually touch the ground each time the water ebbed away, even though I judged it to be high tide at the time. It was harder to keep from being washed into the wall of the hole when the water swept in and out; I had to be vigilant to stay in the center of the pool. It would be even harder in the dark, I knew.

I tried to work out how long it would be before low tide and a meal, but the tide timetables were especially complicated in double moon months and I wasn't familiar enough with Souther Islands to know the patterns.

I tried not to think of Tor.

It was remarkably easy not to think of him, because it wasn't long before I had troubles of my own to consider. I felt agonizing pain in my hand—a pain that was all too familiar. A blood-demon had settled into the rawness on my wrist. I screamed and

wrenched it out. I almost threw it back into the water in my revulsion, then realized that it would just find me again. I hesitated, holding the damn thing in my other hand where it didn't
even raise a tickle. I looked around me, and almost died. The
water was alive with the bastards. I howled, *"Shit!"* which really didn't help much. I tried not to think how many cuts I had:
the old ones that Sickle had made were almost healed, but there
were still ulcers on my back and arms from the yoke, raw skin
on my legs from the shackles—God *damn* Morthred!

I thrashed around to scare the demons off, but I knew I
would soon exhaust myself doing that. In the end, I started to
collect the creatures, stuffing them into the sleeve of the jacket I
had unintentionally removed from the guard. I tied a knot in the
bottom of one sleeve, and every time I caught one of the beasts,
I stuffed it down through the armhole and gripped the sleeve so
it couldn't get out again. I wasn't quick enough to snare all of
them in time. Several managed to wriggle under my clothing
and settle on to my back. Every second that passed before I
could prize them off was unmitigated hell. Still, by the time
the sea was washing around my ankles, I had a sleeve full of
the things, and no idea of what I was going to do next. There
were still more of them and even if the hole dried out entirely, it
wouldn't worry them. They could move across rock as fast as
through water, and they homed in on cuts like a trained Fen Island lurger hunting swamp shrimps.

I thought of trying to throw them, one by one, out of the
hole, but if I missed, then they'd just fall back in. And even if I
did get them on to the lip of the hole, they might very well have
wriggled back in.

Finally, when part of the bottom of the hole became dry at
low tide, I knew I had the solution to my problem. I found a
loose stone and used it smash the blood-demons, one by one,
into little pieces against the rocky floor of my prison. I'd never
before found such satisfaction in killing as I did then.

Once most of the water had gone, I set about clearing the
place of the creatures altogether. I overturned rocks, searched the
pools, looked under the lumps of seaweed and found, as well as
blood-demons, the remains of at least two people, probably more.
There were bones everywhere, bleached white by sun and sea.

In the end, though, I was fairly certain that I had cleared the
area of the bastards. When I sat very still for a time in a final attempt to lure any lurking ones out into the open, I was unmolested.

Only after that did I feel free to look at other things. I examined the sides of the hole and attempted to climb out, but not even a ghemph could have got up that sheer face. It was slimy and as smooth as eelskin, no cracks, no crannies, quite impossible to grip. Worse still, there was an overhang at the top.

I hadn't done much else when my jailers, two of them, arrived back with food and water. They looked down on me without compassion. One of them yelled, "Morthred wants to know how you like the blood-demons?"

I didn't reply.

"He also wants to tell you that your Cirkasian friend is enjoying her task!"

My heart beat faster but I didn't move.

Two bundles, both well wrapped in a tangle of dried seaweed so that they didn't split when they hit the bottom, came tumbling down to splat into wet sand. Their job done, the guards disappeared. I tried not to think about what they had said.

There was a drinkskin of water, most of which I drank immediately. I needed it badly by then. There were also the staples of Gorthan Spit: dried fish, shrimp paste and cooked seaweed. As a meal, I'd had better. I ate more sparingly than I had drunk.

I had barely finished when I heard another sound from above. I looked up and saw Eylsa peering over the rim of the hole. She drew back her lips in what she probably imagined was a grin; she was trying to show me how glad she was to see me in a way that she thought I would recognize, but she made a bad job of it. Smiles did not come naturally to ghemphic faces. Still, I had never been so happy to see the ugly flat features of her breed before.

I smiled back and raised a hand in salute.

"There was someone guarding you back there, did you know?" she asked. I hadn't, but I supposed it made sense. Morthred wasn't going to let me sit out in the open without someone around to make sure no one found me. "I'm afraid I've killed him," she continued. "It's odd how easy it is when you're a ghemph—he didn't expect it, you see. And humans always forget about the claws . . . That's two people I've killed in two days."

I didn't know what to say.

"I'll have to fetch a rope," she added. "I'll be back."

"Wait!" I shouted up at her. "Don't go back to Creed! Get away while you can—"

She grinned some more and was gone.

"Eylsa!" I yelled after her but she didn't come back. I just had to hope that she wasn't going back to Creed. What if she did, and was caught? Much better that she circle around back to the Docks and get some rope from there than risk her neck in Creed. I could wait.

Then I started to torment myself, thinking about Tor. What if I was wrong? What if . . . ? *Don't think about it, you fool.*

I sat down with a sigh. The tide showed no sign of turning yet. I remembered that in double moon months sometimes there was only one tide a day, sometimes four. This looked like being the former. I sighed again. That meant I would have to spend most of the night in the water, fending off blood-demons in the dark, I didn't have the slightest doubt that the incoming tide would bring a fresh batch of the little horrors.

I looked over at the far corner of the hole, where it dipped down on the seaward side—where the water was forced in as the tide rose. That part had never dried out; a deep pool was there still. Presumably under there somewhere was a tunnel that led out to the sea. I tried to visualize how far it was to the open water. And I wondered about the width of the tunnel.

I picked up the drinkskin and looked at it closely. It was made from the swim bladder of a seacow; it was absolutely watertight. The bag part of it narrowed to a funnel, and this had been tightly corked.

I looked back at the pool, and decided to go for a swim, or more accurately, a dive. I found the exit to the sea: here at least it was large enough for a person to enter. The water inside was surging to and fro in response to the movement of waves on the seaward side. I swam in a little way to find that it narrowed quite soon until it was more like a pipe. It was still large enough for a person, but if I entered that narrow part, I'd never be able to turn around. I'd be committed . . . the sea or nothing. And I had an idea that the swim was too far for one lungful of air, always assuming that the tunnel was wide enough for me to fit through all the way to the end. Once out in the ocean, there was the danger of being beaten to death against the rock face, and if I survived that, it would be a long swim to a beach.

All of which made the tunnel a last resort escape.

I came out of the pool and went to sit in the sun to dry out. I felt sticky with salt and wondered just how anyone could live this kind of existence for six weeks. My clothes would stiffen in the sun, and rub my skin. I wondered if it wasn't better to take them off altogether. I had just decided that if Eylsa did not come back to rescue me that day, that's what I would do, when I realized I had company again.

Ruarth.

He flew in and sat on a rock beside me.

"You tell Flame," I said coldly, "that if—*if*—we get out of this alive, I am going to personally strangle her with both hands. Get that? You tell her!"

He just looked at me. He was a mess. He hadn't preened himself for some time. His feathers were as droopy and as listless as the way he stood there, just looking. I sighed and said, more kindly, "But then I don't suppose she's listening to you any more than she'd listen to me, eh?"

He shook his head and then launched into an excited babble.

I interrupted. "I can guess what you're trying to say. And there's no need to explain—I know *exactly* what she's done, the hard-eyed Cirkasian bint, and when I lay my hands on her . . ." I sighed and looked at him. "Thanks for finding me, anyway. Is there anything else you need to tell me?"

He nodded.

I thought for a moment about what he might think I needed to know. "Flame went to see the Keepers after we were taken?"

Another nod.

"And they confirmed they are intending to attack Creed?"

Another nod.

"Good. Now I need to know when. Today?"

He shook his head and held up a foot with two claws extended.

"In two days time?" I asked, praying he didn't mean in two weeks. "The day after tomorrow?"

He nodded again.

I wished it would be sooner. What the hell was Duthrick up to, taking so long about it? Was he hoping that Janko-Morthred was going to turn up at The Drunken Plaice and that he could be dealt with there when he wasn't backed by a village full of subverted sylvs and fellow dunmagickers? But surely Duthrick would have figured out why Morthred had bothered with a waiter's guise in the first place: it was an ideal way to keep an eye on newcomers to Gorthan Docks. Anyone who was anybody would sooner or later arrive at The Drunken Plaice. Morthred, killing time until the full return of his powers, had

wanted to know what was happening throughout the Isles—
what better place to wait than an inn? But once everyone knew
he was a dunmagicker, his disguise was of no more use. Surely
Duthrick, having spoken to Flame, would realize that Morthred
wasn't going to go back.

Then I had another thought: maybe it was my disappearance
that was the problem. Duthrick had said he needed my Awareness. Perhaps, seeing that I was gone, he was going to wait until he could find another one of the Awarefolk to replace me.
Now that would be the ultimate irony—the sort of thing that
had happened too many times in my life for me to be surprised.

In the end I gave up trying to outguess Duthrick.

I continued my questioning of the Dustel. "What time is the
attack planned for? Um, dawn?" Right first time.

I thought about what information I should pass on. In the end
I told Ruarth about Eylsa and added, "Now, I need to know
what I should do if I do get out of this place today. I need to
know where Flame and Tor are. Uh, do you know what
Morthred is making Flame do to Tor today?"

He shook his head.

I told him. If it was possible for a bird to blanch, then he did.
I asked if he had seen Flame that day.

He shook his head again.

"Damn. Then I'll just wait for the ghemph and see what she
says."

Ruarth burst into a flurry of chatter and movement which
meant absolutely nothing to me. I looked at him in frustration.
Then he hopped down to the sand at my feet and began to write
with his beak. The letters were badly formed and then scuffed
about by his own feet, but I managed to make out "I go Creed
find Tor."

"Well, all right. But be very, very careful Ruarth. Tor is probably out of your reach for the time being, down in the torture
chamber with Flame and Domino. Or somewhere recovering
from what she is supposed to do to him."

He nodded.

"And Ruarth, try to get her out of there."

He didn't acknowledge that. He spread his wings in a brilliant
gleam of blue and was gone.

I wondered how he had found me. If he hadn't seen Tor, then
I thought that the most likely way was that he had overheard
some dunmagicker mention my predicament; even so, it was

clever of him to have discovered me so soon. That was one of the few things I knew for certain where Ruarth Windrider was concerned: he was bright. Otherwise, he was a mystery to me.

I trusted him, but I didn't have a clear picture of his character. How could I form an impression when I couldn't understand what he said to me, when everything had to be interpreted through Flame, who loved him? I couldn't even tell what he was thinking by his facial expression: he didn't have one! Nor could I imagine what it was like to be a human trapped in a bird's body, to have been *born* a bird.

In addition, as far as I was concerned, the kind of love Flame and Ruarth had for one another was incomprehensible. How could anyone fall in love with someone who bore a different form? Yet those two were in love in the real sense of that expression, in every way except the physical one. I had often been touched by Ruarth's concern for Flame, and there had been times when he seemed humanlike in his love, but there were other times—while eating flies, for example—when he seemed wholly avian and I had no empathy with him at all, and found it hard to imagine how Flame not only empathized, but loved.

One day, I promised myself, I would learn the Dustel's language. Then perhaps I would understand why a beauty like Flame loved a man who was a bird small enough to hold in her hand.

CHAPTER 22

THE WATER WAS BEGINNING TO SWIRL
back into the hole by the time Eylsa came back. I'd be lying if I
said I hadn't been hoping she would return quickly and get me
out of there. The whole idea of spending a night in those waters
was enough to raise the hairs on the back of my neck. In the
dark, one couldn't see the blood-demons . . .

The only trouble was that she didn't come back to free me;
she came back a prisoner. I never did discover exactly how or
where they had captured her, but I suspect that a guard sent out
to relieve the one she had killed may have seen and caught her.
She had no experience with my kind of life: the sneaking
around, the thinking ahead, taking care to look after one's own
skin before all else . . .

When I saw her, she was standing on the top of the hole between two dunmagickers—genuine ones. One of them called
out to me, grinning. "Thought you were going to be rescued, did
you? Too bad, halfbreed!" And then, with breathtaking callousness, he pushed her over the edge.

With some desperate idea of catching her I leaped up and
lunged forward, but I was too late. There was just a finger-width
of water covering the rock on which she fell; no more than that.

I will never forget the sound her body made when it hit the
rocks.

I kneeled beside her. "Eylsa . . . ?"

She had landed face down. There was blood everywhere. I gently untied the bag she wore on her back and laid it aside. I was too scared to roll her over. I was afraid of hurting her, afraid to see what she had broken.

Above me a mocking voice called down: "Thought you'd like the company, halfbreed!" I didn't bother to look up.

She was alive. She moved her head a little and groaned.

"Eylsa . . . ?"

She moved again and then spoke. "Blaze?"

"Yes. I'm here. How badly are you hurt? Can you move at all?"

She was silent so long, I would have thought her unconscious if I hadn't seen that she was making some attempt to move. Finally she said, "My face hurts. My arm is broken. I hurt inside. Help me on to my back, Blaze."

I did so, gently rolling her over. Then I saw the extent of the damage. Her nose was broken and bloodied, her teeth smashed, her arm was crooked, but none of that alarmed me as much as her labored breathing and the bright frothiness of the blood that oozed out of her mouth. Her ribs had gone through her lungs. God only knows how she managed to speak.

I looked up in rage and hate. The rim of the blowhole was deserted.

"I'm sorry," she said.

She was sorry! "Oh, Eylsa. It doesn't matter. The Keepers will be here the day after tomorrow. Someone will pull me out of here eventually. I can wait."

She nodded faintly. "I hurt, Blaze."

"Yes, I know." She would read my tone, I knew. I was telling her she was going to die. I knew what the froth at her mouth meant, the strangeness of the sound of her breathing; even Garrowyn Gilfeather and his Mekaté medications could not mend that kind of injury. A sylv might have healed the damage, perhaps, but only if they acted immediately.

Her next words told me that she understood and wanted me to know what was important while she could still talk. "Alain—I moved him. I found a ladder . . . Seemed wise. He's hiding—a store shed—on the right as you . . . enter Creed . . . from the south."

It was difficult to follow her; her speech was distorted. I wiped blood from her mouth. "I understand. That was a good idea. When they knew we had escaped, they might have taken it out on him. But where did you go? One moment you were there with us, then you weren't."

"Forgive . . . not brave. Can't fight. Chimney . . . to the roof. They hadn't seen . . . me."

I thought back to the torture room and the wide chimney above the fireplace. I nodded. "You were sensible. You couldn't have changed what happened."

"Wish I could."

"Don't talk if it hurts, Eylsa." I was kneeling beside her, wanting to take her in my arms but afraid to do so, knowing it would hurt her. Instead I held her hand.

"Want to. So much to . . . say. Looked for you everywhere. Couldn't find. Then heard slaves talking . . . followed guards . . . found you." She clutched my hand tight. "Friend."

"Yes. Always."

"Not just Eylsa. We are one. All of us. The pod."

I didn't understand that at all, but I nodded anyway.

"Want to give . . . you . . . something. Raise . . . my . . . head . . ."

I wrapped her bag inside the guard's coat and, very gently, put the bundle under her head. Her breathing eased a little when she was raised. "Want to . . . mark . . . your palm."

I had no idea of the significance of that, but I asked softly, "How?"

"With my claws . . ."

I nodded and put my right hand by her feet. I forbore from mentioning that another cut was going to cause me problems with blood-demons. It was obviously important to her, so I acquiesced. This was the way they did the ear tattoos, I knew— using their claws. I hadn't known, though, just how razor sharp those talons were until they sliced into my palm, leaving a thin trail of blood. Even as I watched, I saw that there was a liquid that dripped through the hollow groove in the center of the claw, so that each time she pricked me, a drop was left behind, mingling with my blood, seeping into the cut. She was in pain, dying, yet she moved her toe—just one—with precision and complete control until she had completed the pattern she wanted. It looked like a curled "M" with a horizontal line behind it.

"That's a bouget . . . symbol . . . water vessel . . . my people. Place your palm in my blood."

I did as she asked. I put my hand face down in the blood that had come from her mouth and now covered her neck. Our blood mingled.

The wound tingled like bubbles were breaking in the cut.

"My name . . . is Mayeen. Remember it."

"Your spirit name?"

She nodded. "Show your palm . . . to my people . . . if you need their help . . ."

I was moved. I kissed her cheek. "Mayeen," I said, "I thank you."

She spoke only once more. A few minutes later, when she reached up to touch my left earlobe, she said, "I wish I could have . . ."

"It doesn't matter," I said, and for the first time in my life, it really didn't. "It has been a privilege to know you, Mayeen."

She didn't speak again, but she was a long time dying.

I SAT ON A ROCK WITH THE WATER swirling around my ankles and Eylsa's body in my arms, stupidly reluctant to release her to the rising water. She was dead, what did it matter what happened to her body? But it did. It mattered like hell.

I still couldn't understand what had made her give me the gift of her name. What had I ever done for her? It was she who had helped me; freeing me from the yoke and then dying in an attempt to rescue me. All I had done was to treat her exactly the way I would have treated anyone else in similar circumstances. I had liked her, it's true, but as she died she made me special to her. I felt inadequate, less than I should have been. Someone had died for me, someone whose kind I had once despised, and now all I had once cared for—the search for citizenship, the wealth, the security—seemed petty. What did any of it matter? I would have given it all to have Eylsa whole and well.

The life of a ghemph was suddenly worth more than all my ambitions.

I WAS STILL SITTING THERE WHEN Morthred came. He wasn't alone: Flame was with him, and so was Tor.

I had eyes only for Tor. He was supported, or rather dragged by two armed subverted sylvs and he was naked and shackled, hand and foot. There were several other guards as well; Morthred evidently enjoyed overdoing the security measures these days. They pushed Tor to the edge of the hole so that I could see him.

I didn't move. I sat where I was, up to my waist in water, still holding Eylsa, but I couldn't take my eyes off him. He stared sightlessly outward, not looking down at me. I could see what Flame had created: eyeless sockets, bloodied mouth, mutilated manhood, but I saw it all as a sylvmagic haze blurring the reality. Only then did I know just how much I had worried that she wouldn't be able to do it, that his mutilation would be real. Only then did I acknowledge that one part of me had feared Morthred really had subverted her a second time.

I don't think I heard the mocking torments they yelled down at me. If I did, I don't remember them now. I don't even remember seeing them anymore; I, who had once not known what it was to weep, was crying too hard.

Then they went away and left me there.

WHAT HAD MADE FLAME DO SUCH AN insanely dangerous thing? To follow us voluntarily into Morthred's lair, pretending his dunmagic spell and her arm had never been removed, pretending his spell really had subverted her? To step voluntarily into the purgatory of an existence at Morthred's side, to be abused by him as he willed? One mistake, one false move and she would doom herself—not to death, but to an even worse kind of perverted, degrading slavery. Her magic was enough to make him see and feel the arm, but it wasn't enough for her to pick something up with it. The deception wouldn't have been an easy one to maintain and one tiny slip was all that was needed for Morthred to guess that her left arm was not real. And if he realized that, he would guess why it had been removed and he would know that she lied, that her subversion was a sham.

I remembered the dunmagic that played over her— Morthred's traces on her skin. I remembered the way she'd flinched when he mentioned the night. No, it wasn't purgatory; she was living in hell already. A volunteer in hell. And she had known what he would want of her . . .

He had already raped her once before. Even if he never guessed at her deception, she had known she would suffer.

She was a paradox: sometimes made of marlin horn, hard and unbreakable; sometimes as soft and as vulnerable as fish spawn tossed in the tide. She could do something so brave it gave me spine-crawls just to think of it, but she couldn't harden herself to the violations of her body. She didn't have my shell. I sensed she couldn't have done it at all if Ruarth hadn't been there to support her: she couldn't stand alone the way I could.

I looked down at Eylsa again.

And I didn't know what I had done to deserve such friends. I still don't.

I released the ghemph into the water.

I PLUCKED EYLSA'S BAG OUT OF THE SEA as it floated past and opened it. She had brought me food and water and a rope. I forced myself to eat and drink; I needed my strength to face the night ahead. The rope was useless—there was nothing around the rim of the hole that I could lasso so I could haul myself up. And doubtless there was now another guard on duty up there somewhere as well.

As I dropped the rope into the water, I caught sight of the mark that Eylsa had etched on my palm. My eyes widened; it had healed already, and there was nothing normal about the scar it had left. It was gold. It shone like the flash of a carp leaping into the sunlight.

You have noticed it, of course. It's still there—see?—just as beautiful as it was that first day. Her gift to me—the bouget, the symbol of her people—and, as I was to discover, a mark that was to ensure me the unquestioning support of all ghemphs from the Calments to the Spatts. A mark bought with her dying blood.

Note from Researcher (Special Class) S. iso Fabold, National Department of Exploration, Federal Ministry of Trade, Kells, to Masterman M. iso Kipswon, President of the National Society for the Scientific, Anthropological and Ethnographical Study of non-Kellish Peoples.

Dated this day 1/1st Darkmoon/1793

Uncle,
I did examine the "bouget" she refers to here. It is exactly as she described it: a tattoo inlaid with gold. The gold is flexible so that it does not hinder hand movements, and it must therefore be paper thin. Paradoxically, it does not seem to have worn away. (Remember, she is stating that it was done some fifty years or more earlier!) If she is telling the truth about how she came by it—which I doubt—then how can it be real gold? Yet it must be, surely, for it was not tarnished. I did ask if we could scrape away a sample for testing, but she refused in a way that made me think it would be unwise to ask a second time.

Shor iso Fabold

CHAPTER 23

THE MORNING BROUGHT STILL MORE horror.

I had wondered at the relative absence of blood-demons during the night. Only one had fastened itself to me and I'd quickly got rid of that.

In the morning the absence was explained.

Eylsa's body rolled in the swell nearby, and her face had been eaten away. What was left of her head was covered in blood-demons.

Even in death, she had kept me safe.

THE TIDE WAS GOING OUT. BY MID-morning, when Ruarth came back, I was standing knee deep. I knew the moment I saw him that something was wrong; there was an urgency to the way he flew. I held out my arm and he alighted, already crying out his agitation.

I interrupted, naming the worst possible thing I could think of: "Morthred discovered her subversion was a sham."

He nodded.

"Damn him to the Trench." I thought of Tor, sightless, tongueless, maimed—for real, this time. I thought of what Morthred might do to Flame. The first thing he would do, in

fact: put another spell of subversion into her body. "He's done it to her again." I said, my voice no more than a whisper.

He nodded. He was shivering, in shock.

Not again. "When? Just now?"

He nodded again. His claws dug into my arm, communicating his fear, his grief.

"Tor?" My tongue felt thick.

He shrugged. He didn't know.

I knew what I had to do. "Listen, Ruarth. Eylsa's dead. I'm going to try to get out of here by myself, through the tunnel where the water comes in, but I may not make it. You will have to fly to Duthrick and get him to attack today." I was already tearing a patch out of my shirt. I ripped open my finger on a piece of shell I'd rummaged from the sand beneath my feet and I wrote a message in blood on the cloth: *URGNT ATTCK TDAY.* Then I found myself frowning. Duthrick would never act on a note like that alone, just at my request, without any reason given. I squeezed some more blood out and added *TO SAVE CSTLEMD* and I signed it in the way I had always signed my personal communications to him: "B." "We'll just have to hope that Duthrick still has enough faith in my judgment, and that he still trusts me enough to take notice of this. Take it and go, Ruarth. If you can't find Duthrick, give it to anyone on the *Keeper Fair.*"

He took the cloth in both claws and I threw him into the air.

He disappeared and I readied for my dive.

I emptied both drinkskins—the one Eylsa had given me and the original one from the guards—and filled them with air, recorking them tightly. I made a cord with material torn from the guard's coat, and tied it to each drinkskin so that I could hang them around my neck. Then I breathed deeply a number of times, and dived into the mouth of the tunnel.

The first part was easy enough. The drinkskins were buoyant, but the tunnel roof stopped them from floating away. There was room enough for me to swim, and there was light.

A little farther in, the horror began. The tunnel narrowed and my body blocked off the light from behind. The light ahead was so far away it was nothing more than a murky suggestion in the darkness. I dribbled air out of my mouth and the bubbles bounced against the rock above me. I had no room to swim properly so I pulled myself along, grasping at the roof and floor. I had some help from the wash of the tide, but there was also an occasional surge of a wave that wanted to take me the opposite way.

And the tunnel thinned still further.

I was running out of air. The rock was closing in on me. I reached a narrow point and had to squeeze my body through, arms and air bladders first, then head. My hips stuck. I needed air. I eased the cork out of the first of the drinkskins and took the opening into my mouth. The sweetness of the breath I inhaled was heaven. I breathed back into the bladder: the air was too precious to waste. I was going to have to reuse it until it was too stale to be of any benefit.

I was still stuck. I kicked desperately; pushed against the rock with my feet. I moved a shade forward—and wedged myself even tighter. In a panic, I tried to move backward, and couldn't. I was trapped. The panic swelled. I didn't want to die like this, to be eaten by blood-demons . . .

I tried twisting sideways. I clawed at the rock with my fingertips, tearing my skin. I pushed and pulled and squirmed. And I remained stuck. Sailors believe hell must be like that: dark and cold and lonely and fearful, without the promise of hope. They call it the Great Trench below, filled only with darkness and the unimaginable.

When the air in the first bag was gone, I switched to the other, postponing death by a breath or two, as unwilling as ever to admit that I was defeated.

Then pain ripped through me, a shocking, unexpected agony so great that it took a moment for me to pinpoint its place: my ankles—both of them—blood-demons settling into the ulcers that constant exposure to sea water had reopened. I couldn't stand the horror of it, being eaten alive, being digested by their disgusting acids, being unable to reach back and tear them from me. My frantic struggles were irrational, but my frenzy brought success. I popped out into the wider part of the passage. The pain didn't end. It went on and on and I still couldn't twist back to get at the cause; the passage was nowhere wide enough. It bored straight on, too narrow to allow me to swim freely, and the light ahead was still dim and distant. I knew I didn't have enough air to make that swim, but I started anyway, driven on by pain, desperate to get somewhere where I could rip those creatures from my feet.

The pain defeated me. I don't know if the air in the second bladder was even finished when I lost it; I was beyond rationality, beyond anything but panic. I opened my mouth to scream—and took in air.

Water surged, bumping me against the roof. I gulped and swallowed some. Again I wanted to scream, again I breathed air. There were pockets of air, air that had been caught in wave turbulence at the entrance, then forced back along the passage by the tide. I twisted over on to my back, pressed my nose to the roof and breathed long, deep, steady breaths.

Rationality returned. I scraped my feet along the tunnel walls until I tore the blood-demons free. Without the pain I could think. I rolled over again and set off for the light, pulling myself along, feeling for hollows in the roof where there would be more pockets of air. I knew then that I would make it.

To shoot up to the surface, to be in the light and air again should have been heaven, but the first thing that happened to me was that I was flung against the cliff by an incoming wave. The tide might have been on its way out, but the waves weren't. I could breathe, but I was in danger of being battered to death. I did the one thing that could save me—I went back down under the water. I dived and caught the undertow out beyond the breaking of the waves.

When I emerged again, I still wasn't far enough out. I dived once more and this time angled myself across the waves instead of directly into them. The next time I came up, I was out of danger. I had also picked up another blood-demon. I rid myself of that by stuffing it inside the pocket of my tunic, and started a long, tough swim back toward Creed.

I was tired. I hadn't slept in well over twenty-four hours; I seemed to have been battling waves, blood-demons and my own grief and terrors for as long as I could remember. I might live, but perhaps the man I loved was being torn to pieces, perhaps the woman I cared for was being turned into something irrevocably evil. My message to Duthrick, my escape, this infernal swim: everything I was doing might be too late . . .

When Ruarth found me I was just beginning to swim in toward the beach close to Creed.

I trod water as I spoke to him. "Did you find Duthrick?"

He fluttered around, nodding. He made some odd movements, and it took me a moment to realize that he was trying to show me something. At first I couldn't see what it was, but when I drifted up on the crest of a swell, I saw it. There were two ships under sail, the first just about to make anchor opposite Creed, a little way further up the coast. "Keepers?" I asked.

He nodded.

Two ships. So that was what Duthrick had been waiting for—reinforcements. Not another one of the Awarefolk, but another ship. And the right combination of tide and current that would enable ships to leave the harbor at Gorthan Docks once more.

I started swimming again, this time toward the nearest of the ships.

I HAD NEVER HEARD SUCH A NOISE. Never.

It wasn't like thunder, although that was the closest thing I could think of to describe it. It was as if the air itself was being rent apart from sky to ground. It was a sound so loud that it could be *felt*. It hurt my ears. I felt the shock of it through the water. It was the loudest thing I had ever heard, and the most unnatural. And yet I couldn't believe it could be man-made. I thought it was some sort of divine intervention—I was almost ready to convert to the Menod, to believe that somehow Alain had called up God himself to vent His anger.

I was barely a hundred paces from the first of the now-anchored ships, the *Keeper Fair*. They were both encased in webs of sylv warding, blue-spun threads and panes of silver shimmer connected the undulating ward pillars that stretched from the mast top to the waterline. I saw puffs of smoke all along the landward side of both ships. The smoke appeared to come from some kind of metal tubes sticking out of the vessels—tubes that hadn't been there last time I had seen the ship—and a moment later I heard that awful sound again . . .

I swam on, almost out of my mind with exhaustion and fear.

Duthrick was on the deck when I clambered up the rope netting they let down for me. He gaped when he saw who it was they had fished out of the water. He didn't notice Ruarth, who perched himself unobtrusively on the rigging above.

I stood there in a growing pool of water and looked at those horrible things that had made—and were still making—all the noise. There was an acrid smell in the air that was almost as bad as dunmagic. I knew then that this was what the Keepers had been protecting so assiduously in the ship's holds.

"Syr-sylv," I said, my voice hoarse, "what is this?"

He gave a superior sort of smile. "Look," he said. "Look, Blaze—at Creed."

I looked. There was another roar of sound, another flash of flame, more smoke, more smell. The deck reverberated beneath my feet. I wanted to run away, to hide, but I did as Duthrick asked. I looked at Creed. And saw the wall of a dwelling *burst*. When the dust and smoke had cleared away, I could see the black gape of a hole—a hole larger than a man—in what had been the wall.

I felt the blood leave my face. I had to clutch the railing to keep myself from falling. I didn't understand a thing. But the connection between the tubes on the ships, the hideous sound they made and the hole in the wall was clear. These tubes were throwing things at Creed just as a bow sends an arrow, but these projectiles moved so fast I couldn't even see them. More than that, when they landed they seemed to do a disproportionate amount of damage.

I'd never felt so utterly at a loss. Tor and Alain and Flame were still there somewhere, and I didn't know how to save them.

I turned to Duthrick. "*Sylvmagic?* Sylv powers should not be used to kill."

He was still smug. "It's not magic. Anyone could do this, were they taught what to use and how to use it."

"Stop it!"

"Stop it? You asked for our attack today! You'll have to tell me about that bird some time, by the way. A Dustel, I assume? I've heard of such . . . Anyway, I assumed you had a good motive for your request."

I hunted around for a reason that would stop him. "Flame is in there. She is your one lead to the whereabouts of the Castlemaid. She alone knows. And she does know. I'm sure of that. In fact," I added, improvising, "there is a good chance that the Castlemaid is in Creed right at this moment."

"You have proof of that?"

"I'd bet my life on it."

"Flame told me she would deliver the Castlemaid if I saved you, you know."

Shit! Why didn't that cockle-headed woman ever *listen* to me? "You agreed?"

"No. She insisted I attack immediately, but we weren't

ready. Besides, I was sure she was lying. If she knew where the Castlemaid was, she would have said so before. No woman would have had her arm cut off rather than give up that information."

I snorted. That's what you think, you cruddy bastard, I thought. Flame's worth ten of you . . .

A moment's doubt flickered in his eyes.

"Trust me, Duthrick," I said. "The Castlemaid is in Creed."

But the look he gave me was heavy with suspicion, not trust. "If I halt the attack now, I lose the element of surprise. The dunmagicker might escape."

"You have the land routes guarded?"

"Of course. With archers. And wards. They were already in place; we'd planned an assault at dawn tomorrow anyway. Blaze, you had better have a good reason for telling me to change the time of the attack. And an even better one for wanting it to stop."

"I didn't know you were going to—to *disintegrate* the village! And Flame and the Castlemaid along with it. Look, Duthrick, what are you worrying about? Even if the dunmagicker escapes this—this bombardment, he will run into your guards." That is, if he doesn't slip past them, blurring himself with dunmagic, if he doesn't flatten the wards with dunmagic . . . The trouble was, Duthrick knew the possibilities as well as I did. Which was why he was standing off the coast, hurling his whatever-they-were at Creed. He'd already lost too many sylvs to this dunmagicker; he didn't want to lose more. "Give me a boat to shore, and an hour and I'll bring Flame off for you. And if I find the Castlemaid, I'll bring her as well. One hour without shooting, from the moment my foot touches the shore, Duthrick."

He opened his mouth to refuse.

Behind me someone said, "I suggest you do as she asks." I turned, to find Ransom standing there. He was pale, but determined. "You will find me grateful, Syr-sylv."

The promise of his words was clear and I could see Duthrick thinking them over. To have the future Holdlord of Bethany further indebted to the Keeper Isles was not a possibility to be passed over lightly. The Councilor stared hard at the Holdheir, then looked back at me, and finally nodded. He gave the signal to his men and the firing stopped. A flag signal went up to the other ship as well. The noise had somehow turned the world upside-down, so that now the ensuing silence seemed deafening.

"I'll come with you on the boat," Ransom said to me. "And I'll wait for you on the beach."

I nodded, too surprised and worn out to feel gratitude. It was the first time he had shown real courage; his need of Flame was giving him backbone, it seemed. In the boat on the way to shore, he asked me if she was all right. He was trying to sound calm, but his voice shook.

"I don't know," I replied. "I think the dunmagicker has placed another subversion spell in her. If he has, you're going to have to persuade Duthrick to let some of his sylvs use their powers to save her before it spreads. She won't give them what they want to know, not now, so you'll have to press Duthrick to heal her anyway. It won't be easy."

He nodded, his lips closed tight in a way that boded ill for Duthrick if he didn't help. It appeared that Ransom was beginning to grow up.

I bent over so that I could speak in his ear without being overheard by any of the six sylvs who were rowing the boat. "What are those terrible things the Keepers are using against Creed?"

He answered in a whisper, pleased to be able to show off his knowledge to me. "They call them cannon-guns. They put a flame to some black powder inside the barrel and it sort of bursts out." He looked puzzled. "I don't really understand how. Anyway, the bursting blows a stone ball down the tube and through the air."

I looked from the ship to the shore. "All that way across the sea to Creed? And can mere stone balls do *that* much damage?" It seemed an unlikely story, not that I could think of a better explanation.

"Some of the, um, projectiles are made of metal and they are filled with the same black powder, or something similar. And some of them have metal nails inside as well. They burst when they hit the target."

"Burst?"

"That's what Duthrick told me. They sort of explode, just as the seed pods of jump-beans explode when left in the sun. Only these things spew forth fire and smoke and nails, as well as the metal that encased them. They do a lot of damage." He shuddered slightly as he looked back at the ship. The mouths of the cannon-guns all seemed to be pointing in our direction.

"What is this black powder?"

"I don't know. They won't talk about it, but I do know where they get it, or perhaps where they get some of the ingredients in it: Breth. I overheard some of the sylvs talking."

Breth. Black powder that made cannon-guns bark and throw things. Cannon-guns so important that the Keepers kept them secret and wrapped up in sylvmagic as though they were the state treasure. Cannon-guns so powerful they could flatten buildings many, many paces away. Cannon-guns and powder. The Keepers desperate to give the Castlemaid to the Breth Bastionlord to keep him happy, against all rules of decency.

Everything fell into place.

I knew now why the Keepers wanted the Castlemaid so badly.

I LEFT RANSOM IN THE BOAT ON THE beach, together with the sylvs who had rowed us across. I didn't doubt that if there was any threat whatsoever to the Holdheir, he would be rowed back to the *Keeper Fair* promptly, whether or not he wanted to go—and I would be left to fend for myself.

I didn't know what to expect as I approached the village. The *Keeper Fair* had continued its bombardment as we rowed in and this had kept people under cover, but true to Duthrick's word, the shooting stopped again the moment I disembarked. I approached the village cautiously, choosing an inconspicuous route through the empty cockle trays stacked in rows between the beach and the first of the houses. Ruarth flew ahead of me, leading the way.

"Do you know where she is?" I asked him.

He perched on a cockle box long enough to shake his head.

"In that case, we'll split up. If you find her, come and get me." When we reached the first street, I pointed to the right. "I'll go this way." He nodded and flew off.

The place was a mess. So many of the lovely white buildings were wrecked, with holes through roofs and walls. Some houses were on fire. There were wounded everywhere, and several bodies as well, most of them slaves. The air was full of shell-dust and feathers, the latter being all that remained of someone's wader flock. Slaves were aimlessly rushing this way and that. Dunmagickers, real and subverted, were giving contradictory orders. No one took any notice of me. I suppose I didn't look too different from most of the slaves: my hair was salt-matted, my clothes torn, my face ravaged with fatigue and worry. I was barefoot too, but that didn't worry me. I'd spent much of my life without shoes.

I grabbed a slave who didn't seem to be doing anything. I had to harden myself just to touch him; the dunmagic bonds that kept him subservient were foul enough to have me gagging. "What's happening?" I asked.

He wrung his hands. "I don't know! The buildings fell down! They say the Master is under that one—" He pointed at the building that contained the torture room.

I was far from elated. Tor was probably also in that building. "Where's the Stragglerman with Awareness? And the Cirkasian sylv?"

The slave didn't know and began to look at me suspiciously, so I left him. I knew that none of the slaves had any will to help me; quite the reverse. If I aroused suspicion, they would tell the nearest dunmaster.

I sniffed the air, looking for traces of sylvmagic, not so easy when the place was saturated with its opposite. When I couldn't smell it, I went instead into the dining hall, which was still intact. My sword was still suspended above the throne and it was the work of seconds to have it down and in my hand. I took Tor's as well. Better yet, away from the people outside, I could smell the sweetness of sylvmagic. It was almost swamped by the dun, but it was there. Flame had to be in the building.

I found Morthred's living quarters on the other side of the hall. There didn't seem to be anyone about. I went from room to room, following the sylv scent.

Without Awareness, I would never have found her. She was in a bedroom on the corner of the building, and the corner had been blown away by Duthrick's damn cannon-guns. The shell blocks of much of the outside wall had disintegrated into white powder and shell-grit; the bottle-glass windows had blown out; the furniture was just so much firewood. Dust hung in the air like stirred-up silt in a wave, and about as breathable. I followed the glimmer of blue.

Underneath all the litter I found Flame.

She was conscious, but shaken. I heaved away some of the debris and gently brushed off the worst of the dust, expecting to find her terribly injured. When I couldn't find anything broken I was afraid to believe it and examined her again, just to make sure. Then I decided that she was suffering more from the force of the explosion, which must surely have flung her across the room, than from any more obvious injury. She was not, however, entirely unscathed. There was still the harm she had incurred before the building had been hit—at the base of her throat there was an angry red patch of dunmagic contagion.

She was beginning to collect herself and smiled weakly at me, but her eyes didn't reflect anything that resembled amusement.

I kneeled there beside her, my throat tied up in knots. I couldn't believe how brave she had been, how much she had been willing to do to save Tor and me.

It was a while before I found my voice. "Of all the crazy, barnacle-skulled *idiots*—do you think I pulled you out of his stinking crimson shit once, just to have you walk back in? *Deliberately?*"

"It was worth a try. Duthrick wouldn't help. I did try . . . But he said he couldn't attack immediately. So I came myself."

"God, Flame!" I helped her to sit up, supporting her as she swayed. "Look where it's got you—and we can hardly amputate this time. Unless you have a hankering to carry your head under your arm instead of on top of your neck."

"You wouldn't have had much fun in bed with Tor next time around if I hadn't come. Allow me that much."

"They've probably done it all to him anyway." Terrified I was right, I was ungracious.

She shook her head. The bleakness in her was wrenching. "No. Morthred is waiting for me to do it—of my own accord—once this subversion takes full effect. He loved telling me that. His idea of fun. Tor's still intact somewhere."

My relief was intense. "You don't know where?"

She shook her head.

I helped her to her feet. "Are you all right?"

"I think so. A little confused. What happened?"

"I'll explain later. Right now I'm taking you to the Keepers." I gestured at the new sore on her body. "Ransom will put pressure on them to use their magic to stop that."

There was a gleam of hope within her. "Will they do it this time?"

"They'd better, or I'll carve them up personally. Starting with Duthrick," I said grimly. "I'm *through* with asking nicely. Anyway, let's get out of here."

"Oh, but I can't! Morthred's warded me again."

I gave a chuckle. "He must have put one of his wards in the corner. It's not there anymore." I waved a hand at the ruins of the wall. There were a few lines of dunspell red flickering aimlessly in the gap, but they had no strength or purpose.

"It's gone?" she asked, hardly able to believe it. "Just like that?"

"Apparently. Believe me, Flame, there's nothing there to stop you walking through that hole in the wall. Let's go." I took her arm and helped her across the wreckage of the room to the gap. But when I peered out I saw a dunmagicker standing nearby giving orders to some slaves. I drew my head back in. "We'll have to wait a moment," I said.

"What's happening here anyway? What's all the noise? Where's Morthred?"

"Trapped under one of the ruined buildings apparently. The Keepers are attacking. Ask Ransom to explain the details."

"What about Tor?"

"I shall try to find him." I remembered the collapsed buildings and wondered if he was still alive anyway. My hope bottomed as quickly as it had crested.

"I can help—"

"Don't be ridiculous. You can hardly stand up straight." I was having trouble doing that myself, but at least I hadn't been half-buried under a wall and I didn't have a poisonous dunmagic sore eating away at me. "You've got to get that spell fixed as soon as possible. The smaller it is, the less energy has to be expended to cure it, and the more inclined Duthrick will be to allow someone to fix it." I sounded as snappish as an irritated crab, so I softened the tone a little and added, "Flame, you've done enough. It's my turn now. All I've been doing so far is sitting around in a variety of prisons playing with my toes." I touched her hair gently. "You've been through quite enough."

Her glance darted involuntarily to what remained of the bed.

I added, "Nothing can touch what you are inside—nothing. Unless you let it."

"Yes. I know. You showed me that. Although . . . it's hard."

I nodded. She slipped her hand into mine, and we gazed at each other in understanding, trying not to remember things that were better forgotten. A chirping from beyond the hole brought us back to the present. "Ruarth!" she cried and he came to perch on her shoulder.

I turned away as her fair head bent toward him and he spoke to her. I didn't need to understand the language to see that this wasn't a moment for a third person.

There was a crash nearby as a burning house collapsed in on itself. I looked out once more, and found the street clear. "Come on," I said.

Flame and I crawled out through the gap in the wall, Ruarth fluttered out behind us and we all headed for the beach. In the confusion, no one took any notice of us.

I took Flame to the boat and left her in Ransom's care. When I told the Holdheir I wasn't coming back to the ship, he shrugged indifferently; it was one of the Keepers who pointed out what I already knew. "The Syr-Councilor will resume the bombardment of the village as soon as he sees the Cirkasian is safe."

I nodded. "I wouldn't have expected anything else of him." My sarcasm was probably lost on the man; those Keeper sylvs all thought Duthrick could do no wrong.

CHAPTER 24

NO SOONER HAD I RETURNED TO CREED than the situation changed yet again. Morthred's acolytes had managed to find their master and they were now pulling him out from under the wreckage that had trapped him, And he wasn't hurt. In fact, by the way he was seething at his dunmagickers, it seemed that he'd had to do most of his own rescuing, using his own powers.

Hidden behind some rubble, I watched from a distance. He stood up, rather shakily, and some trembling slaves brushed off the shell dust that covered him. He was already barking orders and dunmagic billowed forth in his rage. I couldn't help feeling that the bastard had divine protection.

I kept out of sight and debated what to do.

I listened as he shouted at those around him. One of the ex-sylvs had apparently pointed out the Keeper ships and explained that it seemed they were to blame. Not surprisingly, Morthred put the damage down to some kind of sylvmagic, although (like me) he really ought have known better. As I have said before, sylvmagic has no destructive power.

I have to admit that he had the situation summed up in an instant. He spent a moment looking at the ships, frowning, while I wondered—heart in mouth—whether he had regained enough power to simply blast them out of the water. After all, this was the dunmaster who had sunk the Dustel Islands under Deep-Sea. But perhaps he remembered the result of that, because he turned away and began to give orders for Creed to be abandoned. It seemed he was cutting his losses. I waited to hear if he mentioned Tor or Flame or me, but we were apparently not on his list of priorities. He ordered slaves to pack up the things he viewed as valuable, and in the midst of all that chaos, I saw some women rolling up bolts of Yebaan silk inside Mekaté wool carpets, while others stuffed down-filled cushions into a carved chest inlaid with mother-of-pearl. When a jewelry box was dropped, a cascade of whale-tooth necklaces strung with amber spilled out.

While the packing was being done, Morthred sent several dunmagickers to scout out the perimeters of the village, to find out what opposition was hidden in the dunes, and he told several others to find a way to get to Gorthan Docks so that they could place spells on a couple of ship's captains. The man didn't bother to ask or pay for what he wanted: he took. He needed transport, and he would get it, his way. Or he would try. Whether the dunmagickers would be able to pass the sylvs gathered in the dunes was another matter.

I didn't hear any more; Morthred moved away into one of the buildings.

I dithered, wondering how in all the islands I was going to find Tor. I couldn't home in on him the way I had done with Flame.

After a little thought, I decided that the best method would be the most direct. I hid the two swords, then singled out one of the real dunmagickers, one I couldn't remember having seen before, and approached him with the same subservient sidle that the slaves always used. "Syr-dunmaster sir, the Syr-master has told me to see if the Stragglerman, the one with Awareness, is still alive, but I don't know where he is . . ."

The dunmagicker didn't even glance at me. I was a slave, and not worthy of attention. He gave a dry laugh. "You'll be lucky to find him—he was trussed up in the torture room." He indicated the remains of the building behind us and walked on.

I retrieved the swords and went to investigate. In the end, it wasn't difficult to find Tor. It was only the upper part of the building that had collapsed. The underground part, where he had been, was almost undamaged. I slipped in through one of the ground level windows and dropped down into the torture room. Tor was stretched out on the table, his arms and legs bound in leather thongs, but someone was there before me, working on his bonds.

It was an old man, painfully thin, with a blue-tinged cadaverous face that hinted at the imminence of his death, and a beard that looked like frayed sun-bleached rope. He was shabbily dressed in black, smelled bad, and although he wasn't wearing the chain and pendant of the Menod, I thought that must be his allegiance.

"Alain," I said. I might have known that the patriarch wouldn't stay hidden once the Keepers started flattening Creed.

He nodded, his smile strained. "And you must be Blaze. You are very much as I imagined you. Ah, you have a sword. Can you cut these bonds? I have been unable to untie them."

I approached the table reluctantly, afraid to see what they had done to Tor.

But he was grinning at me, that rare grin that lit his face and showed me that he could still laugh at life, that he wasn't always weighed down with the seriousness of it all. "Ah, love, maybe you can tell us both what in heaven's name is happening? Alain here maintains that this is God's punishment for dunmagic evil; my thoughts are more prosaic. I feel that God does not usually indulge Himself with such abrupt expressions of disapproval, as much as He would probably like to."

I explained briefly as I cut the leather and Tor rolled off the table. He took the news almost casually, and he made the same connections that I had. "So that explains the Keeper interest in the Castlemaid, eh? And I see you've brought my sword. Good. You'd better tell me some other time just why you look like you've been shipwrecked." He touched my cheek in tender concern. "Where's Flame?"

"With the Keepers. But Eylsa's dead, as you probably saw."

I didn't get any further. There was a far off rumble, and a second later the ground shook nearby. Duthrick hadn't waited very long before restarting his bombardment. He'd delayed until he'd seen Flame, but he'd obviously put no great faith in my ability to produce the Castlemaid.

"Let's get out of here," Tor suggested equably.

We pushed Alain out of the window ahead of us and, once outside, we scuttled away toward the edge of the village. "If we leave Creed through the dunes, we may be shot by Duthrick's archers," I warned, shouting. The noise of the guns was distant enough, but the village was full of screaming people, falling masonry, thuds—I felt the whole world had gone mad. "Shall we swim to the *Keeper Fair?*" I asked.

"I'd never make it—" Alain began. I glanced back at him, and then, suddenly, he wasn't there anymore. He was cartwheeling through the air, tossed by something unseen, a ragdoll. A split second later Tor and I were flung backward by a blast of air and dust, as helpless as butterflies in a winter's gale. For a moment I stayed where I was on the ground, winded, paralyzed with shock. It was Tor who ran to Alain, who knelt at his side, who took the old man's hand as he looked up with surprize etched in every wrinkle of his face.

"He's dead," Tor said blankly. "Just like that." He turned distressed eyes to me. "What sort of weapon is this, Blaze?" He didn't expect an answer; he wasn't wanting technicalities, but a reason, and he knew I had none to give.

I staggered to my feet, trying not to look at Alain. It sickened me. He didn't have any legs anymore. He didn't have anything left below the pelvis.

"We've got to get out of here," I said.

"I want to say the prayer for the dead, for Alain."

I was incredulous. "Tor, the world is breaking into dust around us, and you want to *pray?*"

"It would mean a lot to him," he said simply.

"Tor—he's *dead!*"

"Blaze, there was a time when Alain and I were very close. I must do this for him."

I threw up my hands. "God preserve me from idiots!" I wanted to be angry, but I kept on seeing myself with Eylsa's body in my arms. I know now that humans are never rational where death is concerned. It is the time when we come face to face with our own fragile mortality . . .

I peered around the corner of the nearest building and looked into hell. The bombardment of Creed was crushing it. People were dying: slaves (many of them still so young), dunmagickers, ex-sylvs. When I looked behind me, out toward the sand dunes, I could see slaves running, carrying baggage, only to be cut down under crossbow fire. Sylv silver arced along the dunes in lacy curtains between twisting ward pillars of silver-blue. I thought I caught a glimpse of Morthred blasting dunmagic at one of the wards. Crimson met silver and intermingled in a clash of light and sparks; I could not tell if the ward succumbed or not. I glanced out over the ocean: the two ships, confident of the lack of retaliation, had actually moved in closer to shore. They were raining their death on us, not caring who it was they killed.

A slave collapsed at my feet, blood trickling down his face. I stood there, shaking, outraged. It was the slaves who were suffering the most. Caught in dunmagic spells, they had no sense of self-preservation. They wouldn't even take shelter, but worked on, trying to do what they had been ordered to do. I felt impotent. I wanted to fight—but I didn't know who to battle.

Then Tor was at my side again, still ignoring the danger, seeing only the carnage. "God damn them," he said softly. "God damn them all." I wasn't sure whether he meant the Keepers or the dunmagickers; perhaps he meant both. He bent down to the slave at my feet. Then he began to drag the man into the shelter of a nearby wall. "Blaze," he said, "I can't leave. These people don't have anyone to help them. Some of them are bleeding to death for the want of a little attention—they never hurt anyone."

I wanted to scream at him: *They aren't our business!* Hadn't we been through enough? I wanted to rest. I was sick of it all.

He didn't even seem to notice my hesitation. He had shoved his sword through his belt and now he moved on to another slave, a woman sprawled in the middle of the street with her tattered skirt rucked up over her head. Silence, of a kind, suddenly cloaked us. The rumble of the cannon guns ceased, along with the corresponding crunch of buildings being hit. The screaming faded and stopped. There was a crackle of flames nearby, a low moaning from a nearby house, the heartrending whimpering of a girl—that was all. Tor didn't seem to notice the change. "Blaze, do you know where we can find some water?"

"I'll get some," I said numbly. I didn't want to stay. I didn't have Tor's compassion. I'd been surrounded by the poor and downtrodden all my life and I'd learned that if you wanted to survive you had to fight, not stay and be a martyr. I didn't want to die in this madhouse of death and dunmagic. And yet I couldn't leave. Not when Tor was still there.

And so I stayed.

I never did get his water to him, though. I found a well, filled a bucket and was on my way back when I came face to face with Morthred and several subverted Keeper sylvs. Morthred was unarmed, but the Keepers weren't. Morthred couldn't believe it was me at first. When he did, he was so enraged he forgot I had

Awareness and flung a spell at me. It was a horrible thing, alive with malevolence. It shattered harmlessly against my shoulder, but I felt its evil. When he realized his mistake, he waved his ex-sylvs on to me and I was fighting for my life in a savage clash of sword on sword, a furious onslaught of cut and thrust that was going to exhaust me if it went on too long. It was all I could do to parry and parry again.

It was really Morthred who won the fight for me. Almost insane with anger, he kept on throwing his spells into the fray, as if he could wear down the protection my Awareness gave me. Instead, he confused and weakened the ex-sylvs when some of the dunmagic rebounded from me on to them. When they faltered I moved in and killed them as cleanly as I could.

Then I turned back to Morthred and what I saw in his face shook me even more, I recognized there the beginnings of the kind of thing that he must have unleashed on the Dustels: his face glowed red with power, but the power was warped with madness and, as yet, only in its infancy. It had been a diabolical insanity that had made the impossible possible a hundred years before. Left alone I knew he would one day have recourse to that kind of power again.

I went for him with my sword, but he was too quick for me. A passing slave was coerced with a spell and the man threw himself between me and Morthred, clawing insanely at me with his hands, trying to rip the flesh from my body with his fingers alone. I tried to ward him off with my blade, but he had been maddened by the spell. When I accidentally slashed his arm he hardly seemed to notice—he fell to the ground and attacked me with his teeth. I kicked him hard under the chin, and he was out of it. But it made no difference—that man was followed by another, sucked in by the magic, drawn to death on my blade. And all the while, Morthred watched, dashing this way and that, shouting encouragement to the men and women he lured to me. He knew what he was doing. He could have coerced twenty of them to fall on me at the same time so that I was overwhelmed by numbers alone, but he didn't want it that way. Even in the middle of the bedlam that was Creed just then, he wanted me to suffer. He knew I hated what I was doing. He saw the desperate ways I tried to avoid killing and maiming—and he laughed.

All I could think of was that while Tor was saving lives, I was taking them.

And then I noticed Morthred's hand, his left hand. The three fingers he had were curled into a deformed twist, yet a moment before they had been straight. I sought to make sense of that, even while I fought off his slaves. What did the old stories say about Morthred the Mad? He had over-extended himself, used too much power and thus been hopelessly weakened. And I had myself thought that it was the uncontrolled release of his own power that had deformed him, twisted his body . . . just as those three fingers were now gnarled. He was weakening himself.

The idea that came to me was born of desperation and exhaustion. I was killing people who didn't deserve to die, and I couldn't stand it anymore. "Why are you doing this?" I shouted at him. "It's not me who's destroying your village and your people! It's the Keepers out there!" I pointed to where the Keeper ships were now silhouettes against the darkening sea of evening. The bombardment had not resumed, but I didn't draw his attention to that. "Why don't you turn your dunmagic on *them*? Or are you so weak that you can't sink a couple of ships? You, who once sank the Dustel islands under Deep-Sea? What's the matter with you, Morthred? I thought you were supposed to be the greatest of all dunmasters!" And so on. That kind of taunting drivel wouldn't have worked with anyone with the slightest sense, but Morthred wasn't sensible. Clever, yes. Cunning, yes. Sensible, no, not when he saw all he'd worked for slipping away between his fingers. Not when he saw the sylvs he had worked so hard to subvert dying around him. His madness controlled him now.

He did what I suggested. He shouted for another couple of ex-sylvs to attack me, then turned from me to fling what he had at the Keeper ships.

And I went cold. What if the Keepers didn't have the ships properly warded? They *were* warded, I knew that. I could see the filigree of sylv blue that stretched from mast top to waterline, but what if it wasn't enough? What if I was wrong about just how much power Morthred had at his disposal? If I had miscalculated, then Flame and the Keepers could very well die. The fact that three fingers had reverted to their previously deformed state was hardly overwhelming evidence that Morthred had overextended himself by his profligate use of power. I was gambling with other people's lives. If I'd had more time to think, I would never have provoked him. I would never have risked killing so many people, Flame among them, on the basis of so little evidence. I wake up sometimes at night even now, in a cold sweat, just thinking about the chance I took. And wondering: did I do it just to save myself? Perhaps. I don't know. When you're scared and tired . . .

I didn't see all that happened. I was still fighting. But I saw enough: the swell of red-brown that brightened to crimson, the way the color enveloped Morthred, then the stream of foul, stinking light that ripped from him and shot across the water toward the ships like wind-driven flames in a forest fire. He was doing what no ordinary dunmagicker or sylvtalent could do: sending his magic away from his immediate vicinity, attacking from a distance. In growing horror, I watched and remembered that it had been a week's sail from one end of the Dustels to the other, and he had submerged all of them at once . . .

Distracted, I was slightly wounded in the arm by one of the ex-sylvs and had to drag my eyes away from the Keeper ships back to my own fight. I killed one of my opponents and concentrated on the other, telling myself that unlike the slaves, these ex-sylvs were better dead.

This last man was a fine swordsman and only the advantage of a Calmenter sword kept me alive. He attacked in quick bursts, then disengaged when I managed to parry, so that the fight was a series of short engagements. Each attack was different, and sooner or later he was going to find one that I didn't know how to counter. I was tiring badly by then.

But luck ran against him; he stumbled over the body of one of the slaves I had killed. It was all the advantage I needed to slip under his guard and send the blade into his heart.

I looked back at Morthred—and found him gone.

I ran down the middle of the street. It was almost dark but I could see him. He was a reddish silhouette against the darkness of the buildings, a scuttling figure that dragged a lame leg and dripped the blood-colored remains of his spell behind him like the slime-trail of a sea-pony. I pounded after him.

As I ran, I spared another glance at the Keeper ships. They were still there, thanks be, although I was appalled to see that the *Keeper Fair* seemed to have lost its foremast and the other had a sail on fire. Morthred's power had indeed been enough to penetrate their shields. Even as I watched, Keeper sailors cut away the burning canvas and it dropped harmlessly into the sea. My gamble had paid off, but only just. One part of me had not

really thought Morthred's spell would even reach the ships. I
started to shake with reaction. It had been so *close*. If Morthred
had had just a shade more control . . .

IF I HAD BEEN LESS TIRED, I MIGHT HAVE
caught Morthred. As it was, I had several wounds and all my
muscles seemed to be screaming their fatigue.

The dunmaster left the village to the east, running into the
dunes close to the beach. I thought I might have him trapped, as
I recalled there was an inlet in there, close to where I had been
tortured. I was right, but Morthred knew what he was doing. By
the time I had struggled up to the top of the dune that overlooked the small bay, he was on his way. Someone had been
waiting for him there at the edge of the water with a laden sea-
pony: a short man. Domino? As the sea-pony swam out into the
ocean with the two men on its back, I saw Morthred's features
lit by his own dunmagic. The right side of his face was no
longer as handsome as it had been; some of the features seemed
to have run together as if they had been melted into one another.
I felt a surge of triumph rise up through my defeat. In his madness Morthred had indeed made the same mistake a second
time, just as I had hoped. He had over-extended himself and,
once he had realized that, he'd been forced to flee. Of course,
this setback was nothing compared to what he had done to himself when he had submerged the Dustel Islands, but it would be
a while before he'd be strong enough to challenge the Isles of
Glory. Or so I hoped.

I stood watching as the sea-pony disappeared into the gloom
with its burden. My sense of victory dissipated, leaving behind
a discontent, a sense of having unfinished business.

I turned and limped back through the dunes to the village.

There were Keepers everywhere now: unsubverted ones.
And what they were doing wasn't pretty. They were scouring
the place for dunmagickers, real and subverted, and when they
found then, they killed them. All the dunmagickers capable of
doing so fought back, of course. I could see splashes of dunmagic and sylvpower flaring in isolated spots around the village
or in the dunes. The Keepers weren't having it all their own way
and some of them died.

One of the first sylvs I saw was Mallani, the pregnant
woman who had come to see me about her baby. I stared at her

in shock. She was huge, and she looked tired. "In the name of all the islands," I said, "What are you doing here? This is dangerous! You should be resting."

"Duthrick said I had to come," she said, and her voice dragged with fear. "If I am in Council service, then a pregnancy should make no difference. Service comes first . . ."

"That's utter eel-slime," I told her. I was as wild as a fish on a hook. "There's too much red shit around here—you'll expose your unborn child. And there are still plenty of dunmagickers. I'm getting you back to the ship now." I looked around, and saw Duthrick was in the main street, directing his underlings, his long aristocratic face without expression, or compassion.

I marched up to him, dragging the protesting Mallani behind me.

He spoke before I could, a brisk, "Do you know what happened to the dunmaster?"

I told him and he looked seaward, but it was completely dark now. There was no point in sending a ship after Morthred. The Councilor's lips tightened into a hard line. "Another failure, halfbreed," he said. "If he gets back to the Docks, he can force a ship to take him elsewhere. You have not distinguished yourself in this whole matter."

I shrugged indifferently. His disapproval had no more power to hurt or disconcert me. He would never make me feel like a half-grown adolescent again. "How's Flame?" I asked, still grasping Mallani's wrist so that she couldn't walk away.

"Recovering. We have rid her of the spell. It hadn't spread much. She will, I trust, be grateful enough to tell me where to find the Castlemaid. This is the second time we've saved her, after all."

I didn't like his chances. I blessed Ransom. God knows what arguments he had used, but they had persuaded Duthrick.

"You look weak," he continued. "The *Keeper Fair* is sailing back to Gorthan Docks shortly, with our wounded. Why don't you go with them? Go down to the beach, and tell the men on the boat there that I said you were to be taken on board." Doubtless it wasn't concern for me that prompted such compassion. He still thought I might help him extract the information he wanted from Flame. He hadn't cared much if I'd been killed during his bombardment of Creed, but seeing I had survived, he thought he may as well keep me healthy enough to be of use.

I glanced past his shoulder. I could see Tor in the distance,

still administering to some of the slaves. Ex-slaves now, I supposed, or they would be once the spells wore off. I doubted that
the magic in them had been of too permanent a kind; that would
have involved too much expenditure of power.

"Yes," I said. "I think I will. Tell Ryder I've gone, will you?"
But I was so tired I didn't care whether Tor knew or not. "Oh,
and I'm taking this foolish child with me," I added, indicating
Mallani. "She didn't want to be left out of things, but I've told
her you wouldn't be happy to have a pregnant sylv exposed to
all this dunmagic."

I nodded amiably and turned away before he would reply.
Mallani had to run to catch up.

"You're sneaky," she said. A child's word, but she wasn't a
child. She was a woman about to have a baby.

I felt old enough to be her grandmother. "That's right."

"I don't think he likes you very much."

"I don't think he likes me at all," I said.

Letter from Researcher (Special Class) S. iso Fabold, National Department of Exploration, Federal Ministry of Trade, Kells, to Masterman M. iso Kipswon, President of the Royal Society for the Scientific, Anthropological and Ethnographical Study of non-Kellish Peoples.

Dated this day 10/1st Darkmoon/1793

Dear Uncle,
Thank you for your comments on the packet of Blaze Halfbreed's recollections that I sent you last week.

In view of several of your remarks, I thought you may be interested to know that, much later, we did visit the village of Creed. We found it utterly deserted. In fact, we had trouble finding a guide in Gorthan Docks who would actually take us there. It was described variously as a bad place, a haunted graveyard, a home to evil spirits and a place where the Sea Devil spawns his young. We finally prevailed on a Kellish aetherial-level priest doing missionary work in Gorthan Docks (the Docks is still a place in need of salvation!) to show us the village. He himself thought Creed was a place that was spiritually dead and therefore not to be visited lightly.

We found it in a state of dereliction, although it was possible to see the scene as it had first appeared to Blaze: the crushed blue shell paths, the white shell buildings. Many of these latter appeared to have been blasted with cannon fire, just as she described. In fact we found some of the cannon balls! We dug out one of the larger buildings and actually came across the oblivion she described. It was all an interesting confirmation of her story.

Of course, in the papers I sent you, she relates events which took place over fifty years ago (did I tell you she is now over eighty?) and we have to make allowances for poor memory as well as her tendency to romanticize the past. Combine that with the innately superstitious nature of these island peoples, and you have this story of good and evil and magic.

You wanted to know more about Blaze as she is now. Well, she is still magnificent. Tall, ramrod-straight in spite of the rheumatism that obviously attacks her joints from time to time, if the way in which she rises from a chair is anything to go by. I guess she could still best be summed up as formidable.

It is very easy to believe that she did indeed do the kinds of things she describes. I made the mistake of once hinting that I didn't believe in dunmagic and sylvmagic. She was amused, and made a point of mocking me at every turn ever afterward, with a decidedly wicked gleam in her eye.

She would say things like, "You won't believe this, of course, but . . ." Or, "I then imagined that Morthred flung a spell . . ." Needless to say, I edited these comments out of the interviews!

I know, Uncle, that you will say it is my own fault, for I broke one of the golden rules of scientific ethnographical studies: I showed disrespect for local beliefs, and I therefore deserved all the mockery I received!

Certainly I learned from Blaze a salutary lesson about field work. She is still a feisty lady. Sometimes I look at my sisters with their needlepoint and fashion magazines, and wonder what she would think of them if she met them. I suspect not much. She has not mellowed with age. And there is an enormous sword, which is kept well oiled, over the fireplace . . .

I enclose the next set of conversations for your perusal. I am almost finished the text of the next talk, and isi Doth has been kind enough to prepare the magic-lantern slides based on the drawings made by the botanist-artist, young Trekan. I have included a drawing of Blaze—or rather, of how she may have looked when she was about thirty.

I look forward to seeing you next week at the Society's meeting.

Aunt Rosris will be delighted to hear that I am escorting Miss Anyara isi Teron to the meeting, and that I will not have need of accommodation with your good selves— I shall be spending a day or two with Anyara's family at their town house. It is just around the corner from the Royal Society, in Second Moon Crescent.

I remain,
Your respectful nephew,
Shor iso Fabold

CHAPTER 25

ON THE SAIL BACK TO GORTHAN DOCKS in the *Keeper Fair,* Mallani went into labor.

I had managed to go to sleep—in fact, the moment I came on board, I just collapsed into the first hammock I found, closed my eyes and was dead asleep in seconds. Some time later I was aware that I was being violently shaken. At first I thought there was something wrong with the ship, and only gradually did I surface to the realization that someone was calling my name and telling me that I was needed. I rolled out of the hammock and followed the sylv responsible, still not fully conscious.

He took me to a cabin with a bunk, and it was only then, when I saw Mallani lying there, that I really woke up. "She wanted you here," one of the sylv women in attendance said.

"I don't know the first thing about delivering a baby," I replied in protest. That was true enough. I'd done a lot of things in my life, but I'd never been present at a birth. Besides, my heart was sinking: I'd just remembered that I was ten to one certain that her baby was non-sylv, and I'd have to be the one to tell her.

Someone said, "She just wants to know if it's sylv or not."

"That could have waited until morning," I grumbled, but the truth was that I was soon caught up in the wonder of what was happening. By the time it was all over I was deeply grateful that I had been there.

I suppose I should have felt the pain of knowing that I could never have children, but somehow all I could do was marvel at this delivery of life, and take joy in seeing a baby's first breath, hearing its first cry. Somewhere along the way, as the head pushed toward freedom, it registered with me that the babe had no sylvmagic, just as I had expected; minutes later when it slithered out and the last life-giving blood pulsed to it via the cord, I realized this was not so. Blue light skittered in fanciful swirls over the child. He was leaking sylvmagic all over the place, so intense that it seemed almost purple. I stared, puzzled over what I was seeing. Then someone was tying and cutting the cord; the flow of magic to the baby stopped, the color calmed.

In the chaos of the room full of Keeper sylvs all exclaiming over the baby and hugging the new mother, I had a moment to examine the placenta, to touch it, to feel the remains of the magic that had been there. I shivered, hating the feel of the residue left. It was *wrong*. Horribly wrong. It may not have been crimson-colored, but I felt the touch of dunmagic, smelled its stench nonetheless.

All the pleasure I had felt during the birth drained away.

Mallani called my name, and someone pushed me forward to her bedside. She was holding the child, now cleaned and swaddled. She pulled back the blanket from around his head, and a bland little face peeked up at me making kissing movements with his lips. He looked pretty much like all new babies look, except that sylvlight played over his features. "Is he?" she asked. "Tell me, quickly!"

"He's leaking sylv blue all over the place."

Mallani gave a squeal of delight and hugged the child to her. Then she looked back at me. "You're sure?"

"Of course I'm sure. He's a strong sylv."

There was laughter, exclamations of delight over the baby, a buzz of sylvmagic as the women around the bed relaxed. I edged my way out of the door, leaving them to it.

Up on deck it was good to breath in the sea air, to feel the cleanness of the wind. I knew if I looked behind me I would see the glow of fire and magic that was all that remained of Creed, so I didn't look. I wanted to think ahead, to a future that was safe and full of things I'd never known. Friendship and love. Joy. Happiness. Freedom.

No Keepers. No dunmagic. No Duthrick.

It should all have been mine. I should have been happy.
So why did I feel so uneasy, so fettered?

I SAT IN FLAME'S ROOM IN THE DRUNKEN
Plaice and watched her as she stuffed her belongings, what little
she had, into her soft leather bag. She was having trouble holding the bag while she put things inside, but I knew better than to
offer to help. She would have to learn to cope.

She was as beautiful as ever. Nothing of what had happened
seemed to have touched her face, except perhaps to give an
added depth to her expression, an added touch of maturity that
was beautiful in itself. Inside there were scars, too many of
them. She hadn't lived hard enough as a child to be unscathed
by what she had suffered. Occasionally, very occasionally, I
glimpsed something in her eyes that made me want to hold her,
to tell her that it didn't matter, that the part of her that counted
was still inviolate. I hadn't done so, and now it seemed I never
would. I hoped that Ruarth was wise enough to give her the reassurance she needed.

"Where's Ruarth?" I asked.

"Oh, around somewhere. I believe there was a local lovely
he wanted to say good-bye to." She meant a Dustel, of course,
but it took a moment for me to understand. She smiled, a lovely
smile of love, and my heart caught at the tragedy—and her
courage.

"Doesn't . . . doesn't that worry you?"

She looked surprised. "Why, no. Of course not. He's a bird.
And I'm human. How can we have more than we have at the
moment? But we both have . . . other needs."

"It doesn't make you jealous?"

She shook her head. "No more than Ruarth was jealous of
Noviss. Holdheir Ransom, I mean. What Ruarth and I feel for
each other is too special to be changed by such affairs. Ruarth
knows that I live for the day when he can hold me in his arms. In
the meantime, I use his name as mine." She said all that lightly
enough, but there was still something in her eyes that told me of
her pain. I don't think she was ever free of it, not really.

"I have found a passage on board a mullet boat going to
Mekatéhaven," she added. "It sails with the tide, around sunset.
So . . . I suppose this is good-bye."

She clumsily tied the strings at the top of her bag and straightened, then conjured up some sylvmagic and made herself a make-believe arm. She held it out to show me. To me, it flickered with silver and I could see right through it, but it was good enough to deceive the non-Aware. "Not bad, eh?" she asked. "Although . . . I'm not sure why I bother. It doesn't seem as important as it did at first." Then she looked at me, serious, and said again, "I guess this is good-bye, Blaze."

I felt almost sick with sorrow. "Yes, I suppose so."

"You'll stay with Tor?"

I nodded.

"I'm glad. Although . . . well, I'm sorry about the two thousand setus."

I shrugged. "I still have part of what the Holdheir gave me." I was leaning against the wall, watching her, thinking how much I'd miss her. She was friend, sister, family, all the woman that I wasn't and would like to be; with her, I was somehow whole.

And in those last moments I couldn't hide from her the truth that I'd kept hidden so long. Something in my expression—a hint of cynical laughter in my eyes?—told her.

"You know, don't you," she said quietly, and it was a statement, not a question.

I nodded.

"Since when?"

"Ever since you told me about Ruarth. And Ruarth's mother. You see, the main reason I felt sure you weren't the Castlemaid was that you knew how to use sylvtalent. I thought the Castlemaid could never have learned, even if she had been born sylvtalented. Then you told me about the Dustels, and how Ruarth's mother had sylvtalent, and I realized that she could have taught you as you were growing up. Would have thought it her duty to teach you, in fact. And the Castlelord and his staff need never have known.

"That was why I didn't want Duthrick to find out about Ruarth—he could have reached the same conclusions as I did. He met up with Ruarth yesterday, of course, when I sent that cloth message to him, but I'm hoping he thinks the connection is between me and Ruarth, not between the two of you. As Keeper Councilor, he must know a fair bit about the Dustels, I would think. You must be careful."

She looked rueful. "No matter how much I admire you, I still seem to end up underestimating you, Blaze. You've been laughing at me all this time, you sodding great lunk of a half-breed."

I grinned. "Rubbish, I'm not so petty."

Lacking any other weapon, she hurled her coin purse at me. I caught it and threw it back. "Of course, once I realized that you could talk to the Dustels, that you had been in close contact with them ever since you were a child, a lot of things about you that had puzzled me fell into place. At times you were so innocent, so lacking in knowledge about the realities of the world—just as a Castlemaid, brought up in close seclusion, would have been. At other times, you could be as shrewd and as cunning as an octopus after the bait in a trap—just as someone taught by the Dustels, who must surely see so much human folly and cruelty, could have been.

"Mind you, I was still puzzled by how you worked the coming-of-age tattoos. In the end I decided that the original tattoos must have been faked—they were a sylvmagic illusion. Somehow you avoided having real tattoos made. I guessed you had reasoned that in Cirkasecastle palace there was little risk of ever meeting one of the Awarefolk who could see through your illusion. I don't know why it occurred to you to fake them, though. Were you planning to run away even then? When you were only eighteen?"

She nodded, threading her coin purse on to her belt. "I was already in love with Ruarth, you see. I knew I'd never want to marry anyone else. We decided to fake the etching of the tattoos . . . I used sylvmagic during the ceremony. The ghemph tattooist never knew it was not really marking my hands."

I chuckled. "Oh, I rather think that it might have done. Ghemphs have a certain amount of Awareness, I think."

"*Have* they? Well, I'll be damned! It never said a word."

"Perhaps it was reluctant to have anyone know that ghemphs have any Awareness. Perhaps it didn't want to get you into trouble. They are very kindhearted."

She gave me an odd look, wondering how I knew so much about the creatures, but she didn't comment. She went on, "Well, after the ceremony, it was easy to maintain a sylvmagic illusion of the tattoos. I didn't flee, though, until my father produced the Breth Bastionlord as a potential husband. Ruarth had insisted I wait until I was older, you see—he wanted me to be very sure of my own mind before I did anything that was irrevocable. After all, he had nothing to offer me except his friendship, and Lord

knows, I wasn't used to material hardships. But when that child-
molesting pervert caught sight of me and pressed my father for
my hand, then even Ruarth had to agree it was time to go. I had
no idea then, of course, that the Bastionlord would go to the
Keepers and ask them to find me, or that they would send someone after me."

"And the slavers always knew you were the Castlemaid, of
course. In fact, you never were a slave."

"That was just a cover. I paid for my passage. The whole
thing was arranged by a palace servant, an old nurse of mine
who sympathized. We pawned some of my jewelry to finance it
all. Mind you, the slavers thought to doublecross me, and earn a
second fee from my father by selling me back to him, but Ruarth overheard them and I flummoxed them with sylvmagic. In
the end they brought me to Gorthan Spit."

I grinned. Those slavers got more than they bargained for
when they took on Flame and Ruarth. I said, "But one of them
told Janko—Morthred—about it?"

"Yes. We ran out of luck. Someone must have told him who
I was, and that I was a sylv."

"He shut them all up with dunspells, and thought to subvert
you to dunmagic. Then, doubtless, he was going to return you to
Cirkase."

She shivered. "Yes. I would have been his pawn. Through
me, he would have controlled both Cirkase and Breth one day.
Blaze, you say he's been weakened. How long will it be before
he's able to subvert sylvs again?"

"How can I tell? I can't even begin to guess. It took him a
hundred years or so, first time around. This time . . . Weeks,
months, years? All I can say is that I feel it will happen, one
day. He is just too powerful to remain crippled. And it won't be
a hundred years, not this time."

"Then he's too dangerous to be left alive. I will never feel
safe, for a start. And with the ability to subvert sylvtalents, he'll
end up controlling the Keepers and the Keeper Isles."

I caught her meaning immediately. "You intend to go after
him," I said flatly. "With Ruarth. Of all the stupid, dangerous,
shrimp-brained . . ."

She nodded. "Yeah, yeah. I know all of that. But I have to.
Because he has to be stopped. And because while he's still
alive, Ruarth is still imprisoned in his blessed feathers." She
looked fierce. "I *need* him, Blaze. Ruarth, I mean. I need him as

a *man*. I don't give a damn if he turns out to be a hunchback with a face like a sea-slug, I want him *human*. I want him in my arms, in my bed, inside of me. You love Tor, you must know how I feel." There was a desperation there, birthed perhaps by her longing, but edged now by the suffering she had endured on Gorthan Spit.

There was nothing I could say, so I just nodded. Inside though, I wondered if I loved Tor quite as much as she hungered after Ruarth. "What makes you think he's gone to Mekaté?"

"Something he once said to me, when he thought I was safely subverted. He has more dunmagickers there, another enclave."

"And you think you can take on another enclave like Creed?"

"No, of course not. If I find them I'll get word to the Keepers. It's just *him* I want. Morthred. He's *mine*, Blaze."

Her ferocity was frightening. Then she relaxed and grinned. "Oh, by the way, Ruarth says that if ever the Dustels get back their islands, he'll make sure you'll be their very first honorary citizen."

I was touched. "Tell him I really appreciate the thought. And there's no place I'd rather be a citizen of either." I fingered my bare earlobe. "Let's hope . . ."

We were both silent for a moment, thinking of what would have to happen before I could ever have that tattoo.

Then she frowned, as though she had suddenly thought of something else. "You knew I was the Castlemaid *before* we went to the *Keeper Fair* to speak to Duthrick. You could have told him. You could have earned your two thousand setus and saved my life—and my arm—by telling him."

I nodded again.

She cocked her head to one side. "You're quite a lady, Blaze Halfbreed. That must have been a hard decision to make."

I looked away. "It was. And I'm reminded of it every time I see your arm. But when it came down to it, I couldn't sell you to them, not even to save your life, not when you would rather have died. It would have been . . . a betrayal." I raised my eyes to meet her gaze, almost unable to speak. "So I gave up the chance to earn some money—so what? You offered the Castlemaid to Duthrick if he would attack Creed. You were willing to sacrifice your whole future for Tor and me, even though you wouldn't do it to save your own life. I'll never forget that. Not as long as I live."

She didn't comment but crossed the room to take me in her

arms, as best she could. We stood like that, hugging each other and, I believe, neither of us was quite dry-eyed.

Then she was gone, her leather bag slung over her shoulder, her fair hair swinging free. She was Lyssal, Castlemaid of Cirkase, royal heir to an islandom, but I knew to me she'd always be Flame Windrider.

CHAPTER 26

I WENT TO FIND TOR. HE WAS IN HIS ROOM and he was also packing.

He looked up as I entered and his eyes crinkled at the corners as they always did when he smiled. He had shaved off his beard and he did not look that much different to the Stragglerman I had first seen sitting by himself in the taproom on my first day in Gorthan Docks. He said, "I have arranged passage on a trader that's calling at the Spatts. I have business there."

"I thought you might want to go with Ransom." In spite of what I had told Flame, I was by no means sure if Tor wanted to have me along. I was trying to appear disinterested, and ended up sounding uncharacteristically tentative.

"The Keepers will see to it that he's returned to his father." He ran a hand through his hair in a nervous gesture I'd never seen him make before. "You know I want you to come with me."

"I know."

He was unusually diffident. "I, er, asked for a passage for two."

I smiled.

His face lightened and he gave that grin of his that chased away all the seriousness. "Are you sure? There's such a lot we have to talk about. There are things I have to tell you. Things you should know—"

Before he could get too carried away, I said, "No more talk of marriage, Tor. It's not possible."

"Well, we need to talk about that, too. Right now, I'm just pleased you'll come. I was so afraid you might want to sail with the Keepers. That you'd go back to their service."

I stared at him, surprised and nettled. After what had happened he still thought I might serve the Keepers? Didn't he realize that it wasn't the Keepers who tempted me away from him now? How typical of a man—it had never occurred to him that I might just have chosen to link my life to another woman rather than follow him.

I said, "You still thought that I might sell the Castlemaid to the Keepers? Could you really have thought that I would serve people who would do anything to get that murderous black powder—so that they can threaten all the Isles with it?"

"No, not really, I suppose. But I know how much having citizenship means to you."

"Not as much as I thought it did. Once, long ago on Calment Minor, I discovered there were some things I would not do to myself for citizenship; here I learned that there are some things I would not do to others. Once I realized Flame was the Castlemaid and I saw that she'd rather die than go back, I couldn't betray her.

"And now, well, if I don't deliver the Castlemaid to Duthrick, I don't think I'll find it very easy to persuade the Keeper Council to grant me citizenship. They don't like failure, especially not Duthrick. I won't gain anything by continuing in service to them."

"I wasn't sure you knew that Flame was Castlemaid Lyssal."

"Did *you* know?"

"Yes, once I saw she had contact with the Dustels. Before that, well, I thought she must be, in spite of the sylvmagic and the lack of tattoos. The information I had made it seem likely that Flame and Lyssal were one and the same person. I even had a description of the Castlemaid that fitted."

Once again there was evidence that he had access to knowledge that was denied most people. Once again that thought came unbidden: who was he? And it was swiftly followed by another: was I so saltwater mad that I was going to become the traveling companion of a man who hadn't yet told me the truth about himself?

I didn't want to think about it. I said, "I must pack my own things, I'll join you shortly."

Back in my own room, I threw the few belongings I had into my pack. There wasn't much; thirty years of living and I hadn't accumulated enough to make any self-respecting thief look twice. I wasn't quite finished when Duthrick came to see me.

I didn't hear him enter the room, but caught the smell of sylvmagic and turned to see him standing there, just inside the doorway. "Don't you knock?" I asked sourly.

"The door was open." He was making an effort to be pleasant. I wasn't. "What do you want?"

"The Castlemaid."

I gave a snort of disgust. "Still? Great Trench below, you never give up, do you? Well, I've got news for you, Duthrick— I know why you want her. I know the price of your foul black powder: Lyssal of Cirkase for the Breth Bastionlord, otherwise the Lord won't sell you the stuff."

I'd shocked him; his face pinched up in surprise. Finally he said, "So you know. Well then, you know how important it is that the Castlemaid is found. Blaze, you've seen what the cannon-guns can do—"

I turned on him in a fury. "Yes, I've seen. It is *unspeakable!*"

He was taken aback. "But you saw what success we had with razing that village—"

"Success? Oh yes, that *was* a success. You killed hundreds: slaves, children, subverted sylvtalents, a Menod patriarch, anyone at all who happened to be in the wrong place at the wrong time, guilty or not. You destroyed houses, anybody or anything that happened to get in the way." Absurdly, I remembered all the feathers blowing around, all that had remained of someone's laying flock of waders. They hadn't asked to die either.

"Do *you*, of *all* people, dare to be righteous? How many people have you killed with that Calmenter sword of yours?"

"When I kill, at least it's face-to-face. They know who's doing it and why. They have a chance to stop me—with their skills or with words. And I know who I'm killing. I am forced to take responsibility for what I do. And I've never killed an innocent who happened to be in the way, simply because they were there." I had an unbidden memory of the slaves who had died on my sword at Morthred's instigation and felt more than a twinge of guilt. I hurried on. "But this—this unspeakable horror of yours—" I almost choked on my words. "Did the people who fired the cannon-guns *see* who they killed? Did they know how many innocents were cut down? How many slaves were buried in the ruins of buildings? Were they forced to see and *care* what they did? D'y'know, Duthrick, I've always been reluctant to use a bow, and now I know why—because it's too easy to kill that way. You can stand away from your victim, and not see the expression on his face. What you did yesterday was immoral. It was *despicable*."

"Those subverted sylvtalents had to be stopped and there was no other way we could do it without risking meeting Morthred and being subverted ourselves. We *had* to do it from a distance. It was necessary. I'm sorry it was necessary. But it *was* necessary. Perhaps if you'd served us better and killed Morthred at the inn, then it wouldn't have *been* necessary." I winced and he pressed home his advantage. "Blaze, can't you see what a wonderful invention this is? With cannon-guns mounted on our ships we can control the sea; there will never be another smuggler or slaver or pirate. With land-based cannon-guns we can force others to obey Keeper law. Our system of law, and equality before the law, will prevail throughout the Isles of Glory. The mere threat of cannon-guns will be enough to stop all petty warring between islandoms. There will be peace enforced by our fleet . . . Can't you see it, Blaze? The kind of society we can build?"

"You can't build a fine society on shit, Duthrick. And these weapons of yours are shit. If you want decency throughout the Isles, then show people that decency works, that it brings peace and prosperity. Don't expect anything but hate when you force yourselves on others. You won't build a decent world when you yourselves lack decency. Practice compassion, understanding, equality. Teach your bloody Keeper sylvs that liberty only works when coupled with right—and responsibility. Learn to *practice* equality, not just preach the myth of it.

"And as for peace, your weapons won't bring peace, but war. That is ever the way of weapons and people who impose their strength on others. And have you thought what will happen when your enemies learn how to use this black powder of yours? That's when you'll find out just how fragile this peace of yours is." My own rhetoric startled me; I wasn't usually given to such eloquence. I thought wryly that I was beginning to sound like Tor.

I concluded, "You damn near killed me with that hellish stuff—don't expect me to bring you the Castlemaid."

"I see." He was snapping at me—voice, eyes, brows, stance, all snapping like a basket of irate cockles. "And just where do you think you're going now? You have no citizenship and doubtless little money. Without us, the only place you can afford to stay is here on Gorthan Spit. If you want Keeper protection, Keeper money, Keeper citizenship, then you have to *earn* it."

"I've earned it twice over at the very least," I said wearily, "but you haven't given it to me. I'm going with Tor Ryder."

His eyebrows shot up off his forehead. "*Tor Ryder?* Ryder and *you*? You're going off with a *patriarch*? Blaze Halfbreed is joining the Menod?" And he started to laugh. Spontaneous, if cynical, laughter, great bubbles of it. For the first time in our relationship, I had brought genuine amusement to Syr-sylv Duthrick's lips. How much greater his mockery would have been had he known how much he had devastated me, had he known that he had just brought my world tumbling down around my ears.

"How did you know he was a patriarch?" I asked. My voice was coming to me across miles of ocean; I could hear the waves creaming in my head.

"I *should* have known right from the beginning—who else wears all black and has the face of a doom merchant, if not a Menod? But it was one of the other Keepers who told me. She knew of him. He's been a thorn in our side for a long while. He's a clever fellow, I'll grant you that. A troublemaker. One day he is going to meet the Keeper Council head on, and we'll have to deal with him. Be careful you aren't caught up in the backwash of that encounter, Blaze."

"Leave me, Duthrick. You've been insulting enough for one day."

He stared at me, hearing the loathing in my voice. "First I want to know about the bird you sent with the message. Was that a Dustel? Are there really still sentient Dustel birds?"

I was too upset to talk to him. "Find out for yourself, for once. Leave me, Duthrick."

He didn't like the arbitrary dismissal one little bit. He said harshly, "If I could be certain that you know where the Castlemaid is, I'd never let you leave this island until you told me."

I pointed to the door. "Out, damn it!"

This time he took the hint.

I slammed the door behind him and collapsed onto the bed. I was shaking.

I'd been as blind as a lugworm in its burrow. How could I have been so stupid? Of course Tor was a patriarch. A Menod priest. It explained so much. His reluctance to kill. His insistence on marriage (how could a patriarch live in so-called sin?). His compassion. His prayers for Alain. His whole relationship with Alain. His wish to see a better world replace what we had. His mental strength and ability to endure, his knowledge—he had the whole Menod network to keep him informed of what went on in the Isles. His conversion to the faith explained the difference between the man who had been the Lance of Calment and the man he was now. And those periods when he was so remote from me, so turned inward—he had been praying, of course.

I felt as if someone had pulled the plug out of my boat in mid-ocean.

HE CAME TO FIND OUT WHAT WAS TAKING me so long.

He stood in the doorway, tall and handsome and happy. The blue eyes looked at me with love. The turquoise sea-snake in his earlobe gleamed in the brown of his skin. I had wondered how a man could be so strong and yet so gentle, and now I knew: his strength stemmed from faith; his gentleness stemmed from belief.

"Are you ready?" he asked.

"Why didn't you tell me you were a patriarch?"

He didn't ask how I knew; it was unimportant. He said, barely above a whisper, "I was so afraid of losing you. I was afraid it might make a difference."

"It does."

"*Why?* I love you." His agony tore at me.

"You love God more."

There was a long silence and I could read his hurt in his face. "That's unfair," he said finally.

"Yes. I'm sorry. It's not quite what I meant. If I shared your beliefs, it wouldn't matter. But I don't. Tor, I can't believe in your God, or your heaven. Under those circumstances, I can't share your life."

He winced as though he had been stabbed. "Blaze, even my

belief is not absolute. I doubt. But I hope that there is a God who cares. Who rewards those who try to make this a better place to live in. If I'm wrong about that, well, I'll still be glad I tried. It can't be wrong to help others be happy."

"No. But I'm not that kind of person. I'm too selfish. I didn't want to hang around Creed helping the less fortunate while Keepers fired cannon-guns at me—I wanted to save myself and get out of there! I don't want to work for others. I want to work for myself. I want *me* to be happy. I want citizenship, a place to live, money to buy my own comfort. Oh, I wouldn't now sail hard over everyone to get it, as I would have once, but I still want it.

"Besides, your association with me has already harmed you—you have fought and killed when your religion tells you it's a sin to kill. You have bedded me, although there has been no marriage. You even offered to torture Sickle and Domino. Your love for me brought you into disagreement with a fellow patriarch." I meant Alain Jentel, of course. I knew now what I had previously only sensed: Alain had pressed Tor to forget me.

He gave a twisted smile. "I never thought I was perfect. And I'm no dogmatist. I'm no Alain Jentel. I've always been at loggerheads with the Council of Patriarchs on a score of issues. I probably always will be. I don't hanker after sainthood; too often it goes hand in hand with being sanctimonious. I'll never believe that something as beautiful as lying in your arms, as loving you, can be wrong. I believe that it's important for the Council to have someone like me around—I challenge the rigidity of their thinking. I want to be the grain of sand that irritates the oyster into producing the pearl, as long as I live. I'm a very unconventional priest, Blaze. You wouldn't find me so very hard to live with.

"And you are too hard on yourself. You have risked your life for others, not for yourself. You are a better person than you think."

"Am I? Perhaps. But I fall way short of your standards, Tor. And I can't serve your God. You are first and foremost a patriarch. I understand that now. You serve the Menod. *I* think the Menod pursue the right goals, but for all the wrong reasons and, for all your pragmatism, often in impractical ways. You do it for God, for a promise of heaven. You do it by love, by example, by unselfish service. How could you travel with a woman who would rather wield a sword against her enemies than love them?

I serve myself first, Tor. But you—you adhere to a different set of values. And you follow the dictates of the Council of Patriarchs. That's what you were doing here on Gorthan Spit in the first place, wasn't it? It was the Council of Patriarchs, not the Bethany Holdlord, who sent you to keep an eye on Ransom. And, I suspect, to look for Alain Jentel as well. You go where your Council sends you. Your stewardship is to the lay Menod, your duty is to the Council of Patriarchs and your service is to God. And if I'm reading the signs rightly, the Council is dedicated to opposing Keepers and undermining Keeper power outside of their own islandom.

"I don't share your calling. I don't believe in your God. And if I'm going to risk my life, it wouldn't be in opposing the Keepers. There are worse evils. I simply don't share your vision of the world, Tor. How can we live together?"

He was silent.

"It was just a dream, Tor. A wonderful dream, but no more than that. I think in my heart I knew it, even before I realized you were a patriarch. We are too different. Our goals are too diverse."

His silence dragged on.

"I'll not go back to the Keepers," I said gently. "I've learned that much. I'm going with Flame."

He spoke then, and there was surprise in his voice. "But she's going after Morthred, surely."

I nodded, impressed that he had read her so well.

He said, "There's hardly money or comfort in that."

"I care about Flame, about what happens to her. And if Morthred dies, I'll be a citizen of the new Dustel Islands. You see, there is something in it for me. There always has to be."

"I would have thought there was something in it for you with me. Quite apart from the fact that the Menod are not entirely without influence when it comes to the citizenship and marriage laws involving its patriarchs and their families." He was trying not to be hurt, but he couldn't hide it.

"The possibility of citizenship was not the reason I wanted to go with you and you know it. I thought it was enough to love you, but it's not, Tor. There has to be a common purpose. We wouldn't even have children to bind us."

He shook his head, in sadness, in resignation. "Every word you say makes me love you more, for what you are. You are all I lack."

"But I *am* right."

"Are you?" he whispered. "Perhaps. But I don't know how I will learn to live alone all over again now that I have met you."

I stepped into his arms and we held each other for a long time. Then he moved back. "If ever I can help you, contact me through the Council of Patriarchs."

I nodded. For someone who had once never cried, I seemed to be doing a lot of looking through blurred eyes lately.

He fumbled in his pocket and brought out a pendant on a chain of black coral. He put it over his head so that the badge of the Menod faith, a spiral inside a triangle, swung on his chest. It was a symbolic gesture, a public acknowledgment of what he was. He said, "You'll be in my prayers as long as I live."

"It can't do any harm," I told him.

We smiled at each other, empty aching smiles. "I won't ever change my mind, Blaze. Remember that, if ever you need me," he said, and was gone.

HAVE I FINISHED MY TALE? WHY NO, I haven't really reached the end of the story as far as Gorthan Spit was concerned. Not yet.

And of course, in many ways what happened there was just the beginning of a much larger story. As I said somewhere near the beginning of this tale of mine, the seeds of change, of *the* Change, were planted on Gorthan Spit. For the Change to occur, it was necessary for me to reject both the Keepers and Tor Ryder and join my future to that of Flame and Ruarth Windrider. For without me, without my sword and my knowledge of the Isles' low-life, they would never have survived long enough to do what they did, and the Isles of Glory would never have been the place it was by the time you people arrived. You might have been greeted by Morthred the Mad when you sailed into The Hub.

And then if I'd stayed with Tor, he might have lacked the drive and the angry passion that impelled him to become the visionary leader he was, that turned him into the kind of man who could challenge both the Menod Council of Patriarchs and the power of the Keepers—and ultimately the very nature of sylvmagic itself. Without my rejection of Tor, you might have been greeted by Keeper cannon-guns when you sailed into The Hub.

Oh yes, in the end we all played our parts in changing the

Isles of Glory: Ransom Holswood who became the Holdlord of
Bethany; Syr-sylv Duthrick who became Keeperlord of the
Keeper Isles and Morthred the Mad who wanted to be monarch
of us all; poor dead Eylsa who gave me the mark on my palm so
that I could enlist ghemphic help when I needed it; even Seeker,
Tunn's mangy dog, played his part too.

But I digress. I haven't told you the end of my tale of
Gorthan Spit.

Duthrick, you see, in his desire to get the black powder for
the Keeper Isles, had not done with us yet.

CHAPTER 27

I DIDN'T GO STRAIGHT TO THE DOCKS, and Flame, after Tor left me at the inn. There was still something I had to do. I wanted to find Tunn, to discover if he was all right. I had meant to ask Flame to look at him, to see if she could help heal his dunmagic whipping, but I'd forgotten and now I felt terrible about it.

I asked after him down in the taproom. The innkeeper, who now practically spat with fury each time he laid eyes on me, told me he hadn't seen Tunn for days. At least, that was what I thought he said; he was actually hard to understand because his broken nose was still puffed up to the size of a sea-cucumber and his mouth was distorted by the dunmagic welts that crisscrossed his face.

I looked for Tunn in the fuel shed, but he wasn't there, so I went to the place where he hid his pet, the place where I'd seen him last. He was still there, crammed into the space behind the fish boxes. Seeker was also there, whining miserably, tail drooping. His mange had improved, but he looked thinner than ever, if that was possible. You could count his ribs with a glance at his flank.

I thought Tunn was just asleep, but when I touched him he fell back out into the open and his eyes were staring, his arms and legs stiffened into a grotesque tangle. It had been a slow

and painful death and he had not been dead long. The worst
thing of all was the look on his face—proof of a fear so great
that it had taken away all his trust in his own kind. He had died
in terror and pain, alone save for his dog. I think it was there,
kneeling by his side, that I first really reconciled myself to what
Flame and Ruarth intended to do; I knew then that I couldn't let
Morthred roam the Isles leaving agony and death like this in his
wake. It was there, on the fishermen's wharf, that my anger became a thirst for revenge. Tor wouldn't have approved of the
emotion, but I was glad of it. It made my fear less important.

I picked Tunn up in my arms and turned to go back to the
inn. Seeker looked up at me hopefully and thumped that huge
tail of his. I was about to send him on his way when I noticed
what I hadn't seen at first—the animal had made a pathetic attempt to feed his dying master. There was a pile of uneaten
scraps at my feet, fish most of it, and quite unappetizing, but
Seeker had done his best.

"You stink," I said. "You're probably the ugliest mutt I've
ever seen. Your coat is a mess. If there's one thing I don't need,
it's to be lumbered with a pet." He swept his tail through the air
with gusto, sending several fish boxes flying, gazing at me all
the while with pleading brown eyes—and I had a pet I didn't
need.

THE FOUR OR FIVE CUSTOMERS IN THE
taproom took one look at me and my burden and hurriedly left.
I laid Tunn on one of the tables. The innkeeper was about to utter an outraged protest when he saw my face and changed his
mind. I said, "I want the lad given a proper burial—no throwing
him to the fish, understand?"

He nodded dumbly.

I gave him some money. "That's for your trouble. And when
I come back to Gorthan Docks next, I shall expect to be able to
see the grave. Understand?"

He nodded again.

I don't know why I bothered. What did it matter what happened to the boy's body after he was dead? I should have done
more while he was alive. I knew it was illogical, but I did it anyway. Guilt, I suppose.

"And now feed my dog," I said.

The innkeeper looked down at Seeker, who was doing his

best to hide under a chair. The chair was small and the animal was large. *"That?"*

I nodded.

I waited while the creature ate probably the best meal he'd ever had in his life. He would have eaten still more if I'd let him, but I was afraid something might burst. His stomach was as bloated as an inflated pufferfish.

Only then did I head down to the docks. Seeker lolloped after me, feet scattering the fish scales in all directions.

Ruarth Windrider and several other Dustels met me halfway and I didn't need to understand their words to know something was wrong. Promising myself that one day—soon—I was going to learn their goddamned language, I hurried on to find the mullet boat that was sailing for Mekatéhaven.

Now that the tides and winds were right, the main docks of the harbor were busier than I'd ever seen them before. A motley assortment of drunkards and vagrants were earning a setu or two loading ships; chandlers along the seafront appeared to be doing good business. The only idle people were a couple of old men sitting on barrels outside one of the chandler shops, and they looked so decrepit I doubted they'd been capable of work in years.

When I found the mullet boat, tucked against the docks between a Gorthan Spit trader bound for the Cirkase Islands and an unmarked ship that had smuggler written all over it, there was enough sylvmagic dripping across its deck to light a mansion on a dark night (for Awarefolk anyway), far too much to have come from any spell of Flame's. "What the shit happened?" I growled at Ruarth. He, of course, could not reply.

The only person on the deck of the mullet boat, leaning nonchalantly on the railing, was Garrowyn Gilfeather. He inclined his head in my direction and adjusted that extraordinary wool garment about his body. "Garrowyn," I said. "I'm looking for Flame—have you seen her?"

"Oh, ay," he said casually. "She was here a while back. Her arm looks just fine. The stump healed beautifully."

I blinked. How could he have seen her stump? He wasn't one of the Awarefolk . . . I wanted to think about that, to think about how he could smell dunmagic, work out the implications, but there was no time.

"What happened to her?" I asked.

"The Keepers came'n took her," he replied. "Luggage'n all. She's not sailing on this boat anymore."

I remembered Duthrick's threat: *I'd never let you leave this island.* He'd finally thought it all through, done all the adding up, including the presence of Ruarth. I'd underestimated him . . .

"Are ye looking for passage to Mekaté too then, lass?" Garrowyn asked. "The captain—"

"No," I cut him off and glanced at the *Keeper Fair.* It was also preparing to sail that night if the activities on deck were anything to go by.

I turned away to hide my whisper to the Dustels, who had lined up on one of the mooring lines. "Ruarth, if you can find her, tell her I'll be with her as soon as I can. After dark sometime. Perhaps just after the ship sails."

The birds flew away and I also turned to go, but Garrowyn spoke again. "I can smell fear," he said, "and she was scared." The look he gave me from under those unruly brows was dispassionate.

"And you didn't help her?" I asked.

"Against Keepers?" His tone was deliberately incredulous. "Lass, I don't mess with magic. Any magic, if I can help it. She's already had more help from me than she had a right to expect."

"You're all heart, Garrowyn Gilfeather," I said.

"I'm a physician lass, no more, no less. Compassion I have no time for. Compassion does not heal the sick, but it does weaken he who feels it. I would have thought ye'd know that."

I turned on my heel and headed for the main street. His voice echoed after me: "Hey, halfbreed, if ever ye come to Mekaté, head for the hills and ask for Garrowyn Gilfeather of the Sky Plains people, the selver-herders. Ye've not seen the best of Mekaté, till ye leave the lowlands behind ye."

I ignored him and set off for the sea-pony pens on the other side of town. Seeker followed, his nose low to the ground, snuffling along as if he was tracking prey. The sea-pony livery kept their mounts in the sea, of course, penned in with netting. The owner, a Bethany Isles man with a wooden leg, was in a black mood when I arrived. He had just been chasing away a crowd of dirty Spitter children whose one delight in life, if he was to be believed, was to tease the animals. He wasn't inclined to listen to me when I said I wanted to buy a sea-pony. I suppose I could have hired one, pretending I was going to bring it back, but I'd been the victim of dishonesty often enough myself to have a distaste for robbing others, with the exception of slavers and suchlike; them, I'd steal from at any time.

I haggled and pleaded and finally beat the price down to something I could pay—just. The amount wasn't lessened by the fact that I had chosen the strongest and largest animal in the pens. I insisted that it be fed well and then I went into the town to do some shopping. I bought food (desiccated fish and seaweed cakes); several large drinkskins; four hide bags, their seams sealed with sea-urchin glue, to keep everything dry; some rope and a few other small items. When I had nothing left in my purse except a couple of small coppers, I went back to collect my newly fed purchase.

My parting shot to the Bethanyman was that he would do well to keep his mouth shut about my purchasing the animal. I tapped my Calmenter blade meaningfully and he gave me a scornful look. "On Gorthan Spit," he said, "everyone keeps his mouth shut about everything if he wants to keep his throat from being cut."

That was probably true up to a point, but if the Keepers actually thought to question him, I doubted that he'd consider it a wise policy to lie, especially when they could use sylvmagic to check that he told the truth. However, it probably didn't matter all that much; by the time the Keepers had found out exactly what I'd done, I'd be long gone.

I rode the sea-pony away, out to sea. The halfbreed children were back at the edge of the pens as I took the animal out through the boom the Bethanyman had opened for me, and they pitched a few rocks in my direction for no reason other than mischief. When I looked back, the Bethanyman was chasing them away yet again.

There's one simple problem with sea-riding—a sea-pony loves to dive and, given the chance, will do so, with or without people on its back. However, there's also a simple solution. The animal will only dive if it can close its airhole, so a special ring, made of animal hide and inserted into the lip of the hole, solves the problem. Naturally you have to keep a close watch to make sure the ring doesn't pop out. I carried extras in case it did.

I also carried Seeker, who whined unhappily inside one of the hide bags. Every now and then he poked his snout out of the top and gave a dismal howl, a strange, undog-like sound that made the hairs on my neck stand up and probably did the same for every sailor in every ship anchored around the harbor.

There'd be a lot of talk about sea-dragons, or sea-sirens and the like, on board ships that night. I cursed him. I might have known he'd be a pest. In the end I tied the top of the bag so he couldn't look out and spoke to him softly until he quietened.

Nightfall found me swimming over to the *Keeper Fair* from the seaward side, in order to tether the sea-pony to the ship with a long rope. The animal was invisible against the darkness of the water; if anyone saw it anyway, well, there was nothing unusual about a sea-pony being in the sea. There were wild ones everywhere, after all.

Ruarth was there, flying about in spite of the dark, to show me where to go. There was actually enough warding on the *Keeper Fair* to make it light as day for the two of us. Fortunately everyone was busy preparing the ship for sailing and the lower deck seemed deserted. The worst of the damage seemed to have been repaired, although I could still smell an unpleasant mix of burned wood and dunmagic.

Ruarth showed me where they had warded Flame—a cabin, with a porthole, and on the lower deck too, seaward side. It couldn't have been better. I asked him to make sure she was alone and he flew up, looked in and then flew back to me, nodding. Then he went back up to tap on the glass and attract her attention. A moment later the porthole was unlatched, and Flame had pushed it open using the handle of her hairbrush so as not to touch the warding. I flung up a hook attached to a rope and a little later still I was wriggling through the porthole, not the easiest of procedures for someone my size. I very nearly left most of my clothing in the sea, but at least I was still unseen by any Keeper.

"This rescuing business is becoming a habit," Flame said mildly. "Although I see this time you did your best to leave your, er, habit behind, so to speak."

"Very funny," I replied, pulling my trousers back up.

"Perhaps we ought to set up a proper business: *Spectacular Rescues Made. Surcharges where dunmagic is concerned—*"

"Do shut up, Flame. You're not rescued yet. Are you all right?" In fact, in spite of her banter, I was appalled by her appearance. Her eyes seemed too large for her face and she looked as though she hadn't slept for a week. It was only a few hours since I'd seen her last, and she looked as if she'd been shipwrecked in the meantime. Beside me, Ruarth was jumping around in that agitated avian way of his, quite obviously just as disturbed as I was.

"That friend of yours has his methods," she said tightly.

"*Duthrick?* What's he been doing?"

"Using sylvmagic to confuse me. He can make you think the world is upside-down, Blaze. He's so much better trained than I am—I'm no match for him." Of course not. The Syr-sylv was, among other things, the chief teacher of sylvtalent use in The Hub Academy. The bastard. "He can make me lose track of who I am, where I am in space and time. It was like being bodiless, without senses. Lost in infinity . . . awful. I thought I was going mad. For a time, I *was* mad."

I frowned. Sylvmagic illusion used this way seemed very much like dunmagic. I asked gently, "Did you tell him what he wanted to know?"

She closed her eyes. "Yes. Yes, I think so. I'm not sure."

Ruarth burst into wild chatter, then abruptly stopped and went to perch on her hand. She raised him to her cheek and he laid his head to hers. "I know, I know, Ruarth," she whispered.

"Who made these wards?" I asked.

"He did. Duthrick."

"Listen, Flame. There's transport out there. All we have to do is to get out of that porthole."

"But the wards?"

"Duthrick is going to have to break them for you. Get him in here. Him alone." I had already noted that there was a key on our side of the door. The door itself was warded, of course. I locked us in. "We'll only open it for Duthrick. Start yelling, Flame."

Obligingly, she started bellowing for Duthrick. For a woman of her size, she could certainly produce a lot of sound. Ruarth flew off her hand quite smartly and went to sit as far away as he could, which wasn't far—the cabin was tiny. I stood behind the door.

We had a couple of false starts. A woman came first and asked Flame, quite pleasantly, through the door, what she wanted. Flame asked for Duthrick and the woman went away. Flame then resumed her bellow, and a few minutes later some-one else came by to explain that Duthrick was busy because the ship was just leaving port and couldn't it wait? This Keeper, a man, actually tried to enter, but Flame refused to unlock the door. Instead, she raised the volume and started shouting gib-berish.

Five minutes later Duthrick came.

Flame insisted he enter alone, which he obligingly did—only to find my sword at his throat. Flame locked the door behind him.

He stared at me, nonplussed. "I thought you'd gone," he said finally. "The patriarch Stragglerman was on that ship that just left—"

"I changed my mind. Break the wards, Duthrick."

"She's the Castlemaid, Blaze."

"That's right. And she's leaving—with me."

"You *knew*?" First he couldn't believe it. Then when he did, he wanted to kill me. He came within an inch of drawing his sword, but, after considering the circumstances, thought better of it and settled for: "You doublecrossing halfbreed Awarebitch!"

I said, "Well, now we know what you *really* think of me, don't we? Break the wards, Duthrick."

"Never."

"There's another way I can do it," I pointed out, almost purring. "Don't make me kill you, Syr-sylv."

"You wouldn't do that." But he was doubtful.

"Oh, yes, I would. For Flame I would do anything."

"You pervert," he spat.

I let him believe it. "You're fussy about such things all of sudden, aren't you? Tell me, Duthrick, which is the perversion: the love between two mature adults, or the fact that you wanted to marry Lyssal off to a man of fifty who likes little boys of five in his bed? But enough of that. I'm afraid some of your friends may grow a little uneasy if we take too much time over this—break the wards, Duthrick. Now." I eased a little pressure on to the hilt of my sword and the tip broke his skin at the throat. *"Now,* Duthrick."

His teeth clamped down as he hissed, "You'll never get away with this."

"Do you know, I think I will? Flame, I'm afraid I'm going to have to kill him . . ." I sighed and gave an irritated tongue click, as if his murder was a mild annoyance. I looked across at Flame. "Sorry. I didn't think it would be necessary." Privately I wondered if I really would be able to do it. Apart from those subverted to dunmagic, I'd never killed a Keeper sylv before. I'd never needed to before. And a Councilor? A few days earlier it would have been unthinkable.

"I don't mind," Flame said calmly. "After what he did to me, I don't care if he dies."

Duthrick snarled. "I'll hunt you down, Blaze, if it takes the rest of my life."

"Don't be so melodramatic, Duthrick. It doesn't suit your cool style. Last chance—this sword is going in now." I smiled at him, a smile as ruthless as I knew how to make it. And he capitulated. The wards came down. To this day, I don't know whether I really would have killed him, but he believed it—and he knew me well.

I dropped the point of my blade and whirled him around to face the door. A moment later he was unconscious on the floor. I knew a thing or two about pressure points: one of Syr-sylv Arnado's handier lessons to an adolescent acolyte with aspirations to be a Council agent.

Ruarth said something and Flame translated, stricken. "He said that—that you have made a ruthless enemy."

I felt a spine-crawl of fear. Ruarth was right. Duthrick was an unforgiving, unscrupulous man. He would lose face over this and he would seek the means to restore his lost pride and prestige. *You'll never get away with this.* "Let's go," I said.

Flame hesitated. "Er, you first."

"No, you. Just in case he wakes up."

"I think you'd better go first."

I looked at her, exasperated. "Will you get out of that bloody porthole!"

"I can't swim," she admitted sheepishly.

I flung my hands up in the air in capitulation. I went first. Flame's bag followed, then Flame, who, by performing a remarkable feat of contortion, managed to follow me feet first. She hung by her five fingers from the porthole for a prayer-filled moment, then dropped daintily into the water. The ship was already slipping away from the docks. I caught her in my arms as she came up.

"Here," I said, handing her the rope I had just cut away from the *Keeper Fair.* "Our transport out of here is on the end of that somewhere. I'll support you while you haul us in." I groped around with one hand for her bag, which was floating nearby.

She asked, with justifiable asperity, "And just how do you suggest I pull myself along when I only have one hand?"

I was still looking for a diplomatic answer to that one when she hit on her own solution by gripping the rope in her teeth in between hauling on it with her one good arm. Still, her mind was elsewhere. She took a mouthful of water, spluttered, and gasped, "You let go of me and I'll never speak to you again."

"You should learn how to swim."

She spoke from between gritted teeth: "You can teach me one day. *But not now.* Blaze, will you please get me the hell out of this bloody ocean!"

Just then there was the most appalling howl of anguish from in front of us. Flame moaned. "Don't tell me," she said, "let me guess. That's the sound of a hungry sea-dragon searching for maidens to devour."

"Then neither of us need worry, need we?" I said sweetly. "Actually, I think it's my dog."

"Your *dog?* Somewhere in the middle of the ocean—in a boat, I hope—you have a dog that howls like a drowned sailor's lost soul in the Great Trench?"

When she put it like that, it did seem rather ridiculous. And what's more, she didn't know about the sea-pony yet.

CHAPTER 28

WHEN DAWN CAME, WE, WERE ON A RE-
mote beach leagues to the west of Gorthan Docks. I built up a
seaweed fire and we sat by it to warm ourselves while we had
breakfast. Ruarth, who had spent the night nonchalantly perched
on the sea-pony's head, asleep, was flitting around catching in-
sects and eating grass seeds; Flame wasn't nearly so happy. I
think it was partially because she was tormented by her failure
to withstand Duthrick. She needed someone to tell her she could
fail occasionally. And it couldn't be Ruarth; not when he had to
rely on her so much because of what he was, because of the
stature he lacked. She needed a friend who was an equal. I was
suddenly glad we were together, although my parting from Tor
was an undercurrent of heartache that all too often eddied
sharply to the surface.

The other reason for Flame's unhappiness was more tangible. The run from the Docks on the back of a sea-pony had been
a non-swimmer's idea of tempting providence, even though I
had tied her to both me and the mount.

I myself was well pleased with the time we had made; sea-
ponies in their element could really move. Too fast even for
blood-demons—although, guessing blood-demons were coastal
creatures, I'd kept us well out to sea anyway.

Seeker was just relieved to be out of the bag. He'd eaten and was now leaping around the dunes kicking up sand and generally behaving like a child who'd escaped from a strict nurse. We'd already had to have a short discipline session with regard to Ruarth and birds in general. Fortunately he seemed to have accepted the idea that chasing, eating or harassing anything with feathers was out of the question. He was nothing if not eager to please.

"Let me see if I have this right," Flame was saying. "You intend that we *ride* on one of those—those sea-*worms*—up to our backsides in water *all the way to Mekaté?* Two or three *days* without stopping? You're saltwater mad! What if we're attacked by sharks? What if we fall asleep and fall off? What if it takes longer than that and we run out of water? What if there's a storm? What if the skies cloud over and we can't read the stars at night?" Her expression was becoming more and more frantic. "God above, what if we miss Mekaté altogether and just keep going until we fall over the edge of the world?"

"The water only comes up to our knees when we sit on the sea-pony," I pointed out reasonably, ignoring the fact that in rough weather it was an entirely different story. "Sharks are scared of sea-ponies. We'll take it in turns to sleep. We'll tie ourselves on. The currents flow directly from here to Mekaté at this time of year, or so the fishermen say. It's not the stormy season. It hasn't rained here in over three months, and the weather is not expected to break for another couple of weeks yet, not until the winds change. And a Menod scholar from The Hub once told me the world was actually round and you couldn't fall off the edge. If we kept on sailing west we would eventually just arrive back where we started from."

She gave me an expressive look.

"Flame, there's no other safe way—"

"Safe?"

"Duthrick is going to scour Gorthan Spit for you—and me—especially now that he knows you're the Castlemaid. He'll sylv-magic everyone in sight to find out if they've seen you. No ship will leave the Docks until he's searched it right down to the bilge water. You can't leave the island any other way but this. The sailors back in Gorthan Docks all told me the good weather will hold. We'll be tied on and we can watch over one another. You were willing to die rather than marry the Breth Bastionlord before. There's very little risk, I promise you."

"Great Trench below," she moaned. "I've got to be out of my mind to listen to you. I've had nothing but trouble since I met you, Blaze Halfbreed."

"Unjust!" I said indignantly. It was *your* trouble right from the beginning, not mine!"

"Yeah. Well, maybe. And I suppose I should say thanks for rescuing me again."

"Don't mention it." That sounded ungallant, so I leaned forward and touched her knee. "After what you did to save Tor and me? Flame—"

She cut me off with a gesture of embarrassment, so I stopped. Some things we really didn't have to say.

Just then Ruarth, apparently having finished his breakfast, came back to us and sat on Flame's hand. He lifted a wing, stretched it daintily so that the tip touched the toe of one foot, and rubbed his beak against his shoulder. "What's he saying?" I asked.

She looked at him, blinked and then laughed. "Blaze, he's just *preening.*"

I felt an idiot. "Oh. Sorry, Ruarth. You *really* are going to have to teach me how to understand Dustel."

Flame said bleakly, "There's not going to be much time for that, is there, except on this crazy ride to Mekaté. I'm sorry I've upset your plans, Blaze. Where will you meet up with Tor again?"

"Well, er, I wasn't actually thinking of joining him. I found out he was a patriarch of the Menod, and I just can't see myself as a patriarch's dutiful wife."

"Ah." She looked at me with compassion. "We did wonder. Ruarth said he was sure Tor was at the very least a Menod lay brother. I'm sorry, Blaze. What are you going to do?"

So I'd been the only blind idiot, had I? That rankled. "Well," I said, feigning indifference, "I was wondering if you and Ruarth would take me along with you."

"You want to go after Morthred? Are you serious?"

"I'm serious, yes. I can't say I *want* to go after him particularly, but it has to be done. And I can't possibly let an innocent like you stick your nose into more of this dun shit without me there to keep an eye on you. Ruarth in his present form simply hasn't feathers enough to keep you out of trouble." The bird cocked his head at me and ruffled his wings.

For a moment she continued to look at me, dumbfounded. Then tears started to trickle down her cheeks. Finally she managed to say, "I've had so few friends—only Ruarth and the Dustels. They do their best, but I have so needed someone who—another woman, who understands. I never dreamed . . . I never thought that you would want to . . . Hell, Blaze. I suppose what I'm trying to say is that I love you, you great halfbreed firebrand."

"Yeah, well, we seem to get along," I said gruffly. Her coincidental use of Niamor's word for me affected me more than I would have thought possible; coupled as it was with her declaration of love, it almost disintegrated me.

I guess she sensed my emotional turmoil, because she sniffed and said in a normal fashion, "But I can't *stand* dogs."

At this point, right on cue, Seeker came running up and flopped down at her feet. A dribble of saliva trickled out of his mouth onto her toes. I could see the reasons for her aversion to this particular specimen at least. A still half-hairless parcel of skin stretched over bones with an oversized tail at one end and four dinner-plate feet underneath, he wasn't an attractive sight. I hoped it might be a different story once all his hair grew back and he'd gained some weight.

"I don't think he's actually wholly dog," I said. "Especially not after I heard him howl. I think he's a halfbreed, like me."

"What's the other half?" she asked, eyeing him doubtfully.

"I don't know, but I suspect he might be part Fen lurger."

She obviously hadn't heard of these marsh-bred canines but she said, "Oh. Well, that's all right then. As long as he isn't *all* dog, I guess I can learn to live with him, can't I?"

We shared a grin. Flame Windrider and I understood each other very well.

Five minutes later we said good-bye to Gorthan Spit and headed out through the breakers toward Mekaté. Far from having made a fortune, I was leaving with less money in my purse than had been there when I'd arrived . . . Gorthan Spit was that kind of place.

For a third time I swore I'd never go back.

Letter from Researcher (Special Class) S. iso Fabold, National Department of Exploration, Federal Ministry of Trade, Kells, to Masterman M. iso Kipswon, President of the National Society for the Scientific, Anthropological and Ethnographical Study of non-Kellish Peoples.

Dated this day 8/2nd Single/1793

Dear Uncle,
I am so glad you feel the second talk to the Society was a success. I am constantly aware that some members have said in the past that the Society's patronage of my voyages and the publication of my subsequent research papers have been entirely due to our blood relationship, and not to any inherent ability of mine, thus it was a vindication to hear the praise given to my paper and presentation. Of course, there will always be detractors; I know that not everyone approves of my methods.

Please allow me here to thank you and the committee for issuing another invitation for me to speak at the spring meeting. I am delighted to accept. I intend to entitle my next talk, The Glory Isles: Magic, Belief and Medicine Prior to Kellish Contact. *And yes, of course I would be delighted if the publicity I am receiving in the press resulted in another sponsored scientific expedition to the Isles of Glory. There is so much more to be done there!*

I will be sending you a new package of interviews shortly. I think you will find these particularly enthralling because they are an account by a Mekaté physician. However, rest assured, Blaze figures in them—you see, I have divined that your fascination with that formidable lady rivals mine! Anyara, by the way, also listens with rapt attention to all my tales of the Glory Isles. I continue to censor Blaze's dialogues when I tell Anyara of them, of course! I do not want to encourage Anyara's liberality too much; fortunately at the moment it only extends to her expressed opinion that we should allow women to be members of the Society. Can you imagine the furor that would cause? As you will recall, we had to fight long and hard just to have women admitted to the public evenings, and that was quite enough, I feel. But I am rambling. It is time I was abed.

My fond respects to Aunt Rosris.

I remain,
Your grateful nephew,
Shor iso Fabold

From national bestselling author

Patricia Briggs

DRAGON BONES

0-441-00916-6

Ward of Hurog has tried all his life to convince people he is just a simple, harmless fool...And it's worked. But now, to regain his kingdom, he must ride into war—and convince them otherwise.

DRAGON BLOOD

0-441-01008-3

Ward, ruler of Hurog, joins the rebels against the tyrannical High King Jakoven. But Jakoven has a secret weapon. One that requires dragon's blood—the very blood that courses through Ward's veins.

Available wherever books are sold or at
www.penguin.com